SPITFIRE RINGERS

A WWII Novel

By Ian R Lindsey

Cover designed by Cover Designer & Sue Stewart

This book is a work of fiction. Names, characters, places, and incidents either are products of the author's imagination or are used fictitiously. Any resemblance to actual persons, living or dead, events, or locales is entirely coincidental.

Printed in the United States of America

First Printing: July 2018
Saoi Consulting
publishing@saoiconsulting.com

ISBN-9781717872494

For My Wife, Courtney, and my three daughters Sydney, Brooklyn, and Marin

CONTENTS

PROLOGUE

January 26, 1936

The sun glinted off the silvery wings of the crop dusting biplane as it sped across the landscape. Somewhat unusually, the sun actually sat in a picture-perfect blue sky, which markedly differed from the normally gray northwest winterscape of Oregon's Willamette Valley. The biplane roared across the empty fields, and then pulled up in a steep climbing turn. Two heads of sandy blonde hair seemed to lean forward against the wind created by the speed of the plane. From a distance, the two heads looked exactly the same, goggles and all. The silver rocket spiraled upward until the radial engine and prop could carry it no higher, then the pilot tipped the nose down and leveled the plane out for a moment before making a mock strafing run on some cows that were too cold to care. The plane banked hard and pulled up over the red barn, missing the motionless weathervane by a mere ten feet, though the weather vane wasn't motionless after the plane sped past.

Finally, the plane came into line with a long straight field that had distinct wheel ruts and started to slowly arc toward the ground. The front wheels bounced lightly over the well-worn field while the tail wheel followed faithfully. After pulling up short of the tree line at the far end of the field, the plane turned slowly and began to awkwardly taxi in the direction of the barn. The plane gracefully soared through the sky, but only meandered slowly on the ground like a squat duck.

Once the plane rested quietly inside the barn, the two nearly identical heads crawled out of the fore and aft cockpit seats onto the wings before jumping to the ground. As it turned out, they were little more than boys, having only turned seventeen the previous September. Of course, they turned seventeen on the same day, like most twins. Dylan Anders was born a scant ten minutes before his brother, Payton, and those were about the only ten minutes he had ever spent alone. They both stood an inch or so over six feet tall, but had yet to put on muscle and fill out as men, though they were both bigger than nearly all the other boys their age. To anyone who didn't know them they looked nearly identical; similar sinewy athletic build, same sandy blonde hair, same hazel-brown eyes. However, differences did abound. Dylan had a bit more square face, and actually stood about a quarter of an inch below Payton. The easiest way to tell them apart, though, were the nearly ever-present smiles. Payton smiled straight across, without showing his bottom teeth, but Dylan smiled straight up and down, showing all of his teeth. Both smiles showed charm and characteristic warmth that radiated from the twins. Someday the girls would notice too, but that didn't matter to them at the moment.

"So do ya think Dad saw us?" Payton more grunted than asked as they struggled to wheel the barn door shut.

"Doubt it, that new truck won't get him back from Portland for at least a couple of more hours, and that's only if he sold everything right away. I hope he gets a couple of Weinhard's in trade though." replied Dylan after the door was shut.

"That is good beer, hope Mom doesn't find out if he does." Payton, as well as Dylan, knew that their mother didn't approve of drinking, but since they had become old enough their dad always managed to slip them a beer or two so they could learn the responsible use of alcohol, or so he said. They both suspected that he just liked having a beer with his sons only three years after the end of prohibition.

"I just hope Dad doesn't find out that we took the plane up without his permission, and cut school to do it. Then Mom and Dad both might be a little unhappy with us."

"But it wouldn't be the first time that's happened! At least it would be only a little unhappy!" replied Payton, with more than just a small mischievous grin creeping across his face, presaging the smile.

"Yeah, it was worth it." opined Dylan. "Dad couldn't be too mad; the engine needed turning over anyway. Did you see the

Smith's cows as I dove for them? They didn't even care! Dumb animals. That was a textbook dive. Anything in the way would have been obliterated if we were flying in a fighter."

"But the biplane means that anything in your way today would have been dusted." teased the taller brother. "I bet fighters are so much different. They are even starting to talk about mono-wing planes in the papers, and all metal! We could have so much fun dog fighting each other if we got our hands on a couple of those. Wouldn't that beat all!"

That is what it came down to; the twins loved flying, and they especially loved flying together. They would have skipped every day of school to fly, but they knew that had to study if they ever wanted to fly with Eddie Rickenbacker and the famed aces of the U.S. Army Airforce.

The twins reached the world about the same time that World War I gave birth to true military aviation. Ever since childhood their father had regaled them with stories of the Red Baron, and the man who shot him down, Eddie Rickenbacker. The stories struck a chord with the two adventurous souls, much to the dismay of their mother. They learned to fly the family crop duster as soon as they could see out of the cockpit. They hadn't quite made it to ace status just yet, but they were both natural pilots, quickly surpassing the flying skills of their father. The only thing holding them back at the moment was the lack of fighter planes to use for their personal amusement. That, however, would come soon enough.

***

June 5, 1936

Again, in complete opposition to the usual weather standard of the Pacific Northwest, this June day stood sparkling blue, with the sun just peaked and starting its downward march to the horizon. Unfortunately, that sun somewhat dismayed Payton as he stared up into it, trying not to get smacked on the head by the baseball arched high into the sky by the rival shortstop. Payton fought the sun as best he could, his glove directly in front of his eyes while he retreated from his third base position into the outfield, but he fought a losing battle. Just then, he glanced down briefly behind the plate, where Dylan was catching. Dylan casually pointed to the sky, directly at the ball so Payton would find it. It was simpler for the twins to work as a team, especially after the years of practice. Payton found the ball by following Dylan's directions, and caught it without anyone else knowing that he didn't have the slightest clue where it was almost until it stuck in his glove.

"Nice catch" muttered Dylan as they both headed into the dugout.

"Yeah, thanks for the help," his brother answered.

"Taylor, Anders, Anders." bellowed the coach to indicate who was up to bat "Let's get some runs and win this thing!" The score was tied headed into the home half of the ninth, so only one run would win it.

The one thing the twins loved nearly as much as flying was baseball. The talents the boys possessed suited both passions. The keen eyesight, lightning hand-eye coordination, and quick decisions served them well, letting them excel at baseball and flying. The crack of the bat lured them almost as much as the rumble of the radial engines turning the prop.

Dylan and Payton had always played on the same teams; Dylan catching while batting fourth and Payton playing third while batting fifth for as long as they could remember. After they finished their chores around the farm they generally played some ball with their friends, if they weren't trying to find a way to take the plane up. Nothing could bother them when they were tossing a ball around or flying, for they didn't have a care in the world. They loved baseball and flying, but they knew their future was in flying, at least they hoped so.

The bat cut the air as Dylan took his warm up swings, waiting for his turn at bat.

"Hey, Dylan, I bet he gives you a first pitch fastball leaning towards the outside. He thinks you won't swing at the first pitch." Payton half whispered to his brother from the dugout.

Dylan turned and replied "It's a good guess, and I bet after that he'll give you a rolling curveball to you first pitch to try and get one over."

"Then we'll just have to teach him not to be so predictable." Payton answered.

Sure enough, after Taylor was put out on a sharp line drive to the shortstop, Dylan sauntered up to the plate and ripped the first pitch fastball for a double into the left-center gap. Then, Payton sat on the curveball and drove it into the right-centerfield gap to push his brother across the plate for the game-winning run. The crowd of mostly family and friends did their best impersonation of a roar with delight, cheering mightily for the hit. Ebbets Field this was not.

After the congratulatory celebration from the team, and the pep talk from the coach, the twins wandered to the backstop in front of the bleachers where their dad sat.

"Nice hitting boys, guessed what he was going to throw you, huh?" queried the elder Anders. "Nothing like getting the game winning hit, always something to remember. Especially today. You boys got some mail." The boys reached through the fence to get the offered envelopes, eager after recognizing the seal of the US Military Academy for the return address. They tore open the letters and read quickly.

"We're in!" they both yelled at the exact same time. They said the same thing at the same time a lot, another quirk of twins. "We're going to WestPoint!"

"Thank God, your mother thought one of you would get in and the other wouldn't. She's been worried ever since I told her the mail was here. Hop in the truck and we'll run home to tell her." With only two Academy appointments per state, it was no small thing that both brothers were accepted.

The boys scrambled into the truck while their father took the wheel. Without showing it, they knew he was proud of them. Maybe they could talk him into a beer to celebrate.

"You know, boys" he said "things are going to be quite different at WestPoint than they are here. New York sure isn't Oregon, and you'll start out as the lowest cadets there are. Just remember, stand up for yourselves and for each other, and always be there for each other. You are lucky that you have each other, so use each other's strengths because you don't have to go it alone. Stick together and you will do far better than you ever could alone. You are in now, but that is just the beginning."

They were in. Dylan and Payton Anders took the first step toward joining the Army, toward making the Army Airforce, toward flying fighter planes. Now they just had to ride a train across the country and start school. Soon they hoped they'd be able to fly back.

***

April 17th, 1940

Four years at WestPoint treated the twins very well. They'd both taken to the physical activity eagerly. The goal of General MacArthur, a previous Superintendent, "Every cadet an athlete" suited the twins just fine. They'd run through the rough and tumble obstacle course as part of physical training, and still kept enough stamina to play on the baseball team. They'd been motivated to keep up the baseball too. One hundred years earlier, as legend told, then cadet Abner Doubleday conjured the game of baseball while on leave from the academy. Thus, the twins were playing on the field dedicated this day to Maj. General Doubleday, and as fourth year co-captains, Payton and Dylan had the honor of serving as catchers as the first pitches were thrown out by former players General Douglas MacArthur and General Omar Bradley. As they both walked out to hand the ceremonial baseballs back to the generals, unintentionally and almost simultaneously they said: "Nice pitch, sir, I'm sure it was a strike."

Both Generals laughed at the curious effect of the same words coming from two people. Bradley chided MacArthur "Douglas, I didn't know you had gotten the school to put out clones that look the same and speak the same!"

"Omar, WestPoint is always trying to build the perfect soldier. Where are you from, boys? What's your field of study?" replied MacArthur as he turned to the young cadets.

"Oregon, sir. We grew up in the Willamette Valley south of Portland" Dylan answered crisply, as only a soon-to- be lowly 2nd Lieutenant can answer a General.

Payton finished off the answer, "and we're both studying mechanical engineering, sir. We want to be pilots."

"Well, I think there will be a future for pilots in the army, especially sharp eyed smart ones. Don't forget the infantry though. Only men on the ground can hold off the enemy. Whether it is Germans or tigers, a plane can only do so much." MacArthur clipped out like only a General can to two not quite 2nd Lieutenants.

"Yes Sir!" both twins yelped as they handed over the baseballs, saluted and trotted back to the dugout for the game.

Besides baseball, Payton and Dylan slogged through the books well enough to graduate with honors in a difficult engineering curriculum. It never hurt to have a study partner, and usually one of them would understand the homework well enough to explain it to the other. They'd learned more about the radial piston engines on their old crop dusting planes than their father could ever have hoped to teach them, but they also knew that he had taught them more than any of the other cadets knew about flying. Some things just can't be learned in school.

As with most college graduates, the endless human struggle to answer the question "Why are we here?" has mostly been distilled down to the immediate future in the most simple of terms.

This time, though, it was Dylan asking Payton "Well, what now after graduation?" However, the question was not unique. Most kids walking out of their university, college, or academy ask the very same question. Only philosophy majors try to answer the more long range "Why" question while still in school.

They both figured that they needed to find someplace where they could fly. The faster the plane the better as far as they were concerned. However, the best planes didn't come from America at the moment. The Germans had the Bf 109

Messerschmitt and the Brits had the Supermarine Spitfire, which were both widely considered the best planes in the world. The USA would catch up quickly, but wasn't close yet.

"We could always check in with that guy in New York." Payton ventured.

"I was thinking the same thing." Dylan offered quickly.

Occasionally the bright lights of New York City beckoned just 50 miles down the Hudson River. An easy train ride took them to Grand Central station where they could spend a holiday weekend wandering between the swanky hotels before ending up at a youth hostel or a room above an Irish bar.

A few weeks earlier, on their self proclaimed last weekend in New York, both young men had a grand time. Stops at their regular haunts, as well as the most expensive dinner they'd ever had at the Plaza Hotel made it a weekend to remember. One particular gentleman they certainly didn't forget. After the expensive dinner, Dylan and Payton had retired to a pub more within their means on the Upper East Side of Manhattan. There, they ran in to this peculiar fellow and struck up a conversation when he started talking about flying. He called himself Colonel Charles Sweeney, but he certainly wasn't part of the United States Armed Forces. He was, in fact, a mercenary. He'd fought in various freedom efforts ever since he'd been kicked out of West Point just after the turn of the century. Both WestPoint and Sweeney considered themselves better off for ending the relationship. He'd fought for the French Foreign Legion, as well as for the Republicans in the Spanish Civil War. At some point along the way, one government or another had appointed him a Colonel, so he used that as a title, warranted or not.

Moreover, on this day, the Colonel was recruiting pilots to help the French. He recognized the glint of adventure both twins possessed in their eyes. That small look singled out pilots to the Colonel above all else. The Colonel didn't need to look too hard for adventurous young men in New York City. The U.S. government turned out to be his biggest problem on more than one account. He had two major problems; one personal and the other policy. The personal problem troubled him little, as the FBI frowned on his mercenary ways and made his life a little difficult. Getting to Europe at the right time would solve that problem. The more pressing problem went all the way back to the Great War. Americans, rightly or wrongly, blamed the debt incurred saving Europe for causing the Depression. Therefore, the US had become more or less an isolationist country during the Depression. Even as the Depression ended and war broke out all over Europe, Congress had passed the Neutrality Act. For the better part of three years it kept America at bay and threatened to fine, jail, and strip any citizenship rights from any American who went to fight with any foreign army. The Neutrality Act seriously hindered Colonel Sweeney's efforts.

However, the shadow Hitler cast fell across the Atlantic. Cadets at WestPoint were more aware than most that this battle would not end at just the European mainland. Hitler was a dark cloud over the whole world bent on ruling a Master Race. He wouldn't stop at the Atlantic or at the Ural mountains, and he had to be stopped. Europe was just the start. Colonel Sweeney felt that way, and so did Payton and Dylan. Eventually, they all knew, the fight would end up at the doorstep of America.

That last night in New York Colonel Sweeney had offered Dylan and Payton the chance to do something about the mustached menace from Munich. At least that is where the trouble started, Hitler actually came from Austria. He offered them a chance to fly some of the best planes in the world, and to get some of the best flight training in the world. They could go to Europe, he told them, and be some of the first Americans to stand up against Hitler. They'd help the French, whom Hitler had invaded a week or so earlier, and they'd fight for freedom. Sweeney argued passionately and persuasively, and at the end he'd left instructions saying that if they wanted to cross the Atlantic they could meet one of his contacts at a hotel in Montreal who could get them to Europe.

Back outside the halls of WestPoint on graduation day, Dylan asked "How do we get out of our service commitments? Is it worth the risk? We could be in serious trouble if anyone in the Army finds out we want to go fight in Europe now."

Payton thought for a moment, and then answered. "I think we need to talk to General Bradley. He'd recognize us from the baseball team, and we might persuade him to give us a deferment of service. We'll tell him we could come back as better trained, battle tested flight pilots after a year or so, and then we could help train American pilots. We might even be able to save some lives."

Much to their surprise, General Bradley agreed with their line of reasoning. He transferred them to General Hap Arnold's US Army Air Force, and gave them the deferment. General Bradley even cooked up a phony reason to put on the deferment paperwork, citing their possible professional baseball careers as a future publicity tool for WestPoint. As far as the army knew, they had baseball games to play, but they really had planes to fly. Now they headed for Europe, by way of Canada. Neither knew what they were really getting into.

CHAPTER 1

May 10th, 1940

Getting across the American/Canadian border was not much of a chore. A train to Niagara Falls accompanied by a story to all that inquired about meeting their girlfriends for the weekend got them close, and then a simple hitchhike across the border and on to Montreal. The driver of the car did a double take when the hitchhiking youngsters asked for a drop off at the Ritz-Carlton Montreal, but still obliged. Dylan and Payton were dressed in their smartest non-military suits, but the quality of those suits was not nearly what one would expect at The Ritz. The boys did a double take when they inquired at the front desk and were told that a room had been reserved under their names for the night and that the bill had already been paid. Colonel Sweeny spared no expense taking care of them to insure a smooth trip across the Atlantic. As a mercenary, Colonel Sweeny received payment for every recruit he sent over, which more than covered the expenses he incurred. When the twins reached their room they found another surprise; a note to meet a Mr. Eriksen in the Jardin Du Ritz garden restaurant for dinner.

With a couple hours still to kill, they threw their bags on the beds and wandered out of the hotel lobby. Upon hitting the streets, the Golden Mile Square section of Montreal stretched out ahead. Imposing mansions lined the streets of this impressively wealthy area that housed the financial magnates and decision makers controlling the economic fate of Canada. Though some in the neighborhood had relocated out of downtown Montreal, and the area wasn't quite at the peak anymore, it was close enough, and the residents still controlled a large portion of the national wealth. To the east sat the prestigious McGill University, and so the twins headed in that general direction. It had been eight months exactly since Canada had declared war on Germany, so Montreal looked like a city pushing and prodding its way to a wartime footing. Posters exhorting young men to volunteer in both French and English plastered the windows of the buildings around McGill University. As the twins meandered on to the campus they noticed a general excited murmur around them as students spoke quickly and quietly, and all seemed headed to the center of campus and the massive stone building there. The placard on the building said that this was the Arts Building and noted that this was the oldest building on campus, dating back to 1843. Several other very impressive stone buildings surrounded the art building. Some looked like gothic churches with impressive spires, while others echoed the stern columns of the

Roman Senate, but it all worked to bring a stately, elegant feel to the campus.

The central structure of the Art Building consisted of dark grey stone and rose three stories, then another two stories with a small watchtower and rotunda atop. The roof appeared the same shade of green as the Statue of Liberty, so it must have been oxidized copper. The rotunda on top of the watch tower reminded the twins of Monticello, Thomas Jefferson's home in Virginia, which the twins visited during school. Two story wings extended from each side of the building, presumable housing the classrooms and workshops. Students were gathering in the main foyer and listening to a radio broadcast over the loudspeaker. Unfortunately for the English speaking brothers, the broadcast was in French. A few words rattled over the stone foyer unmistakably: Hitler, France, Blitzkrieg. Knowing that they planned to join the French air force, the boys sought more information from one of the co-eds at the fringes of the group.

"What's going on?" inquired Dylan.

"Hitler has invaded Belgium and is running down towards France." replied the chestnut haired girl. "He just went around the Maginot Line. Paris is in a panic. They are rushing troops north."

"They're never going to stop them. If the tanks are in Belgium already the Blitzkrieg is on. Tanks and planes will pound their way to Paris in no time." commented Payton.

"The radio anchor is optimistic and talking up the Belgian Army, maybe they can hold." replied the girl. "I am Anne Fields,

17

by the way. My brother Jack is with the Canadian army in France. He said that any Germans that set foot in France will be thrown back, just as in the last war."

"My apologies, Ma'am. My name is Payton, and this is my brother Dylan, it is a pleasure to meet you. I hope your brother is right, but he didn't mention that it took 4 years to throw the Germans out in the Great War. When Napoleon went east it took even longer to throw him out of Germany. Any war in Europe is going to be a long-term affair."

"Nice to meet you both. You must be Americans, since I've never seen you around campus and most of the other boys in town are off training or at least in a uniform." Anne said.

"Yes, Anne, we are Americans. But, we are just up here on a school break. That's why we wandered over to the campus. Thought we might find something interesting. I would think that this certainly qualifies." Payton noted.

"Well, I hope you find something more interesting to do than talk about the war. The constant war talk can be tiresome. My friends and I try to find some distractions occasionally." she replied with a wan smile.

Even though it by no means constituted an invitation, Payton didn't waste an opportunity.

"Let us entertain you later, then. We have a dinner planned with a family friend this evening, but we would certainly be happy to take you and your friends for a drink later." Payton interjected happily. Dylan had always been more inclined to social planning, but Payton felt an immediate shine to this evidently smart and beautiful girl.

Dylan didn't mind letting his brother handle the planning and added "Our father gave us a little bit of money to make sure we had a good time up here, and we appreciate you translating the French broadcast for us. We'd like to return the favor."

It wasn't exactly true. Colonel Sweeney provided the money. Payton and Dylan were forced into these little white lies because America was still a neutral country. The start of the Second World War occurred when Germany invaded Poland on September 1st, 1939. Two days later, Great Britain, France, Australia and New Zealand declared war on Germany on September 3rd, 1939. Two days after that the US declared Neutrality on September 5th. Five days later, September 10th, Canada declared war on Germany as well. Even though Dylan and Payton had the unofficial approval of General Bradley, any US citizens caught fighting for a foreign country could, in theory, forfeit their citizenship. The State Department loathed prosecuting any such charges since they knew the US might eventually have to enter the war, but making a claim to go off fighting while on foreign territory, even friendly foreign territory, simply asked for trouble. In public at least, the twins wanted to keep a low profile and stuck with their traveling students on break story. Besides, the few dollars that Colonel Sweeney had given them for the trip might as well be put to good use.

"Well, that is a little forward since we just met, but it does sound like fun. All right, I'll bring my friend Donna and we'll meet you at DePorte, a little bar just down the street from here. When shall we meet you?" Anne said.

"Our dinner is at 6, so how about 8:45 or 9?" replied Dylan.

Anne happily responded with her bright smile, "Thank you boys, I'll see you there at 9."

***

A couple of hours later the boys sat in their room preparing for dinner with Mr. Eriksen. Payton shined his shoes, more for the impending date with Anne and her friend than for Mr. Eriksen, while Dylan looked in mirror looping his tie into a knot that reasonably resembled the usual military double Windsor. Neither wanted to look overly crisp and presentable, the usual protocol at the military academy at all times. They hoped not to arouse any suspicions by looking a little less than perfectly turned out, but not many people in Canada paid much attention so the efforts mostly fell for naught.

"How are we going to recognize Mr. Eriksen?" Dylan asked.

"I'm hoping he recognizes us. Otherwise there is no way we are getting in to one of the nicest restaurants in town with no reservation. We'll just inquire at the front when we get there."

A few minutes later the boys walked in to the elegant Jardine Du Ritz. The dining was al fresco in the expertly manicured patio garden. White wrought iron chairs surrounded the light blue linen covered tables on the patio. In the middle sat an impressive fountain and pond, complete with a family of ducks sedately paddling through the water. Beautiful sunflowers adorned the center of each table and augmented the native greens of the garden finally shaking off the Canadian winter in late spring. As the name suggests, the restaurant drew heavy influence from the French cafes so common in both Paris and Montreal, but in much more of a fine dining setting befitting The Ritz.

The Maitre D took one look at the young pair as they entered the garden and the frown turned to a smile look on his face indicated that these must be the set of twins that Mr. Eriksen had generously tipped him to look out for and greet warmly. The boys needn't ask, and he ushered Payton and Dylan to a prime table right next to the pond. At the table Mr. Eriksen rose to greet them. He stood several inches shorter than the boys, perhaps 5'9" or so. Though he was impressively and properly turned out for a dinner at The Ritz, he had an unruly head of curly Italian hair. It looked as if the barber had sheered it as close as possible, but the scissors were not up to the task. The remaining hair looked a bit like a ball of yarn tightly wound, but with several curly locks dripping out. A hat would cover it, but the man had no care for what others thought and moved with pride and dignity none-the-less. His suit fit him immaculately, even though he tended to the smaller side of lean everywhere on his body but the middle, as happened to men on one side or the other of middle age.

"Messieurs' Anders, my name is John Eriksen, it is a pleasure to meet you." He said in a deep voice with an accent that was hard to place. It sounded as if he might be American, but he spoke with a slightly different intonation that hinted at a continental upbringing.

"Nice to meet you, sir" both twins responded at the same time.

"An unusual habit you have of speaking together, and please, call me John" replied a mildly surprised and slightly amused John.

"Sorry, John" said Payton "it isn't intentional. We were just raised together so closely that sometimes we have the same reaction and response at the same time. It does sometimes make for an interesting conversation piece."

"I know the feeling" John mused in his subtle accent. "Some people comment on my accent as well, and it does make for a good conversation starter on occasion."

"I didn't want sound ignorant and say anything, but I couldn't place your accent either. You don't sound quite Canadian, or American, or Italian. Where are you from?" Dylan inquired.

"You would not be ignorant to ask, as my accent is my own, and my acquisition of it a unique circumstance. I was born and raised in New York, where my father was born and raised as well. However, he traveled the world as a student studying for his doctorate in Roman History. During his travels he met my mother in Malta, a small island off of the Italian mainland. When he returned home to teach at Columbia University he brought her with him. I was raised with the regular New York accent most of the time, a mother who spoke Italian and Maltese at home, a university education at Cambridge, and to finish off the mix I've spent the last several years teaching Military History here at

McGill. I like to say that Montreal is where both the French and the English are a little off."

"That's quite the melting pot of languages. We both speak a little bit of German from high school, but other than that it's just plain English. It must be useful to know all of those languages. How do you know Colonel Sweeney?" asked Dylan, further testing their new acquaintance.

"Ah, the good Colonel. We met several years ago during the Spanish Civil War fighting against the fascists. Since then we have stayed in contact and occasionally I will help him with some of his recruits. It is much easier to take care of certain travel arrangements from here. He has a zeal for war that I do not share, Spain cured that, but I have no love for fascists, so I am happy to help my friend."

A waitress approached carrying a large tray "Monsieur's, your meal. Two filet mignon and one rack of lamb."

"The service here is excellent, we haven't even ordered yet and they came out with something for us." Dylan joked.

"I took the liberty of ordering you both steaks before you arrived. I figured you may not have such a chance once you enter the fray in Europe." Mr. Eriksen admitted. "I hope that you will enjoy them."

"There is no doubt of that. We appreciate your help as well. The only information Colonel Sweeney gave us was to meet you here. He didn't tell us anything about our destination or who we would be flying with." said Payton. "We're hoping that you can tell us what's next."

"Do not worry" John said. "It is standard operating procedure to pass you from one link in the chain to the next with each link only able to tell you the next step. That way if your trip goes awry the whole chain is not blown. I have arranged transportation for you to Portsmouth, England. A Mr. Hobbes will meet you at the docks. Your trip is slightly unusual for me in two ways, but actually both make my job easier. First, I usually have to set up descriptors and codes so that Mr. Hobbes will recognize his men to pick up. You will be easily recognizable as the young men who are twins that he is to meet. The other reason has to do with your transportation. You are quite lucky in that I have procured for you a spot on the Empress of Britain. Up until last year it was one of the finest first class cruise ships on the oceans, and then it was to be converted to a troop transport. At least that was the story. It was only partially converted, and has served as the backup trans-Atlantic ship of British King George VI. He has just completed a secret inspection of Canadian troops here and the Empress of Britain has peeled off from the Million Dollar convoy to take him back to England. I have procured a spot on his shipboard serving staff for you."

Trying to hide the hint of excitement creeping in to his voice Dylan said "You mean that we'll be traveling on a luxury cruise liner with the King of England? That doesn't sound like a bad deal."

"Well, it is not exactly a luxury cruise liner anymore." Mr. Eriksen offered. "It was converted last year to a troop transport and painted the standard naval grey. It has peeled off from the other luxury liners of the million dollar convoy returning from New Zealand to return the King to England. Not many know of his secret review here to encourage the troops, but with today's invasion by Hitler I'm sure he is glad he came to muster the allies even more. I'm guessing he won't be leaving Great Britain much in the days to come with Hitler pushing westward. Britain and France will need all the help they can get."

"We heard on the radio. It sounds like he is blitzing down through Belgium as fast as he can." Payton noted as he cut in to the steak left in front of him.

"It is Hitler's style; blitzkrieg. He strikes like lightning with tanks and planes and browbeats his adversaries quickly. He does it while orating and while fighting. I don't think he knows any other way." Dylan added. "It will be interesting to see if he can sustain anything other than an attack. Occupation is just as hard as the attack, at least that is what they told us at WestPoint. Is you steak as good as mine?"

"Absolutely. It is as good as anything we ever had in New York," replied his brother. "Thank you for dinner again, Mr. Eriksen, this is a real treat."

"It is my pleasure. We can only hope that what you say about occupation is true. He seems very good on the attack at the moment and stands to occupy nearly all of Western Europe." Mr. Eriksen said with the enthusiasm trailing off in his voice. "Nevertheless, he must be stopped. That is why we must get you to Paris as quickly as possible. The retrofitted ship is still somewhat fit for the king. There should be ample space, as the passenger list merely contains the King, his family, servants, and the crew. There will be fewer than 50 people on the whole ship. The royal outfitting of the ship should be comfortable, but not opulent by any means. You need to be at the dock tomorrow morning at 07:45, sharp. Here is a little bit of money, have the hotel set up a taxi to ensure your arrival. I do not know what your duties will be, but I do know that you will be serving the King himself. The trip will have some danger from the Uboats. The Battle of the Atlantic still rages, but this is a secret trip by the King, and I'm sure the

Royal navy will take every precaution. It seemed like the safest way to get you to Europe."

"Does he know who we are?" inquired Payton with an aim at getting straight to the point. "I don't think he can cause us trouble in the US, but he will eventually talk to the President, and we don't want to lose our citizenship. He may not intend to, but he could say something that would get us in trouble."

"An astute question, my young friend, and one with good foresight. The politics of the US have made your adventure somewhat of a risk to your status as US citizens, but my guess is that FDR is only biding his time until he can get in to this war. At that point, it won't matter who you fight for as long as it is one of the Allies. However, to make sure you are safe, I have arranged for fake passports for you. The King thinks you are young students at McGill, but your parents are in Britain on business, so you are going to join them. Your names are Ryan and Justin Stewart. You might do well to spruce up a little on the surrounding area to make your cover pass. You should be able to easily enter both England and France with these Canadian passports. If you run in to trouble, dash to Ireland with your American passports. The Irish are officially neutral, so you shouldn't have any trouble there."

The waitress returned again carrying a huge tray of desserts, which all three customers waved off. Mr. Eriksen quickly paid the check and began to rise, "I must be off. My wife and children are expecting me at home. I enjoyed our dinner, and I wish you the best of luck in your adventures. If you are ever back this way, please do not hesitate to look me up. Your fight is a just one, do not forget that or let politics get in your way."

"Thank you, again, sir, hopefully things will go smoothly." Payton and Dylan intoned at the same time. Mr. Eriksen just chuckled to hear them both as he walked out of the garden.

CHAPTER 2

May 10th, 1940

With at least an hour left until they were to meet Anne, Payton and Dylan retired to their room. Payton figured it was time to let their father know of their plans.

Dear Dad,

I know that Dylan and I haven't written in a while, but I guess you could say we have been busy since graduation. I'm not totally sure how to tell you this, but we are on our way to Europe. The week after graduation we enlisted with Colonel Sweeney. I'd like to tell you that he is in the military, but he is just a well-connected mercenary. He is an American, and a patriot, but he isn't willing to wait around for his government to declare war. He says he has talked directly with FDR about it, but he may just be a braggart. Even so, we signed up. He has arranged for us to go to

France and start fighting the Germans. Since we know how to fly, we got the best possible deal and will fight with the French Army Air Force. They are apparently flying the Curtiss P36 Hawk, an American plane. It has a powerful Pratt and Whitney engine (Colonel Sweeney said it could muster 1200 horsepower!) so we should be flying faster than we ever have before! It will be better than when we used to steal your old bi-plane for sure.

It also has six machine guns. We've had our regular rifle training at school, but neither of us has fired anything from a plane. It will feel weird to shoot down another plane. It seems like every flyer everywhere should root for all other planes to stay in the sky, otherwise a day might come where it is their turn to go down. It would be sort of like when the whole country was rooting for Jesse Owens. When he won, we all won. When one aircraft stays in the air, all pilots win. We heard that the Messerschmitts have cannon as well as their machine guns, so hopefully the Hawk will stand up.

We know that there are risks, both of getting killed and to our standing in the US Army, let alone our US citizenship. I am glad to let you know that at least some in the US Army see the possibility of entering in this conflict, or are at least hedging their bets. General Bradley cooked up a story about playing baseball so that we could quietly leave West Point. It would have been nice to try out for the Dodger's and play like the story he made up, but this is more important. He instructed us to learn everything we can about flying and engaging the Germans and to report back regularly to him. If the US enters the war, then we will have a leg up in our training and can share that with others in the service. It might prove invaluable since the Germans started training their Army and Luftwaffe long ago, and they now have more than 9 months of battle testing. If we must go to war with Germany, then we must be prepared. The "Sitz Krieg" is over and so our commitment to the greater service of our country must now include fighting for another country.

I am sorry to have to write you this letter. I could not write it to Mom, so I hope that you will break the news to her gently. In the end, Dylan and I both hope to return safely, and I believe we will. We'll see you and Mom again as soon as we can. I will write as often as possible to let you know where we are and what we have been up to.

Love,

Payton

***

As Dylan and Payton wandered in to Deporte a few minutes late, they saw Anne and her friend sitting comfortably in a corner booth waiting for them. In scale, the bar tended towards cozy, but it was certainly big enough for the dozen or so patrons evenly divided between the classic long oak bar with brass fittings and the five or six booths situated against the brick walls opposite the bar. Heavy dark wood beams held up the ceiling and ran the length of the bar, giving a somewhat dark but charming ambience. Deporte looked like the type of place that could hold a boisterous crowd on the right occasion, or a smaller place where patrons could sit comfortably and converse. On this night, the latter was true as the few groups talked quietly amongst themselves. It did not require a translator to realize that most of the talks centered on the invasion of France. Much of the world surely talked of the same thing. Hitler was moving west.

Anne turned and raised her hand to wave the boys over to the booth where she and her friend sat side by side. Both girls stood to greet the twins when they neared the table. Anne had been wearing an overcoat and hat earlier in the day which had allowed just a hint of what was underneath, so it was just now that the boys could see how pretty she really was. Her long chestnut locks were parted at the side, rolled up in the front and curled down the back just above her shoulders in a very fashionable way. When she smiled her high set cheeks flared out and showed a slight dimple. She was slender and stood at just over 5'5" in her heels. Her few freckles just added to her appeal as prettier than the girl next door. She smiled with her eyes as Dylan and Payton greeted her.

"Anne, we are so glad you made it. It is nice to see such a familiar face on an otherwise interesting day." said Dylan.

"Interesting is a delicate way of putting it." replied Anne "I would have said dreary. At the very least this may bring the whole world to bear on Hitler. Now the West can't ignore or appease him. Excuse me, where are my manners? This is my very good friend Donna Henri. Donna, these fine American gentlemen are Dylan and Payton, though I can't for the life of me tell you which is which."

"I'm Dylan Anders" he said as he reached out to shake the absolutely beautiful girl's hand. "We are hard to tell apart, but it

31

becomes easier the more you get to know us, I promise." Donna's classical beauty stunned both boys as she stood to meet them. She stood a couple inches taller than Anne with wavy dark brunette hair and contrasting shimmering blue eyes. She epitomized the tall and lithe model ideal. The twins shared a knowing glance saying that they had stumbled on to an evening with two contrasting but exceedingly beautiful girls.

"It is a pleasure to meet you both as well. Anne so kindly invited me tonight so that we both might have a distraction on this dreadful day. The invasion has the whole campus buzzing, and especially those with familial ties back to France," Donna replied. It was evident by the way she looked down as she said the last sentence that she did indeed have family in France even though her accent was definitely still French-Canadian. "I am hoping that this unwarranted attack will help bring the US in with the Allies. After all, France is America's longest standing ally, dating back to your war for independence, and other than Canada, Great Britain is your closest ally."

"Sound reasonable to me, and I wish it were so" Payton responded as he thought her statement all the way through. While Dylan tended to be more outgoing, Payton tended to allow his analytical though process more sway, but both could certainly share the other's strength and play the socializer or the thinker when necessary. "The problem is that many in the US remember the last war, what it cost, and see this as strictly a European problem. There are plenty of isolationists in the country, and notably in the Senate. Roosevelt is no war hawk, but he is looking for a way to stop Hitler. FDR just needs to convince the rest of the country that we need to join the war, especially before re-election. Unlike Hitler and the fascists, FDR can't just declare war and invade. That is a definite plus for democracy overall, but it means it will take a little longer in this case. I do believe it is only a matter of time before the US enters the war, and when it does there will be plenty of young men willing to fight."

"I hope you are right, but how would you know? Are you willing to fight?" Anne commented half in jest.

"Actually, yes." Payton replied rather dryly. "And I don't say that lightly or to try to impress you. I'm sorry if we gave you the wrong impression when we met earlier, but we are not students anymore and we came to Canada for a couple of days waiting for a ship across the Atlantic. We graduated from the United States Military Academy earlier this month and then signed up to fly against the Germans in France."

"I'm terribly sorry for joking, then" Anne said, showing that she was more than just a little embarrassed. "I didn't mean anything by it, I was just teasing."

"That's okay, Anne. We know, and we are not exactly broadcasting our intentions while we are here. If we are caught by United States military officials, we could be banned from future military service when the United States enters the war and lose our citizenship. At the very least that would make it hard to travel since we would be nationless individuals." explained Payton.

"Nationless? What does that mean?" Donna asked.

"It means no passports and no place to land." Dylan explained. "But enough of that now, we just want to go and do our part to stop Hitler. I believe you called the day dreary earlier, why don't you brighten it by telling us a little bit about yourselves. Where did you come from? How do you like McGill? Anne, you said you had a brother in France, but that is just about all that we know about you."

"I'm not sure that anything I have to say will brighten the day, but thank you for asking. My family has a ranch in Alberta where we herd cattle. My older brother in France is my only brother. He signed up for the Army as soon as Hitler invaded Poland and England declared war. He knew that we'd be in the war as soon as England declared. The realm always sticks together, I suppose. He's a first lieutenant since he attended McGill here before me. He studied history and I'm studying art. Father always said that we'd be the first two in our family through university. He never went, but he's done a remarkable job building the ranch up. It's twice as big now as when his father ran it."

"So, you're a good old-fashioned cowgirl after all then?" Dylan teased.

"Yes, but only in the most Canadian sense of the term!" Anne shot back playfully.

"I tell her the same thing all the time." Donna offered. "And I've visited her on the ranch. She rushes around there on her horse like she was born on it. Seeing her around the city here you'd never guess it, but she keeps up with the men on that ranch as easily as she pleases. I don't know how she does it."

"Well that is funny to hear, I never would have guessed either." Payton said with a laugh. "We grew up on a farm in Oregon, the northwestern part of the US, so I guess we have something in common. We don't raise cattle, just crops, so I guess you are one up on us in the toughness department. Now tell us about yourself Donna."

"I'm just a city girl. I grew up not far from here in Montreal. My father is a businessman in town and I'm an only child. My parents are originally from France, having moved here just before I was born." Donna offered.

"She's being modest." Anne interjected. "Here father owns and runs the biggest newspaper in town. The journalism building on campus will probably be named after him soon."

"I don't know about that. I'm not in the journalism school anyway. Anne and I are in the same art program. I truly enjoy the art history curriculum. So much has come out of Europe and especially my parent's homeland. I hear stories about Paris in the 20's and I long to be there. I hope the fascists feel the same. Politics should not interfere with great art, and if they destroy anything it will be a tragedy." Donna concluded.

"Well, I think you have reason for hope and reason for concern." Payton offered. "I've heard the much of the Nazi leadership are patrons of the arts. Göring, in particular, values the arts. We had a guest lecturer at the academy who had served as an attaché in Berlin and he described Göring's country house, Carinhall, alternately as a palace and a museum. The

Reichsmarshall apparently displayed his art collection rather proudly."

"That says something, but then what should cause my concern?" Donna asked.

"It's a war with bombs. Explosions do not discriminate what they blow up. They just obliterate everything in their path. Blitzkrieg relies heavily on air support and bombs to soften up an opposing army during an advance, so anything in the way will suffer," Payton finished saying. Silence hung over the table like a thick fog. Both the girls thought of the destruction and involuntarily lowered their eyes.

"I'm sorry if my brother has upset you. It is just conjecture." Dylan offered.

"It is all right. We are glad to hear some straight answers and not propaganda. To date all we have heard is that the world needs our boys to go over and fight for freedom." Anne said.

"Donna, where in France is your family?" Payton asked, hoping to deftly change the subject.

"They live in Carentan. It is a port city close to Cherbourg in Normandy. It is at the base of the Contentin Peninsula and the Douve river runs through town and down in to the channel. It is a small town, with maybe four thousand people. It is a bit inland, but there are causeways that run down to the beach, which is beautiful. It is quite lovely in summer. We went over when I was a child for a summer with my parent's family. I have fond memories of those days with my cousins there. My father is from a big family, so there are plenty of Henri's in Carentan. It would not surprise me if my parents moved back there one day." Donna answered. The town sounded idyllic; the kind of place where the sun shines on grandchildren visiting their grandparents for the summer and where families would visit to get away from the rigors of life. Donna spoke of a small coastal town like thousands ringing the seas and oceans of the world.

"That does sound wonderful." Dylan grinned "We are aiming to go in to Le Havre after sailing to England. I'm not sure what we do after that, but if we get the chance we'll have to look up your family when we get there."

"That would be splendid, and if you do make sure to write me back. Father has been worried sick about his family there all day. If you walk in to any shop or tavern in Carentan I'm sure you will run in to a Henri."

"Thank you, Donna, we will certainly write you and Anne both, if that is okay. If we have a place that you can write us, we'll pass it along as well. Any letters that you can spare would be gratefully accepted." Payton offered with a hint of boldness.

"Of course, we will write back. Letters are gratefully accepted here as well. Hearing the truth unfiltered will only help our countries, so hopefully lots of the boys will take the time to write home." Anne declared.

With all four glasses nearing the bottom, and no one making a move to order more, the enjoyable evening that happened purely by accident of radio and invasion looked to flit off in to the darkness like a lightning bug flashing in fits and starts. Dylan paid the bill and offered his arm to Donna as they all walked out of the bar in a mood buoyed by good companionship but with a dark cloud hanging above them, even as the night sky above showed no sign of overcast and twinkled with stars.

CHAPTER 3

May 11th, 1940

Dylan and Payton awoke early the next day and packed the few things that made the trip with them before checking out and hailing a cab. They had no reason to rush, but keeping the King waiting seemed like bad form. They reached the dock several hours before the scheduled noon boarding, and an hour before the prescribed 7:45 arrival. The slate gray ship rose above them like the thick, dense evergreen forests they knew not far from the farm at home. Both blocked out the sun rather effectively. The boys walked the length of the ship down the dock side by side in silence. Both took in the massive ship with just the slightest bit of awe. They scanned the lines of the ship more thinking about their aeronautics classes and how the water would flow around the prow of the ship than the beauty of such a ship capable of supporting a small city at sea. Air and water behave the same way whether sliced by a wing or a prow. Water is just heavier, that's all. The twins knew that no ship this big could outrun a torpedo, but they could also tell from the shallow rake of the prow that this ship wouldn't maneuver out of the way of anything very easily, either. Torpedoes and icebergs could outmaneuver this ship. The thought surprised neither Anders boy, as this ship started life built for luxury, stability, and steaming in a straight line between New York and London. The designer's task did not include thinking about self-defense. With a full head of steam, though, it might outrun a Uboat.

The twins returned the length of the ship and headed a few blocks away for breakfast to a restaurant recommended by the cab driver. After ordering some scrambled eggs and hash browns, with Dylan adding bacon and Payton opting for sausages, the two finally decided to have the conversation that they'd been avoiding all morning.

"So, this is it. This is our last chance to walk away." Dylan offered.

"I'm not so sure how General Bradley would take it, but we could probably find our way back in to the Army if necessary." Payton responded. "We could probably come up with a plausible reason for not going to pacify him."

"Does that mean you think we should turn back?" Dylan asked.

"No, we made it this far, so we should see it through. We made our decision long before we left New York. If you're in, then I'm in. And, if I'm in, then you're in. We've never done it any differently, so why start now."

"I think you're right. No reason to turn back now, and imagine what we might miss sitting back here." Dylan replied nonchalantly, and his half jesting declaration hung in the air as they finished breakfast. The twins did not agree on everything, and when they didn't the exchanges could get a bit testy, but more often than not they were on the same page. After all, they had grown up together with the same nurturing family around them, attended the same schools with the same teachers instructing them and shaping their outlook. They had similar experiences and a similar predisposition shaping them, but they were not exactly the same and had fraternal reads and reactions to life just like they were fraternal twins. Either way, just as in life, they were in this together.

***

After wandering around the docks for a while longer, the twins arrived at the gangplank precisely on time for WestPoint, which is to say fifteen minutes early. Without much else to do, they loitered on the dock while the crew loaded the provisions for the trip. With such a small passenger list the loading took only a fraction of the usual time. After just a few minutes, a large military truck, known as a deuce-and-a-half for its two-and-a-half ton cargo rating, pulled up next to the loading dock. The driver yelled for a foreman to come over and oversee the unloading of some very expensive looking steamer trunks. Both boys noted the Royal Coat of Arms on each of the steamer cases. The distinctive crowned lion stood guard atop the crowned knight known as the imperial crown proper and was offset by the lion rampart and Scottish unicorn supports holding either side of the quartered shield. The unicorn was chained because it was believed that a free unicorn was dangerous. Each quadrant represented a part of the realm; a harp for Northern Ireland, a lion rampart for Scotland, and a double set of three guardian lions taking up two quadrants for England. The ancillary parts included a surrounding garter with the motto "Honi soit qui mal y pense," ("Shamed be He who thinks ill of it.") The base looked like a meadow with shamrocks, the union rose, and the motto "Dieu Et Mon Droit," ("God and my Right.")

The large, dark leather trunks gave way to two small pink trunks. The young princesses' luggage made it aboard without incident the same as the rest of the royal party's luggage. Mr. Eriksen had not indicated with whom His Royal Highness was traveling, but the smaller pink trunks gave away that his family accompanied him on this trip. On December 11, 1936 King George VI ascended to the throne of England after his brother, Edward VIII abdicated so he could marry the twice divorced American Socialite Wallis Simpson. Dylan and Payton read the many articles in the New York Times delivered to West Point that day. The articles ranged from the diplomatic ramifications of the abdication in Washington DC to a profile of the new Queen and her devotion to her family. The raft of articles also included a contrast of the retiring King, and his brother, the new King.

Where Edward VIII (with a given name of David) was described as outgoing and friendly, George VI (with a given name of Albert) was described as shy and reserved on account of a pronounced stammer. However, Albert had proven a fine family man, according to the articles. George called Princess Elizabeth, his oldest and now heir to the throne, his Pride and his younger daughter, 10-year-old Princess Margaret, his Joy.

In the last year, the boys estimated, the world benefited from King George's stewardship of the monarchy. King George served in the navy and air force during WWI, so he knew both the horrors and necessities of war. He backed Chamberlain in trying to avert war, and now he would help Winston Churchill, announced the day before as the new Prime Minister from his position as First Lord of the Admiralty, muster all the resources of the realm against Adolf Hitler and the Third Reich. Despite their previous disagreements and differing views, the tall saturnine monarch King George VI and shorter, rounder politician Prime Minister Winston Churchill now stood together as veterans of The Great War to try to stave of Germany again in what amounted to the second act of the conflict twenty years prior. If the battle lines in France cannot hold, let alone developing the momentum to forcefully turn back the Germans, which seemed unlikely based on the news so far, then King George VI, Sir Winston Churchill and the British Isles would stand as the last holdout in northern Europe against Hitler and the Third Reich.

Once the luggage loading finished, the large truck rumbled away back towards the town. Payton checked his watch and indicated to his brother that it was time for them to board. They approached the gangplank manned by the steward. The steward smiled as they approached, indicating that perhaps he knew the twins.

"You must be the young charges of my friend Mr. Eriksen." The steward said in a very proper English accent. "Of course, it is easier to recognize two instead of one. I am Mr. Collins. I'm the head steward on the ship in charge of caring for the King and his family from the time he steps on the ship until he steps off."

"Good morning, sir." the twins intoned together in response. "I'm Ryan Stewart, and this is my brother Justin." Payton offered on his own. "We appreciate you taking us on board, and we are happy to do anything to help serve the royal party."

"Excellent. You are, in fact, extra serving crew. We had a full complement of stewards and pages aboard, but we also have a relatively empty ship. Mr. Eriksen told me your true purpose once you reach Europe, so I am pleased to offer any help to those that wish to help Great Britain. I assume Stewart is not your real name, but everyone else on the ship will never know. Your duties should be light; though I'm sure I will find some things for you to help out with around the ship. The King and his family are due to the ship in another quarter hour, so I will show you to your quarters and to the livery for your uniforms in short order. This way please."

The steward walked briskly up the gangplank while deftly handling the gentle sway of the ship in the ebbing tide. Dylan and Payton carried their small suitcases holding the few belongings they brought with them up the steep gangplank keeping pace with the steward. All three walked with the ramrod straight posture belying a military background. Once they reached the top, the steward turned sharp left and led the twins to a staircase leading below decks. After descending only a few flights, the steward surprised the twins by turning towards the outer set of rooms. He stopped at room 910. The twins expected small servant's quarters near the engine, but the small sailing party meant that they were afforded a beautiful stateroom with excellent views out of the starboard side portholes. They would enjoy a southerly view from their stateroom for the trip across the Atlantic, which in these early summer months meant plenty of sunshine as the sun arced from one horizon to the next. The stateroom yawned larger than expected in front of the twins. The retro fit to a troop transport had stripped some of the luxury from the stateroom, but this particular stateroom must have been for higher up officers because many of the amenities remained. It had a private bath with gleaming copper fixtures, as well as a desk set complete with pen and paper emblazoned with the Empress of Britain logo. Opposite the desk sat a very large and ornate headboard suitable for a king size bed, but the bed had been replaced with two slightly offset twin beds indicating shared officer's quarters.

"Sir, this room is more than we deserve. We are just grateful for the ride and glad to help in any way that we can." Dylan said a little sheepishly.

"Mr. Eriksen indicated that you graduated from the US Military Academy. That means you are officers and at the very least I can try and accommodate you as such. Most of the help on the ship have nice state rooms as well, so it is not overly generous to give you this particular room." Mr. Collins kindly replied. "Please, after you put down your things, follow me to the livery where we store the uniforms. Mustn't be late for the King" Mr. Collins urged the twins. "I know that you are due your commissions from the US Army, but I'm afraid the best rank I can give you here is that of Midshipman. Technically you'll rank above the enlisted Petty Officers, but most Midshipman are new and still do what the older Petty Officers ask of them. It is a bit like a new lieutenant in your army listening to the veteran Sergeants. I hope that will not be a problem."

"Of course not, thank you for the deference in asking." Dylan politely answered.

"Excellent, follow me please." Mr. Collins said and turned to resume his brisk pace down the hallway.

As the boys hustled to catch up, Payton asked his brother "Did you catch the room number we're in?"

"I did, apparently the same as you" Dylan answered.

"Yes, 910. Our birthday, September 10th, or 9/10. Probably a good sign for the rest of the trip, I'd say." Payton elaborated.

"Let's hope so." Dylan replied.

CHAPTER 4

May 12th, 1940

After a day at sea Dylan and Payton began to find their sea legs. The massive ship plowed through the calm seas with little rocking or effort, but Mr. Collins wanted to make sure that any seasickness the boys might endure, after all this trip marked their maiden voyage on a seagoing vessel, was left in their stateroom. Fortunately, the intestinal fortitude for flying carried over to the seagoing motion and neither twin found any trouble from the gentle and constant swaying of the ship. They spent their time instead exploring the ship and learning where to find everything aboard. They avoided the Royal Family, but otherwise engaged the rest of the crew to learn as much as possible about both the goings on of the ship and the elite passengers. While on this specific voyage, the name of the ship changed from the standard RMS Empress of Britain, denoting a Royal Mail Ship, to HMS Empress of Britain showing that his was now indeed His Majesty's Ship. The ship measured 760 ½ feet long by 97 ½ feet wide at the widest point. At the bow of the ship and running back for 150 feet of the stem the outer steel plating measured double the normal thickness to deal with the ice of the North Atlantic. When all four propellers pushed the ship forward it could reach a maximum of 25 ½ knots, but most of the time only the inner two screws turned for more efficient running at closer to twenty knots. In its configuration as an all first class luxury cruiser it could carry 700 passengers in style, or when dressed down it could carry just fewer than 1200 passengers combined between first class, tourist class, and third class. The stately ship looked off painted slate grey and not the standard blacks and reds of the cruise line, but the ship continued to slip along the calm waters peacefully. The trip would take eight days total, but the first part stayed mainly in the St. Lawrence River before heading in to the open ocean where the dangerous Uboats waited like wolves looking for easy prey. Running straight ahead and fast on the river and into the Gulf of St. Lawrence made up some time, but zigzagging across the Atlantic slowed the voyage considerably. Zigzagging helped avoid Uboats, and helped convoys run away if they did hit a Uboat trap. The type VII uboat, the most common in the German Kriegsmarine, topped out at 17.7 knots on the surface and only 7.6 knots submerged on battery power. The converted cruise liner carried no defenses save for the speed advantage. The large cruise liner target could only run for safety like a hare from a wolf.

With so few passengers aboard, the ship ran on a skeleton crew. The captain and several officers ran the bridge with only a few more men down in the engine room. The King's staff took care of the galley and personal services under the guidance of the Head Steward, Mr. Collins, so more than just the nooks and crannies remained empty on the voyage. Knowing the ship from stem to stern might help the twins in their duties, but it also helped pass the time. The twins fought off their natural proclivity and walked the upper decks first, but then the twins naturally gravitated to the engine room. After studying the inner workings of steam turbine engines in their interminable thermodynamics classes at West Point and touring some smaller navy boats in the nearby Hudson River, they wanted to see a big one for themselves.

The Empress of Britain had four Parsons Turbines, one for each propeller. The turbine engines used high pressure steam from the ships boiler to create the horsepower required to turn the propeller screws. The double reduction turbine system for each screw actually consisted of two turbines to increase the efficiency of the system. One turbine took the high pressure steam directly from the boiler while the second turbine then took the lower pressure steam from the first turbine. The steam forced over the turbine blades forced each turbine to spin at over 1000 rpm. If the propellers spun at that high rate, the ship would shake apart. So, a very precise set of reduction gears reduced the revolutions output by the turbines to a speed suitable for the screws. The turbines strengths lay in its relatively small size and its proven reliability. The former attribute meant smaller engine rooms and more room for passengers, while the latter meant that the properly maintained turbine would hum along peacefully for many years. The twins spent a couple hours touring the engine room and peppering the engineer on duty on how the whole system worked. They talked about firing up the boiler, pre-heating the turbines, and how the coils helped condense the superheated steam back through the system. The fact that simple steam pushed the mammoth ship ahead at such a fast clip simply amazed the boys. The technology spawned decades ago, starting the industrial revolution, still pushed modern society forward powering ships across the vast oceans.

The second day dawned and the twins reported promptly to Mr. Collins to receive their duties for the day. Dressed in the standard issue naval uniforms, the twins wore the standard navy blue open collar shirt, navy and white striped kerchief around the neck, matching pants and white circular hats with blue headbands.

"We look a little bit like Donald Duck" Dylan had muttered as they put on the uniforms that first morning. The British Sailor suit was the template for most sailor suits in the 19th and 20th century, so the sentiment did not stray much from the mark.

"Gentlemen, good morning, I hope you enjoyed your first day on the ship. I'd say at sea but we aren't quite there yet. I believe we leave the Gulf of St. Lawrence sometime this morning. A pleasant way to start the trip, I believe, as we pass between

Newfoundland to the north and Nova Scotia to the south before we get to the North Atlantic ." Mr. Collins said by way of greeting the twins. "The Royal family should begin stirring in a few minutes, so I'll have one of you take in the morning tea to his Grace while the other takes it to Her Royal Highness. Incidentally, I should remind you that the King is always referred to as his Majesty or his Grace, the queen her Royal Highness, and the children as Princess or your Royal Highness as well. Americans seem to muck up these things, so I thought it best to let you know."

"Thank you, sir. I had no idea. Hopefully we won't embarrass ourselves now." Payton said. "We hope to keep a low profile."

"King George usually takes no offense, and I've even heard some lower nobility refer to him simply as Albert, his given name, but servants should know their place." Mr. Collins continued. "And, I don't think your American accents will help your quest for anonymity." he noted rather dryly.

The twins followed Mr. Collins directions to the mess and then took the silver tea sets quickly up to the royal suites while only pausing briefly to admire the exquisite hand etched silver sets marked with the royal crest. Dylan turned left and headed for the Queen's stateroom suite while Payton turned right and entered the King's stateroom suite. These staterooms obviously avoided the troop transport retrofit. The Kings Suite stretched the length of the two largest staterooms and had a separate sitting area with the bedroom through a door in the rear of the first compartment. Elegant artwork bolted to the mahogany paneled walls showed several seascapes and naval scenes throughout the front room. Payton immediately recognized a scene depicting the Spanish Armada fighting vainly against gale force winds, and Adm. Horatio Nelson's Battle of Trafalgar depicted on another wall. The two greatest British naval victories no doubt hung on the walls for good luck both on this voyage and, hopefully, throughout the war.

His Royal Majesty was not in sight as Payton entered the room, so he set the serving tray down on rather ordinary looking captain's desk bolted to the wall adjacent the door. The middle of the room held a simple sitting area with a comfortable looking love seat across from two Spartan armchairs. None of the furniture shifted even the slightest with the gentle cross motion of the ship, so they too were bolted to the floor.

"You are lucky that we are still in the river, or that tea would surely be on the floor by now." Payton heard from behind him. He turned, snapping to attention, and there stood a man around six feet tall with a long narrow face, dark hair parted to the side, and ears slightly too big for his head. He wore a simple naval captain's uniform with little in the way of markings. Payton knew that the one ribbon on his chest came from his action in the Great War during the battle of Jutland. The King had drawn some praise for his work as a turret office during the largest naval battle of World War I.

"Your Majesty, my apologies. This is my first sea voyage. I will make sure to be more careful in the future." Payton said rather embarrassed.

"You must be one of the Americans that Mr. Collins was telling me about. I was hoping that he would send you up this morning. Mr. Stewart, isn't it?" The King replied.

"Yes, Your Majesty. My name is Justin Stewart. My twin brother Ryan Stewart is in serving Her Royal Highness the Queen." Payton answered.

"I know that is not your real name, as Mr. Collins has told me your true purpose. Don't worry; your secret is safe with me." His Majesty graciously responded. "Mr. Stewart, we are pleased to have you and your brother as part of the war effort. France appears to be faltering, but you are more than welcome to join our forces there. I see that Mr. Collins has given you the rank of Midshipman, which seems appropriate for a Westpointer, I served as that rank more than two decades ago. Therefore, on this ship, you can simply call me sir like any other officer."

"Thank you, sir. We appreciate the ride over on your beautiful ship. She stands well against anything I've ever seen in New York Harbor. The invasion of France makes our trip more urgent, so I'm glad we made the trip with your party. I am pleased to be at your service throughout the trip." Payton answered.

"I'm pleased you are here as well. Before the trip is out I'll want to sit with both you and your brother to learn something of the mood in America. I may be King of the Realm, but I know we

53

will need all the help that your country can give to defeat the Nazis." King George replied with some force in his tone. When he spoke with even this modest passion no hint of a stammer came through in his speaking. "And, the least I can do is offer some help to you." His Majesty continued. "We sail in to Bristol, up the Avon River from the west coast, below Wales. I'll have orders for you to accompany us to London, and then have a car run you down to Dover. You should be able to catch a ride across the Channel from there."

"Thank you, sir. That is very kind of you." Payton replied.

"That will be all for now. Thank you for the tea, Mr. Stewart." The King said as Payton saw the stack of dispatches and other paperwork awaiting the His Majesty on the desk in his ever present red briefcase. Even on the voyage home royal duties never ceased.

***

Payton met Dylan again outside Mr. Collin's office. With their simple morning duties done the steward sent them off after their own breakfast. Seated in the main dining salon with just a few of the other crew, the twins quietly spoke about the experience of meeting royalty for the first time without having the other by their side, a unique circumstance for the twins at a major life event.

"It's not so bad that we get to eat in the main salon. I'm sure the crew usually eats below decks. I guess there are advantages

54

traveling with such a small passenger list." Dylan noted. "Tell me about the King."

"He was very gracious, and same kind of command presence as General Bradley, but more so. I guess the royal upbringing tends to foster that in anyone. He said to call him sir, so I guess we don't have to worry about the official titles on the ship, anyway." Payton responded. "Incidentally, he knows we are frauds, and that we are going to fight in Europe. He didn't ask our real names, but he wants to talk with us about the mood back home. He knows that beating Hitler will take a team effort by the Allies, and the biggest Ally is currently sitting on its hands. Not that we know that much, but he at least thought to ask. Tell me about the Queen."

"She was quiet, but pleasant. She read her dispatches, which I gather were mostly newspaper stories of interest that her staff sent. I imagine the King gets the same." Dylan said.

"Yes, the substantial stack on his desk drew his attention as I started to leave." Payton answered.

"The Queen said little while I set up the tea, but she did light up when the princesses entered the room. She genuinely enjoyed seeing them to start her morning. The girls were cute and quite well mannered. They curtsied to me in their dressing gowns." Dylan continued with a slight grin. "I'm sure they will grow up to be proper ladies. Elizabeth doesn't act like a future queen, but just like a care free young girl. She only stepped seriously in to the line of succession when her uncle abdicated, so I'm sure she may not understand fully the implications yet. She is

55

only 14, so basically a freshman in high school. She's not quite 8 years younger than us."

"A lot happens in 8 years. We played our first varsity baseball games 8 years ago, so not nearly as momentous as learning the monarchy of a thousand year old country in the last three years." Payton said. "What do we tell King George? Everyone at WestPoint knows that this war will consume the globe. I'd even venture that Dad and most of the regular citizenship knows the same, but everyone older than us wants to avoid a fight after The Great War. The people that remember the pains 1918, and know that we are still fighting out of the Depression, sit in Congress and would vote against any war. Simply put, isolationism at its finest. Monroe would be proud. He just said if you don't mess with us we won't mess with you. So, Europe is left to handle itself."

"Seems like the Senators from the North Dakota, Michigan, and Wisconsin would prefer Europe left alone. They think that we entered the Great War just to sell more bullets. We have the Neutrality Act at the moment, so nothing is imminent, but I'm sure the King will want to know how much Roosevelt and the people really believe in it. Roosevelt and Secretary of State Hull both have said they dislike the limitations of the Neutrality act, but they may just say that to tweak the Republicans." Dylan said, thinking aloud. "At this point cash and carry is out, so the Allies can't get guns, planes, or ships from the US. Unfortunately, all they get are you and me." he finished with a chuckle.

"Kind of a raw deal, that's for sure." Payton smiled back. "I'm sure His Majesty will understand. Let's grab our gloves and go up to the deck and see if we've hit the ocean yet."

CHAPTER 5

May 12ᵗʰ, 1940

Even before Dylan and Payton climbed to the top deck the increased sway of the large ship told them that the safety of the gulf lay behind them, and the North Atlantic waited ahead. Nova Scotia receded down the starboard side of the ship, and on the other side of the border Maine receded as well. The coastline reminded both boys of the Oregon Coast back home, more than three thousand miles away. The craggy, rock-strewn beaches hugging brilliant green forest covered hills had a harsh beauty set in stark relief against the furious weather hurled against this coastline by the North Atlantic. Trade the Atlantic for the Pacific and the pattern repeated in Oregon for a similarly beautiful coastline etched by the storms over millennia. The harsh winter weather made days such as this all the more beautiful. The sun shone brightly and bathed the coast with a virginal glow.

Fishing trawlers trailed behind the great ship, merely looking for the days catch and sustenance for the men and women that inhabited the harshly beautiful area. The sunrays may as well have felt like pure hope for a bountiful summer, and on the ship as hope that the light would find its way to Europe to ward off the darkness of the Third Reich. The final glimpses from North America, Canada, and the United States fell behind the twins as they headed for Europe, showing the way for the light to follow. The act of sailing towards a war took courage, though neither Dylan nor Payton thought much about it. Artists use beauty to inspire the masses, while generals use courage to inspire their soldiers. Courage was not the goal of war, but winning a war required courage from the young, and war brought out the greatest expressions of courage the most often.

The boys worked their way to the rear of the ship to avoid the breeze both off the ocean and from the ships forward velocity before pulling their old brown leather gloves from the back of their waistbands. The coastline fell below the horizon and ocean surrounded the ship in every direction as far as the eye could see. Payton pulled a baseball from his pocket and ground it in to the double loop of leather strips forming the web between the thumb and index finger. The glove gleamed an oily deep chocolate brown showing the care with which Payton maintained the leather. The fingers on the square glove splayed out somewhat as Payton gripped the laces of the ball slightly dingy from travel in a suitcase. With a motion honed by years of practice, he turned his shoulders perpendicular to his brother, stepped lightly on line with his shoulders, and casually flung the ball to Dylan. Continuing the light warm up, Dylan repeated a similar motion and easily tossed the ball back at about half speed. After a couple more easy exchanges, they began to unleash hissing missiles at each other. Throwing the ball back and forth let the twins relax in something that they knew and loved, something that they played together as far back as either could remember. It reminded them of home, of their parents watching them play catch in the yard, and of why they chose to enter the battles of Europe and protect those freedoms.

Lost in thought, Payton held the ball a split second too long and skipped the ball just in front of Dylan, who took one step forward, bent his knees, and cleanly picked the short hop just as it rose off the deck. Pivoting back towards his left and sweeping his arm and hand back to cushion the ball in the pocket of his glove, Dylan felt an abrupt thud on the back of his hand as it struck a knee, just as if he had tagged a runner.

"I don't know the rules of baseball very well, but I suppose this means I'm out." His Majesty the king noted with a sly grin.

"Your Grace, please excuse us. I'm terribly sorry. Are you okay?" Dylan stammered out while flushing a deep crimson red in embarrassment. Payton rushed to his brothers side, though he turned the shade of the other stripe on the American flag, white as a ghost in embarrassment as well.

"A bump on the knee won't do me any harm. I did play a little bit of cricket at the Naval College. I was never very good, but enjoyed it nonetheless. You gain advantage on the ship though, otherwise my guards would have toppled you quickly so I could escape the imminent danger of your baseball." The King replied in jest, laughing despite himself. "My God, you two do look so much alike. I'm glad I can just call the both of you Mr. Stewart and not worry about with whom I'm speaking. I am also glad that I ran in to you, as I do want to chat. Perhaps you could teach me to throw a baseball like a proper American while we talk a little bit about your home. Who served me earlier?"

"My brother did, and by way of belated introduction I am Ryan Stewart. I'd be very pleased to add baseball coach to the King of England to my list of accomplishments, sir." Dylan said as he handed the ball across his body to the Kings right hand. King George surprised both boys by switching the ball to his left hand, and gripping it properly across the seams. "Well, sir, you have the first steps down already. I thought you were right handed from watching you take tea, but it is important to throw with your dominant hand, and you naturally gripped the ball correctly." Dylan continued.

"Yes, most people think I'm right handed because I was forced as a child to learn penmanship with my right hand. Only in sport did no one try and correct me." His Majesty answered.

"This will actually make it easier, sir. You can just stand facing me and mirror what I do. Justin will stand on the other end to catch your throws, though I'll have to catch the return since we don't have a left handed glove for you. I'll mime the motions for you, but the important part is the release. Just let the ball roll off your index finger and your middle finger."

Payton stood twenty or so feet away from the duo miming each other as if facing a mirror. The slightly shorter King of England followed along as Dylan turned his shoulders, raised both arms with elbows bent mimicking a scarecrow, and then bringing the ball up behind the back air before pivoting and whipping the arm through. The Kings first throw sailed wide to Payton's left, but he shuffled his feet quickly and grabbed the ball one handed before it escaped in to the Atlantic. Dylan adjusted the kings arm angle to a more vertical position and the monarch's next several throws found Payton easily.

"I can see the appeal in this. Simply throwing something and hitting your target. It's somewhat like archery crossed with lawn tennis, but simpler, and the ball comes back. I am glad that you are doing the catching, as it appears that your brother is capable of returning the ball with somewhat of a furious pace." His Grace observed. "As I've indicated, I would very much like to know what you think of Herr Hitler, and perhaps the mood of your country in general. After the debacle in Norway, I have accepted the resignation of the Prime Minister. Mr. Chamberlain knows quite well that we must unite to win this war, so he has stepped down. First Lord of the Admiralty Sir Winston Churchill will take over as Prime Minister at my request. We both firmly agree that there will be no peace until Germany surrenders fully. No armistice will end this war without total capitulation by the Third Reich." The King continued, working up a slight glean of sweat on his forehead from both throwing more vigorously to Payton and his strident appeal against the Third Reich. "However, France may not hold out, Russia has signed a non-aggression pact, and it appears that Great Britain alone stands against Hitler ruling all of Europe. While all of our heart and might shall fight onward, we must find help."

Standing next to King George, Dylan saw the determination in his face, the determination to uphold the realm that he ruled, to protect the people in his charge, and to make the world a better place. The gravitas automatically bestowed upon a king suited this man well, and he evidently intended to use it well.

"Well, sir, our personal viewpoints stem from our education and I'm sure you understand by our actions that we personally agree with you. We are not merely seeking an adventure across the pond, but truly intend to help defeat Germany. We took the risk to our statehood, our lives, and our future with the US Army because we agree with you, but we also took the risk with the blessing of General Bradley; whom, I'm sure, would agree with you as well." Dylan answered after a moment of thought. "I'm also sure that you know the resistance from many of our Senators and congressmen. They'd rather avoid a war. President Roosevelt probably disagrees, but must unite the country for a war effort before the US can offer any help."

"We personally may not truly represent the American mood at the moment, I'm afraid." Payton jumped in as he walked toward his throwing mates. "However, I would venture that we have a couple of other perspectives that might prove useful to you. First, our father lives in Oregon, on the West Coast, and has farmed his whole life. We grew up helping him. He lived through the Great

War, and he pulled our family through the Depression. He's an intelligent, hard working man, and he's supported us in whatever we've chosen to do. In his last letter to me, he indicated a reticence to endanger the lives of American soldiers, but also noted that when all else failed, it might be necessary to risk those lives to do what is right. Of the common folks, I'd wager that most of them agree. America's roots are partially in Europe, so most can relate. Even the German-Americans are American's first, so when it comes down to it, you can rely on the US common man. The Midwesterner, the West Coaster, the Southerner, they'll all do what is right."

"And the other perspective helps back that up, sir" Dylan continued for his brother. "We spent some time down in New York while in school. The city comes alive at night, and there are plenty of places to find a debate. Before he invaded Poland, some just saw Hitler as trying to pull Germany out of a rut. Now, no one debates it. Everyone agrees he must be stopped. Some debate how, but most know that England can't stop him alone. It's a hard truth, but still the truth."

"Thank you, Gentlemen, both for your honesty and for your courage. Your difficult decision to leave behind your country with no knowledge of the future, the progress of the war, and whether or not your country might eventually enter the war took a bravery I'm not sure many hold. Some go to war to seek glory, but I see that you don't feel that way. I sense that you know right from wrong and will not stand for wrong." His Majesty stated quite elegantly.

"Sir, we hadn't really thought of it that way, but we appreciate your kind words. General Bradley asked us to keep him informed and send back any pertinent information, so part of our task aligns with yours. We'll send back anything that might help the US Army in the event that we join the war, but as we said we do think we'll have to join the war effort at some point. The Allies are strong, but America can add the deciding factor, manufacturing. Supplies fuel a war. Winning requires guns, tanks, planes, jackets, boots, and bullets as well as men. WestPoint hammered that idea home. Napoleon ran short on all of the above when he stretched his supply lines so far east, and the French could not make enough to keep up with the war machine. Let's hope the Allies can hold out and the President can persuade congress to allow us to supply the side of right." Payton said, reiterating their belief that Germany did not stand in the right.

The historical significance of the current conversation never really struck Dylan and Payton. They were discussing the shape of the world, right and wrong, with the King of England, a title that for centuries dating back to the dark ages determined right or wrong for much of the Western Hemisphere. The issue of Hitler did not include shades of grey for the twins or for the King. However, that was not always the case for the German people. Hitler fought in The Great War as a foot soldier for Germany, even though he was born across the border in Austria. At 32, he took over leadership of the Nazi Party, and two years later attempted to seize control of Germany in the Beer Hall Putsch. When his attempted Coup d'état failed, Hitler found himself in jail. While imprisoned, Hitler wrote *Mein Kampf*, his memoir that gained him support throughout Germany based on its nationalistic viewpoint. Hitler took control of the German government after appointment to Chancellor by then President Hindenburg in 1933 at the age of 43, after huge wins by the Nazi party in general elections.

The Versailles Treaty that ended World War I had crippled Germany economically and morally. Hitler's fiery oration and fierce pro-German stances found favor with citizens wallowing in depression. Germany missed the roaring '20s while recovering from the war, and so when worldwide economic depression hit in the '30s, Germany took the hardest hit. Germans felt that he fought to bring Germany back to its former glory, so many followed him simply for giving them a reason to feel good about Germany again. The supposed backing of the common man let Hitler take control of Germany, and lead as a total dictator. With total power, Hitler showed the evil within. He knew that to protect his position and power, to dig Germany out of depression, and to follow through on the promises he made to become Reichsfurher, Germany must re-arm and control continental Europe. Hitler craved power, and more land meant more power. First, Hitler had German forces re-occupy the Rhineland industrial area in 1936, which was taken after WWI by the treaty of Versailles. The industrial area held the key to re-arming the Wehrmacht. Then, Germany annexed Austria in 1938. Later in 1938 Germany occupied The Sudetenland and Czechoslovakia. During this time, British Prime Minister Neville Chamberlain, wishing to appease Hitler and keep him from further pushing out the borders of Germany any more, made a deal that Germany could keep the lands it currently occupied in violation of the Treaty of Versailles as long as they went no further. Hitler, however, did not keep up his end of the bargain. He merely used the time that the appeasement bought him to continue building up his military forces.

The Fuhrer continually used his political acumen to gain his ends, and his subterfuge with Chamberlain was only one example. Knowing that he was not yet ready to execute a full war on two fronts in Europe, and not wanting to only rely on his army, in 1939 Hitler signed the Pact of Steel with Italy forming the Axis Powers, and in a surprise move signed a non-aggression pact with Stalin and the Soviet Union. No longer fearing a response from the Soviets, Hitler invaded the half of Poland that the Russians agreed to, drawing declarations of war from Britain, France, Australia, and New Zealand.

King George VI sought to understand from the twins whether or not America would stand with the Allies or would simply keep its sphere of influence to the westerly side of the Atlantic. Many in America blamed the Depression on the residual effects of interceding in Europe during The Great War. Before WWI, Great Britain dominated the world with its navy. However, that war ushered in the modern era of warfare which relied heavily on manufacturing and inventiveness to produce the weapons required to win a war of machine guns, submarines, tanks, and airplanes. Great Britain could only produce so much on the island, so King George needed the industrial war machine and all the resources of the United States on his side. Staving off German rule of Great Britain stood in the balance. The Goths of ancient Germany had toppled the Roman Empire, and King George VI wanted to make sure that they did not topple his already tenuous empire as well.

"Well, Gentlemen, I appreciate your insight. Let us do hope that America can join the Allies quickly. Otherwise I fear this war will drag on." His Majesty said. "And I really can see why baseball is such an enjoyable sport. It is somewhat cathartic to throw repeatedly. Let's off some of my obvious frustration with the Fuhrer. Next time I'm in America I shall have to enlist someone to take me to an actual game. You are fine instructors, thank you for teaching me."

"I'm pleased you enjoyed yourself, sir, next time we can work on catching the ball, as well as some of the finer points of the game." Dylan said, with a half teasing look in his eye at the rudimentary introduction to simply playing catch.

"I should enjoy that very much. I'll leave it to you to arrange a left handed glove." The King teased back. "I must return to my correspondences, for the moment. Otherwise I shall never see my daughters at all on this trip. Thank you again."

As His Majesty, King George VI, strode back down the length of the ship, both twins knew that they had made themselves an ally should they ever need help of their own as they tried to provide what little help they could fighting against the Nazis.

CHAPTER 6

May 16ᵗʰ, 1940

The next few days went by quickly for the twins. Mr. Collins required very little from them, serving the royal couple from time to time and lending a hand at a couple of meals, so they found different ways to spend their days. They rose early enough for double time runs around the deck, though the monotony took its toll. Eventually, they set up a game where they would race from far below decks by the stern to the upper decks of the bow at the end of their usual run. The stakes were low, so the loser simply had wounded pride and had to make the beds the next morning. Dylan wrote a letter to Anne describing the King and their anxious anticipation for the unknown that lay ahead. Mostly, he surmised to her, they didn't know so they could only wait as the ship slowly crossed the Atlantic. They spent as much time as they could on the deck of the ship, catching the early summer sun that shone brightly across the slight ripples in the chilly water.

This day the ship settled quietly in to the usual afternoon routine. The royal party finished their lunches and retired below decks to rest in their staterooms. After helping with lunch, Dylan and Payton held no responsibilities for the rest of the day. On the ship for nearly a week, the boys knew the Empress of Britain inside and out. They found the best views on the short stern of the ship behind the three massive funnels, so when relaxing they tended to see what lay behind. The vast expanse of water stretched behind the two boys as they idly discussed nothing at all. The boys sat in chairs above the great propellers below, at the very end of the ship. Dylan faced slightly port of dead astern and Payton faced slightly starboard. The midday sun splattered rays from behind the twins as it marched from bow to stern since the ships last turn put it back on an almost direct easterly course.

Half way through a sentence to his brother, Payton stopped suddenly and squinted out to the southwest.

"What's going on?" Dylan asked as he turned toward his brother.

"Out there, a consistent reflection. I've seen it twice, spaced out about 15 seconds each time." Payton answered as he pointed out to a spot in the ocean about three thousand yards out. As he said it, the small flash showed again in the exact same spot. Knowing almost exactly the angle his brother looked out on, and sharing the same remarkable eyesight, Dylan saw it too.

"I see it. That's too bright to be a reflection off the water or a fish. That's glass." Dylan said.

"Right, Uboat. Let's get to the bridge." Payton answered as both boys knocked their chairs to the ground simultaneously going from sitting with no movement to as fast as they could run. Running along the port rail and bounding up the stairs, the boys reached the bridge in near world record time for the 100 yard dash. The midday watch officer lead the twins straight to the captain.

"Sir, there appears to be a Uboat bearing down on us." Dylan ventured to the captain. Usually the low ranking officers serving as stewards did not speak much to the captain, but the twins had spoken with him several times, allowing him to show his pride in the ship while sharing his knowledge of the Empress and of the North Atlantic. The boys impressed the captain with their knowledge of engineering and their willingness to listen. Since they had become friendly, the captain did not dismiss them immediately as green sailors mis-sighting a piece of rubbish floating aimlessly on the high seas.

"Show me, please." The captain commanded as he stood and reached for his binoculars. The boys led him out the back of the bridge and angled his view to the last spot sighted. The captain leaned forward and rested his arm on the rail to steady himself against the slight swaying of the ship. After a few seconds staring, the captain saw the bright flash and stood straight up while pivoting and nearly ran to the bridge himself. The flash had moved several hundred yards closer, nearing the range for a torpedo shot. With the stately cruise liner steaming ahead without a course change, the Uboat commander had no reason to believe that he'd been spotted.

As the captain arrived back at the bridge he addressed the crew, "Gentlemen, we have a tail gaining on us from the southwest. His angle is acute enough that he will overtake us and have a sure firing solution for his torpedoes in roughly 30 minutes." The mental arithmetic involved in coming to that conclusion showed a keen mind by the captain, and years of experience at sea. The calm tone with which he delivered the statement showed his fortitude.

"Shall we sound the alarm, Captain?" The office of the deck asked with only a hint of tension in his voice.

"Not yet." The Captain responded. "This submariner is going to try and get in as close as possible before taking his shot. He's underwater, so he's moving slowly. We want to get our outer two screws turning so that we can make a hard turn and run away from him before he thinks we know he's there. Otherwise, he'll let loose his torpedoes from further out and still have a decent shot at getting us. We can't have that. He's played at deception, and now it is our turn."

"Sir, you've only got one engineer, and it would take him nearly an hour to get the boilers going in the engine room." The officer of the deck reminded the captain.

"We can help, sir. We know something of boilers and turbines and at the very least could add two extra sets of hands." Payton offered.

"Excellent, report to the Engine room and tell the engineer that he has 15 minutes to get the outer screws turning or we will be known as the ship that sank with the crown aboard." Dylan and Payton left the bridge and hustled as quickly as they could to the engine room.

On arriving in the boiler room, the twins heard the engineer arguing mightily with the captain.

"I don't care who will sink with us, it takes at least thirty minutes to even get the boilers heated, and another ten after that to get the screws turning. We need another plan!" the engineer practically yelled in to the radio.

The twins knew the logistics involved in firing up the remaining boilers. The water in the boiler must first boil and turn in to steam, and then the steam must be heated and brought up to a very high pressure before it passes over the first set of blades in the turbine. After passing the first set of blades in the turbine, the steam passes over a second set of blades at a lower temperature before condensing back in to water. As the steam is passed over the blades due to the pressure gradient, it turns the gearing system that in turn delivers power to the screws of the ship. If the steam isn't at the correct pressure, the gears won't turn and the screws will sit motionless or worse yet, the water won't turn to steam and it will damage the turbine blades. If the steam is heated too quickly and overheated causing a much higher pressure, it can blow out the bearings and seals in the system, also damaging the turbine beyond repair.

"Mr. Scott, the captain sent us to help." Dylan said as the engineer slammed the radio receiver down. The boys knew the Irish engineer quite well from the hours they'd spent going over the engine room peppering him with questions. The short, round, red-haired Irishman was glad for the company at the time, and didn't mind answering the questions that helped the boys go from theoretical knowledge learned at WestPoint to practical knowledge learned on an actual ship.

"I'm glad you both are here to help, but I don't think it will do much good. We can't cheat physics in this case." Mr. Scott responded as he cooled down somewhat from the heated exchange with the bridge. "At least you've seen everything here and know where to find everything. Hopefully your time spent down here already won't have been for waste."

"Well, sir, in this case we might be able to cheat physics just enough to get out of here." Dylan continued, somewhat boldly.

"If you've any ideas I'm happy to listen." Mr. Scott said, and his voice indicated that his desperation meant he would listen intently.

Payton knew exactly what his brother was thinking and answered Mr. Scott. "In school we had a class dealing with turbines, and one of the professors took us down on the Hudson River to a smaller ship. He wanted us to get some hands on learning. One trick he taught us was to pre-fire the boiler tank in two stages. He said this was for emergencies only because the first stage uses a blow torch to heat the casing until it is hot, but not hot enough to melt metal, and the second stage requires a little more pop."

"And by that he means a controlled explosion." Dylan finished for Payton.

"That's crazy. You want to turn the boiler tank in to an internal combustion engine." Mr. Scott said with a stunned expression on his face.

"He did say it was for emergency starts. I'd say this qualifies. You pump some of the blow torch gas in to the top of the boiler tank and let it blow to vaporize enough of the water for a kick start. The first heating makes sure that the water is warm enough that it will vaporize quickly, otherwise the boiling will get out of control. I'm hoping you have methyl acetylene and propadiene, MAPP gas, in your blowtorches here for the underwater work. It's less volatile, so should work better for this scheme."

"That's correct. I've no other ideas, so let's hope that we don't explode the royal family. If we don't try, the torpedo surly will. There are two blow torch tanks attached to the bulkhead just outside the boiler room. You each take a boiler tank, and I'll monitor the pressure gauges here. We're down to eleven minutes to get these started."

"That should be about right." Payton answered.

"Good luck and Godspeed then. Off with you." Mr. Scott said as a brief farewell and half prayer.

The boys hurried down the half hallway between the engine monitoring room and the boiler room, grabbing the blow torches on the way. The boys felt fortunate that two protective masks hung next to the blowtorches instead of the usual single mask per station. Dylan entered the room first and broke to the left, heading for the dormant outboard port boiler dragging the fuel tank behind him. Payton broke to the right, aiming for the cold outboard starboard boiler with his fuel tank in tow as well. Working quickly to light the torches for each other in between the two boilers, each twin returned to his boiler and methodically started heating the outer tanks. Payton kept a tally of the time on his watch, and reported the minute long increments to Dylan. They moved the blow torches in long circular motions around the bottom of the boiler tanks and worked their way to the top. They managed five full passes each in the six minutes they figured they could spare. Then each twin extinguished the torches flame, but left the gas flow fully open. The twins quickly opened the water overflow ports and held the torch heads in the tanks. As the MAPP gas and oxygen mixed above the water in the tank it started to become more volatile. The twins needed to mix just the right amount of gas in with the oxygen in the tank to reach the flash point and vaporize the top layer of remaining water. Without enough gas, any spark will fall harmlessly in to the water. Too much gas and the resulting explosion will blow the doors off the boiler at least, and possibly blow out the hull of the ship as well.

"How long do we fill these things?" Payton wondered aloud.

"Well, the Professor said 1 minute, but that tank probably wasn't even half this size. I say go two and half minutes. Better to overfill at this point than to fizzle and wait for the torpedo." Dylan answered.

Besides guessing at how long to leave the gas flowing in to the tanks, Dylan and Payton had another problem.

"Do you have idea how we are going to light the fire in the tanks? I seem to be fresh out of fuses." Dylan told his brother.

"I've only got one idea, and it isn't great." Payton answered. "It does, however, give us the best chance of not blowing ourselves up."

"Let's hear it." Dylan said without hesitation.

"Call it a variation on flicking a cigarette. We'll loosely attach one of Mr. Scott's cigars to the valve handles that are directly above these openings. See the spokes in the handles? It shouldn't be too hard. Then, we'll each take a baseball and throw it from over by the door at the pipes. If we both hit it the angle next to the valve on cue, the cigars should drop in and light the gas." Payton offered.

"You're right, that isn't a very good idea." Dylan deadpanned back at his brother. "We need these doors to slam shut on impact. How you going to manage that, Houdini?"

"Simple, balance them straight up instead of flopping them all the way to the side. We can wedge a wrench underneath with some grease so it is barely holding and the first rumble of the explosion should slam them shut. They are self locking, so we won't have to worry about them re-opening." Payton said to his brother as he began to warm to his own plan.

"Well, it's this or no plan. And, like Dad always said, a bad plan well executed is better than no plan at all. Let's give it a shot. Overfill your tank since some of the gas is bound to leak out while we are getting everything set up." Dylan said, also warming to his brother's plan. "I'll radio Mr. Scott for the cigars. We've only got about two minutes left."

Mr. Scott arrived with two lit cigars and a mass of confusion. "The tanks are warm, but we'll need quite the explosion to get us going, lads. I don't even want to know what you need the cigars for. Hopefully for a victory celebration, but it seems a little premature to ask for them to be lit already."

"I'm sorry, sir, but the cigars are a sacrifice to the boilers." Dylan said with a playful tone belying the pressure of the situation. "You may want to head back to the monitoring room. We're not sure this is the safest place to be."

Mr. Scott required no further prodding and turned tail back to the control room. The twins each affixed the cigars above the overflow opening by gently balancing the burning embers in the spokes, and they both hoped a stray piece of lit ash didn't start the explosion early. Having already balanced the doors open, they then turned and both walked slowly back towards the bulkhead door to avoid shaking both the doors and the cigars. Just before they reached the bulkhead, each produced a baseball from their pockets.

"Don't forget to duck." Payton said as the boys turned simultaneously and unleashed their best fastballs at the pipes overhanging each boiler. With the release of the ball, the twins planted their left foot and dove for the bulkhead door. Payton scrambled through first, followed by Dylan slamming the door behind him. Their throws both flew true and straight, and struck the pipes as intended. The poor plan executed flawlessly ignited the gas and slammed the doors shut. The boys knew they'd gotten it right by the simultaneous clang of the baseballs on the pipes followed by a loud cracking explosion, just like the fireworks on the Fourth of July.

Even before the twins could make it back to the control room, Mr. Scott burst out in to the hallway and exclaimed "You've done it!" He grabbed both boys and hugged them with such enthusiasm that Dylan thought the burley engineer meant to break their spines. "Both turbine leapt to life and are humming along. There are no indications of a leak or damaged blades. The shafts and propellers should start turning full bore in moments." The nearly giddy engineer continued.

"Now it's just up to the captain to get us out of here." Dylan smiled.

"If you don't mind, Mr. Scott, we'll head up to see if Mr. Collins needs us." Payton said, more relieved than anything that the plan worked and they hadn't sunk the ship before the Uboat had a chance.

CHAPTER 7

May 16th, 1940

Dylan and Payton took more time returning to the top decks than they had descending to the engine room. With the rest of the ships fate out of their hands they could walk off some of the tension inherent in setting off an explosion in a very explosion unfriendly place. During the actual work neither thought of the gaping hole below the water line possible from their actions, but walking back up gave them a chance to think it over. Both counted themselves lucky and moved forward with only enough reflection to note that at least they'd thought quickly, worked together as a team and succeeded. Their absolute faith in each other to execute the plan allowed each to perform under pressure. Neither twin would let his brother down.

The twins managed to track down Mr. Collins in the main salon with the royal family and most of the traveling party.

"Excellent, I was looking for both of you. I was afraid the young Misters Stewart had gotten lost. We seem to be in a touch of trouble, the Captain has asked that we remain in the Salon while there is a Uboat in the area." Mr. Collins said by way of greeting and obviously relieved to see his young charges.

"Sorry for our absence, sir, and thank you for your concern. The Captain had us helping in the engine room." Payton answered.

King George overhead the twins speaking with Mr. Collins and inquired "I heard a muffled explosion from the direction of the engine room, is everything all right?"

"Yes, your Majesty. We caused the explosion on purpose in the boiler tanks to help start the turbines for the outer two screws. It was a bit tricky, but I think it worked." Payton answered the King while understating the risk involved in their startup.

"The Captain is trying to lull the Uboat in to not firing until we can get all four propellers spinning. Then we can take evasive action and sprint away from the slower boat while it is still underwater." Dylan added. "I'd expect the captain to give the orders shortly."

"You started two turbines in such short order?" The King asked, vaguely remembering the tedium from his days in the Royal Naval College at Dartmouth. "I'm rather impressed."

"Thank you, sir. It was a bit hairy, but it worked. Unfortunately, now we must sit, wait, and hope that the Captain is right." Payton said. As he finished, the ship shuddered like someone with a cold feeling running up the spine. The whole ship shook as the captain had given the orders for the port rudders to full reverse and the starboard rudders to full ahead. The engine noise, usually at a low murmur throughout the trip, markedly increased in intensity and throbbed through the ship. The cruise liner certainly could not turn on a dime, but stressing the propellers and shafts with this maneuver gave the ship the quickest pivot. Once turned, the Captain could order full ahead on all four propellers to run away and hide.

"I'd suggest we hold on to something." The King instructed everyone in the room as the ship began to tilt back to starboard from the massive forward inertia and the port propellers pulling that side down. The twins rather gamely took at seat at one of the bolted down tables and held on to the edge, knowing that the legs were available for back up handholds. The king took four strong steps toward his family and secured his two daughters on a padded booth seat against the near port bulkhead. The King made a sensible choice since the starboard side of the ship already hung noticeable higher than the port side.

As the angle increased, the few loose items such as forks and spoons began sliding towards the port bulkhead. The rest of the traveling party held on a little tighter as the angle of the ship continued in to an uncomfortable tilt. Though the ship was far from capsizing, those not accustom to the sea felt anxious at least. Payton and Dylan grinned at each other and sat totally at ease. They'd twisted the old crop dusting plane to much steeper angles at home. Some of the traveling party looked with horror at the large grand piano as it creaked loudly like old floorboards with the rising angle, but it remained anchored firmly in place.

However, as some looked at the piano, Dylan and Payton eyed a large silverware cart that carelessly left out in the haste brought on by the Uboat sighting. As it began rolling towards the royal family, Dylan started to rise to his feet and say something to his brother.

Payton cut him off "I see it, too." he said as he stood up also. Dylan stood closer to the rolling cart, so he took the three steps across and at an upward angle to intercept the cart. Payton stepped around the table and followed close behind his brother. The large thick oak cart matched the walls of the dining Salon, and still held the full complement of the ships silverware after lunch. Not only did it look heavy, it was heavy, befitting the class and style of the regal ship. Dylan grabbed the handles of the cart as it approached him, but knew that momentum would betray him. The cart slammed in to Dylan knocking him abruptly backwards and threatening to run him over. Trusting his brother, Dylan neatly reverse pivoted to the side of the cart and threw one hand up for his brother to catch while holding on to the cart with his other hand. Payton had already wrapped one arm around a support pillar and reached out to perfectly catch his brother's wrist in midair. It looked like perfectly choreographed trapeze artists in midair beneath the big top. The collision with Dylan slowed the momentum enough that in tandem the twins could hold on enough to stop the cart before it barreled in to the King and his youngest daughter. Dylan and Payton swung slightly to the side and lowered the cart to the bulkhead wall as gently as they could manage.

"Thank you. That could have turned out rather badly." The King said to the twins with obvious relief and his daughter hugging tightly to his side. The twins noted that the King moved round himself at the first sign of trouble to help shield his daughter. He would have taken the brunt of the blow in an effort to protect his child, just like any other parent. "It looks like you may have practiced that pirouette before. I hope you are not injured." His Majesty continued.

"I'm fine, sir, and thank you for asking. The pivot was just like turning a double play in baseball from second base. I mostly played catcher, but have made that play before. It's also similar to spinning away from a tackle in football, at least our football. You just plant your inside foot and spin out." Dylan answered politely.

"I'm not sure that you would usually throw your arm up to be caught in either of those moves." The King observed.

"That was just faith in my brother, and a bit of luck." Dylan lightly added.

As Dylan spoke, the sound of the ship stopped pulsing as all four screws slowed momentarily. The Captain was allowing the port screws to slow from all back and accelerate to all ahead without the starboard screws continuing to push the ship into its turn. By allowing all four screws to accelerate together, the captain hoped he'd gain enough torque to accelerate quickly enough that any torpedo fired half cocked would fall behind the ship. The passengers in the main salon all breathed a sigh of relief as the ship began to level out. With an even keel, the engines shuddered again and fully came to life. The lumbering behemoth did not leap forward, but it did make a small, reassuring surge on its new path. Several more minutes passed in tense silence as everyone prayed that the ship would avoid the watery depths.

"Well, we've made it this far, the Captain must feel better. I haven't heard any torpedoes pinging after us yet, so we are at least putting distance between us and the sub. I'm sure the tension up on the bridge must be unbearable. Fortunately down here we have Mr. Collins and that fine piano." His Majesty observed, breaking the mood. Unbeknownst to the twins, Mr. Collins was also a highly accomplished pianist who played for the King and his family often. "Mr. Collins, if you would, let's have a song. Girls, you can sing along. Camp Town Races may be appropriate for our recently won five mile turn and run!" He continued enthusiastically motioning Mr. Collins to the piano and addressing his children at the same time. Mr. Collins took his place at the piano and played a brief entry before breaking in to the familiar tune. Both the princesses sang the melody with sweet soprano voices, and before long the whole room joined in to the song. The salon rang with boisterous if slightly absurd music born of the relief that only a near miss with mortality and escape back to life can bring.

As the song wound down, the officer of the deck stepped in to the room with an announcement. "I'm terribly sorry for the inconvenience, everyone. The Captain appreciates your cooperation and hopes you understand that he is only looking out for everyone's well being. We are now out of range of the submarine, so you are free to go about your usual business." As he uttered the last phrase the room erupted in applause, not the least of which came from His Majesty himself.

"Excellent, please pass my heartfelt thanks to the Captain and all the crew. A jolly good show by everyone. I'll remain in the salon for a while, so please let the crew know that I'd like to thank each and every one of them if they have time to stop by here." The King commended the beaming officer and showed his intention to commend all the crew. After all, even on the ship, it wasn't often that one had an audience with the King.

Dylan and Payton sat against the wall of the salon quietly. They were pleased that their efforts had helped aid the escape in a key role, but they knew the ultimate outcome came from a good plan by the Captain and a healthy dose of luck. The salon still buzzed from the escape and the dissipating tension, so Dylan and Payton quietly slipped out the side door to avoid stealing the show from the Captain and regular crew.

CHAPTER 8

May 19th, 1940

The day broke crisply as the sun seemed to bounce in to the sky faster than normal. All aboard the ship anticipated the mid-morning arrival in Southampton eagerly. Many wandered to the bow of the ship straining to catch the first sight of their home realm. Not long after breakfast, the watch office spotted the first glimpse of their destination through his binoculars. Soon after, the passengers on the bow could see the first bump on the horizon with their naked eyes. A small cheer rose from the decks and then quickly vanished as everyone hurried back to their staterooms to put the finishing touches on packing and readying for arrival. With little to pack, Dylan and Payton took their last chance to stroll around the decks, enjoying the sun and relaxation settling over the ship. After the Uboat incident most of the passengers tensely waited out the last days of the journey, but with land in sight everyone could breathe deeply again.

What most of the passengers did not know was that hours ago in the middle of the night they had already passed in to the English Channel. Montreal sits at roughly 45 degrees latitude while Southampton sits at roughly 50 degrees latitude. Since the ship came up slightly from the south and it was the middle of the night, the passengers never saw Falmouth on the western tip of southern England.

Normally, the cruise liner would pull in to Southampton opposite the Isle of Wight, but since the King's name topped the passenger manifest this particular voyage would continue for about an hour more on to the Royal Navy yard at Portsmouth which sits 19 miles southeast of Southampton. The city of Portsmouth, such as it was, mostly occupies Portsea Island. Portsmouth, an island city, serves as one of the main seaports traversing the English Channel to mainland Europe and on through the Mediterranean Sea from the United Kingdom. The island sits in a cove shaped like a C tipped down so the opening faces south. Portsmouth Creek completely cuts the island off from the mainland in the north, but several bridges easily cover the distance and give Portsmouth the feel of a peninsula rather than an island. The true Portsmouth harbor lays west of the island, with the Naval Base sitting on the western edge of the island. Many fingers of the harbor intrude on to Portsmouth proper and the mainland on both sides of the island, looking like a leafless tree in winter from above.

The low laying industrial city did not particularly stand out on first inspection from the sea liner. No sight emerged of a pretty coast line with white beaches and a forest behind like in Sussex, or any striking geological feature like the Cliffs of Dover. The low docks and piers had some small hills behind and that was that. However, on closer inspection one could see the history of the city as its best feature. Once closer to the city South Sea Castle stood proudly and defiantly on the southern tip of the island projecting the military might of the British Empire. Portsmouth played a key role in the naval history of the British Empire, and any future king surely knew the symmetry of sailing in to this port with his latest version of the Empire at stake.

The strategic value of Portsmouth first showed in 1194 AD when King Richard the Lionheart gathered an army there after returning from imprisonment during the crusades. The French invaded and sacked the city in 1338, the Black Death first struck in 1348, and the French sacked the city again in 1369, 1377, and 1380. The fortifications necessary throughout the years eventually led to Portsmouth boasting the most fortifications in all of Britain, and possibly the world, surrounding the city. As the main Naval base for the Realm projecting its power on the high seas the necessary fortifications were continuously built and improved throughout the 16th, 17th, and 18th centuries. In 1787 eleven ships sailed to settle the first European colonies in Australia, and thus began the infamous prisoner transports.

The city also boasted two unique literary ties to two of the more famous authors of the 19th century. Charles Dickens was born in Portsmouth on February 7th, 1812. The famous author's family moved away shortly after his birth a hundred or more miles to Chatham, southwest of London. Portsmouth still claimed him as a native son, though his socio-economic views and his fight against child labor were formed later on in London. The other famous author was more closely linked to Portsmouth. Sir Arthur Conan Doyle moved to Portsmouth to start a medical practice in 1882 when he was just Dr. Conan. With few patients and little money at first, he spent his time writing. In 1887, Sherlock Holmes made his first appearance in *A Study in Scarlet*. Four years later Doyle moved to London as well, but Sherlock Holmes was born in Portsmouth.

Knowing their naval history, the twins also knew the most famous fact about Portsmouth. In 1805, Lord Admiral Horatio Nelson set sail for the last time from Portsmouth. He led the British fleet against the combined fleets of the French and Spanish Navies during the Napoleonic wars in one of the most famous English Naval victories, The Battle of Trafalgar. At the time, Napoleon had the greatest land army in the world, but the British had the greatest Navy and controlled the world's oceans.

In the middle of August 1805 Lord Cornwallis had detached the core of the fleet from the English Channel to sail towards Spain and engage the enemy fleet in a decisive battle. That fleet began by blockading Spain. Nelson joined the blockaded sea lanes off of Spain in his flag ship HMS Victory and took command in the middle of September. Nelson had twenty seven fighting ships to meet the thirty three fighting ship Spanish/French fleet off the

Cape of Trafalgar in southwest Spain. Napoleon badly wanted to invade Britain, so Nelson sailed to defeat the enemy fleet, maintain control of the English Channel, and thwart any chance of an invasion flotilla safely crossing to Britain.

The decisive battle came on October 21, 1805. After several hours of maneuvering and build up to the battle, at just before noon, Nelson sent out the signal "England expects that every man will do his duty." Fifteen minutes later, the Spanish Admiral opened fire. Nelson played out an audacious plan. General high seas warfare of the time indicated that the two fleets faced off in single battle lines, broadside and parallel, firing away until one side sank or ran away. Instead, Nelson divided his line in two and ran one line straight for the heart of the opposition line while the second line headed for the rear. The Spanish and French could fire at the oncoming lines, but the British could not return fire since their broadsides would not point at the enemy ships. If the British could survive the run to the lines, then they could envelope the enemy ships and engage them individually with their superior seamanship. Nelson even had his ships painted in a yellow and black checkered pattern so they would recognize each other in the melee. The risks were huge, but the English Empire stood in the balance.

The plan succeeded spectacularly. Not one English ship was sunk or captured, but only eleven enemy ships escaped. Nelson's genius plan, and the execution of the British sailors, won the day handily. Slightly more than sixteen hundred British sailors were killed or wounded, including Nelson who died on

HMS Victory, but that paled in comparison to the more than 13,000 Spanish and French sailors killed, captured or wounded.

The decisive battle denied Napoleon any chance at invading the Island. HMS Victory survived the Battle of Trafalgar and still sat in Portsmouth harbor as a museum. As the converted cruise liner steamed past the retired wind driven ship, Hitler's and Napoleon's dominance of continental Europe drifted over the minds of the twins. King George now hoped his military could deny Hitler the same attempt in the first real threat of invasion since Napoleon. Britain stood at the precipice of trying to stop another tyrant controlling the Old World, but the King knew that this time he'd need the help of the New World. The Uboat episode proved that the Royal Navy no longer ruled the high seas and that Britain could no longer stand alone. The Battle of the Atlantic indeed.

By the time the ship docked and the gangway was lowered in to place the twins had taken care of their final duties and packed. They returned their uniforms to Mr. Collins and thanked him profusely for his hospitality on the ship. The steward admired the sincerity and effort the boys brought to the tasks he assigned and with a twinge of sadness bid them goodbye. He knew they meant to help fight Hitler, so the twinge of sadness was tempered by hope that their fight would help bring more like them. These two risked as much as all the British soldiers already fighting.

Custom called for the Captain to wait by the gangway and give permission for the King and the Royal Family to disembark first. With the Royal Family not yet ready, Dylan and Payton loitered on the top deck waiting for their turn to amble down the gangplank. As with most of the trip, the mid May sun competed only against the blue in the sky. As they stood near the stern of the boat, the boys managed to conceal their surprise when the King wandered toward them. Neither had said goodbye to the King or his family, figuring that such familiarity might not suit their place. However, the King walked directly for the twins with a smile on his saturnine face.

"I'm glad to find you both." he said by way of greeting.

"We're pleased to see you as well, sir. I thought you'd be busy finishing up any duties before disembarking." Dylan answered.

"Fortunately for me, my wife is quite adept and rounding up the details as well as being a Queen. She does everything she can to help me, and I adore her for it." The King said. "Even for a King, a loving wife and family bring me more joy than anything else. You are young now, but you'll find that in time I'm right on this one." He finished with a slight nod of the head indicating knowledge hard earned over time.

"Our father always told us that the right woman makes all the difference, so I guess he must have been right, too." Payton jokingly replied.

"Smart man, your father, teaching you so well" The King smiled back. "I do wish to discuss something with you for a moment. I appreciate your advice on the mood in America as well. The throwing lesson was just an added adventure inside what I believe you call The National Pastime. I understand your great sacrifice and risk coming here to help, so for that I'd like to do everything I can to help you. My people tell me your real names are Dylan and Payton Anders, but I hope you don't mind me inquiring about that."

"I believe in your discretion sir, so no, it isn't something for us to worry about. And, just so you know, I'm Payton and he's Dylan" Payton answered gesturing at his brother with only a hint of surprise and a touch of pride that the King had bothered to find out who they really were.

"Excellent, then I have two things to hopefully help you on your way. I understand you are to meet a Mr. Hobbes here." The King inquired.

"Your information is very good, sir. That is correct." Dylan replied.

"The Monarchy has its benefits. His only job was to put you on a bus to London and instruct you to find your way to Le Havre. His services are not needed, as I've arranged for you to take one of my cars here and have you delivered to The Savoy. You may stay there as long as you like, but with your intents you'll probably be gone within the week." His Majesty continued.

"Thank you sir, that is more than generous of you. That's the second lift you've offered us which is more than we deserve." Dylan offered graciously in return.

"I wish I could offer you a third, but I'm afraid I can't arrange passage to France for you. Imposing on the Royal Navy would be quite bad form at the moment." The King concluded. "I can, however, offer you these." He said reaching in to his breast pocket and extracting to letter sized envelopes with the royal seal engraved on them. "These are letters of recommendation I've written for you both. They indicate that you have my full support in your endeavors, and that whomever you present these to should offer you whatever assistance you require. If you are in a hard place, you can use these as a last resort."

"Your Majesty, thank you, your kindness is an honor. We can only hope to live up to the responsibilities such honor requires." Payton said failing to conceal his stunned feelings.

"Your modesty is a virtue. You helped save me and my family from that Uboat, and you offer your services to my country and mankind without asking anything for yourselves. My actions are from gratitude." His Majesty said with all sincerity. "Please, if you are in and around London throughout your efforts call ahead to Buckingham Palace to see if I am there to meet you. I'll very much like to hear reports of your efforts."

"Of course, thank you again, sir. Nothing would delight us more than to see you again."

"Splendid, then we shall meet again. I'm sure my wife is looking for me now, so I'm off. Good hunting to you both." The King finished as he left with the stride of a man determined to accomplish the task ahead.

"Well, I guess we have something to write home about. Dad will never believe how this trip started. The King of England believes in us, so we'll have to make sure not to disappoint him." Dylan offered wryly when His Majesty was out of earshot.

"Hopefully we don't have to use them, but these letters should help." Payton said to his brother. "It can't hurt, at least. I'm glad that he remembered the car, though. I'm sure if it is one of his it's a nice one. If I recall from the paper he's a bit of a car buff and has helped design several of his personal limousines."

"We'll see soon enough. It appears that the Royal Party is headed down to shore if you look over to the gangway. Let's start heading that way, at least. The ship's been fun, but the sooner we're off it the better." Dylan indicated.

"I'm with you. Let's get the rest of this show on the road." Payton answered his brother as they both walked unhurriedly but with a hint of a purpose to the gangway amidships.

The Captain lingered by the gangway after the Royal party departed, so the twins offered him their thanks and goodbyes before heading down the steep plank to plant their first steps on European soil. Neither took much note of their first steps because they kept walking down the docks enjoying dry land for the first time in more than a week. As they edged off the dock and walked over the seawall the twins smiled at the beautiful automobile that pulled up to greet them. The King's automobile's reputation preceded itself nicely as a midnight black limousine with the long hood gracefully stretching across the horsepower inside slowly stopped a few feet from the twins. A smartly dressed chauffer stepped out the driver's side on the left and introduced himself to the twins.

"I'm Mr. Smith, your chauffer. May I assume that you are the Misters Anders that the King has asked me to take in to London?" The chauffer asked succinctly.

"That's correct. This is a beautiful car." Payton said.

"Thank you. This is one of the Kings two limousines from the Lanchester Motor Company, owned by Daimler. The limousine is all aluminum, so it is lightweight, and the coachwork was done by Hooper, Royal Warrant Holders. The King himself contributed to the design." The chauffer answered; obviously proud of the car he drove.

The car deserved the praise. On the tip of the car stared out the hood ornament that appeared to be a saint of some sort. Below that four headlights showed the way, but with the bigger standard lights nearly the size of a beach ball sitting between the fenders and the hood. Below the larger lights sat a horn on each side, and then the smaller lights attached to the front bumper. The vertical slats in the front grill sat below the long black hood covering the straight eight engine. The rakish fenders flowed back like waves on either side of the car. The front almost looked like two big eyes with the grill as a nose and the smaller lights as nostrils just above the smile extending from the bumper through the front fenders. The running boards tapered from the front to the rear of the roomy box shaped coach, and the spare tire nestled behind the front fender. The car exuded the height of elegance and certainly befit the King.

Mr. Smith took the boys bags and strapped them down in the trunk as the boys climbed in to the back seat.

"How far is it to London?" Dylan asked.

"It's a little over sixty miles. We should make it in a little over an hour, perhaps an hour and a half." Mr. Smith responded. "The countryside is beginning to bloom this time of year, and the weather should be good, so please enjoy the ride. If you have any questions feel free to ask me. I grew up in London, but my mother is from here, so I've been this way many times."

The car swept out past the dry docks where workers furiously fussed over repairs of ships needed for the war effort. Navy ships stood naked above the water where even the smallest ships showed their massive girth. The twins settled in to the back seat and watched the port turn in to the port town and eventually the countryside. Neither twin said much as each quietly contemplated the next steps in their journey. The stop in London sounded fun, but the ultimate goal lay in France. They needed to find a way to get to Le Havre so they could help.

CHAPTER 9

May 22nd, 1940

Three days later the twins grew more anxious the longer they stayed at the Savoy, but the hotel held no fault. The twins knew that famous folks such as Charlie Chaplin, Judy Garland, and Babe Ruth had all signed the guest book as well as literary giants such as HG Welles and Oscar Wilde. The boys also enjoyed the music of George Gershwin, and knew that the 1925 British debut of "Rhapsody in Blue" came in the elegant River Restaurant of the Savoy with the BBC broadcasting it across the country. The musical connection fit nicely because originally the hotel was built next to the Savoy theater and financed by funds from Gilbert and Sullivan operas. Over the years many, many brilliant musical acts had entertained the guests at the Savoy.

Located northeast of Westminster Abbey and Trafalgar Square in the heart of London; England's first and most famous luxury hotel loomed across the north bank of the River Thames. The south facing rooms overlooking the river had splendid views of the waterway below. Claude Monet enjoyed the view so much he even painted views from his room of the Thames. The hotel styled itself after old world opulence with deep mahogany colored wood paneling on the walls of the foyer with white columns and gold trimmed seating as well as a well-appointed main courtyard off the Strand leading in to the building. However, the hotel as always had dashes of art deco modernism splashed throughout such as the back lit Savoy sign above the courtyard entry.

Dylan and Payton counted themselves lucky because the King arranged for them a magnificent river view suite. On this day, the slightly overcast sky lent shimmering patches amidst the grey slate river where the sun poked through. The near magical scene did not sway the twins from their restless state. They made no progress as all trying to obtain passage to Le Havre since their arrival. Their visits to the docks proved fruitless as no one dared even discuss taking civilian passengers near the war zone.

Unable to make progress and unable to sit still, the boys grabbed their baseball gloves and walked out the luxury hotels front door, gaining a few odd looks from the upper crust walking by. The baseball gloves slung under the twin's arms as they walked out slightly raised the eyebrows of the usual patrons. They walked around the hotel across the Strand and took up their positions on the embankment parallel to the Thames. Starting slowly and closer to each other, they softly tossed the ball back and forth. Eventually they worked up to full speed and stood roughly a hundred feet apart. As far as they knew, they were the first ever people to play catch with a baseball next to the Thames, but that surely was not true. It was still, however, a rarity. The throwing helped to sate their frustration at their inactivity and two fruitless days searching for a boat to France as well as their slight annoyance that Colonel Sweeney had not quite delivered them the entire journey as promised.

As the sweat began to glisten on their foreheads most people walking along ignored them or steered well clear fearing a run in with the ball. The twins stayed in their own cocoon throwing back and forth together, the same as always. They might as well have been back home on the farm procrastinating on their homework or their chores. Without notice from the twins, one man stood a short ways off and stared at them whistling the ball to each other with a rapt look on his face. The man stood no more than 5 ½ feet in shoes, so he had no reason to worry about the ball as the much taller twins threw well above his head as he approached them. In any case, the tweed flat cap he wore offered little protection except to keep the sunlight off the shock of red hair that drifted out beneath the brim. He dressed modestly in brown trousers, a matching well worn leather jacket and a white open collared shirt. The twins continued to take no notice of him until he reached within ten feet of Dylan. Catching his brother's last throw one handed Dylan turned slightly to the man as he approached. The man looked older than the twins, but not by much.

"Hello there, boy-o. Couldn't help but be impressed with you slinging that thing back and forth." The man said in a thick Irish accent. "You throw that thing like a gun throws a bullet."

"Uh, Thank you, I think." Dylan hesitated as his brother walked toward the stranger.

"You must be American, then." The stranger continued. "And look here, there are two of you. I couldn't tell that without your second walking over here too." He said as Payton arrived next to his brother.

"Yes, sir. We are American and we are twins. You must be Irish." Payton answered politely but without offering any further information.

"That, my young friend, is my blessing." The stranger laughed. "My name is Timothy O'Ryan and I hale from the Emerald Isle. I've only seen a ball travel with that pace during some of our hurling matches."

"I'm Payton and this is my brother Dylan" Payton said warming to the increasingly jolly new acquaintance but guarding their true last names at least a little bit.

"I've heard of hurling. It sounds like a rough and tumble sport. It's like baseball in that you hit a ball, but only to pass it. Otherwise you carry it and I think there is a goal for scoring on either side like in soccer. It seems like the dastardly little brother of cricket." Dylan mused excitedly.

"You are well informed, but you left out that you can also score by hitting the ball over the bar of the net. A goal is worth three points, and over the bar is worth one." Timothy explained as the three began to bond over sport. "I must admit, I know nary a thing about your baseball. At least I assume that's what you yanks are tossing back and forth."

"That's right. This is a standard Rawlings baseball. All you have to do to score is touch all three bases and return home. Couldn't be any simpler." Payton joked. "The hardest part is getting to first base."

"Why's that?" Timothy asked.

"Because to get there you have to hit a round ball with a round bat, and the ball is usually traveling more than ninety miles an hour. It's the hardest thing to do in sports. A great player fails seven out of ten times." Dylan explained.

"Hurling requires you to hit that ball while you're moving and someone is trying to tackle you, but at least you get a flat paddle and you toss it to yourself usually." Timothy said. "It looks like your baseball is roughly the same size as the sliotar, the hurling ball, so the target is the same size at least. What are you two doing playing catch out here in this part of town?"

"We're staying at the Savoy, actually. A very kind friend has lent us a room there for a few days." Payton said.

"A very kind friend indeed, to put you up in such a swanky place. I should make such friends." Timothy teased.

"We planned on lunch in the Grill Room, if you want to join us. You can tell us about Ireland and hurling." Dylan offered.

"Well, it appears I have made such friends. I'd never pass up a meal in such a fine restaurant." Timothy answered, pleased with the prospect.

The three new acquaintances walked back across the street with the twins standing a full head taller on either side of the shorter Irishman. They went through the riverside entrance and continued on to the Grill Room on the opposite side of the hotel. Although not as elegant as the River Restaurant, the Savoy Grill had gained a reputation as the place to have lunch amongst the powerful in London. On any given day you might see the new Prime Minister, Sir Winston Churchill and his cabinet, or several Generals of the British army amongst other well to do upper crust aristocracy. They came for the excellent food ranging from steaks to sandwiches, for the beautiful art deco style, and to be seen by other powerful elite.

The Maître D whisked Dylan, Payton, and Timothy quickly to a table since he happened to know the twins stayed under the patronage of the King even though the twins failed to mention it. All three settled in to the fine table in the middle of the room and perused the menu that was printed anew each day. Dylan and Payton again ordered steak since they remained ready to leave at a moment's notice and didn't know how long the excellent meals would last. Mr. O'Ryan ordered a simple shepherd's pie because he knew that even a simple dish would get the special Savoy Grill touches to make it splendid.

"Thank you kindly for the lunch. I've never been in such a fine place." Timothy said. "I'll try not to run up your tab too much!" He finished with a laugh.

"Well, actually our bill is covered, so don't hold back on account of us." Payton answered a little sheepishly.

"Your kind friend must be the King to lavish you two like this. It's good to be friends with his friends!" Timothy exclaimed.

"He's something like that." Dylan said with a slight grin, but trying to conceal the truth. "Tell us about yourself, Ireland, and how you left the land of your blessing."

"I guess you could say I work in shipping, as a sort of the family business, and that's why I'm in London. My father is a distributor of fine spirits and wine in Dublin, so I handle the procurement and handling of the merchandise until it reaches his warehouse back home." Timothy explained.

"So we've made friends with a liquor smuggler." Payton said matter-of-factly, hoping that he'd correctly read the tell tale words that Timothy used.

"That you have." Timothy said plainly with no shame. "And you're sharp to pick up on it so quickly; most folks wouldn't have understood what I just said. I don't mind telling you, as I don't think a couple of Americans will get me in any trouble."

"You're right that we won't get you in to any trouble. We've got our own secrets as well." Dylan said with a little bit more reserve.

"At least you can trust a man who has his own secrets. I'll drink to that." Timothy raised his glass, gaining the confidence of Payton and Dylan even if he was a smuggler. At least he was affable and unapologetic of his place in life.

"You don't seem to mind being called a smuggler." Dylan noted.

"We just run booze so as not to pay the taxes. It's an age old Irish tradition. At first it was to avoid paying taxes to England, and now that Dublin is its own government we just do it to be stubborn." Timothy explained further. "We don't get mixed up in anything more dangerous than whiskey, champagne, and wine. We don't run beer because Guiness can't be beat anywhere else in the world. Whiskey does okay for us, but Bushmills is hard to beat as well. We make most of our money running wine and champagne in from France. We can sell it a little cheaper to the bars and hotels this way, and we make a decent living doing so. Everyone does it, and most of the time big brother turns a blind eye. They've bigger things to worry about up north." He finished by referring to the Protestant Northern Ireland that was still controlled by the British. The Irish Republican Army and a host of other militant groups made Northern Ireland a bloody place for the British as they wanted to throw the English off the whole island.

"But why are you in London, then?" Payton asked.

"It's easier to make deals here with the French. I make most of my arrangements here and then sail for France from a variety of places. We usually return in Northern Ireland where we can pay off the inspectors and then haul the stuff discretely across the border in to the south. The Irish inspectors in Ulster don't much care for the British either, so they don't mind taking a small cut to let us through."

"How often do you go to France?" Dylan continued with his brother's line of questioning.

"Every couple of weeks seems like. But I'd guess we'll go as much as possible at the moment to get out everything we can before the Germans run over the place. I think we sail from Dublin next, in about a week." Timothy explained, happy to discuss it with the twins. Most of the time the young Irishman could not talk about his business except with his father, so the opportunity to blow off steam and talk about what he really did helped ease whatever stress he felt. However, to look at his easy going manner one could not easily see any stress on the affable lad.

As the meal arrived the twins let the subject die for the moment. The talk turned back to sport as the three compared notes between baseball, football, soccer and hurling. They laughed as Dylan noted that Hurling seemed like it was a drunken attempt to combine all three of the other sports in to one. Hurling had the large field and goal posts like football, the goals like soccer, and the bat and ball like baseball. The three agreed that Hurling was as rough as football, but without pads, and that baseball required a very difficult combination of precise skills. Each boasted a little of games past, as well as oversold their accomplishments to a small degree. Timothy spoke lively about games played against rival counties while the twins remembered their dominance of the Naval Academy. The talk lasted throughout the meal and in to the dessert course before talk returned to nature of Timothy's family and its business.

"Tell us about your father." Payton said to their new friend.

"He's a barrel of a man, not much taller than he is around. He's worked hard his whole life to provide for my sister and me as well as Mother. He has his moments, but our saintly mother mostly keeps him in line. Pop's liquor business is well respected around town because he always deals with his clients above board. I know, sounds wrong for someone getting the liquor the way he does, but he keeps an honest relationship and accounting with the people who buy from him, so the respect that." Timothy said, so obviously hoping to live up to his father one day.

"Sounds a little like our father. Works hard on the farm to provide for the family, plays fair with those he does business with, and enjoys life to the fullest." Payton noted. "My best guess is that our fathers would get along just fine."

"Indeed they would. Do you have any other family?" Timothy asked.

"No, just the four of us at home in Oregon. You said you had a sister?" Dylan said.

"That would be my younger sister Clara. She's about your age, and a firecracker. I'd tell you to stay away from my sister, but honestly it's probably best that I warn you off first. She's ravishing, but she'll drive any man mad!" Timothy exclaimed with a twinkle in his eye. "I'm not sure anyone can handle her. She likes to go out with the boys during the day and play the lady at night. It'll take a lot to keep up with her, for sure she's not easily pleased."

"I accept your challenge!" Dylan jokingly replied.

"You'd have to come to Dublin to accept the challenge. She's still there with my folks finishing up her studies at Trinity College. She's studying history there, but I suppose Dad put her up to it to keep her busy and away from the business. I think he's afraid that she'd end up liking the adventure as much as I do." Timothy said, again smiling to himself for admitting that he enjoyed the life he led.

"Actually, I wanted to speak with you about Dublin anyway." Payton said in hopes of taking advantage of the opening. "We told you earlier that we had secrets as well, but now I think it's time to share why we're here with you. We aim to get to France and join the French Air Force fighting Hitler. We've hit a roadblock, however, in that we can't seem to get from here to Le Havre despite our best efforts."

"Ireland is officially neutral so far, and so is America." Timothy noted. "I've no love for the English, but I've even less for the Nazi's."

"And I'm sure a Nazi occupied France would be hard on your wine and champagne importing business." Dylan added. "I think our aims might align nicely in this case even if they are not necessarily those of our governments at the moment."

"You make an easy case sound persuasive. What exactly would you like from me?" Timothy asked with nary a dark undertone.

"We'd like to hitch a ride to Le Havre when you sail next week, if you don't mind." Payton said breezily.

"You certainly don't beat around the bush. Straight to the point it is." Timothy laughed.

"We'd happily work for you over the next week to pay our way." Dylan offered.

"You don't need to convince me." Timothy said. "I'll be happy for the help and the company traveling to Dublin. Pop might need some convincing, but we'll see to that when necessary."

"Excellent!" Dylan exclaimed with a quick clap of his hands as the frustration at just sitting in a luxury hotel while a war was on lifted from his shoulders. "I wish there was something we could do in return for your help."

"Now I'm glad you brought it up." Timothy said with a rueful smile. "There's an aristocratic lady here in town that I would very much like to impress. Might you be able to secure a reservation for this evening? I'm sure she'd have some friends along for a triple date I guess you could call it. Nothing wrong with a bit of fun before you head off to fight for the side of right."

"I think we can arrange something. Give me a moment and I'll see what I can do." Payton said as he excused himself and headed to speak with their acquaintance the Maitre D. Dylan and Timothy continued to chat amiably as they finished the last bits of dessert and waited for Payton to return.

"Who's the girl you want to impress?" Dylan inquired clearly aiming at needling Timothy a little bit in good fun.

"Her name is Simone Courtney, and her father is an Earl of something or other, Crawford I think, up in Scotland. She's definitely out of my class, but still humors me. At least she is Scottish and not English. My family would never forgive me otherwise." Timothy said with a sigh. His consistent lack of shame easily avoided Dylan's good natured ribbing.

"You'll forgive my ignorance, but where does Earl land on the scale of titles? All I know is that the King is at the top." Dylan admitted.

"The King is a Duke and an Earl and all the rest combined. Otherwise it goes Duke, Marques, Earl, Viscount, and Baron in that order, are the actual peers and the upper level of the nobility. The lower nobles are Baronets, Knights and Dames, and then Esquires. Some titles are hereditary, some are not. Some titles are based in Ireland or Scotland; some are based in the whole United Kingdom. It depends on the title, as well as how and when they earned it. Baronets, for example, were basically created to raise money. James the 1st created the level and sold the titles." Timothy explained.

As Timothy finished, Payton approached the two with good news. "We are all set for this evening. The Maitre D has us down for the best table in the house, overlooking the river, for 7:00 pm sharp. I hope you've a tuxedo to wear, Timothy. He offered some spare footman tuxes but he didn't think he had one that would fit you, sorry. We are also in luck, as they have a special guest for the music tonight. The Glenn Miller Orchestra is playing. It should be one heck of a show."

"Splendid. I'll call up Simone and make the arrangements with the ladies." Timothy enthused. "I'll bring them around to meet you here at about quarter of seven so we can get a drink in the American Bar first. I'm sure they'll want to dance, and I'm sure we'll need a couple drinks to have the nerve to try dancing with ladies of such refinement. I hear they have some excellent drinks there."

"Perfect, my friend, we will see you this evening." Payton finished, genuinely looking forward to the night of fun now that they had made arrangements to get on with their journey.

CHAPTER 10

May 22nd, 1940

Again with some time to spare before dinner, and having already written to his father of their safe arrival in London, Dylan sat down to compose a report to General Bradley. He did not presume to write it as a personal letter, but did his best to model it after a military memorandum.

To: General Bradley

From: former Lt. Dylan Anders.

RE: Findings of trip from America to London and English disposition

The purpose of this memorandum is to inform the General of relevant notes from the trip my brother and I undertook from Montreal to Southampton by ship, and then on to London by car.

We also wish to inform the General of our plans for advancement on to Le Havre.

There are two notable pieces of information regarding our steam across the Atlantic. The first is that we sailed with the King of England, and had a chance to interact with His Majesty. The King was very courteous and sought our opinion about the regular American's view on the war. We informed him that we thought the average American would see that Hitler must be stopped and of our opinion that America would eventually join the war. We believe that President Roosevelt feels the same way (though this is speculation) but he must overcome an adverse congress to do so. The second notable event was the necessity to avoid a Uboat attack in transit. Should America be required to ship massive amounts of arms and men across the Atlantic then the Uboats must be destroyed to protect shipping lanes and the Allies must maintain control of the seas.

Furthermore, we were failed by Colonel Sweeney in that he had no way for us to get to France. We have made contact with an Irish national that imports wine from France and makes regular shipping runs there. We will travel to Dublin with him and attempt to cross the English Channel in his company. Will advise once we have reached France.

Payton, on the other hand, took the opportunity to write Anne back in Canada.

Dear Anne,

I hope that this letter finds you well and having already finished your final exams. You would be pleased to know that we have made it to London and are staying at a hotel where Monet painted. I'll complete the story, but the King of England has kindly put us up at the Savoy on the river Thames. Between the Ritz in Montreal and the Savoy here we have stayed in some pretty swanky places. I'm not sure we deserve it, but don't mind staying here either way.

Our travel from Montreal to England wasn't a pleasure cruise, but it certainly was interesting. I could not tell you at the time, but we served as extra stewards on The Empress of Britain and the only passengers were the King of England and his royal traveling party. His majesty very graciously spent some time with us and offered to help us in any way he could. He is a fine gentleman and I am pleased to have met him, and he befriended us when he certainly had no reason to do so. I look forward to telling my grandkids about that one day in that no matter how high you climb in life it never hurts to act kindly to others no matter who they are or what they have done in life.

How are things going in Canada? I hope everyone still feels that this is a war that must be fought. I know the war news here sounds dreadful, but the spirits of the people from the King on down still remain high and they understand the mission they must undertake. Hitler is blazing his way through France and if he is not stopped then it will take years to dislodge him. Propaganda or no, the task remains tall

We have only had a slight hiccup in our travels in that we must find our own way to France from here as our arrangements were not as thorough as we'd thought. We've just today found a glimmer of hope that we'll be able to get to France with an Irishman that we've made acquaintance with at the hotel. We should strike out for Dublin soon and sail from there to Le Havre. If I can I'll write you from Le Havre, but don't be too concerned if mail service is sporadic going forward. Please give our best to Donna as well and tell her that we promise to try and visit Carentan if we get a chance.

Sincerely,

Payton

***

As the boys exited the elevator on their way to meet Timothy they walked out looking resplendent in their borrowed attire. Each had beautifully crafted pleated tuxedo shirts and black bowties under white dinner jackets that, fortunately for borrowed clothing, fit them well enough. Both felt they had lucked in to close matches offered to them by the afternoon Maitre D, but in reality the Maitre D had snuck over to the costume department at the Savoy theater next door to help out his new friends. The only luck involved was that he had picked the right size for the twins out of the masses of costumes available.

With excellent timing, the twins strolled in to the bar and ordered drinks just as Timothy and three exquisite young ladies entered behind them. Timothy walked as tall as any man as he swept in to the luxurious bar with such beauties surrounding him. Most men in his position would feel the same, and his sly grin certainly confirmed his feelings. The three beauties on his arm were each a different level taller than him. The first stood barely above him and minus the high heeled shoes probably fell below him. The other two were at least two inches taller than Timothy with or without high heels. The taller two were also obviously sisters. Timothy found the twins at the bar and introduced everyone.

"Simone, Maggie, and Caroline I am pleased to introduce to you Payton and Dylan Anders, my two new American friends, so we obviously must meet them in the American Bar. Don't, however, ask me to tell you which is which. Maggie and Caroline are sisters as well, and both very beautiful, but not twins." Timothy concluded.

"Ladies, thank you for coming to dinner with us and entertaining we wayward travelers. We have just ordered Manhattans but can surely have the bartender up the order if you would like something to drink." Dylan offered using his best manners.

"Why, the pleasure is all ours." Simone offered as she flashed an engaging smile. The perfectly voluptuous red lipped and white toothed smile only enhanced the striking deep green of her eyes and pulled up blonde hair. She might have been able to light the whole room herself, so it was no wonder that Timothy wanted to impress her. She wore long white gloves as well as a stunning ball gown, red to match her lips, which swooped and clung in all the right places. "What exactly is in a Manhattan?" She asked.

"It's a cousin of the martini, but instead of vodka or gin it has rye whiskey as the base. We've had our fair share of them actually in Manhattan during our time in school, but I'm sure the bartender here will make a splendid drink." Payton added.

"That sounds lovely, I'll certainly have one." Maggie offered. Although she and her sister weren't twins, they might have been able to pass as such and were certainly no more than two years apart in age. They shared the same dark coffee colored eyes and auburn hair that was also swept up for the fine dining occasion. Maggie's face seemed a little more angular than Caroline's with her nose a touch more pointed and Caroline's slightly more rounded. Both girls shared small creases indicating a wealth of smiles in the past but otherwise held perfect complexions. Without knowing their actual age, both boys guessed that Maggie was slightly older. Maggie wore a similar dress to Simone but in turquoise, and the so far silent Caroline wore a slightly more modern dress with a lower cut in blue. She seemed slightly more shy than the other three girls, but may just have been the younger sister tagging along. All three girls were lithe and striking in their own right and the twins hoped their minds and personalities could match their stunning appearances. It appeared that the sextet were off to a fine start to the evening. All involved seemed pleased to entertain and be entertained for those around, with only Timothy on a real mission.

"If there are no objections then I will add to the order." Dylan said.

"Not me, my friend." Timothy said. "I'll just have a Bushmills neat."

"Certainly, far be it from me to change the drink of the man in the business." Dylan joked.

Shortly after the drinks arrived their reservation came up and all six adjourned to the dining room with glasses in hand. Again, their new friend the Maitre D had come through as promised on the best table in a place where all the tables were coveted. The waiter led the group to a large round table in a semi-private corner of the art deco inspired restaurant overlooking the River Thames. As they sat, Dylan asked a question that one of the twins had asked countless times on the trip of the new people they met along the way.

"Ladies, tell us about yourselves." Dylan queried after everyone had settled in to their seats. "We only know the little bit that Timothy has told us about Simone. He said your father is an Earl?"

"Yes, of Crawford. The actual title is linked to lands about fifty miles south of Glasgow on the River Clyde. The old castle is a ruin now, and it used to be known as Lindsay tower after David deLindsay was awarded the title Earl of Crawford for helping William Wallace and Robert The Bruce during the battle for independence." Simone said as a way of running through her standard family history lesson.

"That's fascinating. No one in America has such a long family history, and if they did it would probably tie back to here." Payton said.

"Now Crawford Castle is just a nice country house, not much of a castle. We spend most of our time in Edinburgh or London. My father is a noble, but a businessman none the less." She finished.

"And what about your family, Caroline?" Dylan asked in a deliberate effort to draw out the quietest of the three girls.

"Our family isn't quite as noble, but we did grow up here in London. Father is a banker and a minor baron who sits in the house of lords, but to be honest that is all I really know of his business. We met Simone at boarding school." She answered quietly but confidently. "Where in America are you from?"

"We are from Oregon, on the West Coast just above California. The biggest city is Portland, but we grew up south of there in the Willamette Valley which is named after the main river that flows south to north between the Cascade Mountains and the Coastal Mountain Range. The Valley boasts some of the most fertile soil in the world, so of course we grew up on the family farm." Payton explained. "Once we graduated high school we went to university in New York, north of the city on the Hudson River."

"I know of Oregon and the Willamette Valley. Isn't that where everyone went heading West? I believe it was called the Oregon Trail, wasn't it?" Maggie asked, furrowing her brow a little trying to remember a trivial fact from her boarding school history.

"Yes, that's right." Dylan said, pleased to hear that she knew some of the same history that he did of his home. "I didn't think they'd teach that in history classes here."

"I took an American History class in school as an elective. I very much enjoyed the geography related portions. I guess it might be the explorer in me." Maggie said.

"I didn't know that about you." Simone said with mock astonishment.

"Caroline and I used to explore all throughout the city. Father hated it because he never knew where we were." Maggie said.

"I always enjoyed the adventure, even when we got lost." Caroline added.

"The only University I know of on the Hudson is the US Military Academy at West Point, though that would explain what you said about having manhattans in New York earlier." Simone said.

"That's also right." Dylan answered. "We're just here on a holiday after graduating in June." He finished with a lie to keep up appearances.

"I hope this is just a holiday, because if you two are all that the US Army sends as aid to fight the Germans then Heaven help us all!" Timothy joked.

"Oh, we'll see if we can find a way to help out." Dylan deadpanned back returning the good natured barb with a sound sense of humor.

"I'm sure they'll make us write some kind of a report when we get back." Payton added in jest.

As the joking subsided the meals arrived and the six settled in to individual conversations between couples with Timothy talking to Simone, Dylan speaking with Maggie, and Payton to Caroline. Each nominal couple seemed to enjoy their company and soon enough the dessert service came and went.

"I think the band is about to play." Maggie said. "I haven't been dancing in ages. Do you gentlemen know how?"

"An Irishman always knows how to dance!" Timothy declared with a hint of triumph.

"I'm certainly no Fred Astaire, but wouldn't turn down a chance to dance with such beautiful company." Dylan offered.

"That's okay, I'll act like Ginger Rogers and you just follow along!" Maggie enthusiastically teased.

So the men rose from their seats and extended a hand to each of their respective dates as the Glenn Miller Orchestra began to play its distinctive style. Eschewing the normal big band style, the Glenn Miller Orchestra became famous for organizing the melody around a clarinet and a tenor saxophone. The set started with the bands new hit "In the Mood" which got all three of the couples weaving around the dance floor to an almost foxtrot beat. A few more songs played and everyone danced in their own swing style such as the Charleston and the Lindy Hop as the girls swung and spun of the ends of their partner's hands. Dylan and Payton kept up well enough, but only well enough to not step on their partner's feet or drop them during a spin or dip. It was a humbling experience for such precise athletes. Finally, the band slowed down and played another of their hits "Moonlight Serenade." The boys were able to execute a box step waltz perfectly, for once leading as they thought they should.

"Again, I'm sorry you have to dance with such a poor excuse for a partner." Payton said for probably the hundredth time to Caroline.

"You are more than just passable, and how hard you try is sweet." Caroline offered. "And your waltz is splendid. Twenty years ago you wouldn't have had to dance any of the rest of this. At least for dancing, you were born twenty years too late."

"Where did you learn to dance?" Payton asked as the waltz continued.

"At school. We had social events with some of the boys boarding schools, but mostly they taught us there. One of our finishing teachers was only a few years older than us, so she didn't mind teaching us about swing dancing, which was new at the time. I think she used to sneak off and go out on the weekends, so she wanted to teach us at school."

"I think you did her proud. I'll let the generals at WestPoint know that they failed us in at least one part of our education!" Payton smiled back.

As the music drew to a close, the sextet returned to their table, each with the glow of standing so near to someone of the opposite sex while dancing as only the young could. They all decided a walk along the river might make a fine end to the evening. So, the boys escorted the girls to the coat check room and then across the Strand to the River Thames embankment. The night stayed pleasantly warm but with a slight chill that hinted at the barest need for a jacket like only an early summer evening can. The girl's thin shawls were enough so the boys had no need to offer their jackets.

Timothy and Simone walked a few paces ahead of Payton and Caroline while Dylan and Maggie brought up the rear an additional few paces back. Even after only meeting him that afternoon, Dylan and Payton easily saw that Timothy continued working hard to impress Simone. They could hear his voice rise and fall as he excitedly tried explaining something or another to her, or as he reached the crescendo of some story. He laid out all his charm in a gentlemanly way that came off as sweet.

"I don't think I've ever seen someone try so hard to court a girl like that." Dylan remarked to Maggie.

"It's sweet. He really likes her. She's such a proper lady, though, that he can't tell that she likes him back. I think she's a little nervous about her father liking him too, but that will come in time." Maggie observed just as sweetly. "It might be that you've never seen a proper courting while at an all men's military academy, too." She finished with a tease.

"That may well be. I hope that I haven't disappointed you this evening. They don't teach chivalry like they used too, I guess." Dylan answered. "At least it wasn't a course that I saw offered at school."

"You've done just fine, I think. Most of the boys around here are a little bit on the dandy side, so it's nice to have a pleasant evening and a normal conversation with someone not so concerned with themselves." She replied. "I guess the ranks of young men still here are slim because most of them are fighting in France."

"I hope I'm not a stand in for someone fighting right now. That's not a very gentlemanly thing to do." Dylan said feeling a pang of guilt if it were true.

"Oh, don't worry; I don't have a boyfriend, military or otherwise, if that is what you're asking." Maggie said with a slight grin.

"My conscience is clean, then." Dylan laughed and let the sound waft back to Payton and Caroline behind them.

"Apparently your sister is quite funny, judging by my brother's laugh." Payton joked to Caroline.

"Most people say that. She can be quite funny, which is nice to have in an older sister. I can usually just let her break the ice." Caroline said, offering a little bit of insight in to why she may seem reserved compared to her sister.

"Funny thing, siblings and how we compare at some points." Payton noted. "My brother and I have been nearly inseparable since birth and couldn't be closer. We play the same sports, have similar ambitions, but there are differences. It just takes a while to see them. I'm a shade taller but he weighs a couple pounds more. He jumps to action and I tend to think a little longer before I do something." Payton offered as a little insight in to his brother and himself.

"That's interesting, but I would guess that most twins are the same." Caroline said.

"Not really. Just like any set of siblings it depends on who you are. I know some twins that hate each other. They don't do anything together and may as well be strangers. It's rarer, but I've seen it." Payton said. "Maybe they have too much of a sibling rivalry."

"My sister and I are much closer to how you and your brother are, but it can be a strain at times." Caroline noted.

"We fight, too, but mostly about little stuff and it is easily forgotten. He's the only person that I've ever punched in anger, but that was when we were younger. It's much easier working as a team, and to have someone that I can trust no matter what may happen. He'll always be there for me and I'll always be there for him." Payton replied easily.

"You are lucky, then. Not many people have someone that they can trust so absolutely." She said quietly in return.

"I like to think so. A good family makes anyone lucky, I figure. Although, I think anyone might feel lucky walking along this river with you right now." Payton complimented Caroline.

"That's very kind of you, and I've had a splendid evening as well." She complimented back.

The three couples continued strolling along the river quietly until they'd made a full circuit back to the hotel. Dylan and Payton thanked all of the girls for entertaining the wayward travelers for the evening and the ladies all agreed that the American friends of Timothy were more than welcome to dine with them again should they ever come back to London. Timothy promised to come round the boys up in the morning for their trip to Dublin, and everyone said their good-byes.

"Not a bad evening." Dylan noted to his brother.

"Not bad in the least. I hope Timothy impressed Simone." Payton said.

"According to Maggie he should be all right. Apparently at the upper levels of society it just takes a little longer."

"Good for him. The sisters were pleasant as well." Payton yawned at his brother as they walked back in to the hotel.

"I for one will have very good memories of London. Something to remind us of what we're fighting for, I guess." Dylan replied.

"That is true. We've met several nice young ladies on this little trip of ours so far. It won't do us much good once we get to France, but no complaints from me." Payton said.

"Now we just need to get to France and figure out what Colonel Sweeney has set up for us." Dylan continued the thoughts of his brother. "The next step is tomorrow, when we head for Dublin. There is nothing to do but sleep until then. We'll have to bid farewell to another luxury hotel, but it's time to move on."

With the thought of Dublin and then on to France looming, the boys retired to their fine suite for the evening and both quickly fell fast asleep.

CHAPTER 11

May 24th, 1940

Timothy had kept his promise and collected the twins the next morning at the Savoy, and the arrangements he'd made for travel to London could not have been better. The three took a train directly to Holyhead, which sat directly across the Irish Sea from Dublin. The train took about six hours to travel from London to Holyhead, and the twins saw a great deal of the English countryside on the trip, including passing by the impressive Conway Castle and a beautiful stretch of the North Wales Coast. The three then stayed the night at a small local hotel before hopping on a ferry on this particular Friday morning that sailed directly to Dublin. The ferry ride was a scant three and a half hours, so they arrived in Dublin around lunchtime.

"Ceade Mille Failte, my friends. That's Irish for A Hundred Thousand Welcomes. I am pleased to have you in my home country." Timothy said. A car awaited them that then whisked the three to lunch at a fine restaurant. No doubt his father's liquor distribution serviced the establishment because it seemed that no one paid the bill when they left.   Dylan and Payton both wanted to meet Timothy's father to insure their passage on one of his boats running to France. Although Timothy had plenty of power in the family business, the final say always rested with the father in Ireland. The patriarch of the family, however, was currently engaged out of town. Timothy's father left for a business meeting unexpectedly up in Northern Ireland while his son tarried in London, so when the three boys arrived in Dublin they found waiting one more day a necessity. So the younger Irishman repeatedly assured the Americans that he foresaw no trouble, the boat to Le Havre would sail without a hitch, and that they'd go meet his father first thing in the morning.

Timothy took the twins from lunch down through the heart of Dublin to show off his hometown. The name Dublin derived from the ancient term "Dubh Linn" meaning dark pool in the native tongue. The town had started around a deep, dark pool of water that had since been covered over as the city grew. The town sat at the mouth of the River Liffey, where it emptied in to the Irish Sea. Throughout its history, the town has served as an important port city for the Emerald Isle. The low hills to the South gave way to rich farmland to the North and East. The River Liffey split the town into North and South, with the north part considered working class and the southern considered middle to upper class.

"It reminds me a lot of Portland." Payton said. "The weather is pleasant in the summer, and you said it doesn't get overly cold in the winter. It even has the river running right through it. The only difference is Portland doesn't open up to the sea like this, the Willamette just pours in to the Columbia River to the north. Plus, Portland is split East/West instead of North/South."

"I'd imagine Portland is smaller, too." Dylan added.

"If it is anything like Dublin, it is a grand place." Timothy said showing his pride hail from Ireland and from Dublin in particular. "The town stays always green, and the occasional dusting of snow just enhances the mood. Most of the year is mild and no month is particularly rainier than the next. I find the town ideal. I'm always happy to come back after traveling, and always displeased to leave."

Timothy seemed determined to show them all the sights in one afternoon, so the twins happily followed along. They'd already walked past the Guiness Brewery and compared notes on beer with Timothy. All agreed that when debating beer, no one actually lost. Next they walked along the outer walls of Dublin Castle which the British built in the 13th century to defend the King of England's land, men, and treasury. It remained one of many reminders of the former British rule. Each corner of the massive stone walls held a circular tower and the whole thing looked exactly like one would think a castle should. From there they found their way down to Trinity College and its famous Long Room library, where they saw the even more famous Book of Kells. Around 800 AD Irish Monks set about crafting a beautifully illustrated and illuminated copy of the Gospels. The resulting book of Kells has survived and is the finest example of art and scripture from a time well before the printing press. An illuminated text consists of vellum, which is stretched calf skin, instead of paper giving it a slightly translucent quality allowing light to show through for the illumination. Using beautiful calligraphy for text gave the pages words. However, the true beauty of the illuminated text came from the illustrations. Each page contains exquisite borders in geometric or natural patterns, all hand drawn. Finally, several full-page illustrations interspersed in the accompanying text compared favorably to even the finest artwork of the time and showed the skill and passion the monks put in to each work of art. Each illuminated text took months if not years to finish. The four books of the Gospel never looked better than they do in the Book of Kells.

As the three walked out of the library, a striking red haired woman spied the them and made a direct line towards their path. As she got closer, it became obvious that this was Timothy's sister Clara. She stood an inch or so taller than her brother, even in the flat shoes she wore. They shared the same fiery red hair, though hers flowed down between her shoulder blades and perfectly matched the warm summer day. Where Timothy may seem stocky, his sister could only be considered slim. She wore a light weight blue and white check dress in a fashionable cut that perfectly offset her green eyes and red hair.

"Hello, there, Tim. I thought you were still in London." She said by way of greeting her brother.

"I made my way back this morning to show my friends around town. These two Americans are Dylan and Payton. I've said it before, but don't ask me which is which." He replied.

"You both must be a good influence on him. I never thought I'd see my brother coming out of a library, let alone a university library." She teased her brother lovingly.

"I don't know much about that, but he did just show us the Book of Kells, which is indescribable. I'm Dylan, this is my brother Payton and it is a pleasure to meet you." Dylan answered while simultaneously gesturing at his brother.

"I'm pleased to meet you both as well." Clara said with a small smile indicating that she really was pleased to meet someone maybe a little different.

"For your information, I've been in several libraries in the past. Too many books, though. I like the Brian Boru Harp inside, though, so I showed them that as well." Timothy laughed. "You got the brains in the family, but I got the good looks!"

Clearly, the brother and sister played off each other well. The smile from Timothy showed his pleasure at seeing his sister, and her body language indicated the same. Dylan and Payton recognized siblings that liked each other immediately because they knew how lucky such a family circumstance helped anyone work their way through the world. No matter the circumstances, the twins knew that they had each other, and now they saw the Timothy and Clara had each other as well.

"What brings two Americans to Dublin?" Clara asked, ignoring her brother easily.

"We started in London, where we met your brother. We're actually trying to get to France." Payton said, minimizing the details intentionally.

"Ah, young adventurous Americans then. You certainly look the part. What do you hope to accomplish there?" Clara replied with a slight edge.

"We are hoping to fly airplanes, actually." Dylan replied matter-of-factly.

"Easy sis, these boys graduated from West Point. They know what they are doing." Timothy added in a soft tone that he must have used often to settle his sister down.

"We want to help, not just seek out an adventure. Adventurers often end up dead, and that is not our goal." Payton explained. "We are hoping that we can hitch a ride on your brother's next boat to France, so we are in town to speak with your father."

"Forgive me, but I am a little tired of the college boys around here talking a lot but not acting. I've no love for the English, but even less for Hitler." Clara said, echoing the sentiments of her brother. "I'm sure my brother has told you that I don't hide my emotions."

"No offense taken. All talk and no action can rile anyone." Dylan graciously replied.

"Will you be having dinner with us tonight, then?" the boys heard from Clara with what seemed a hint of hope that they actually would say yes. Apparently they hadn't made too bad of an impression.

"We plan to follow Timothy's lead. We know no one else in Dublin, so we sit at his mercy." Dylan dryly noted.

"Absolute power, my favorite kind!" Timothy cracked wise in return.

"Absolute power corrupts absolutely." Payton quoted the old proverb back to finish the joke.

"I won't let it go to my head. Clara, I think we planned to eat out on the town tonight, and you are welcome to join us. We'll meet with Father as soon as he returns tomorrow." Timothy said to his sister.

"I'm only coming if I choose the spot." She coyly demanded of her brother.

"As usual, I submit to your tastes. I am but a lowly man humbled to your finer sense of food, decor, and dress. My absolute power has found its bounds." Timothy melodramatically intoned with a wicked grin.

"Excellent, I'll meet you at the Horseshoe Bar at the Shelbourne, 7pm sharp. I assume my brother has you there. It is beautiful and overlooks St. Stephen's Green." Clara commanded more than asked.

"Yes, that's correct. We'll look forward to seeing you this evening." Payton said as Clara turned to leave.

"I'm off to class, don't be late this evening." She said as she was off with the breeze.

"I warned you about my sister." Timothy mirthfully said.

"She was very pleasant; you needn't warn anyone off on her." Dylan said sincerely.

"Just wait for tonight. I have no idea where she'll take us, but I would bet my hat that we'll have fun." Timothy answered.

"You won't hear us complain about that. We rarely turn down a night of fun." Payton said with a bright smile.

"Excellent, we'll send you off to your hotel to relax a little bit before we catch up with Clara then." Timothy finished.

***

Clara certainly knew what she was talking about with regards to the Shelbourne. Just a short walk south of Trinity and on the other side of St. Stephen's green, the Shelbourne exceeded every expectation, and the twins streak of fine hotels continued with this majestic landmark hotel. Where the Ritz showed a new world elegance, and the Savoy integrated art deco in to its traditional styles, the Shelbourne represented old world charm and elegance in its finest form. Built in 1824, the beautiful brick building with a Georgian facade and grand marble columned entrance stood out among the best hotels in Europe. The inside exceeded the outside with its high, sculpted ceilings, marble foyer, and continued columns throughout.

"A man could get used to staying in places like these." Payton noted as they followed the bell hop up to their room.

"There is no doubt to that notion." Dylan replied. "I thought the Savoy would be our last decent place to stay. I was wrong."

"That is for sure. Between Colonel Sweeney, the King, and Timothy we have had some extremely generous patrons." Payton finished his brother's thought.

Taking Timothy at his word, the boys spent the rest of the afternoon relaxing in their hotel room and generally recovering from the continuous travel they'd endured. Neither spoke much and they mostly avoided any war news on the radio. As the appointed hour drew near they heeded Clara's advice and readied themselves early enough to make it to the bar on time.

This time, however, Timothy and his sister had already beaten the boys to the bar. There was no formal dining on this evening, so all four were dressed casually with the boys in collared shirts and nice slacks while Clara still wore a knockout blue dress highlighting everything right about her figure. They were, of course, each holding a Manhattan drink.

Without batting an eyelash, Dylan walked up to the bar and said "Since we are drinking to the home of our counterparts, we'll each have a bushmills."

"A brilliant idea, my friend!" Timothy exclaimed. "I was just explaining the Manhattan to my sister and how you came to know it from your time at WestPoint."

"It's a fine drink, but a whiskey neat can't go wrong. Besides, when in Ireland, drink like the Irish!" Payton said as he raised his glass to the small group. "Cheers!" he exuberantly said to the small group.

"Slainte!" Timothy and Clara responded back. "That's an Irish toast for good health." She explained.

"We may need all the wishes of good health we can get, so many thanks." Payton replied.

"I can't resist, sis. Where are we going after this?" Timothy asked.

"Why should I tell you?" His sister replied feigning a tart annoyance. "There's no need to impress you, so I'm taking the boys someplace for them." She finished and gestured towards the twins.

"No need to impress us. The Irish reputation for hospitality continues with our fine treatment. We are impressed already." Dylan said.

"I just need to know if we need a car." Timothy said, deftly hiding any irritation since he knew his sister just wanted to tease him some.

"We do not need a car." She said simply to avoid letting on their destination.

"Perfect, I love the Brazen Head." Timothy said confidently.

"How did you know?" Clara exclaimed, flustered that her brother figured through her subterfuge so easily.

"It's within walking distance, and I called earlier to check. They said you'd already called ahead for a table." Timothy said triumphantly. He never failed to mark a win against his sister in their good natured sibling rivalry.

"That's cheating!" Clara pouted.

"What's the Brazen Head?" Payton asked.

"The Brazen Head is the oldest pub in Ireland. It was established just before the turn of the century, the 13th century." Clara explained. "It's around the corner from Christchurch Cathedral, northwest of here. They play wonderful Irish music there nearly every night. I believe the band tonight even has a bagpiper to go with the fiddle and the whistle. I go there as often as I can for the music. The history is just a nice addition to the atmosphere."

"Sounds wonderful, so I'm glad you chose it." Dylan said. "Do we have time for another drink here or should we head over?"

"The table is set for 7:30, so we best head out." Clara answered.

As the three approached the pub the twins saw why Clara spoke glowingly of the establishment. The low front entrance looked like the ramparts of a castle with a stone facade and open slits along the top mimicking a crown. The stone facade belied the original use of the building as a stable house. Behind the low slung building stood the more recent addition of a three story whitewash building housing the bulk of the pub.

As the quartet walked in to the newer building they heard the happy blaring of the band at least one room over. Dylan and Payton had expected a dark pub with low oak beams overhead, but the Brazen Head seemed more like a fine country house inside with dark wood paneling half way up the walls and interesting pieces of artwork hung on the plaster walls above it. Fortunately, the paintings, signs, and old maps making up the bulk of the artwork were securely fastened to avoid having the music vibrate them off the wall and on to the ground. The Americans happily followed their Irish hosts in to the large central room with the band and sat at a table along the outskirts of the dance floor. The band played traditional Irish dance music, in this case a reel in

4/4 time, and several bonnie lasses stood on the dance floor executing the exquisite footwork with nearly still upper bodies characteristic of the style. The band did have a bagpiper, but in these songs the whistle and fiddle fought back and forth to lead the way with the simple hand drummer keeping everyone on pace. The next song switched to a jig in 6/8 time and several more dancers joined the fray. The syncopated fight between the whistle and fiddle continued unabated and only intensified as the song played on. Payton and Dylan dared not even attempt this folk dancing passed from generation to generation in Ireland since it was much more intricate and required keeping pace with the rest of the dancers, but they certainly enjoyed the show. Dancing in London seemed a breeze compared to the highly stylized and athletic moves required of both the reel and the jig.

As the flagons of ale arrived at their table, the band switched to a slow lament casting all the dancers back to their tables. The bagpipe took the lead and pulled at the crowd with low and long notes.

"Timothy, you certainly know what's right for you following your sister's lead around here. This place is fantastic." Dylan enthusiastically crowed above the band and crowd noise as the four quaffed Guinness imperial pints.

"Thank you, Dylan, I like playing the hostess and taking people to new places. I truly appreciate the compliment." Clara answered for her brother. "I'd be a terrible hostess if I couldn't show guests a good time, and the Brazen Head generally fits that bill."

"It does indeed. Can you dance like that?" Payton asked while nodding to the currently empty dance floor.

"Of course, I'm a good Irish lass. Father wouldn't have it any other way. Timothy runs the ambiguous parts of the business so Father can dote on me. At least that's what he'd like to think." Clara said.

"And you don't subscribe to that notion?" Dylan asked.

"Not exactly. I'm my own woman now, but I certainly respect my father and try to abide by his wishes." Clara responded. "Father is by no means a hard man, but he softens up for me, so I must guard against taking advantage of him. To him, I'll always be his little girl."

"I'm sure he's scared off some suitors, then!" Dylan joked.

"Not as many as I have!" Timothy retorted, playing the proud and over protective older brother. "She handles herself, though. Dad and I have no control." He relented.

"It sounds like your father and mother just care about you, and raised you right. We try to listen to our parents too, while forging our own path. They know why we are here, and they support us." Payton said. "I very much look forward to meeting with your father."

"I'm sure he'll like you as well. He enjoys men of action." Clara said as encouragement. Between the confidence of her brother and her encouragement the twins both began to breathe easier about getting to France to prove they were in fact men of action.

The food arrived and the band picked back up with livelier music and the two sets of siblings ate well, drank well, and generally enjoyed the company. The twins tried their best to regale Clara with stories of America in general and New York in particular. Dylan especially tried to impress the younger O'Ryan as his brother noticed that he'd taken a keener interest in her than even the fine ladies of London or their first meeting with the friendly Canadians. Of course, Payton enjoyed her company as well, but the twins had long ago established the unspoken ground rules in any situation involving the fairer sex; if one is far more interested he can make the first attempt, but in the end let her choose. The situation worked out well as they had never really fought over a girl in the past.

As the night wore on the twins ended up at the table by themselves as Clara wandered over to speak with a school friend and Timothy heeded the call of nature.

"Clara is certainly wonderful." Payton said, broaching the subject with his brother.

"That she is." Dylan answered.

"Best to be careful while we are still trying to win over her father." Payton cautioned.

"I know what we came for, and in the end we'll be in France. So, yes, I like her, but it doesn't matter much beyond tonight. No need to worry." Dylan assured his brother. While some brothers may have seen Payton's comments and inflammatory, both twins knew that each had the best interests of the other in mind, so the simple exchange was quietly and quickly executed to the satisfaction of both. They didn't so much need to say the words as confirm that both felt the same for sure. For a smaller matter, they wouldn't have even needed the confirmation, but in this case their singular goal might tip out of their favor, so they both knew that a quick chat kept them on track.

The night wound down after one more round of drinks. The night had swung past the point of being young, so Timothy made arrangement to pick up Payton and Dylan in the morning. Timothy then pointed the Americans in the right direction to their hotel and walked his sister back to her school.

CHAPTER 12

May 25ᵗʰ, 1940

The next morning the twins woke a little later than usual, but still not long after the sun rose. Throughout the trip they had little chance to exercise save for a few double times around the top deck of the ship and some pushups in their hotel rooms. This morning they took advantage of the early sun and renewed their relationship with morning running and calisthenics nurtured over the years at WestPoint. They drew some funny looks as they trotted along the River Liffey, and even a few wry looks from the few early bird students at the library as they went through their basic calisthenics on the lawn out front. After they'd worked up a good sweat, the twins headed back to the hotel to quickly get ready for the day and meeting Mr. O'Ryan.

However, as the twins got ready in their room the radio continued to relay distressing news from France. The Wehrmacht continued to overrun a greater portion of France with what seemed like every passing hour. In the two weeks since the twins had sailed from Canada the Germans completely bypassed the

Maginot line by overrunning Holland and Beglium first, and then systematically made their way to the sea. On the 20th of May, the first German forces reached the western coast of France. The German spearhead cut off the French 1st Army, the Belgian Army, and the British Expeditionary Force from the rest of the French forces to the south. The Germans then turned north and threatened to envelope the whole of these forces and prevent them from escaping. The day before, the newsman reported, the Wehrmacht surrounded the forces in the small harbor town of Dunkirk in the north of France, not far from the Belgian border. The report simply said that the soldiers were cut off, but continued to battle valiantly. The twins knew that this was simply a code so as not to hurt the national moral. The Battle of France was going very badly, but the twins needed to find out how badly.

Timothy arrived promptly to gather the twins at 9am for a breakfast meeting with his father. Despite his position as a relatively powerful businessman in the community with influence over much of the local liquor dependent business in Dublin and other pockets of Ireland, Mr. O'Ryan preferred to do business from the back of a small restaurant owned by one of his childhood friends. A solid dark green awning covered the glass and mostly dark wood front of a small restaurant tucked on the ground floor between tall brick buildings. The twins followed Timothy in the front door of the rudimentary establishment. Several booths sat against one wall, a couple of tables in the middle, and a long bar with a brass rail sat on the opposite wall. In the back corner sat an impeccably dressed man in a corner booth. Mr. O'Ryan wore a dark pinstripe three piece suit with just the hint of a pocket watch chain hanging out of the front of his vest. None of his suit looked out of place or as if it came from a pretentious aura. He dressed smartly and it fit him. When he stood to graciously greet the twins they saw he was bigger than his son, but not by much. He looked exactly like his son, but thirty years older. His face betrayed a life of smiles and laughter based on the creases around his eyes and smiling mouth. He'd enjoyed life and his family, and his demeanor showed it.

"Gentlemen, I'm Mr. O'Ryan, and it is a pleasure to meet you. I am sorry that I was away yesterday and that you had to wait." The older Irishman said by way of greeting.

"Thank you sir, it was no problem to wait. Your son and daughter showed us a wonderful time around town yesterday and last night. They are fine hosts for sure." Payton answered.

"I absolutely agree with my brother. I'm more than happy that we got to see some of Dublin yesterday. I never thought that I'd get to see such a fine place on our little adventure." Dylan added.

"Yes, my son filled me in on your plans." Mr. O'Ryan said. His demeanor changed in just the slightest way with the news he had to deliver. "I applaud your effort. Our governments seem to have the same philosophy in this war at the moment, but yours can make a difference."

"Thank you, sir. Based on what we know of our military and president I would venture that the United States will get in to the war one way or another." Payton said.

"I'm pleased to hear that. Unfortunately, it seems that our business in France is about to dry up. My travel yesterday was to go meet one of my main suppliers out of France who has simply fled the country. The news reports, while not totally false, are somewhat misleading. The Allies are in full retreat. There is no hope for staving off the Germans." The elder Irishman stated stoically.

"Is it really that bad, Da?" Timothy asked.

"Yes, it is. The Allies are surrounded in Dunkirk and barely holding out. The Germans halted their advance yesterday, and only Hitler knows why. They could roll over the whole force in the next couple of days. The hasty retreat had men running for the hills and beaches. They left behind all their heavy equipment to try and escape. There are hundreds of thousands of men waiting on the beaches in Dunkirk. There is no war for you boys to go help out with." Mr. O'Ryan finished.

"A day late, then, for us to help out in France." Dylan said slightly dejectedly.

"I'm sorry for your business. What will happen to all the men in France?" Payton offered.

"We'll be all right. We have other sources and plenty of reserves. We won't be going to France anytime soon. I'm not sure about the men. The Royal Navy will need to launch some sort of rescue operation, but I'm not sure what they'll do since I'm not sure they could hold that many men if they used every ship in the fleet." Mr. O'Ryan said.

"You said you brought your friend back, maybe you could use your fleet to pick up some soldiers as well." Payton said. "I know the Irish and the English don't get along, but if Hitler can launch an invasion of the UK from a base in France Ireland will surely fall."

"I've been thinking the same thing, my young friend. Hitler is bad for business, which at the moment outweighs usual British issues. My problem is that I have three ships and only two crew at the moment, and that is counting Timothy as my captain." The Irishman said.

"How many hands does it take to run one of your ships?" Dylan asked.

"A skeleton crew of just one can do it. A captain only and no first mate. Usually we have more, but they just load the holds with liquor cases." Timothy answered for his father. "With only one on the ship we'd have more room for passengers."

"I appreciate your enthusiasm, you three young ones, but there is also the very real possibility that our ships would be attacked in such an effort. Best to let the Royal Navy handle it." Timothy's father said with an air of finality.

"Thank you for your consideration, and for the information, sir." Dylan said politely while hiding his disappointment.

"I'm sorry to end your adventure early. Please, have dinner at our house this evening, though." Mr. O'Ryan said. "I'd love to hear some of London from the two of you and from Timothy. Mrs. O'Ryan would love to meet you as well." He finished by way of ending the conversation.

"Of course, how very kind of you." Payton said as the three boys rose from the table to leave. "Thank you again for your time."

***

The day came and went with the twins left to their own devices as Timothy attended to business with his father. They wandered the city a little bit, and mostly talked about what they might do next. They discussed heading back to London but dismissed that for at least another day. They discussed heading back to America, but dismissed that outright. They'd come far enough that turning back was not an option. They needed to find more options, but they didn't find any that afternoon. They thought about playing catch again, but didn't have the time or space. They stopped outside a fenced in field to watch as a team of school age boys practiced hurling. They ran across the field, in to each other, and batted the ball at the goal. The sport looked fun and the twins vowed to give it a shot if they stayed in Dublin much longer.

After drifting through the afternoon they readied themselves at the hotel to meet Timothy. As usual, he picked them up exactly on time out front of the hotel and drove them southeast. His parent's home sat in a prestigious residential area known as Ballsbridge, so named for the bridge originally owned by Mr. Ball that spanned the small River Liffey tributary named the River

148

Dodder. The three probably could have walked from the hotel, so the drive took almost no time at all. The fine neighborhood consisted of mostly elegant Georgian homes with their two story box style and symmetrical window layouts. The elaborate front doors with crowns and pillars in varying styles set in the middle of the brick or stone houses dated back a century or more. Most of the houses also sported chimney's on either side of the house, almost like antlers of a young deer sprouting above the roofline. A few also had dormers growing out of the roofline, which the twins correctly guessed used to house the servants in these stately houses. Further burnishing the reputation of the neighborhood, many foreign embassies sat within the boundaries of Ballsbridge including the US Embassy and the British Embassy. The proximity to the central parts of Dublin south of the River Liffey yet without the bustle of the city center made the part of town very appealing to the upper class.

The O'Ryan's house fit in nicely with the rest of the not quite mansions on the street. The house claimed neither the largest nor smallest titles from the neighbors, but it obviously housed a family financially comfortable to say the least. It looked as if the house could comfortably sit on a large country estate in either the United Kingdom or the United States but instead it sat just on the outskirts of central Dublin.

"This house is splendid." Dylan said as Timothy pulled the car as close as he could to a neighborhood designed well before the automobile. They parked next to what clearly looked like a carriage house. "Did you grow up here?" he asked of Timothy.

"Yes, this house has been in my father's family for several generations. I believe my great, great grandfather built the house." Timothy answered.

"Did he run the same kind of business as your father?" Payton asked.

"No, my grandfather started the liquor distributing. Before that my ancestors traded in a variety of things, but the ties to France built the necessary connections to do what we do today. Here we are then" Timothy said as the reached the front door. With a single rap butler swept open the door and escorted the boys in to a drawing room that looked more like a library. The twelve foot high bookshelves stretched from floor to ceiling and had the rolling ladder to prove it. The shelves ran over nearly every inch of available wall space save for the windows and two exquisite paintings of Dublin harbor on opposite walls. Every shelf held a neat row of leather bound books and each shelf held the maximum number of volumes possible. Were it not for the perfectly crafted oak construction the shelves surely would sag in the middle from the weight. If the room was meant to impress visitors as they entered, then it succeeded with Dylan and Payton. The three boys took seats in some wingback chairs across a small table and continued chatting amiably for a few more minutes before Clara swept in to the room in a stunning dress. She wore a crimson red full length gown that not only reached the floor but trailed slightly behind her in a small pool of silken elegance. Her upswept hair perfectly offset the dress that peaked at the point of her shoulders and gracefully dipped in a shallow v shape in the middle and then the rest of the dress fell straight to the ground. The dress relied on its bright color and shape to stun since it held no other adornment except for a few pleats where necessary around the bust line. Dylan especially perked at her entrance.

"I'm glad you boys could join us tonight." Clara smiled.

"We are certainly pleased to be here." Dylan said.

"Father and Mother are in the dining room, please follow me." She said and turned to lead the group again. They walked down the central hallway lined with photographs of family members in oval frames behind beveled glass and more beautiful paintings of countryside unknown to the twins. They turned a corner and walked through a grand set of double doors in to an impressive dining room, but not quite a dining hall.

"Gentlemen, it is good to see you again. This is my wife, the mother of my two wonderful children." Mr. O'Ryan greeted the boys while standing next to his chair at the head of the table.

"Ma'am, I must agree with your husband. Your son and daughter have been perfect hosts to us with only Irish hospitality as a reason to treat us so." Payton said graciously.

"You are too kind, dear." Mrs. O'Ryan said and gestured for the group to sit. The six dinner guests only filled half the table in the room with Mrs. O'Ryan sitting on the left side of the table with Timothy and the twins sitting on the right side with Clara in between them. The butler and a maid served the dinner party from silver platters with a soup as the first course.

"I'm hopeful that you had a good day despite our conversation this morning." Mr O'Ryan offered.

"Thank you sir, we did. We walked around some more of Dublin and even saw some of your lads practicing Hurling." Dylan answered.

"Excellent, Timothy told me that you'd met around sport and discussed hurling and baseball. I used to run up and down the pitch as a lad, but didn't amount to much." Mr. O'Ryan said.

"Hurling looks fun, but tough." Dylan returned. "We've played baseball all our lives and played at WestPoint during our schooling there. In fact, the last month or so may count as the longest since I've swung a bat that I can remember."

"We finished our last game more than a month ago and haven't picked up a bat since then. I guess you are right." Payton finished the thought for his brother.

"Yes, Timothy also told me about your time at WestPoint, something he hadn't mentioned earlier." Mr. O'Ryan continued and something in his tone showed that the fact seemed important to him.

"Sorry Da, lots of other stuff going on." Timothy apologized.

"Not to worry, it didn't really matter this morning, but it helps tip the balance a little bit this evening." The elder Irishman said.

"How so?" Timothy asked.

"I spoke with my man in London this afternoon. He's close to some Admiral or another and said that they are on the verge of a complete disaster. As we discussed this morning the whole of the armies in France are in full retreat, but the admiralty is only planning on getting out maybe one tenth of the men in Dunkirk. There are 450,000 men over there, and the admiralty is hoping to get 45,000 of men off the beaches before the Germans overrun them. This is the whole of their plan called Operation Dynamo." Mr. O'Ryan said with no effort to hide his displeasure at such a dim effort.

"That sounds horrible." Clara said. "They plan to abandon those men?"

"Not exactly. They'll keep sending ships as long as they can, but they don't hold out much hope for having enough time." Mr. O'Ryan continued. "They just don't have enough ships, so they are quietly appealing to anyone with a boat big enough to make the crossing to help."

"So you are reconsidering our plan from this morning?" Payton boldly asked.

"In fact, I am." Mr. O'Ryan flatly stated. "As long as the Germans are halted we must do everything possible to bring those troops home. They might be the only thing keeping Hitler out of Dublin, so I'd rather have them fighting in England as a buffer to Ireland than sitting in some prison in France." He finished with a sigh.

"We'd still be happy to help." Dylan offered.

"I'm counting on it." Mr. O'Ryan countered. "Tonight we'll eat as family, and tomorrow we'll head up to our house in Howth to show you the ships and how to run them. Then, we sail for France. Timothy will run lead in his ship, and each of you will have a ship. Our house is equipped with its own dock and radio, for our usual purposes, and I'll run the radio and keep you informed as best I can from there." He finished.

"While the ladies just sit here and wait?" Clara interjected with an air of annoyance.

"Actually, no, my impatient daughter, you will have a role as well. We must sail around the south of Great Britain, and then back up to Dunkirk. We've no choice to start, but I'm sure the Brits would rather we drop them in London than in Dublin. I'll have you go meet some of your brothers contacts in London and arrange drop off points and resupply along the coast at Dover." Mr. O'Ryan said as his daughter beamed at the thought of being included in the mission.

"Re-supply shouldn't be a problem. Dunkirk is farther north than we usually run, but we'll have plenty of diesel to get us there, drop the soldiers off, and back to Dublin." Timothy noted.

"We may need to make more than one trip back to France." Payton quietly pointed out.

"Exactly." Mr. O'Ryan sighed. "There are almost half a million men over there. It's only a shade over forty five miles from Dover to Dunkirk, so with our ships pushing 20 knots that makes each way of the trip at about two hours. I don't know about the seas, or the onslaught you'll face, but you should be able to manage more than one run a day."

"You're offering up a lot, sir, but we appreciate your confidence." Dylan said to their host. "You risk your family and your business for a noble cause."

"You risk your life, as well." Mr. O'Ryan quickly retorted.

"I find no fault in your plan. The only thing left is getting to your boats." Payton said as the dinner finished.

"Yes, as you say that I was thinking an early start tomorrow might work best. If you'd like, please stay here tonight and we can leave first thing in the morning for Howth." Mr. O'Ryan offered.

"We'd be delighted to have you." Mrs. O'Ryan added.

"Yes, of course, please do stay." Clara said as she turned to Dylan and put her hand on his arm.

"Your hospitality is greatly appreciated. We would be honored to stay with you tonight. I'll leave Dylan here as collateral and go gather up our things at the hotel if Timothy would be kind enough to take me back." Payton said after exchanging a knowing glance of confirmation with his brother.

"It's settled then. We'll depart first thing in the morning." Mr. O'Ryan cried with enthusiasm. "Our two adventures will merge as one and we will let the Almighty decide our fates." He finished with a fist thump on the table.

***

As Payton and Timothy pulled out of the drive on their way to the hotel, Dylan and Clara found themselves alone in the drawing room. Dylan walked along the rows of books and noted some works of the famous Irish authors including Bram Stokers classic *Dracula*, Victorian plays such as Oscar Wilde's *The Importance of Being Ernest* and Nobel Prize winner George Bernard Shaw's

Pygmalion, and native Dubliner James Joyce's famous novel *Ulysses* as well as his recently released *Finnegan's Wake.*

"Your father has quite the library." Dylan lightly said to Clara.

"He loves to read. Something he passed down. That's why I took up history. I wanted to read some of the great stories of the past because most of the time the true historical accounts are more fantastic than some of the fiction." She revealed back to Dylan. "Take the Arthurian legends, for instance. Most people think he was just a feudal king centuries ago, but he may actually have been a Roman centurion simply trying to bring justice to the brutal island of Briton."

"That is quite a tale. American history only goes back a couple hundred years, so the old stories aren't quite legends yet." Dylan noted with a small smile.

"Are you aiming to make yourself a legend with your adventure over here?" Clara asked sternly, but with a look of tender concern in her eyes.

"Absolutely not." Dylan answered quickly and sternly.

"I'm sorry, I didn't mean to offend you. That may be the second time I've done so when asking why you are here." Clara sighed after realizing the brashness of her question. "It's just, I seem to like you more than I should. I'd hate to see you try for something foolish and get hurt." She quietly admitted.

"Do you think your father would mind if I took you for a walk now?" Dylan asked in his most chivalrous tone masking the increasing pace of his heartbeat.

"I don't care if he does. I'll just tell the butler that we are stepping out." Clara said in a fashion true to what her brother had warned Dylan about in London.

Without much thought the two stepped out the front door moments later. Dylan felt a little embarrassed to not know much of where he was, so he was forced to let Clara take the lead. The night held just the smallest hint of a chill, so Dylan offered his jacket to Clara mostly because he thought it the gentlemanly thing to do. He hadn't noticed that it capably covered up her red dress that had drawn the attention of other passersby. Both the tall boy and striking red haired girl failed to notice much else as they hovered in the glow of the first inclination that both felt the same about each other.

"How on earth did we end up here?" Clara wondered in amazement after several blocks.

"Um, I was following you." Dylan said a little confused. The generally self assured military man acted less so in the presence of this particular Irish girl.

"No, I mean how did you and I end up walking together tonight? You're an American from Oregon, graduated from WestPoint and yet you somehow ended up in Dublin with my brother and I just met you walking out of the library at Trinity. Somehow I meet a boy at school who isn't actually from my school." Clara explained her wonder to Dylan.

"I'll just consider myself lucky. You're brother did try to warn me off while we were in London." Dylan teased.

"Funny, he tried to warn me off of you as well before dinner last night." Clara laughed.

"I think he might have been trying to play the reverse matchmaker. Apparently we both fell for it." Dylan cried out with a deep belly laugh. "I'm now required to trust you, though, as I have no idea where we are. I'm not usually this bad with directions, but I guess I usually have my brother to co-pilot us back home. I guess I've only been looking at you this whole time."

"We are almost to the bridge. The River Dodder isn't big, more of a small canal most of the time, but the bridge provides a nice view out towards the south of town. We've also already passed your embassy and a couple of others." Clara said sweetly. Dylan looked ahead and saw for himself that she had led them to the namesake bridge of the town. The short two arch bridge couldn't have been more than thirty feet across and ten feet high, but the craftsmanship of the old grey rock bridge belied its age.

"This is such a pleasant evening. You'd hardly believe there's a war on." Clara said as she leaned against the side of the bridge with her back to the water. Dylan leaned over the side to look out at the river and bent at the waist with his elbows planted on the rock parapet.

"Calm before the storm. Tomorrow you'll head to Dover and I'll be on a boat I have yet to see." Dylan cautioned. "I'm happy to just think about tonight. Tomorrow will bring what it may bring."

"Very philosophical of you, my dear. Do they teach you to trust the fates at WestPoint?" Clara teased.

"We have a world class English and Philosophy department, but I only took the one critical thinking class required for graduation. The rest of the time I was looking at machines or playing baseball." Dylan declared.

"And yet I still seem to like you." Clara chuckled.

"I'll take that as a compliment, and count it along with the rest of my blessings tonight." Dylan wryly responded.

"Where do we go from here?" Clara asked.

"Again, I'm still fairly lost, so you'll have to lead us back." Dylan deadpanned back.

"No!" Clara cried. "I mean, you leave tomorrow on my father's boats. I'll hopefully see you in Dover, but I don't know."

Dylan knew no answer could possibly suffice in such a moment, so he simply stood and pulled Clara close. With one hand on her hip and one hand gently cradling her fine features he kissed her slowly and gently. To Dylan's great joy, she kissed him back as he felt her body melt in to his. The two lingered in the embrace and glow of their first intimacy for several beats past a usual first kiss.

"You showed great restraint waiting this long to kiss me, but I'm glad you didn't wait longer." Clara sighed with a happy smile as she stayed in his arms and linked hers around his waist.

"I'm pleased you liked it. I felt a little forward. Plus, if I was wrong you could always shove me off a boat tomorrow!" Dylan cried with a little chuckle to himself at the relief of avoiding outright rejection. The two held each other for a while longer leaning on the parapet overlooking the small river.

"Walk me home slowly." Clara stated more than asked. "I don't want this to end but I also don't want my father to start wondering too much."

Dylan took her hand in his and ambled in the right direction back towards the house belying his protests that he was lost. He slowly led her along the sidewalks as she dropped his hand to take his arm and walk more closely to him. Anyone observing the two could quickly surmise the situation of two young people finding love for the first time. They walked slowly and closely, and neither wanted the walk to end.

CHAPTER 13

May 26th, 1940

Early the next morning Dylan and Payton woke in the comfortable guest room at the O'Ryan household to an unseasonably cold and foggy day. Mrs. O'Ryan provided a brief but filling breakfast for everyone and then they all managed to squeeze in to Timothy's car and head for Howth. They wound their way north through the center of the city and over the River Liffey before bending north east and aiming around Dublin Harbor. Howth lay a scant 10 miles northeast of the city proper, so the drive took less than an hour. The road to the O'Ryan's country house passed through the small village of Howth and curved along the high cliffs overlooking the harbor so the twins saw the mist slowly crawl back out to see as the sun began to beat back the grey and bring out the blue sky above. They arrived just as the whole harbor revealed itself and the splendid house shown like a jewel on the cliffs above the water. The main house stood a hundred yards or so inland from a thirty foot cliff that jutted out to the Irish Sea. The small spit of land out in to the water created a small south facing natural harbor below the house and the O'Ryans had built a set of stairs down to a very serviceable dock that the twins only saw once they'd gotten out of the car and walked past the boathouse to the cliff. The secluded dock fit perfectly and aided the clandestine liquor running for the family business. On the North side of the spit the waves crashed below the emerald green carpet covering the estate that gave the island its signature color and lush texture. In all the reading the twins had done on European History during school that included descriptions of Ireland, this spot perfectly fit what they'd imagined Ireland to look like.

"I'm not sure what our ancestors were thinking, leaving this place." Dylan quietly sighed to his brother as the two stood alone on the bluffs.

"I think lack of potatoes had something to do with it." Payton wryly noted.

Dylan chuckled a little bit as Clara walked up behind and took him by the arm. She said "I'll show you around the place. I love it here, and have explored it since I was a child."

Payton noted the affection between Clara and his brother, which confirmed the news his brother had shared as they drifted off to sleep the night before. Then and there, Payton gave up on his warning to his brother and with a smile at Clara and glance to his brother mentally wished them the best in their burgeoning relationship.

As they turned back to the house, Clara slipped her arm around Dylan's waist and he put his around her shoulder. Dylan said "This house is gorgeous. I can see why you love it here."

Clara led the two boys back past the small boat house toward the immense main house. The original stonework cottage stood out front of a large brick addition with three peaks in the Victorian style. Five white shuttered windows hung on the second level symmetrically with the same pattern repeated on the first floor save for the black door with a small pillar and portico replacing the middle window. The three peaks signaled three dormers on the third floor protruding from the rooftop which must have had splendid views of the countryside to match the awe inspiring cliff top ocean views from the rear of the house.

"Father bought this to try and get us out of the city more when I was five years old." Clara explained. "I guess it is a second home, but honestly I feel more at home here than anywhere else. I learned to read here, and to swim as well."

"A place to feel at home; you are lucky because that is a special thing." Dylan said to her tenderly. Clara fairly beamed back at him with a smile so bright it could outshine the lighthouse they saw up the road. The trio continued around the grounds with low rock walls and a small garden in the back. Payton asked what they grew and Clara simply noted that going forward they'd grow more foodstuffs even though Ireland had no rationing issues. Clara pointed at all the places she'd ever fallen off the walls, scraped her knees, or played a trick on her brother. After a good half hour tour they finally made it back to the main house and found Timothy on the back porch waiting for them.

"Gents, I hope you enjoyed the tour of the grounds. I'll take you down and show you the boats now, if you please." Timothy said jovially.

"Of course, to the boats. Clara, thank you for the tour, it was marvelous. I hope I can return the favor and give you a tour of our humble farm if you are ever in Oregon." Dylan said.

"I'd be delighted, but I fear you won't be there anytime soon to show me around." Clara replied with a hint of melancholy.

"Splendid, to the docks then." Timothy interrupted the moment blithely trying to ignore the look he saw between his sister and Dylan.

"I'll be inside with mother." Clara cheerily noted while she herself ignored her brother as the three boys walked off towards the cliffs.

Timothy led his American friends to the back of the property and down the wide stairs cut into the cliffs. Hauling cases of liquor up the stairs must have been hard work, even if the stairs were intentionally cut wide enough for the task. That truth revealed itself as they got to the bottom of the stairs because someone tired of hauling had built an ingenious dumbwaiter elevator pulley system to handle the heavy lifting. The platform looked big enough to carry a couple men or a dozen cases of liquor at least.

"Nice little lift you've built here. It must save your back." Dylan said to Timothy.

"Indeed it does. My father and I built that when I was a teenager. We designed it together after I'd complained long enough about lifting cases." Timothy chuckled to himself. "You'll see the boats are over here on the dock." He gestured towards the three covered boat slips tucked beneath the cliffs protecting an unusually calm little cove. The three boys walked out on the docks and came to the first of three identical boats, each bearing a meaningful Irish name. The Eriu was for the goddess of peace, the Eirinn was for the ancient name of Ireland, and finally the Etain was for the heroine of a famed Irish legend. Each boat looked to be about 40 feet long and a third of that or so abeam. The weathered boats looked like the hundreds of other fishing boats that trolled the seas off the Emerald Isle the same as their ancestors for thousands of years before them. The worn white painted hulls sported a thick black strip around the top of the gunnels and the bridge mirrored the hull with mostly white paint and a black stripe on top. Just behind the bridge stood a sturdy two post tower that on most boats would hold the winch and feed the nets out to sea, but on these ships a careful inspection revealed that special modifications meant they could be used as cranes to easily load illicit goods quickly and quietly in to the holds below decks. Instead of fish, these boats carried booze.

"Each boat is equipped with twin screws matched by 300 HP diesel engines." Timothy explained.

"Seems like a lot for a fishing boat." Payton smiled.

"We may have modified them in the event that more horsepower is required to evade any entanglements." Timothy grinned back. "But, in the case of our little mission it means we'll be able to run in and out of trouble quick enough."

"There is a lot of room in the stern for passengers, so hopefully we'll get a few men off the shores." Dylan noted.

"We usually run these up to the docks of our suppliers, so we'll see if we can get a pair rubber inflatables for each boat and then recruit a few of the soldiers to run them in and out of the beach bringing back their compatriots. We should be able to get within a couple hundred yards." Timothy continued. "The small boats should be easy to lift in and out with the cranes, and we can deflate them to store below decks when the boats reach passenger capacity. Each of these boats is rated for 40 men, but I think you can squeeze fifty on, plus yourselves, in relatively calm seas."

"That's better than catching fish, I suppose." Dylan deadpanned.

"Indeed." Timothy said back matching Dylan's wryness.

"Do we know the conditions on the beach?" Payton asked.

"Not much information is leaking out." Timothy replied.

"Best to prepare for the worst, then." Payton continued. "What can we do to protect both the bridge and the men on the open decks from shrapnel or any Luftwaffe planes lurking about?"

"Good point. What can we add as armament without adding too much weight or slowing us down?" Dylan wondered.

"I thought we'd turn the bridges in to our own little fox holes. The earth is the soldiers best friend. We'll use some of the pallets in the boat house from moving liquor and line them with burlap. Then we'll fill them with a lining of mud to disperse any shrapnel and mount them on the windows of the bridge. We can have one smaller piece that is removable in the center so we can see to steer and then put it up when we get close to the beach and just look through a cutout then." Payton explained.

"That's not a foxhole, that's a tank!" Dylan exclaimed. "Now we just need something for the open decks. I don't think the tank theme will work there. Let's use the same burlap but coat it in lacquer and tar, then arrange it like curtains around the boat using the fishing riggings. We can then raise and lower it around the sides and like a dome over the top to protect against some of the shrapnel. It won't repel a direct hit, but it will at least provide some protection."

"Splendid thinking. I never would have thought of armament and probably would have been shot for my troubles!" Timothy laughed. "We'll need three sets before the tide turns this evening. It will take us at least a day to get to Dover as our jump off point. Best get to work. Payton, come with me and I'll show you the pallets. Dylan, you can go round up Clara to show you where the rolls of burlap we use for making the sacks are stored."

Dylan and Payton dutifully complied and set about their tasks with a vigor they knew well from all the early mornings spent attending to the mountain of tasks required of every cadet. Payton took the twelve pallets required for the four boats and began digging up a slurry pit to cobble together the mud and straw mix he envisioned for the make shift mortar inner barrier layer of their armor. He mixed sand, dirt, straw and water with the precision of a drunken master chef mixing the world's largest soufflé in a ditch with a shovel and pitchfork. Timothy rounded up all the twine and packing material he could to enclose the slurry mess and covered all but the top of each pallet and lined them up to receive their slurry infusion. Payton and Timothy worked together patiently until each pallet sat full and drying in the afternoon sun.

Next, the two needed to find a way to easily secure the pallets in to the windows. Dylan remembered an old trick his father taught them for securing plywood sheets over small barn windows during the wicked winter storms that swept down through the Willamette Valley when he was a small boy. His father called them Hurricane Clips because he'd learned how to make them from a friend that had used them in the south before moving to Oregon. Dylan found some old steel flat springs that probably had been used as the suspension on a carriage before his birth and with Timothy's help cut them in to foot long lengths with hacksaws. They then were able to bend one end in to a rough C shape with the help of a vise while leaving one leg out that they filed some sharp grooves in to form teeth. The odd shape looked something like half of an upside down rocking chair with vampire teeth on one end. Using one clip on each side of their armament they slid the pallets in to the C shaped portion and used the protruding end as a tension leg to press fit the pallets in to the window frames of the bridge windows.

"The beauty of these hurricane clips is that the more pressure you put on the pallets, the harder they will dig in to the windowsills. The tension legs can act like springs as well, which will allow a little give when something hits them and absorb some of the impact. However, if you release the tension just a little bit the pallets will slide right out of the window frames" Payton explained.

"Clever little pieces of hardware." Timothy said admiringly. "We get some real blows through here, so perhaps when we get back father and I can build out some protection for the windows. I can't tell you how many times I've nailed boards over the seaward windows here."

Meanwhile, Clara and Dylan had nearly finished installing the protective apparatus for protecting the open decks. They'd used the rest of Payton's slurry, covered the long reams of burlap, and sealed it in with the shellac that was usually used for sealing in old liquor barrels. The resulting fabric was by no means an impenetrable chainmail, but it had some deflective ability while maintaining its flexibility and lightweight. The two had also fashioned a set of riggings for each boat so that both sides could be raised together with one rope much the way a sail could be raised. When fully extended, the two sides came together in an oblong dome covering the rear of the boat up to the top of the bridge ten feet off the deck. Each ship looked like a turtle with a mottled shell on its back and the bridge and nose of the ship sticking out like the eyes and beak of the famously defensive and steady creature.

The four young ones reconvened with the elder O'Ryans for an early supper. The mood did not quite become jovial, but all involved clearly enjoyed the company of the others. Mr. O'Ryan told tales of his younger days running wine and fighting against the English which enthralled Payton and Dylan while boring the rest of his family that had heard his hero's tales many times before. Mrs. O'Ryan quietly listened but clearly had to hide her concern for Timothy every time she looked at her son. She'd seen her husband risk his neck on these boats many times up against the local law, but now her son would sail in to a war zone far more dangerous than anything her husband had ever seen. If her son felt the gazes he did not show it, and he did not show any fear at the prospect of danger in the mission ahead.

As dinner finished the party broke up in to separate groups. Payton retreated to the library to write one letter each to his father and Anne. The two letters included a brief description of their plans and then a description of the Dylan's blossoming romance with Clara. Payton wrote with a touch more sentiment and tenderness in his letter to Anne, perhaps mirroring the feelings he knew his brother felt for Clara but he had denied himself with Anne previously.

Dylan and Clara walked along the cliffs discreetly holding hands, though everyone else on the property knew what was transpiring between the two. They settled together on the lawn in the early evening low hanging sun overlooking the calm ocean below.

"When will you leave for Dover?" Dylan asked.

"I'll take the ferry tomorrow morning and easily beat you there." Clara answered. "My trip won't take me much more than half a day."

"I'll hurry there as fast as I can." Dylan said only half joking. "I am pleased that we don't have to say goodbye just yet."

"I've been thanking God for the same thing all day." Clara sighed as she leaned her head in to Dylan's shoulder. "I've never really considered that I'd feel this way about someone, you know. I've sworn up and down to my mother that I didn't need anyone else."

"I've always had my brother. Having a little help isn't a sign of weakness. Our father used to tell us that as a whole we are greater than the sum of our parts and I truly believe that. I'm blessed with at least one person in this world that I can wholly and totally depend on no matter what." Dylan offered. "Having a big heart isn't a weakness either, and I can see that you possess that as well. I'm just surprised that it seems to be falling for this boy from Oregon."

"I am envious that you have someone to trust so completely. Timothy and I get along well, but I'm sure it's not the same as having a twin brother." Clara said, ignoring the bait.

"I've known twins that didn't like each other at all. I suppose we just got lucky." Dylan modestly answered.

"Will we ever be that way?" Clara asked hopefully.

"Time will tell, but I'd like to try." Dylan answered as he reached to kiss Clara again. "We'll figure it out when I get back from France. I have to see through what I've come to Europe to do if only because it led me to you, but we'll find a way for you and me in this mess." Dylan promised Clara as their moments together began to wane.

"I'd rather start now, but I'll wait." Clara sighed as she held Dylan even tighter.

CHAPTER 14

May 27th, 1940

The tide turned as it always did so the boys set out in their modest armada for Dover as planned. They sailed through the night with each taking a turn leading the way and keeping watch while the other two slept as their boats kept pace on automatic pilot settings. The trip passed blissfully uneventful and a helpful current plus prevailing tailwind combination meant the boys arrived in Dover sooner than anticipated. Clara performed as promised and had berths and fuel lined up for all three boats.

"Have you heard anything from France?" Timothy asked his sister after the quartet had reconvened at a nearby pub for a late lunch.

"I've seen a few soldiers on the streets and they look weary, at best. So far there seems to be a slow trickle in to town. I spoke with one fellow who said that men are huddled all around the town close to the beach. Some units have broken up, but most have stayed together. So far the wounded have been moved out on the Naval ships while the able bodied are scrambling for anything that floats." Clara answered. "He reported intermittent shelling in the town and at the beach, though he said none had fallen near his boat. He also said it felt like there were a million men waiting to get to the boats."

"Sounds about as we expected it would." Payton said. "We need to get the inflatable boats loaded and back on the road, so to say."

"When does the tide go out in France?" Dylan asked by way of agreeing with his brother.

"About six thirty." Timothy said offhand.

"We'll want to run the rubber boats during slack tide, so we'd need to be there by about five thirty then, I'd guess. That way we'll have about an hour to run troops out to the boats before we sail home. If we hurry we'd get back her at about dusk." Payton said to continue laying out the schedule.

"So we'll sail at about three. Excellent, then, we'll rest for an hour and then return to our posts." Timothy declared.

Dylan and Clara sat together and chatted quietly for the hour on the Eirinn. Timothy busied himself on the Etain securing the rubber boats, and Payton instantly fell asleep on the Eriu. Anticipation made the hour pass quickly for all four, and soon enough the three boats pointed their bows toward France and left England at their backs. They soon found that they were not the only boats heading to Dunkirk. Dylan spied medium size sailboat about two-thirds the size of their boats on the same heading and about a half mile southwest of their trio. Their new tail craft clearly looked like the pleasure craft that it was with long sleek lines and a highly polished teak hull. Twenty minutes later Payton radioed that he had spotted another bigger fishing boat steaming ahead of them at a slightly slower pace. The Spanish Armada it was not, but England would muster whatever she could to save the troops.

The waters remained calm, so again the trip progressed smoothly and quickly. As they drew within two miles of Dunkirk, the air began carrying muffled rumbles like far away thunder. As they continued closer to the beach the muffled sound increased like a thunderstorm rolling towards the ships. When they reached the close confines of the beach and shallow depths the rolling thunder turned in to the staccato booms of heavy artillery along with the occasional chatter of machine guns. All three boys press fit their make shift armor in to the windows and said a little prayer to seek protection for their boats. Anyone on shore could tell them that they'd need all the prayers they could get.

The sun grew increasingly dim, but not because dusk had arrived. Smoke billowed out of no fewer than ten buildings that the twins could see, and probably more inland added to the dark haze blotting out the blue sky above. Flames flickered towards the sky on the bluffs above the beach. Carnage reigned up and down the coast line as an ironfisted rule with no exceptions. The only hope came from the steady line of boats headed to shore, like a trail of ants each taking their little part of a monumental task bigger than any single one could handle. Each boat did its part without question amongst the chaos.

Over the radio, the three boys decided that as the best seaman Timothy would stay with the three boats tied loosely together while Dylan and Payton ran the rubber boats to shore.

"I'll just tow the two boats in a nice little oval pattern while I wait for you." Timothy said easily enough belying the difficulty of towing two boats behind his. Timothy threw a tow rope to Dylan, who tied it to the bow of his boat, and then repeated the action by throwing a rope to Payton. Timothy set his autopilot in a quarter mile oval and hoped that he wouldn't drag his tail in to any other boats because his maneuverability wouldn't amount to much.

Dylan and Payton each lowered their rubber boats over the sides on to the gently rocking sea below. Their planned arrival hit the slack tide perfectly so they wouldn't need to fight the currents heading in to or away from the beach. The little twenty horsepower outboard motors roared to life after only a couple pulls on the starter chord. Only minutes after their arrival on the scene, the twins were flashing across the short stretch of water to the beaches ahead. Small geysers occasionally leapt up in the distance from errant artillery shells, but they felt no danger as they closed on the sands. They did, however, fear landing on an empty beach to find no soldiers making this risky trip all for naught.

Once they hit the beach, that fear evaporated. A crouched over man in a British uniform ran towards the boats to greet them. He knelt next to the bow of Dylan's boat with a hand on his helmet to keep it on as he looked up. Dylan saw that he wore the three star markings of a captain.

"Gentlemen, thank you for coming. We've little time to waste. I'm Captain Lawrence and at this point I'm in charge of the beach evacuations for this sector. How many will fit in your boats." Captain Lawrence stated briskly.

"Fifteen in each of these inflatables, counting ourselves, and about fifty on each of the three fishing boats we have waiting off shore." Payton replied in the clipped military fashion they'd learned at the academy for quickly conveying information to a superior.

"Excellent, I'll prepare three sets of men for you. Captain Lawrence said and began to turn away.

"We can stay here until the last trip if you include an officer to run these boats out for us." Dylan offered.

"Our boats offshore won't be hard to find, you can just see them offshore now." Payton added.

"That would be ideal. Thank you for your bravery. Most of the injured are getting priority on Royal Navy ships, so you'll have able bodied men." Captain Lawrence said in an understated way as he finished his turn and sprinted to the edge of the beach. Not thirty seconds later, a small cadre of men raced out to the boats with Captain Lawrence in the lead. The men moved as a unit as fast as they could straight to Dylan and Payton. Captain Lawrence said "Leftenant Gore will lead your boats out, please point him in the right direction and then follow me."

"Head straight for the three boats in line circling at 11 o'clock, you can't miss them." Dylan said while pointing out to where Timothy held their boats.

"You'll need to maneuver in to the boats for unloading. There is only one man out there so he won't be able to change course much." Payton warned.

Leftenant Gore nodded and hollered at his men to push out the boats and go. Dylan and Payton followed Captain Lawrence as a smattering of machine gun bullets pelted the beach behind them where the boats used to sit. The three ran for the cover of a small cottage just past the sandy beach. Captain Lawrence wisely chose the cottage for its protection and for its commanding view of the beach and sea below. No other boats had closed on his sector, so the three sat quietly at a table with a large window quite like they were having a late afternoon tea. In the cottage the twins could see that Captain Lawrence was older than themselves, but still well short of middle age. He had dark hair that hinted at ancestry that ran back to the Vikings with piercing blue eyes to prove it. He seemed to carry on despite the indignities around him and proved a jovial host, offering tea and biscuits to round out the illusion that they were in fact just having tea at the beach.

"As I said before on the beach; thank you for coming here to help with the evacuation. Your three boats will fit an entire company of men. I've assigned you C Company, of which Leftenant Gore is in command at the moment." Captain Lawrence said amiably with no trace of stress from the ongoing war around him. "We've had a good bit of luck in that the Wehrmacht halted three days ago and have not tried to attack the city in force. We can survive the bombardment well enough, so the longer they sit the more men we'll get off these beaches."

"Any port in a storm, I guess. I can't believe they aren't pressing their advantage." Dylan said with a hint of incredulousness at the German misstep.

"I couldn't hear on the beach, very well, but you're Americans." Captain Lawrence said with his own hint of a question at the peculiarity. "What on Earth are you doing here?"

"We'd originally intended to come fight with the French Air Force, but that plan seems a bit outdated at the moment." Payton explained to their new compatriot. "So, the next best alternative looked like helping bring back as many soldiers as possible. You'll be even more stunned by our friend out in the boats. He's Irish."

"That is a bit stunning, an Irishman helping out the British Army." Captain Lawrence laughed at the thought.

No more than ten minutes passed before they saw the boats return again with only Leftenant Gore towing two empty boats behind him. Captain Lawrence didn't even rise to coordinate the next round. The battered soldiers still maintained their discipline well enough to sprint from where they had hunkered down in make shift foxholes on the beach and meet the boats exactly as they hit the shore. They turned the boats and left with no wasted time as the Englishmen and the Americans continued chatting. The twins told Captain Lawrence about Oregon as well as WestPoint. The Captain spoke of his home back in Moffat, a small town in Southern Scotland, as a father of two children and a solicitor, or in American terms an attorney. The war had intruded on his sedate small town lawyer's life, but he performed his duty to God and King admirably.

"The next ride will be yours." Captain Lawrence said. "Your assistance is greatly appreciated."

"We'll be back in the morning." Payton said. "What time is slack tide?"

"Splendid." Captain Lawrence said genuinely with an enthusiastic smile. "I'll expect you here at half past nine in the morning. You are now officially part of Operation Dynamo, the evacuation of the British Expeditionary Force from Dunkirk"

"Thank you sir, we'll see you then." Dylan said as the three rose and shook hands. Dylan and Payton walked through the side door of the cottage and then sprinted in a crouch to meet the rest of the soldiers as they ran to the last set of boats returning. The twins commanded the first two boats as this time Leftenant Gore was pleased to follow them out after his last trip to the beach.

Timothy had successfully avoided all collisions so the rendezvous went off without a hitch. Payton and Dylan were pleased to see that their fortifications had held up with the dome covering the soldiers and the bridge windows cracked in a few places but held together by the pallets. The soldiers quickly and deftly pulled the rubber boats out of the water, deflated them, and stored them in the cargo holds. The three ships loosed their tow ropes and pointed the bows westward. The mood of the departing soldiers began lightening with every mile they traveled away from the beach, and it noticeably improved when they lowered their protective curtain and saw that the sun did indeed shine outside of the crucible they left behind.

Each man thought of comrades left behind, but all thanked the Lord for their deliverance and barely contained their jubilance two hours later as they neared Dover. The three ship's captains expertly pulled in to their slips and tied up for the night while dusk descended on the English Port. Soldiers piled out on to the docks, some kissing the ground, some looking skyward and saying silent prayers, but all smiled in relief at returning home alive. Dylan and Payton grinned at each other for making it through their first run, and prayed their own prayer that their luck would hold. They knew the next day might not be so easy.

***

May 28th, 1940

The next day dawned crisp and clear. The three boys had declined the invitations from the many thankful soldiers willing to buy them drinks and instead spent the night sleeping on their boats. After nearly twenty four hours of continuous sailing any bed would do for them, but a few blankets in the bottom of the rubber boats made for a shockingly comfortable mattress. Within minutes Payton and Timothy slumbered away at the rest of the good and weary. Without Timothy's knowledge Clara had snuck aboard with Dylan and curled up beside him. Dylan didn't stay awake much longer, but he was pleased for the company throughout the night and promised Clara he'd return for the next night. She promised to look for an inn where they could all stay even though Dylan protested that the boat was just as cozy as home.

The three boats set sail again promptly at 7:30 to avoid any tardiness for their appointment with Captain Lawrence. They arrived on time and repeated the process of tying the three boats up and lowering the rubber boats down to the slightly choppier sea before speeding and bumping to the same spot on the beach. Another Leftenant met them with a full complement of men, obviously well briefed by Captain Lawrence, and turned the boats around nearly as fast as the twins could step out of them. They scurried across the beach and met Captain Lawrence in the same cottage again.

"Good to see you again, my friends. You are quite punctual." Captain Lawrence noted.

"We didn't want to leave anyone hanging around the beach, sir." Dylan said with a slight grin. "The beach has a few more pock marks, so I'm glad you survived the shelling."

"Yes, the Wehrmacht intensified the shelling last night. They either intend to come in after us soon or are content to pound us from afar. At this point the best we can hope for is the pounding from afar. Can I offer you some breakfast?" Captain Smith asked.

"Actually, sir, we brought some for you." Payton said with a smile as he pulled open the messenger bag he'd slung across his back. "We noticed your tea ration was limited yesterday, so

Dylan's lovely girlfriend provided a fresh box of tea, some oranges because I'm sure fresh fruit is in short supply, and several crumpets. She is also going to scour Dover this morning looking for more supplies that we can bring back on our next trip."

"Brilliant. You continue to amaze me. You have gone above and beyond. This tea will be cherished, and I shall share it with my men. It's the small things that keep them going at this point. Please, thank you girlfriend for me. Food is always welcome, but please have her look for medical supplies on her next outing. Bandages, morphine, plasma, and penicillin would all greatly help. " Captain Smith implored.

"Of course, I'm sure many of the men here just hope to get back to their wives and girlfriends, so we'll do anything we can to help." Dylan said with a sigh. He, of course, hoped to get back to Clara unscathed.

"Thank you again, as it seems I can't thank you enough. You mentioned flying on your last trip here. Do you have any further plans once this debacle is over?" Captain Smith inquired.

"Not really, sir. At this point we can only focus on the task at hand." Payton answered.

"Well, it occurs to me that I might, for once, be able to help you. It's not much, but my Great Uncle is Air Chief Marshal Dowding. He runs the RAF." Captain Smith said.

"We know the name well. He is a champion of modern fighters and pilots." Dylan said excitedly.

"He was set to retire a year ago, but they've kept him on so far and he's managed to push his retirement back to July at least."

Captain Lawrence explained. "I've written you an introduction letter so that once you return to England you can take it to him directly at RAF Bentley Priory, his headquarters just outside of London."

"Thank you sir, that was very kind and thoughtful of you." Payton said appreciatively.

"Our ride is back, we'll see you again this evening?" Dylan asked of Captain Lawrence.

"Yes, same as yesterday evening if you please. Off with you now." The elder officer said.

On their way back to the fishing boats Dylan and Payton noted the intensified gunfire both on land and at sea. Several Luftwaffe planes circled lazily in the sky waiting for any RAF fighters to engage them, but none ventured out. The twins also noted with pleasure that there were nearly twice as many small boats perched off the coast waiting to run soldiers back across the English Channel. Again their luck held and they met up with Timothy easily enough to carry another company of men back home to their home island. The fishing boats stood staunchly over the gentle waves, though Dylan and Payton had obviously missed some close misses. The sides of the ships had some deep marks above the waterline from shrapnel, and the make shift domes had some obvious pieces of wood and metal hanging where the cloth and lacquer had repelled the injurious intentions of the German gunners.

"At least we know our little armor works better than nothing." Payton muttered to himself.

Steaming west again, the men aboard this time seemed more subdued from an additional nights shelling, but still happy none-the-less. Two hours later the men again clamored over the sides as soon as the boats berthed in Dover and thanked God and their rescuing ships for returning them home safely.

"I hope there are lots of trains or buses out of here." Dylan joked to Clara. "All we do is bring them back, they are on their own after we drop them on the docks."

"The bartenders in town seem pleased that you are bringing them. Apparently most of the soldiers last night got good and sodden drunk before even thinking of finding their way back to any kind of a military base. Most relayed a desire to take another crack at the Germans post haste, so I'd assume they'll find their way home soon enough." Clara laughed in return.

"We've the afternoon again before we head back. What would you like to do?"Dylan asked tenderly.

"Let's just find a place away from this blasted war." Clara said with more than just a hint of bitterness. "Every time you leave I'm afraid you won't come back. I run around looking for provisions to make sure that I don't think of the possibilities while you're gone for five hours or more. I count the seconds to your return, and God forbid you are ever late because I'd go mad." She finished fighting off tears.

"I know." was all that Dylan could muster in response, feeling torn between his feelings for her and the responsibility he felt to help defend England in general and Clara specifically against the Germans. He justified leaving her by knowing in the long run it deflected danger from coming anywhere near her. "All I can offer is lunch in a quiet pub. Will that do for now?"

"Yes, of course. I'm sorry." Clara said pulling her emotions under control.

"You've nothing to be sorry for." Dylan quietly responded.

The two quietly walked off the dock arm in arm behind the boisterous crowd of returning soldiers. The two young people in love tried to act like they didn't have a care in the world through a quiet lunch and they just sat together in anticipation of another parting. The time apart fell short of a considerable challenge to overcome, but each departure grew increasingly more difficult and painful. The sweetness of arrival paled under the shadow of another departure.

The time for another departure came near, so Dylan and Clara held each other close and kissed for a few seconds longer than that morning. Timothy and Payton knew that their siblings were fighting through the tough situation, but also knew they must press on as well. The appointed hour came and the three ships sailed again out towards the desolate sea in search of weary men longing for home.

CHAPTER 15

May 31ˢᵗ, 1940

The morning and evening trips to the war zone in France continued unabated with each trip bringing back a company sized unit of men, so nearly a battalion of men in total, during their seven voyages. With every voyage they brought needed food and medical supplies that Clara managed to scrounge from around Dover as well. Each trip brought an increasingly weary cadre of men home. They told tales of huddling in drainage ditches through the night as shells fell around them. They told stories of men packed in to basements with houses above them rumbling with each new barrage. Each man looked back at France with glassy eyes as they pushed westward to at least momentary safety. Captain Lawrence continued providing a steady stream of well briefed men running upon their arrival. More than anything, his leadership made their trips successful. Each trip saw new carnage on the beach, and increasing shrapnel wounds to their little flotilla of three boats. All of the glass on the Eitan showed cracks from direct shrapnel hits, and the Eirre and the Eiru looked only marginally better. Each time they heard a thud on the pallets the boys silently drew a deep breath of relief that their fortifications held strong. The hull of each boat showed scrapes and gouges from multiple shrapnel wounds, but none had punctured below the waterline so their seaworthiness remained strong. The danger had become monotonous, so each of the three had to remain vigilant to avoid mistakes like sailing to close to shore or forgetting to put up their make shift armor.

The morning run went smoothly again by the Grace of God, and the boys spent their afternoons in the usual way with Timothy and Payton napping while Clara and Dylan spent time together quietly dreading the next voyage.

As they arrived for their evening appointment Dylan and Payton knew something was amiss. A well trained group of men failed to hurry to the boats to meet them, and they realized the beach around them had been heavily shelled with large caliber guns since their last trip. Large burrows in the beach deeper than they were tall littered the landscape as if a huge steam shovel bigger than any steam digger they'd seen in New York had run rampant on the beach. The sunken craters rivaled those on the moon for size and frequency. Not a soul ventured out to meet them.

Not wanting to wait around in such a targeted zone, the boys drug their boats in to the nearest crater to secure them and quickly set out for Captain Lawrence's cottage. When they arrived, they stared grimly at a charred hole in the ground surrounded by rubble where the Captain's one man command post once stood. They searched for any sign of Captain Lawrence around the grounds. Finally, they found his dead body some twenty yards from the main house under an immense boulder. Either the initial shell had killed him or knocked him unconscious while the boulder finished the job. The boys quickly knelt over his body and mourned the loss of their friend. His upper torso appeared perfectly preserved but they could not even see his lower body below the boulder that now rested on him. They met only four days previous, but their work together saved more than a thousand lives to fight again for Britain. They gathered what few of his belongings they could find. They tucked his dog tag, campaign ribbons, what appeared to be a journal and side arm in to a rucksack they found and headed further inland to find some more passengers. Along the way they picked up some wayward rifles just in case they needed them, as well as a couple of British field jackets to insure no sentry mistook them for Germans.

After searching the closest houses to the beach they found themselves facing an inland road with large houses on either side about three quarters of a mile from where they'd landed. In textbook infantry fashion they searched each house until they came to the fourth house on the left. After knocking on the door, then kicking it in, they searched throughout the house until they came to the basement. Inside they found several groups of men huddled together. It turned out that they'd stumbled on the poker house. Each group sat around a small table playing cards seemingly oblivious to the war outside.

"Ah, some more players." Stated what appeared to be a Major as the boys entered the room with rifles raised so as not to threaten the soldiers. "Does anyone have seats at their table?" The major inquired brightly. The resounding silence spoke loudly of the packed houses sentiment, but the fact that no shelling accompanied the sentiment could only come as a welcome sign.

"Actually, sir, we're looking for passengers. We have three boats ready to take men back to England." Payton said

"You must be the Americans my friend Captain Lawrence spoke about. Where the devil is he? We're just waiting for his signal to come to the beach." The Major replied.

"I'm afraid he's dead sir, it looks like his cottage took a direct hit from a large caliber shell. I'm sorry, he was a good man." Dylan offered up the bad news as best he could.

"Well then, boys, time to hit the beach. Please follow these gentlemen." The Major ordered ignoring the death of his friend as he must in war time. On command, the men in the cellar rose and formed up to follow Dylan and Payton. They quickly exited the building and moved swiftly down the open lane. As they approached the intersection with the beach Payton saw a flash out of the corner of his eye followed by a pop. In the next horrifying second he heard his brother grunt and saw him stumble forward to the ground.

"DYLAN!" Payton yelled but his brother did not respond. As he quickly moved to his brother he saw the dirt where he'd been kick up from the next round fired by the sniper targeting them.

"Everyone down! Mr. Carlisle, there is a sniper at our seven o'clock. Please eradicate him." The Major calmly ordered as his men scrambled for cover. Mr. Carlisle lay prone next to the major taking aim at the upper windows of the house holding the infiltrated German sniper. As he released a long slow breath the English soldier fired his rifle before confidently rising to continue down the road. He knew he'd gotten his man.

Payton knelt over his brother fearing the worst. Blood pooled on the ground under his left shoulder and he was afraid to move him. Dylan moaned and rolled over to look at his brother.

"I guess the British uniforms weren't the best idea. He may have left a couple civilians alone." Dylan cracked wise after seeing the look on his brother's face. "Check and see if there's an exit wound. I'd rather not have a bullet in me."

"You're just lucky it's your left shoulder. You might still have a baseball career after all." Payton joked back clearly relieved. "One bullet left two holes, so no lead left in you at this point. Try to remember to duck next time."

"Thanks for the advice, now go get something to patch me up." Dylan ordered as the shock wore off and the pain set in a little more.

"Lucky for you, I saved a couple things from the stash that Clara sent." Payton said as he pulled out bandages, sulfa powder, and a small vile of morphine.

"I knew you were good for something. You'd make a fine nurse." Dylan laughed as his brother expertly administered the sulfa powder, bandages, and finally the morphine.

"Let's get going. The longer we stay here the more chance you have of getting shot again. On your feet." Payton commanded as he reached for his brother's good arm more to motivate his brother than anything else. Dylan did struggle a touch to keep up, but through his fortitude they all managed to reach the beach together. The Major ordered the initial wave out to the boats, but with Dylan injured the twins left with first round rather than the last. They rendezvoused with Timothy again and unloaded the men before sending the rubber boats off again. Payton helped Dylan up to the Etain, his boat, and stayed with him instead of returning to the Eriu.

Timothy came to the stern of the Eirrin and shouted "What took so long? I've been dodging shells for more than an hour. It's getting a little more hairy out here. Dylan you're bandaged!" he exclaimed as he noticed Dylan's arm lashed to his chest.

"This is just a scratch. I'll be fine. I ran afoul of a sniper. Captain Lawrence is dead. We had to go inland." Dylan reported.

"You've come just in time. There is a lot of debris in the water from all the shelling. Get those boys turned around fast and let's end this day alive." Timothy said with his usual jovial self overcoming the worry at the twins delay. The soldiers needed no further urging as the shelling intensified again.

The major himself took all three rubber boats back to the beach and returned with the second wave of soldiers. The beach continued taking numerous thunderous hits from the big guns, so on the beach the Major decided against a third for his own safety and that of his men. Instead, he loaded the boats over capacity and then the rest clung to the sides for dear life and surfed their way out to the big boats. The Major managed to leave no man behind but skip the last trip.

"No reason to tarry about." the Major said as he returned and the men began unloading on the Etain. "These men are Royal Marines; they should be used to the water. If you don't mind, let's head west." As the major finished his last words a whistling screamed from above. "Take cover!" he screamed at the tell tale sign of an incoming shell. The seasoned soldiers dove for the decks, and those still in the water just submerged and hoped the water would slow down any shrapnel.

With a crack louder than thunder the incoming shell found a target and struck the Eriu squarely amidships. The boat exploded from within in spectacular fashion. First the initial explosion lifted the boat several feet in the air on a geyser of white water and then the ship blasted apart from the center as the fuel tanks sparked. The additional fuel added twice the original power to the explosion and nearly obliterated the Eriu. Trailing only fifty yards behind the Etain, the Eriu's explosion lashed the passengers with flying wood and metal debris. The stern of the Etain took a peppering, as did the protective screen covering the open decks. The explosion shredded the burlap and lacquer covering, but the extra cover did its duty and slowed the shrapnel enough that only minor scratches and lacerations befell the men already on the ship.

"Cut the tow rope before it takes us under!" Payton shouted to the men on deck. Only the very bow of the boat remained intact, though it quickly took on water and started slipping under the sea. One of the officers in the stern of the ship quickly withdrew a bayonet from his holster and in one swift movement lowered a strike sharp enough to sever the rope.

"I guess that's how it feels to dodge a bullet." Payton said with only a hint of soberness, shrugging off the idea that he normally would have been on the Eriu when the shell hit.

"I wouldn't know." Dylan joked while gesturing at his wounded shoulder. "Good thing you are up here with me."

"And thank God that none of the men had started boarding back there." Payton added quietly.

"How are we going to handle the extra men?" Timothy bellowed back at the twins before they even thought of the dilemma.

"I hope they like a bumpy ride, we'll just have to tow them in the rubber boats. Fortunately, the big boat here blocked the debris from puncturing the rubber boats. Not a fun ride for two hours but they'll survive. I'll go tell the Major and tie up two in back." Payton replied. "Cut us loose and let's get out of here." he instructed his brother. Dylan complied and passed the tow rope over the side to one of the rubber boats while Payton headed astern to attach the remaining two boats.

Not a single marine complained about riding in the rubber boats. All thanked their luck for simply getting out of Dunkirk. In a bit of a surprise, it appeared that mostly officers filled the trailing boats having deferred the easier voyage to the enlisted men. For centuries a rigid class structure ruled Great Britain, but this small act of kindness showed that war does not discriminate based on wealth, but can bring men together across normally strict boundaries.

The trip that normally took two hours drug on for an extra hour and half due to an increasing headwind and the fact that the two big boats slowed to keep their towed passengers from bouncing out of their small crafts not built for the open sea. Fortunately, the hardened marines avoided the effects of a bumpy ride and neither of the twins saw any heads perched over the side from sea sickness.

After the long trip, the cadre of men pulled in to two slips at Dover, leaving one empty. The small rubber boats bobbed behind until the soldiers pulled them in by their tow ropes. They arrived nearly three hours later than anticipated. Clara burst across the docks from the shore looking white as a ghost with apprehension at only two boats returning. She quickly scanned the boats and gasped when Dylan emerged from the tattered bridge of the Eitan a little wobbly from the lost blood staining his clothes.

"I'm so glad you're back." She cried as he stepped off the boat.

"Did you miss me too?" her brother asked jovially as he walked over from his boat.

"Yes, but not nearly as much." she zinged him back. "What happened?"

"Our main contact was killed, so we ventured inland a little where Dylan got dinged." Payton explained. "And then the Eriu took a direct shell hit before we could get it loaded. Fortune shined on us and we all made it out alive, so no complaints from me."

"I'll be okay." Dylan added, though he was starting to feel more pain as the morphine wore off. Clara hugged Dylan tightly to relieve the stress building in her over the last three hours spent fretting and worrying. "Not so tight." Dylan grunted. "Really, I'm fine though."

"Nonsense. Come with me, I'm taking you to a hospital." Clara demanded.

"Yes ma'am. I'm a military man, I know how to follow orders." Dylan grinned as Clara gently took his good right arm to lead him down the dock.

"I wouldn't have said no to her either. Your brother is right smart to follow that one, its best for his health to listen to my sister." Timothy said. "Not because she's taking him to a hospital, but because she'd have hurt him even more if he'd have ignored her good advice!" Timothy finished about his sister with a good natured laugh showing even his relief at returning to Dover in one piece.

"Did you talk with your father on the way back?" Dylan asked.

"Yes, I found a radio signal that worked for about twenty minutes just before we made port." Timothy answered. "I think my mother may have been more worried than Clara. She convinced him to rescind our sailing orders. After losing a boat I think he'd rather not lose another. I didn't even tell him about Dylan and he still gave me a line about fulfilling our duty and asked us to sail home tomorrow morning if possible. He said the Royal Navy sent out advisories warning of the danger to smaller boats yesterday."

"He'll get no argument from me." Payton said. "If the Royal Navy can handle it from here then we should let them. The Major told us on the way back that the beaches were to be closed with the rest of the men shipped out of the harbor. I'd imagine they'll still get some off the beaches in the next couple of days, but the shelling may deter that even more. Our little boats would just clog up the harbor at this point."

"I agree. Tonight we celebrate and tomorrow we head back to Dublin." Timothy said.

"I'll certainly drink to that." Payton said. "I've no idea where to go in Dover, but I'm sure we'll find a place."

"It's only an hour and half to London. Let's check the train schedule and see if we can make it up there for the night. Our last encounter in London went reasonably well, so it could be fun again." Timothy replied. "Besides, I'm sure there will be more than a few soldiers up there that would happily pay for our service in drinks. And, I could call Simone."

"Now we come to the real reason you want to go to London. You want to see her again!" Payton teased.

"Of course I do. I'm surprised it took you that long to catch on!" Timothy chuckled. "Don't worry, I'll have her invite Caroline as well so you aren't a fifth wheel."

"Your intentions are certainly noble, how could I refuse? We may have to warn off Maggie about your sister and Dylan. Where do you think she took him anyway? Let's go round them up and see if we can catch a ride up to London." Payton enthused warming up to the plan. They juxtaposition was lost in the moment, but the boys had gone from real danger and intimate proximity to German shells no more than three hours ago to making plans for an evening on the town in London. They quickly forgot the stress only the way the young can leave the immediate past behind while looking at a bright future, even if this future only included one night.

"The hospital is just up the road. We'll have him sprung out of there in no time." Timothy answered. "Most of the wounded went to the military hospital, so I'll guess that he'll get quick service in and out at the county place. I'll go get us a cab."

"Perfect, I'll finish tying everything down here and we'll be off." Payton said as both boys hurried to their tasks.

Timothy's prophecy proved true. They found Dylan and Clara exiting the hospital less than an hour after entering. He looked no worse for wear, and at least he now wore a clean shirt minus the blood stains.

"Glad you boys turned up. The hospital surgeon gave me a clean bill of health. He just stitched up my shoulder and said I was good and fine to heel. He didn't even prescribe any more pain medication, but did make Clara promise to keep the wound clean by re-dressing it every day." Dylan said by way of greeting.

"Good to hear. Father has called us off. We thought we'd head to London for the evening before sailing back to Dublin tomorrow." Timothy explained without much in the way of greeting for his sister or friend.

"We won't be there until close to 10:30 tonight if we leave right now." Clara protested mildly.

"All right then, we'll leave right now. The taxi is waiting and we've already gathered our things in to the trunk. Not the shortest taxi ride, but the cabbie said he'd give us a break on the long trip because he wants to go to London anyway. Where shall we have him drop us?"

"The Savoy, of course." Payton interjected quickly. "We'll have to pay for it ourselves this time, but might as well. Hopefully they'll remember us there."

"The Savoy it is, then." Timothy confirmed as the four piled in to the taxi and headed to London.

CHAPTER 16

June 1ˢᵗ, 1940

The previous night at the Savoy veered from the original plan only in that Simone and Caroline failed to join the group because of a previous engagement, but the four followed the rest of the celebratory plan un-hindered. The staff at the Savoy cheerfully greeted the twins after instantly recognizing them from their previous visit and arranged two splendid rooms for the group. The manager remembered their connection to the king so they were well taken care of from the moment they arrived. By the time the bell hop had delivered the twins to their room someone had already found and laid out perfectly pressed and fitted tuxedoes for them. Timothy and Clara found the same treatment in their rooms and so the four were properly outfitted for dinner in the River Restaurant again. Throughout dinner, Timothy occasionally cast a glance at the door hoping Simone might appear, but her arrival never came, so he satisfied himself with beer and the knowledge that the last few days stood firmly in the past and that memory included the survival of the whole group.

After a wonderful dinner and some waltzing for Dylan and Clara as well as a few dances for Payton and Timothy with some lovely single ladies at dinner, they all met again in the morning for breakfast. With his duties held off-shore, Timothy finally had a chance to discuss the scene onshore from the last trip with Payton.

"They really sat there playing cards?" Timothy asked incredulously.

"Yep, though I think the major ended the last hand so quickly because he was losing overall. I think he just wanted to cut his losses in more ways than one!" Payton joked, but quickly turned serious again. "Havoc dominated the entire coastline, and that might only cover half of it. They happily took our piecemeal solution because of the dire situation. They'll need better leadership if they ever want to keep Hitler off this island, let alone if they ever think they can take France back from him." And then, absently and to himself, he thought out loud " I should tell the King first hand."

"You'll have no argument from me." Timothy confirmed Payton's thoughts. "But I'm not sure there's much to be done about it for us. I've cabled father that we'll be home the 4th. I'm in no rush to get home, but I'm not sure there is much that we can do. You might need the King to sort out something like this."

"You might be right. You say we don't need to head back to Dover until the day after tomorrow, then?" Payton asked.

"That's right. Unless you think you can gain an audience with the King for tomorrow we'll content ourselves with the good that we've already accomplished." Timothy teased.

"I will let you know how my call with His Majesty goes and if he has a time to meet us tomorrow." Payton quipped with a large smile to match.

"What are you two going on about the King?" Clara interjected.

"Payton thought he'd call up the King to explain the troubles in France." Timothy explained lightly.

"He seemed like the right man for the information." Payton noted dryly.

"Of course." Clara said with her curt answer showing that she really didn't believe him or find the joking as amusing as her brother.

"Let's go find you a dress for meeting the King." Dylan offered, joining his brother in the joke to the chagrin of Clara.

"I won't pass up the chance to find a nice dress in London, but I don't think it's funny to joke about meeting the King. Father would be mortified for his Irish offspring to joke about meeting the King of England." Clara said not hiding her irritation.

"My apologies, my dear, but why don't you and Timothy go shopping as you say. Payton and I do need to write a couple of letters back home and to the General officer who helped us get here. The sooner we can accomplish that the better." Dylan offered to pacify Clara.

"All right, that will be fine. We'll meet again after lunch, then." Clara said with her tone a touch calmer. "Timothy, we'll go to Saville Row. I'm going up to the room to change and we'll make our way over."

"Yes Ma'am." Timothy said accepting his orders with grace.

***

Once Timothy and Clara left, Dylan set to work writing back to General Bradley.

To: General Bradley

From: former Lt. Dylan Anders.

RE: Findings of trip from London to Dublin and and English disposition in France

The purpose of this note is to inform the General of relevant notes from our continuing mission in Europe. Upon last communication we were traveling to Dublin to secure passage to France. Upon arrival in Dublin we learned of the failing British Expeditionary Force and German occupation of nearly all of France, as I am sure you are by now well aware. Without the possibility of joining the French Air Force we began running rescue missions on the boats of the Irish friend mentioned last dispatch. We made eight runs between Dover and Dunkirk from

27 May through 31 May. On the last run we lost one of our three ships and sustained one slight wound that will fully heal in two weeks.

The British in Dunkirk were beaten soundly, but remained resolute in their defiance. All queried said that they would return to England and defend their homeland from Hitler. Overall, spirits were low and leadership was lacking. The beaches and evacuation were scattered and disorganized at best. Will endeavor to also inform the King of such. If Hitler crosses the Channel now the outcome would be in doubt.

In the course of rescue mission, we made contact with an associate of Air Marshall Sir Hugh Dowding. He provided an introduction letter for us to take to the Air Marshall. We plan to enlist his aid in joining the British Royal Air Force instead of the overrun French Air Force. We believe this will suffice for our mission as discussed with you before our departure.

Continuing updates to follow.

***

In all reality, Dylan and Payton had no idea whether or not General Bradley approved of their current path, but had no way of getting feedback from him. General Bradley had a reputation for being a GI's General, in touch with the common soldier, so the twins hoped he'd agree with their decisions. They also had baseball in common. Bradley had played as an outfielder with a cannon arm and a slugger at the plate for three years at WestPoint, including on the 1914 team where ever member that stayed in the Army went on to become at least a General. Bradley graduated in 1915 along with Eisenhower and the rapid rise of that preeminent class now foreshadowed the true leaders that must guide the United States Military in this time of trouble. Army Chief of Staff General George Marshall lead the whole military, but the class of 1915 would advise him and lead the American forces in the field. Payton and Dylan hoped to add a little perspective and on the ground intelligence for General Bradley, but they knew that their little mission did not amount to much in his world. So, they moved forward with their plan undaunted and determined to see it through.

Meanwhile, Payton left Dylan to his writing and found the concierge to assist him in making two phone calls. The first call turned out as a much simpler task than the second, though Payton never thought calling the King could go more quickly than calling an Air Marshall. Payton returned to the room as Dylan sealed his dispatch to General Bradley in an envelope and readied it for the mail.

"Are we all set, then?" Dylan asked his brother.

"Yes, we'll go up to Bentley Priory this afternoon, and the king has about fifteen minutes available for us at 11:00 am tomorrow. That call was easier. The concierge connected me directly to the King's secretary who knew immediately who I was. For Sir Dowding I had to talk my way through two sergeants of the Women's Auxiliary Air Force before getting his actual Chief of Staff to schedule us only because I said we'd had a letter from Captain Lawrence for him. I tried to avoid that angle, but in the end I'm sure he wanted us to meet Sir Dowding. At least we can deliver the few personal effects we have for the family." Payton explained.

"What time is the meeting?" Dylan asked.

"Two O'Clock. The timing should work out to make it back here before Clara and Timothy return. Good thing that the hotel pressed our suits last night. Too bad we can't wear our uniforms." Payton lamented.

"Better get a move on if we want to make it. I have no idea how long a cab will take to get us there." Dylan said.

***

The ride to RAF Bentley Priory took less time than then twins thought it might as it was in the London Borough of Harrow, so they arrived with plenty of time to spare. The large square grey stone building housed RAF fighter command. The guard took their names at the gate and a rather stern WAAF corporal escorted them to an anteroom where she told them to wait. The boys sat down on the metal folding chairs against the wall and set Captain Lawrence's rucksack on a third chair. Though they had arrived only thirty minutes early, they waited nearly an hour for the return of the WAAF corporal. She ushered them quickly down the hall and in to a book lined room that, although plenty large enough, seemed small to serve as the office of a man such as Air Chief Marshall Sir Hugh Dowding. At the far end of the room, behind a good sized desk, the stood the Air Chief Marshall whom the twins hoped could help them. He was of medium height and had kept in excellent shape for a man nearing sixty. His well groomed mustache spread across his narrow face below deep, piercing eyes. The boys walked over and stood at attention in front of his desk.

"You must be the Anders boys that my great nephew wrote me about. I am sad to report that shortly after his letter arrived I was informed that he was killed in action." Dowding said with very little introduction. "You are definitely military, of some sort. I can tell by the way you are standing. Please, relax and have a seat." He finished and motioned toward two chairs opposite his desk.

"Yes, sir, we know. We were the ones who found him." Payton offered quietly as they sat down. "We've brought a few of his things for you in the hopes that you can pass them on to his family." Payton said and handed over the rucksack.

"That was rather kind of you. Thank you. I'll see to it that his wife gets them, and I'm sure the children will one day be pleased to have some of his things to remember him by. I'm worried about his wife, Elsa, but our family in Moffat will make sure to look after her. Captain Lawrence mentioned that you wanted to help out the war effort as pilots, is that correct?" Sir Dowding asked, coming directly to the point.

"Yes, sir, that's correct." Dylan replied. "Our background is in mechanical engineering and we've flown planes on our father's farm since we were teenagers."

"Flying a crop duster is not the same as flying a military fighter plane." Sir Dowding noted sternly.

"No, sir, we understand that. We studied the fighter crafts in our Mechanical Engineering classes at WestPoint." Dylan offered.

"Ah, that makes more sense. I thought you might be military but no one had mentioned WestPoint before. Do your Generals know you are here, even though you are technically neutral?" The Air Chief Marshall asked.

"General Bradley is aware of our intentions, but no, no one officially knows our current status." Payton answered diplomatically. "We hope to train with your men and then, should America enter the war, and we think she must, the US Army Air Force would have at least some fighting experience."

"In essence, you are trying to borrow the experience of the RAF, then? Fortunately for you, I've spent the last month fighting to save every plane and pilot I could for home defense. Churchill wanted me to waste them in France, but once Hitler ran through Belgium the outcome was already determined. We need pilots and planes to defend the Island. My great nephew spoke very highly of your bravery in Dunkirk. I'll have you tested for basic flight training and if you pass that you'll be posted to an operation training unit to learn to fly the Spitfire. That run is usually a year, but you'll most likely have two to four weeks before being posted to a squadron. You'll learn fast or crash quickly, we've no time to do it any other way at this point. You'll be commissioned in the RAF as flight Leftenants and most likely end up at Middle Wallop, north of Southampton. I'll have my staff put together the paperwork. Tomorrow is Sunday, so please return here Monday at 0900 hours." Sir Dowding clipped out in rapid succession.

It was more than the twins could have hoped for, but the RAF pilot shortage made it possible. Sir Dowding's long held belief that you could replace planes faster than pilots worked in their favor, and without much in the way of an interview he'd just bestowed on the twins the chance to fly much more readily than they could have gotten back home.

The boys stood in preparation to leave and both said at the same time "Thank you, sir, we won't let you down."

"If you are as disciplined as that cadence and can stick together as such in flying formation, you'll do just fine. You'll meet my chief of staff Monday morning. He's just down the hall. Thank you again for Captain Lawrence's affects, and for your service to Great Britain." Sir Dowding concluded and stood to shake hands with the boys.

As the twins exited the office, the rather strict looking WAAF corporal looked far less daunting than when the entered mostly because the boys could not believe their luck. With one meeting they took the first step in accomplishing their true purpose on the journey that had started with a small idea back in New York. The chance meeting with the late Captain Lawrence turned in to a stroke of luck, though they wished he'd been there to celebrate the triumph with them. They hadn't even needed the help of the King's letter, so they could meet with him the next day in good conscience. With their path laid out before them, the twins would now know whether or not they could truly make the cut as fighter pilots, and thus make a difference in this war.

***

After nearly floating out the gate of RAF Bentley Priory, the twins hurriedly caught a cab back to The Savoy to meet up with Timothy and Clara. As they walked past the front desk, the manager politely got their attention.

"Mr. Payton Anders? I have a letter for you sir." The manager said from behind the desk. He walked back to the cubby holes behind him and produced a small white envelope with Air Mail stamped on it, but no return address.

"Thank you." Payton said as he took the letter from the manager.

"Who's it from?" Dylan asked.

"Don't know, I'll have to open it to find out." Payton answered more than just a little intrigued. "It doesn't look like Mom or Dad's handwriting, and I can't make out the postmark. I'll open it when we get up to our room. Timothy and Clara are expecting us soon for dinner."

Once in their room Dylan rang up Timothy on the phone and arranged a low key dinner at a nearby pub. Payton sat at the desk and carefully opened the first letter either of them had gotten since they left New York. It was dated May 29th.

Dear Payton,

I received your last letter postmarked from the Savoy, so I hope that this letter will find you there. I know we only spent one actual evening together, but it was one of the better nights of my life and I long to see you again. I certainly cherish the letters that you send me, so thank you a thousand times over for sending them. They seem to be growing more affectionate, and I must admit my feelings for you are growing as well. I sound like gushing school girl, but it doesn't bother me. I can't stop thinking of you and worrying about you, so I will come quickly to my point. I finished my exams at McGill last week and promptly joined the Red Cross and volunteered to work in London, which was the closest they could get me to France as a citizen of a combatant country. They'll train me as a nurse there, and then I shall come find you. My mother has promised to forward all of your letters, so even if I miss you hopefully there will be enough information to meet you somewhere. I know this is a slightly crazy idea, and very impetuous, but I want to help the war effort as much as my brother and I want to find you. This plan will hopefully accomplish both of those things. I fly out the day after tomorrow (I'm a little nervous for my first plane trip, but the Red Cross is desperate for nurses so they'll happily fly me) and I arrive in London the evening of the 1st of June. Father has promised to put me up at the Savoy for the first two nights before I report for duty on the 3rd. Hopefully this letter reaches you first and I will meet you there.

Yours Truly,

Anne

"Well, that's a bit of a shock." Payton muttered to himself after he read the letter.

"What?" Dylan asked as he hung up the phone.

"Anne. She'll be here in London, at The Savoy, tonight. She finished classes and joined the Red Cross. Says she wants to help the war effort and see me." Payton replied a little dumbfounded. He'd denied his feelings that night, but now that she threw off the shackles of distance he now knew what his brother must feel for Clara.

"I thought she might like you, but I never thought she'd end up here. It actually will work out fine for tonight. Timothy just told me that only Simone could make it for dinner tonight, Maggie and Caroline are unavailable. Are you happy she's here?" Dylan inquired.

"I'll certainly be happy to see her. You've known this whole time that I liked her. I guess you and Clara sort of proved that we don't have to put our lives on hold to fly here. I'm worried, though, that she's coming to London when Hitler might be on his way here soon." Payton said thoughtfully.

"I know how you feel. Clara insists that she'll go wherever we go next, but I think Ireland might be best for her if things get sticky here. I doubt she'll listen, though." Dylan commiserated with his brother about the headstrong women in their lives.

"Well, at the very least we'll have a say in holding them off." Payton concluded. "At least she can tag along for our meeting tomorrow, too. I don't ever really try too hard to impress a girl, but I'm sure she'll be impressed by the King. Clara might be too when she finally believes us."

"She won't believe us until we pull in to Buckingham, I suppose." Dylan chuckled. "Dinner starts in ninety minutes, so you best check and see if you can find Anne so she can join us."

"Right, I'll run down to the lobby." Payton said and stood with the letter still in his hand. With an added energy in his step, Payton quickly left the room and headed for the elevator and then the lobby several floors below. He emerged from the elevator in to the lobby that, while not exactly a bustling tube station at rush hour, still contained a fair number of people. The extra people checking in before dinner complicated his task of finding the chestnut haired girl he'd often thought of since they first met a little more than three weeks prior. His heart thumped a little faster as he searched, and he quickly rehearsed in his head what he might say, though he rejected each iteration as quickly as he thought of it.

Payton scanned the crowd quickly and as his eyes swept over the front doors one more time he finally saw Anne glide easily in to the hotel. She wore a light cotton dress in navy with small white trim on the hem and neckline and the faintest polka dot pattern in between. She looked slightly tired from the travel, but to Payton she radiated the calm, serene beauty he noticed the first time they met even though the radio announcements at the time would rattle anyone. His heart rate oddly slowed down once he saw her. His nervousness stemmed from thinking that she might not be there more than anything, and now that he saw her he relaxed and walked directly through the crowd to meet her. As he approached, she finally saw him coming her way and broke in to a wide, warm smile.

"I didn't know if you'd be here." She said quietly with a look of relief on her face. "The whole way here I kept imagining the worst."

"I just got your letter today. We only returned here last night. We hadn't even planned on returning. I think fate meant for us to meet here." Payton said with a smile to match Anne's own.

"Are you pleased to see me?"Anne asked sheepishly as the two stood still in the middle of the lobby while everyone else seemed to stream around them.

"Yes, of course I am." Payton said and gently held her close for a kiss. "I'm very pleased to see you. I didn't know if we'd ever meet again, but I'm lucky to have you here now."

She blushed slightly at the romance of their first kiss and said "I thought you'd be in France when I wrote the letter, but then prayed you weren't when I heard that the Germans were overrunning the country. You said you just got back, were you there?"

"It's a bit of a trek, but we ended up in Dublin when we heard the news about France. We ended up sailing to France several times to help with the Dunkirk evacuation. On the last trip Dylan didn't duck in time and got scratched by a bullet, then one of our three ships took a shell before anyone was aboard." Payton summarized the action quickly.

"Is that all?" Anne said with a bit of a laugh.

"Actually, no, it isn't. Through a contact in France we met with the Air Chief Marshall this afternoon. We report back to the RAF on Monday. I think I wrote you about the King as well, we have an audience with him tomorrow." Payton said, then he remembered "Oh yeah, and Dylan fell for a girl in Dublin, Clara."

"That is quite the tale. It's only been three weeks and so much has happened." Anne said with a bit of a gasp. "War will do that, I suppose. The only news I have is that my brother is okay. He cabled home that he'd made it out of France and would be reassigned to another camp in England."

"That's excellent news." Payton said, genuinely pleased. "Let's get you checked in. I'm very pleased you are here. Thank you, my dear, for coming." He finished as he guided her to the front desk. The clerk helped Anne check in and gave her the best room remaining in the hotel without even a request. The twin's unfailing politeness to the staff even outshined their connection to the King and had garnered them more than just the usual excellent service at the fine hotel.

Payton led her to the room on the upper floors overlooking the river and left her to recover from the trip as much as she could in the hour before dinner. He left her with the note that they'd have a casual evening at the pub with their new compatriots and to meet them in the lobby. He then went up the two floors to the room he shared with his brother as though he were floating.

"You look happy. You must have found her." Dylan said with a grin as Payton entered the room.

"In fact I did. I'm quite pleased." Payton answered.

"I can tell. I'm ready to go meet Timothy, Clara, and Simone, though you've got a few minutes to get ready. This will make for a lively dinner, I suppose." Dylan said. "Do you need me to stall them for Anne or will you two go it alone this evening?"

"No, we'll be there. She's getting ready right now. She might as well dive in with the rest of us. That's what she came here for." Payton said as he headed for the shower.

Three quarters of an hour later Dylan and Payton headed down to the lobby to meet everyone. They found Simone just walking in the front door, but did not find anyone else yet.

"Hello Simone, it's a pleasure to see you again." Payton said as she walked towards them.

"I'm quite pleased to see the both of you as well. I didn't know if we'd ever get to meet again after our wonderful evening." Simone said with genuine pleasure at seeing the boys again.

"Thank you and we're happy to be back here as well. We didn't know it at the time, either." Dylan said. "But, I guess we never really know where we'll show up."

"As long as you show up at the opportune moment then you don't need to worry about where you show up." Simone observed.

"That's quite right, and very astute." Payton said.

"My father says it all the time. The right time can make up for the wrong place, and the opposite as well." Simone smiled sheepishly for a moment, but then broke in to a wider smile as she saw Timothy and Clara approaching.

"Hello, Simone." Timothy said in his best dashing voice.

"Hello, Timothy." She replied coyly. "And Clara, I haven't seen you since you last came down with your brother more than a year ago."

"I haven't been to London since, but I haven't tarried so long to forget to splendid time we had. It is so very nice to see you again." Clara said as she leaned in for a familiar peck on the cheek with Simone.

"Everyone, please let me introduce Anne." Payton said as she approached. "We met Anne before we left Montreal at McGill, and she's come to England to join the Red Cross as a nurse. Anne, these fine folks are Timothy, Clara, and Simone that I've told you about."

"Bless you, dear, for coming over to help." Simone said sincerely.

"Payton spoke of you in Dublin, but he didn't say that you'd be here." Clara said.

"Thank you, Simone. Payton didn't know. I sent a letter but I think he just got it today." Anne blushed as she explained. "I'm just happy that I found my way over here and caught up with him."

"Ah, not just the Red Cross then, you've come for Payton!" Timothy teased even though he'd known Anne for less than five minutes.

"Timothy!" his sister scolded.

"That's all right." Anne said. "I did want to come help, but I also wanted to find Payton. These two boys leave quite an impression."

"I'd agree with you." Clara laughed.

"I've no idea why." Timothy poked a little more fun at his friends.

"Okay, enough. We give up." Payton said playing along with the joke. "Let's get to the pub before this gets out of hand!"

With the introductions done they all made their way out of the lobby for one more evening together without knowing what lay ahead for Europe, for London, or for their little group quickly becoming fast friends.

As they walked to the pub Timothy and Simone lead the group, followed by Dylan and Clara. Payton and Anne fell behind the others for a moment alone.

"Thank you for coming." He said feebly as he held her hand.

"I couldn't stay behind this time. I felt that way after my brother left, and now we don't know where he his other than in England. I'll try and find him soon." Anne answered. "If you disappeared too, I'd never know. I couldn't have that." She finished.

Still lacking a decent answer, Payton replied "I'm glad he's okay, and I'm so happy to have you here. I fell in love with you that first night, and have not stopped thinking of you since." He let rush out all at once. "I guess that might be a little forward." He finished sheepishly.

"No, I felt that same way. I love you too, Payton, and I'm here to prove it." She said boldly with a smile.

With that, he leaned in as they walked and kissed her with a passion reserved for the young in the first blush of true love. She kissed him back as the warm glow enveloped them both, cementing that love amid a world of chaos.

CHAPTER 17

June 2nd, 1940

The next morning for breakfast at a little restaurant near the hotel nearly the entire expanding little group felt the after effects of the raucous evening at the pub. They'd drunk and danced even though the worldly events hovered like a shadow. The young love of each couple pushed the shadow aside somewhat to allow a little sunshine. The girls got along famously, with Clara, Simone, and Anne quickly acting like the best of sisters. Clara especially welcomed Anne with her warm and gracious manner. They recognized the kindred spirit of toughness and rebellion in each other easily and truly enjoyed the shared kinship. Simone's gentle grace fit in nicely with the two feistier girls to round out the better halves of the boys in the group. By the end of the night, no one could tell that the three had started out the evening with introductions.

The twins seemed in the best shape in the morning even though they'd matched everyone else drink for drink and then some. The small old pub reminded them of their days back in Oregon more than anything else on their adventure so far. Timothy especially looked the worse for wear, but still sported a contented smile as he picked at his morning eggs and steak.

"We did mention yesterday at breakfast that we'd have a meeting today." Dylan said to break the quiet as everyone finished their food.

"Yes, you thought you were funny saying we'd meet the King today." Clara said with very little amusement.

"That is correct. We have an audience with the King at 11:30 am." Payton said.

"Really?" Anne asked.

"Yes, really." Payton answered. "Clara, will you and Simone please help Anne find something suitable to wear? I'm not sure what the etiquette for meeting the King is."

"You can't be serious." Timothy said.

"I think he is." Clara followed with the realization that the twins wouldn't continue with the line of joking for so long if they weren't serious.

"We are. Our shipment over from Montreal was in the King's service and he asked us to report in to him with any interesting news. I think what we saw at Dunkirk qualifies." Dylan answered.

"Excellent, I'll meet the King with a hangover. Father wouldn't have it any other way." Timothy said.

"Come on, Anne, you look like you are about my size. We can find you something at my house." Simone said. "Clara, bring your things and I'll have father's car come round and take us back there. We can all get ready there, though it would have been nice for a little more notice. We'll have to do each other's hair because I don't think my salon is open today."

"That should work nicely. The King has arranged for a car to pick us up here at 11 am. We'll have it stop at your place on the way to Buckingham Palace to pick you up." Payton said.

"We'll make it work." Anne said gamely. "I'm sure the King will take us as we are."

"Thank you, ladies; we'll see you in a couple hours." Dylan said by way of farewell as the three women hurried out of the restaurant back to the hotel.

***

"Sirs, it's a pleasure to see you again." said Mr. Smith the chauffeur as he opened the door to the same Lanchester limousine that had ferried the boys to London previously.

"I'm glad to see you again as well, Mr. Smith. Nice to have a familiar face take us to such a grand place." Dylan said with a smile.

"Buckingham Palace is grand, indeed, but you'll find the King just as welcoming as could be there." Mr. Smith replied.

"You two seem to have made a lot of friends since you got here. You know the whole town." Timothy said wryly. "Perhaps you'll run for mayor of London next!"

"That includes you, my friend." Payton noted with a glimmer in his eye.

"We're just like moths to a light, I guess, or for the ladies like bee's to honey!" Timothy laughed.

"People see two of us and just get curious, so it's easy to strike up a friendly conversation. I've found it costs us nothing to be kind and friendly." Dylan said explaining the phenomenon that Timothy was joking about.

"True, very true." Timothy admitted. "Let's pick up the girls. Making the King wait might be bad form." So the three boys thanked Mr. Smith again for his service and tried their best not to crease their suits as they clamored in to the back of the limousine. After a short ride, they arrived in time to gather the girls each dressed in splendid, fashionable dresses perfect for the late morning audience with the King. Simone's closet turned out a dark navy blue beaded dress for Clara that perfectly offset her hair, a dark green shimmering dress for Anne that highlighted her eyes wonderfully, and deep purple dress for Simone herself that flattered her in every way possible.

"Ladies, you look smashing." Timothy said as they descended the steps from Simone's house to the car. Dylan and Payton failed to come up with any words at all. Along with the fine gowns they each also had long white gloves, velvet shawls to match their dresses, and the appropriate baubles as accessories. Simone dripped diamonds from her ears and neck, while Anne had opted for sapphire earrings and a matching deep blue sapphire pendant hanging from a loose strand of pearls. Clara, of course, chose very elegant emerald drop earrings and an enchanting gold necklace emblazoned with emeralds.

"We barely had enough time to do our hair." Simone complained slightly "But Anne is a wizard so at least we are presentable."

"I had to learn how to do my own hair on the farm. We were a long way from the salon." Anne explained as the women swept in to the limousine followed by the boys. "And Simone was so kind to loan us these exquisite ensembles. Thank again, my dear, you are a kind friend."

"Think nothing of it." Simone replied demurely, though she seemed genuinely pleased with the compliment.

"I know the shortest way to the palace from here." Mr. Smith said "So we should make it in plenty of time for you to find your way to the Royal Quarters. The King's Butler will meet you at the car park and escort you up to his office."

Within minutes of leaving Simone's they'd arrived at the regal Buckingham Palace. The twins had only a passing idea of the place after reading about it in school, but the citizens of the Commonwealth were all in utter awe as they passed the familiar guards and finally glimpsed the gleaming white Portland Stone face and famous balcony of the massive building up close. The Palace had served as the official Royal Residence since Queen Victoria moved in just over 100 years prior. The Royal Court remained nominally at St. James Palace as it still held the title of ceremonial home to the monarch, but when in London the King stayed at Buckingham Palace. The Palace consisted of 775 rooms in all, including 19 state rooms and 52 Royal and guest bedrooms.

The butler did indeed meet them promptly at the car and escorted them through the labyrinth of corridors until they arrived at a specific door where he knocked sharply twice in quick succession. The Kings secretary answered and showed the party of six in to a large anteroom to wait for His Majesty. Of course, the room looked like it should be in a palace with high gilded ceilings and fine woodwork around large windows overlooking the garden. Even though they were outside his private office the room was clearly meant to impress visitors, and it succeeded easily.

"His Majesty will be with you in a moment." The secretary said before returning to his seat behind a desk in the corner. Not three minutes later a small buzzer on the desk sounded indicating the King was ready for his guests. The secretary opened the door and waved for the group to enter. In stark contrast to the anteroom's impressive appearance, the king sat in a simple but elegant office behind a large desk that wouldn't look out of place in the office of the head of an accounting or law firm.

"Misters Anders, it is a pleasure to see you again. I'm pleased that you've taken me up on my offer to visit when in London." The King beamed as they entered.

"Your Majesty, we are quite pleased to see you again as well." Dylan said as politely as possible without showing how pleased he was at such a warm greeting from the King.

"I see you've made a few friends along the way." The King motioned at the rest of the group.

"Please excuse us, Your Majesty, our manners have left us. These are our friends, Mr. Timothy O'Ryan and his sister Miss Clara O'Ryan from Dublin, Miss Anne Fields from Alberta, Canada by way of Montreal, and please forgive me if I miss the title, but Lady Simone daughter of the Earl of Crawford from London."

"Well done, you are correct." Simone smiled sweetly.

"We've brought them with us to help tell you what we've seen since we last met." Payton added.

"Thank you all for coming and I'm very pleased to meet you the King said as he indicated places for everyone to sit while he returned to his seat behind the desk. "I'm very interested to hear what you have to say. I'd assumed that you'd make it to France, though you didn't have much time to get there I'm afraid."

"That's right, we never made it to France, at least in the way we expected." Payton responded. "In trying to get to France we met Timothy here in London. His father has an import business and offered us a ride on their next scheduled cargo run between Dublin and Le Havre." He finished after stretching the truth only a little to cover exactly what and how the O'Ryan's imported their goods.

"Very resourceful of you to find a ship crossing the Channel during wartime." His majesty commented, full well knowing the implications of business going to France at such a time.

"As you noted, we never made it. Upon our arrival in Dublin we found that France was falling." Payton said.

"Timothy's father found through some of his contacts that Operation Dynamo was in the works so volunteered his three boats to help out. Clara went down to Dover to arrange a base for us as we sailed down from Dublin."

Dylan picked up the story "On our first trip, we met a Captain Lawrence. He was nominally in charge of the beach we landed on using rubber boats to cover the shallows. He arranged for several platoons of men to ferry out to our boats and we sailed back to Dover."

"I am deeply in your debt. I know that some small boats helped, but I didn't know you were a part of it, and to the extent that you did help." His Majesty said. "Those boys will mean more men safe here than trying to defend a falling country. We'll need them to fend off Hitler from our island. We've repelled the Spanish Armada, and we'll repel the Germans too." He finished quietly but with great resolve.

"Yes sir, we concur that the men are more valuable here for defense. We made seven more runs with the assistance of Captain Lawrence and ferried back almost a company of men each time." Dylan said.

"That is truly astounding. God Bless you for your efforts." The King said in astonishment.

"On our last trip we found, unfortunately, that Captain Lawrence had been killed. We ventured further inland and found the men he'd intended for us. We made our way back to the beach and our ships, however one ship took a direct hit from a shell. No one was aboard so we avoided casualties, and everyone made it back to Dover safe." Dylan continued, omitting his own injury cleverly hidden under his jacket.

"We'd like to comment on the fitness of your forces, if we may sir." Payton said.

"Of course, we need to know the moral of the men to know the fighting ability of our army." The King answered.

"We only saw the men at the beach as well as a few stragglers on the road in to town. The morale and discipline of the men ran high, and they particularly seemed defiant to the Germans. However, they were saved by the Germans stopping on the outside of town and that is the only thing that allowed their escape." Payton reported in the same clipped military style he'd used before.

"I do not want to seem presumptuous, sir, but there seemed to be a very distinct leadership void. Captain Lawrence acted nearly autonomously in his area and we believe his leadership alone enabled the men we brought back to get out of France alive. All of the men we spoke with talked of disjointed efforts to organize the men for an orderly withdrawal, but in the end it turned out to be every company for itself, if not every man for himself." Dylan finished his brother's description.

"Yes, I quite agree. It is a miracle that we've gotten so many men out." The King thought out loud. "Operation Dynamo is still ongoing, but it is beginning to trickle to a stop. To date, we've brought home nearly a quarter million men, and little ships like yours must have played a big part. We hope to bring home another seventy five thousand or so from today in to the next few days, but that's all it is, a hope. We must address the leadership at the top. I'll speak with Lord Beaverbrook about it. Thank you for the information. What will you do now?"

"Captain Lawrence kindly put us in contact with Sir Dowding, and he's offered us training positions in the RAF. We report Monday. Anne has come from Canada to join the Red Cross as a nurse." Payton said.

"I'm going to join her." Clara interjected while Timothy shot her a sharp glance knowing that their parents would want her to finish school.

"That would be wonderful. We can go through together, knowing someone there will make it easier." Anne smiled at the thought.

"A very kind and valiant thing to serve as a nurse and I dare say you'll be needed more than I wish. Lady Simone, have you any plans?" The King asked.

"My father has asked me to organize several gatherings to sell war bonds, Your Majesty." She answered somewhat quietly to avoid comparison to all that the others were doing.

"Any effort helps the war." His Majesty replied kindly enough. "Misters Anders, what do you suggest I propose to Lord Beaverbrook?"

"We are but lowly second lieutenants." Dylan said.

"Who are freshly graduated from one of the finest military schools in the world, where you probably graduated higher in your class than I did in mine, and with a firsthand look at the latest war front. Please indulge me and act like this is a class exercise." The King commanded.

"Of course, sir." Payton said while glancing at his brother. "We'd recommend centralizing your command structure, preferably here in London to defend the coast. You'll also need to work with whoever is left in the French government to have them cede most of the control to your supreme commander. They'll need a figure head, but should report to your army at the moment."

"I'd find your most organized senior General and put him in charge. This is a massive logistical undertaking, and no detail can fall through the cracks." Dylan added.

"All good points strategically, but what of the tactical situation at the moment?" His Highness astutely asked.

"Make Dover look like a fortress to scare off the Germans, and rely on the moat you have in the English Channel. Any submarines you have should be deployed to act like sharks in your moat. Maintain mobility for your armies and hit like a sledgehammer at the initial landing point with all you've got." Payton pointedly answered.

"The longer you can hold off any attempt they'll make at crossing the Channel, the better chance you have of rebuilding your army both physically and from a morale standpoint." Dylan continued. "And the greater chance you have of the United States entering the war to aid you."

"Thank you for your candor. Most people won't tell me the grim reality. Winston seems to be the only one willing to give it to me straight." The King lamented. "Thank you, again, for your visit." He continued rising from his desk. His busy schedule brought their brief meeting to an end. "Good luck in your flight training, and in your nursing training ladies. You must visit again when you have some time. Next time I'll arrange for all of us to have dinner here with my wife and family." He finished as the group moved toward the door.

"Thank you for seeing us, Your Majesty, and we will make every effort to take you up on your kind offer again." Dylan said as they departed through the thick oak door where they had entered.

***

"I can't believe you weren't kidding around!" declared Clara in mock anger as the six poured out of the limousine for lunch at the Savoy.

"I can't help that you didn't believe me." Dylan protested mildly. "I hope you enjoyed the visit though."

"Of course we all did." Anne interceded gently. "This war..."she said trailing off. "What will happen to us next?" She finished after a moment.

"Ours is not to wonder why, ours but to do and die." Payton answered.

"*Charge of the Light Brigade.* At least you know your poetry close enough. Tennyson wrote roughly that almost a century ago." Clara said as if she were lecturing to a class. "Hopefully there will be no futile rushes across barren fields. Please don't die, my love." She finished playfully with only a hint of seriousness added for Dylan's benefit

"No, a century ago the war could only take place on the ground. Tomorrow we start training for war in the air, for war at 350 miles an hour." Dylan offered earnestly. And, he was correct. The last war hinged on men in trenches willing to hurl themselves across no man's land into a barrage of machine gun and cannon fire. In the last war, few machines helped the effort, but in the two decades since the end of the First World War technological advances furthered the ability of nations to bludgeon each other in to submission. Hitler's entire war making effort hinged on these advances. The Blitzkrieg simply could not blitz without the aid of machines. Dive bombers roared ahead and softened enemy lines for tanks to crash through and envelope whole armies in days instead of the traditional maneuvers that took weeks or months to execute on foot. Generals from the old days could not imagine the speed and ferocity unleashed by such machines and suffered massive defeats because of it. The tactics of war shifted swiftly from fixed fortifications with thick walls and big guns to speed and mobility above pure firepower. The French offered the simplest example of the shifting tactics. They had bet heavily that the Maginot line would stop any German invasion cold in its tracks before it even got started. The line of fortified gun emplacements meant to keep the Germans out lead the French army to believe they could withstand any frontal assault across the border and the Rhine River. However, the French did not anticipate the Germans simply bypassing the

Maginot line and coming through Belgium and the Netherlands. The mobile Wehrmacht and the gaping hole left by the undefended boarders to the north rendered the Maginot line useless to the French Army, the march to Paris simpler for the Wehrmacht, and the Dunkirk evacuations necessary for the British Expeditionary Force.

Dylan and Payton saw the problem the moment Anne translated the news from the radio for them. At WestPoint they'd learned the virtues of firepower and mobility in the new age of warfare and had taken the lessons to heart naturally because they knew that an airplane combined the best of maneuverability with great firepower. Plus, they loved to fly so the never questioned their desire to join the air corps. No longer could a country simply throw concrete and men against an enemy and hope for victory. Now only machines skillfully employed with the armies behind them could take and hold land. Moving so a big gun couldn't hit a soldier and then taking it out from the air seemed far simpler than running straight at the barrel. Now, Dylan and Payton would learn to fly at speeds never dreamed of by generations before them with an invasion looming that they could only hope to beat off. They would learn the limits of speed and warfare in the most intense crucible possible.

CHAPTER 18

June 4th, 1940

After a long afternoon spent in the glorious sunshine of London with the awe struck ladies recounting their encounter with the King, the little band of young people split off in to pairs for the evening and each couple had a quiet dinner forgetting their impending split and challenge to their newfound romances with many promises to write and reunite at every possible moment. The twins promptly reported back to Sir Dowding's aide at Bentley Priory on Monday morning where they'd endured a battery of physical tests on everything from their reflexes to their eyesight which both passed rather easily, Dylan's shoulder not-withstanding. Sir Dowding's aide gave them one more night off by informing them they'd report back in the morning for transport to the training grounds at Middle Wallop.

With one more found day they met Clara and Anne back at the Red Cross in London for the evening. Both girls made it in to the newest class of nursing students and arrived to meet the boys with looks of relief on their faces now that they could for certain help the war effort. The night went quickly with brief bursts of chatter about updates on the one day of action but mostly with quite moments spent glancing back and forth hoping for time to stop though all involved knew that time marches on.

The Red Cross took the ladies back in, and the boys reported for their transport again in the morning. Middle Wallop sat between its brother and sister parishes Over Wallop and Nether Wallop in Hampshire the three of which run in a roughly north south line along the stream known as Wallop Brook. Situated southwest of London and due north of Southampton, the transport took a little more than ninety minutes to cover the roughly seventy-five mile trip. The newly opened airfield east of the village housed Nos. 609 and 238 squadrons which were part of 10 group RAF fighter command. The former flew the smashing new Supermarine Spitfire, and the latter flew the RAF workhorse Hurricane MK1. The Spitfire descended both in name and form from a sleek racing plane with the best fighter engine in the world, the Rolls Royce Merlin Mark VIII. The combination of the two made for a fast, maneuverable predator of the sky. Where the Spitfire was fast and smooth, the Hurricane was rugged and strong. It plowed through the sky on shear might and thunder warding off attackers instead of evading them.

The twins saw both of these planes close up as the transport pulled along the hangars before dropping them off at the main base headquarters. They also saw several pilots practicing touch and go landings before pulling back up in to the sky. The whole aerodrome buzzed with activity punctuated by the humming of engines turning to buzzing and then to an all out roar as a plane hurled past those earthbound mortals on the ground. The twins smiled at the roar because it reminded them of home and mock strafing the cows in their old crop duster biplane. The driver dumped them off at the front door with just a point to show them the general direction they should head. The twins grabbed their rucksacks and followed the modest directions in to the front door. The clerk shuffled them off to the WAAF secretary of the 609 squadron commander. Without their knowledge, Sir Dowding assigned them to the training squadron for the most advanced airplane the RAF had to offer. The luck of such an assignment for new recruits, not to mention new American recruits, stood beyond measure. Both stood ramrod straight and managed to avoid cracking a smile as they waited for their meeting with the commander of the group. Flight Commander Dreth buzzed his secretary to usher the new recruits in to his office.

"Gentlemen, welcome to 609 squadron." The small man behind the desk said while half standing to greet them. "You'll need to forgive my brevity. We are quite busy around here at the moment, training pilots up as fast as we can. I see from your file that you've been in Dunkirk, so you certainly understand the urgency of our training."

"Thank you sir, yes, we understand the urgency." Payton answered.

"Excellent. You'll have two weeks of flight training, including gunnery, followed by a week of flight training in the Spitfire. The rest of your training will take place within your squadron. It is not the best situation, but we do what we must." The commander said as he stood. "Please report to hangar C, and you'll begin instruction immediately. I'll have my secretary arrange for your bags to be delivered to your bunks in Barracks No. 3. Good day and Good luck."

"Thank you sir!" The twins said in unison as they saluted and turned to exit.

Dylan and Payton marched directly from the office to the large metal hangar emblazoned with a crimson C over the doors. Inside the arched cavern they found a meeting room with several desks arranged like a classroom. Two men sat by themselves inside while the twins followed a third in to the room. All five waited several minutes until a weary yet hard looking man strode purposely through the door. The recruits stood and saluted crisply the new man wearing the Captains insignia above flight wings. The captain saluted back quickly if not quite by the book and studied the men before him. The first recruit was a small bespectacled man with a shock of red hair pushed to the side. The small man seemed quite by nature, more scholarly than anything, but he looked at the Captain with an intent gaze of determination. He had a small round nose and ice blue eyes. To his right sat a barrel chested round man with dark curly hair and a mustache turned up slightly by a self knowing smirk. He proudly thrust the barrel chest forward so everyone could see the name Baker on his uniform. Finally, behind those two sat an older gentleman gray around the edges with deep set dark eyes and a wrinkled brow. He seemed as if he was hiding his nervousness by concentrating heavily on the desk in front of him. His name was not as proudly displayed as that of Baker, but his tag read Wallace none the less.

Finally, the captain spoke in a clipped British Public school accent "Welcome to flight school. I'm Captain Benson. Usually we fill out this class every three months with the finest military men. However, now we begin the course once every three weeks with all willing and available men that can pass a written test. Does anyone here have any flight experience?" Payton and Dylan both raised their hands while none of the others obliged. "What type of plane?" Captain Benson commanded more than asked.

"A crop dusting biplane." Dylan answered succinctly.

"American?" Benson followed up.

"Yes, sir. From Oregon via WestPoint." Payton answered this time.

"As I suspected. You are the Flight Leftenants Anders I presume. There are precious few crop dusters in England. We are training to fly the Supermarine Spitfire, so you'll find that the only similarities are that you have a stick and rudder pedals in both planes. Going from a biplane to a Spitfire is like going from a bicycle to motorcycle. Knowing how to ride one does not necessarily mean you can operate the other. Please keep that in mind." Captain Benson instructed.

The small man raised his hand and Captain Benson nodded at him to speak "Sir, you said three weeks?"

238

"You must be flight sergeant Quarles. That is correct I did say three weeks." Benson responded. "You will learn to fly one of the most technologically advanced fighter aircraft in the world, including take off, landing, and basic gunnery in the next three weeks. We will work from dawn until dusk out on the airfield and then regroup for flight breakdowns after dinner. Once you are assigned to your squadrons the veteran pilots will teach you dog fighting tactics. The situation is not ideal, of course, but we soldier on as we must. Now let's begin with a review of flight theory."

The small group spent the next two hours reviewing basic tenants of flight including Bernoulli's principal and wing section theory. Bernoulli applied the universal gas law to theorize that air moving at a faster speed must be at a lower pressure. It took scientists and engineers several more centuries to put the principal to use with the theory of wing sections, or airfoils as the cross sections of a wing are called. By curving the top of an airfoil in roughly a tear drop shape while leaving the bottom flat and creating a faster flow of air over the top of that wing the first aeronautical engineers could create a pressure differential between the top and bottom of a wing. Bernoulli said that air had to travel faster over the top of a wing with a bigger bulge, and that the air moving faster was at a lower pressure. That meant the higher pressure air under the wing pushed up, creating lift. The bulge or asymmetry from the leading edge of the airfoil up to the top peak of the wing shape was known as the camber and determined the speed differential between the air on the bottom and the air on the top of the wing. The higher the pressure on the bottom of the wing the greater the lift, so the greater camber created a bigger pressure difference between the top and the bottom of the wing. That meant a wing with more camber, to a point, could create more lift. Therefore, the camber of the wing defined the lift a wing could create. However, with all engineering there were trade-offs. More camber created more lift in a wing at slower speeds, but also created more drag at higher speeds.

To get the steady air flow over the cambered surface wing meant the aircraft had to move forward at sufficient speed. The great engineering feat of the Wright brothers was to create an engine at a light enough weight with enough horsepower to turn the propellers fast enough so they could produce enough thrust, or forward propulsion, to allow man to consistently pull away from the grasp of Earth's gravity. That first simple flight had advanced in the forty years since to the sleek modern mono-wing all metal aircraft the scorched across the sky at nearly six hundred miles per hour. The fear of every pilot came when the airflow over the wings became insufficient to hold the plane in the air, which usually came on steep climbs, and the airplane stalled out before quickly falling back to earth.

Captain Benson did not delve much further in to the theories behind flight, keeping it simple to the four main opposing forces affecting the aircraft: Gravity as defined by weight, lift to overcome that weight, thrust to create forward motion and drag pulling against that forward motion. The only other thing he mentioned was the complexity of moving through space in six dimensions. Whereas automobiles moved in two defined dimensions (forward, back, left, and right) an aircraft had to be controlled in six dimensions. Added to the standard two dimensions of the automobile was the up and down component. In addition each of the standard three dimensions of movement the aircraft needed to control the rolling or side forces exerted in the unbounded space high up in the air. With regards to the tip and tail of the plane any sideways force created yaw, which meant the nose or tail of the play would slide to one side and conversely move the other end of the plane in the opposite direction. All planes controlled this with the vertical tail flap that could move left or right forcing the nose in the opposite direction. With regards to the wings any up or down force created roll, which pilots controlled by adjusting the horizontal wing flaps on either wing up or down. Finally, a vertical force applied to the nose or tail created pitch, forcing the nose of the plane up or down and controlled by the horizontal tail flaps.

After understanding these fundamental forces acting on an airplane flight became more about feel and art than the hard science keeping the fighters aloft. Captain Benson, and to a certain extent Dylan and Payton, knew this and the accompanying hard truth that only flight hours logged could truly teach a pilot how to fly, and fighter pilots needed more time than any others to master the speed and agility of their advanced machines. Captain Benson must shepherd the small class, all of whom were on a true military airbase for the first time, from mere novices to hardened pilots flying for their lives each time they left the ground. Three months usually barely covered the basics of flight, but now two weeks covered the gamut.

So, with the morning finished and the basics covered, the small class adjourned to the supply office for flight uniform fitting. The RAF standard issue war service dress consisted of the dark blue wool short jacket buttoned over matching dark blue wool trousers. The uniform was identical in cut and style to the standard Royal Army Battle Dress uniform save for the color. The jacket was really a waistcoat with two pockets on the front and a collar that could be worn either opened or closed. As officers, the twins were also issued collared shirts and ties to wear with the jacket open at the top while the enlisted men would button the jacket all the way up to the neck. The boys had seen Eisenhower wear a similar style jacket the last time he appeared at WestPoint. Black leather boots and slouch hats known to military men the world over finished the uniform. As aircrew, all of the men were also issued blue coveralls for flight operations, thick turtleneck sweaters and sheepskin lined leather jackets to help combat the blistering cold at altitude. With their gear in hand, the soon-to-be pilots followed their escort to change in the barracks that would serve as their home for at least a fortnight.

After lunch, Captain Benson met the class of five back at the hangar, but instead of sitting in the class room he had all five crawling around a two seat trainer airplane. The Miles M.14A Magister Hawk Trainer III, built of plywood encased spruce, had two open cockpits and impersonated the similarly low slung wings of the Spitfire adequately. On the ground few people would mistake the two planes for each other, and in the air the difference only grew. It looked like a child's rudimentary drawing of the sleek Spitfire, but as a first entry into the monoplane world of flight it served perfectly.

Dylan and Payton took turns in the front trainee cockpit looking at the basic gauges and simple controls. Each moved the stick back and forth to control the rudder and tale flaps to get a feel for the movement of the control surfaces. Captain Benson sat behind each recruit and talked them through the basics of controlling the aircraft and reading the altimeter, horizon gauge, and airspeed. Since Dylan took the last turn in the cockpit, Captain Benson took the opportunity to impress upon the group the necessity of learning quickly by ordering the plane pushed out to the landing strip.

"Gentlemen, we start flying today. We don't have the luxury of time to wait." The Captain ordered. Dylan took the orders in stride and went through his pre-flight checklist quickly and efficiently. He was saved by the fact that the trainer had more or less the same pre-flight routine as the old biplane at home since they'd only briefly touched on the routine before lunch. With Captain Benson's approval from the rear cockpit, Dylan fired up the engines and taxied to the end of the runway. While pushing the throttle all the way to the stops as he released the brakes, Dylan felt the light trainer plane leap forward down the runway. He felt the familiar roar of the engine vibrating up his spine as the plane gathered speed running down the asphalt strip. At precisely the right moment, Dylan heaved back on the stick and the plane slid up in to the sky.

"Well done, Flight Leftanant. Not many men know the correct time to leave the ground. We call that the rotation speed. However, taking off is the easy part. We'll see how you do landing." Captain Benson said over the intercom. "Please climb to a height of ten thousand feet and a bearing of 210."

"Yes sir, heading southwest and climbing." Dylan responded back promptly. Captain Benson took Dylan through some simple maneuvers that Dylan executed easily. After impressing the Captain with his airmanship, Dylan landed the plane expertly and taxied back to the hangar.

"Young man, you have the flying part down. It will be much faster in combat, but your feel for flying is second to none." Captain Benson beamed. "I can teach you some dog fighting tricks and you will be a useful pilot for the RAF."

"Thank you, sir. I actually always thought that my brother was a better flyer than me. Please teach us everything you know. It might save us one day." Dylan answered modestly.

"The RAF is lucky to have two of you. We'll need every man we can get in the air. The Luftwaffe is coming, of that I can assure you." Captain Benson finished as he walked in to the hangar to fetch the next recruit.

***

Directly across the Thames from the Palace of Westminster stood St. Thomas' Hospital, a large square building looming over the river. On the north side of the hospital Clara and Ann took up residence in nurses' housing before beginning their training. Unlike the long open barracks of the military, the nurses' dormitory more resembled what the two were used to from university where they shared a small room down the hall from a common area and bathroom. Unlike the other new girls starting with them, at least they knew each other and thus could room with a familiar face. The hospital, founded nearly a millennium earlier, housed the Medical College and had a partnership with the Red Cross to train nurses. With the start of the war, the nursing school had doubled in size, with new classes starting every three months.

"I'm not sure that this is what my father had in mind when he sent me down from Ireland." Clara noted idly as she finished putting her few belongings in to the small dresser provided.

"I'm not sure my father knows where I am!" Ann joked. "I'll have to send him a letter. All I told him was that I wanted to help with the war and that I was going to London."

"Timothy will have to tell my parents where I am when he goes back to Dublin. For the moment I think he is going to stay around here to see if there is anything he can do." Clara thought out loud at the plans of her brother.

"Or he just wants to see if Simone will have him!" Ann laughed mischievously. "It certainly doesn't hurt that he brought her in to see the King. That will impress a girl."

"It impressed me, that's for sure." Clara said. "And I'm Irish! Where did those two American boys come from? They can't be true, right?"

"I suppose they are true enough." Anne sighed. "I just hope that they don't get themselves killed flying against some silly Germans."

"They'll handle themselves well enough. My brother told me that they never flinched at Dunkirk. I never understand men that seek out a fight like Hitler, but at least in the air it will be on the boys' terms. I'm mad at Hitler for putting them at risk, but then I think that we'd never have met if Hitler had stayed put. All we can do is keep saying our prayers." Clara replied with a touch of melancholy in her voice. Ann too shared the melancholy of not knowing what the future held while knowing that the immediate future looked bleak indeed. They'd both decided to help as nurses, but in reality the nursing would help them grapple with their immediate future by giving them something worthwhile to do instead of just sitting and waiting. The Germans might jump across the Channel sooner rather than later, but at least they'd be able to help in their own way, just like Dylan and Payton were.

After lunch the twenty-five or so girls starting at the school that day gathered in one of the classrooms adjacent to the hospital. They each were issued their nurses uniforms and after a lecture about the importance of cleanliness in the hospital the head nurse paired the girls up and sent them off with a more experienced nurse to observe rounds at the hospital. By the time the class reconvened two hours later, four girls had dropped out unable to stomach the blood and pain presented to them. None of the girls thought less of those that left, but none of them really knew that they might soon see worse. Even Clara, after hearing the stories of Dunkirk and tending to Dylan at the hospital after their return, did not fully understand the challenge ahead.

With the first day nearly done, the head nurse of the school delivered a stirring speech to her charges. She spoke of the true horrors she'd seen during the Great War and how she never slept without thinking of the poor souls missing limbs, burned horribly by mustard gas, or those simply left dead there. But then, with a bit tenderness, she spoke of the healing power of love, and how she'd seen men near death hold on either for the love of someone back home or simply because a nurse cared for them like a loved one. She implored all of the students to remember that they could save lives both through the great medical advances since then, and also with the oldest medicine of all. She said that she could teach them all the latest techniques, but that each nurse would have to find the love in their soul to care for these men. All the students had to pull up the ends of the aprons to dab away tears as the head nurse finished. Clara and Ann both knew where their motivation and love would flow from, and how they'd use every bit of it to help the patients they saw in the hopes that they would not have to see Dylan or Payton as one of their patients.

CHAPTER 19

June 18th, 1940

Aviation gunnery school, like flight training, started on the ground. In between flight maneuvers in the previous two weeks the pilot trainees also learned to shoot. Although Dylan and Payton had occasionally toted around a rifle at home on the farm, and had been taught military gunnery at WestPoint, they knew little of the complex geometry and dynamic nature of firing a gun moving in six dimensions at 330 mph.

A cockpit type apparatus had been set up on the ground with both stationary and moving targets, and just to make things interesting the cockpit moved too. Out the front windshield lined up with the nose of the plane sat the gun sight, just a metal ring really. However, the gun sight on an airplane differed greatly from that on a rifle. On a rifle, the sight lined up with the barrel and the stock so the bullet flew true and straight. The bullets from the plane could fly true and straight as well when not moving, but a single bullet, or even a few bullets flying in a straight line, would never bring down a plane because the plane moved so quickly out of the line of fire. Instead the machine guns on a plane were set at an angle to converge and concentrate the firepower about thirty yards in front of the plane. With the light caliber Browning guns on British Interceptors, chosen so that they could use the same ammunition as the rest of the military, the number of rounds required to bring down an enemy aircraft could reach in to the thousands, so getting all of the rounds possible on target took the highest priority. After the rounds crossed paths, they spread out again like a shotgun blast hoping to get a lucky hit on a vital piece of an enemy aircraft.

However, the biggest challenge in aerial gunnery was not the angle of the machine guns fired from the wings, but actually the inertia exerted on each bullet by the maneuvering plane. A stationary target with a stationary rifle took a straight line and little skill. Adding a moving target increased the difficulty, but not by much. Like a quick draw or shooting from a horse in the old west, adding some movement to the gun increased the difficulty even more. Now, adding airplanes flying about half as fast as the bullets, both as targets and as firing platforms, along with the uninhibited maneuverability of both tested the laws of physics. Bullets flew in arcs and curved at angles determined by gravity and rolling planes that seemed impossible. No smart pilot would let an enemy directly behind him for a clean straight shot, so the impossible angles stood as the only real chance at shooting down the enemy.

The gunnery simulator moved along a track while the targets moved as well. Each of the students learned to anticipate the targets from whichever angle they moved and fire accordingly. Dylan and Payton handled this part of the training as well as the other students, but tried to get as much extra practice as time allowed because they knew that a missed opportunity in a dog fight might mean the end of their plane at least, and possibly themselves. The best shot turned out to be Flight Sergeant Quarles, the small bespectacled man that the twins noticed first in the initial introduction to the training. As the twins befriended him that first day they'd learned that he knew a thing or two about cricket, and that he taught as a professor of physics at a small college in Wales. Although his flying did not match that of Payton and Dylan for the level of instinctive feel, he easily rated above the rest as the best gunner in the group. Owing to his exceptional eye sight and understanding of what the movement he exerted through the training simulator would do to the rounds loosed from the machine guns he hit all targets much more often than the other students.

"It's really quite simple." Flight Sergeant Quarles tried to explain. "You rounds will never fly straight unless you are moving straight as well."

"Why's that?" asked Baker loudly.

"Because it will move a little in the direction you are moving, and a little in the direction it was moving originally when you fired it." Quarles said, leaving out the technical aspects of Newton's first law of motion. Baker was a true fighter and just wanted to go fast in planes so he lacked scientific inclination and curiosity to care too much about the details. The idea of vector mechanics sunk to the depths of Baker's mind like a stone in water never to see light again. "Think of it like rugby. When you are running with the ball and have to pass to a teammate you have to account for your running and the running of your teammate. The ball will curve." Quarles finished sensing that Rugby might be more understandable to Baker than physics.

"That's right." Dylan noted. "In baseball when you throw on the run the ball doesn't go straight. It bends and curves depending on how fast you are running, the angle you throw from, and the angle you are running at compared to your target."

"Very good my young friend, that is precisely right." Quarles congratulated Dylan. "The force you are exerting on the ball comes from both the throw you are making with your arm, the rifle, and the speed you are running at in a different direction with your legs, the plane. Those two forces, plus gravity, determine the movement of the ball. It is the same in an airplane, except the forces involved are much greater, and the bullet is much smaller, so the total effect is quite large."

"Is that why you are so good on the range?" the elder recruit, Wallace, asked. "You are anticipating the bends?"

"Yes of course, that is all I am doing." Quarles smiled at the thought of helping his fellow pilots. "I anticipate where the target will be as it moves, and then just imagine the arc the tracers will travel towards the target and try to line up the sight with the high point of the arc. Physics takes care of the rest."

That afternoon Captain Benson noted a marked improvement in the gunnery of the group as a whole on the range. The best pilots in the world can run out of trouble, but without shooting down enemy planes and pilots, eventually their luck runs out. The best fighter pilots were flyers and gunners all at once without ever thinking about either.

Two weeks after their arrival at the training field in Middle Wallop, Dylan and Payton graduated from the training planes to the fastest plane in England. The Supermarine Spitfire began life as a failed bid to a military contract. The Supermarine company answered an Air Ministry request for a new short range high performance interceptor plane in 1931. The resulting Supermarine type 224 failed miserably with too big wings, an open cockpit, and fixed landing gear. Lead designer RJ Mitchell learned quickly from his mistakes and re-modeled his next attempt after the sea planes the company entered in the hallowed Schneider Cup races. The refined iteration closed the cockpit, retracted the landing gear, and shortened the wings while thinning them out and adding the trade mark elliptical shape. Finally, the new design included the Rolls Royce Merlin engine that eventually pushed the plane over 350 miles per hour. The resulting Supermarine type 300 prototype would become the spitfire, one of the two interceptor planes along with the Hawker Hurricane, the factories of Great Britain rushed to manufacture as quickly as possible.

Equipped with four Browning machine guns in each wing, the Spitfire was the first real fighter plane that the twins had flown.

Now all the trainees would start to put together the flight skills and gunnery acumen drilled in to them over the fourteen straight long days at the airfield. Payton climbed the ladder up to the Spitfire cockpit with a renewed energy and excitement for the first flight, just like a knight of old climbing on to his best warhorse for battle. The thought of flying such a machine made him feel invincible.

Just after takeoff, Payton pulled the plane in to a steep climb north of the airfield. Following the flight instructions given to him by Captain Benson before leaving the hangar, Payton executed several evasive maneuvers in the new plane. Finally, he spotted one of the training planes towing a training target behind it off to the east. Payton took three different strafing runs at the target simulating different angles of attack and peppered the plywood frame each time. The pilot of the training plane towing the target appreciated the marksmanship on the target and not his plane.

On his fourth and final run he dove after the target from high above in the classic Red Baron attack out of the sun. However, on this run, Payton found one of the fatal flaws in the Spitfire. Hoping for superior horsepower and less maintenance, the Spitfire design included a simple carburetor instead of the new fighter standard direct fuel injection. When Payton took such an extreme downward angle on the target he created a negative G force in the engine which, effectively weightlessness, forced all of the fuel out of the engine and starved the powerful Merlin Engine of its combustion. Payton sprayed the target below him just as the engine on his plane sputtered and coughed to a halt as he tried to pull back on the stick. It did not take long for Payton to realize the danger he faced flying a plane pointed at the ground with no engine to pull him back in to the sky.

As he hurtled toward the ground the altimeter spun like the scoring on a pinball machine as the feet quickly disappeared beneath the plane. The negative G forces also made Payton feel like he was floating in his seat with only the harness keeping him in place. Though the rapidly approaching ground never left his sight, Payton narrowed his eyes to focus on what the plane was telling him both through the instruments and the feel of stick and seat. Panic never crept in to his thoughts because panic would kill him.

After falling more than two miles Payton knew the plane was doomed. He just had to level out the flight path enough so that he could open the cockpit and bail out with his parachute after doing his best to point the plane at an empty field. Payton quickly deployed the flaps on his plane to maximum angle to try and slow his descent and increase the lift he could generate. He also lightened his touch on the stick while he pulled back so the tail might level the plane out long enough to jump without jerking the plane back and forth in any wild maneuvers. At about seven thousand feet Payton's efforts paid off. The plane eased back from a straight nose dive to slightly more gradual descent and he wasted no time popping open the canopy and exiting the plane as fast as he could. He crawled from out of the harness holding him to the plane and pushed off from the side as hard as he could.

Leaping clear of the plane Payton just hoped that his parachute would deploy above him as the plane continued its tragic fall from the sky. As he pulled the ripcord on his chute Payton said the same little prayer as ever person that had ever exited an airplane while still in flight. "Lord, please let this chute open!" he murmured to himself as he approached terminal velocity.

Blissfully, the Lord answered his prayer. The chute billowed out behind him and jerked Payton back as the canopy fully deployed. The white silk looked like gossamer above him as he began floating towards the ground. He watched gratefully as his plane continued on course right at the empty field he aimed at before disappearing in a fireball on the ground. Relaxing only a bit, he looked down to see where he might land. Fortunately, this part of England consisted mostly of farmland, so he only had to worry about the low stone fences separating plots. Barely pulling on the riggings above him put him down dead center in a meadow empty except for one cow lazily feeding on grass in the far corner.

The last pass at the flying target had brought Payton close enough to the airfield that Dylan and the other recruits could see Payton's plane as it began its final strafing run. From the observation deck of the airfield tower Dylan saw immediately that his brother had lost control of the plane and before anyone else noticed a problem he ran down the stairs. Dylan jumped in the closest car, a major's staff car, and revved the engine while he peeled out in the direction of Payton's descending plane.

Hurtling out on to the country lanes outside the airstrip Dylan swerved back to the left side of the road to avoid a motorcycle heading in to the airbase. He looked up in relief as he saw the snow cone shape of his brother's parachute deployed and wafting gently to the ground. He saw the fireball rip in to the sky from the exploding Spitfire and thanked God himself that his brother made it out of the plane first. After another frantic few minutes trying to pinpoint exactly where the parachute deposited his brother Dylan found Payton calmly sitting on a low rock wall with his parachute bundled together in his lap.

"Thanks for coming to pick me up." Payton half smirked at the understatement but with evident relief in his voice.

"Nice landing." Dylan chided his brother in response.

"I've had better landings, that's for sure. Hopefully this doesn't qualify me for jump school. I don't want to be a paratrooper. I'm not sure any sane person should jump out of a perfectly good airplane." Payton joked to ease the edge from his near fatal experience.

"Hopefully the Captain doesn't dismiss you for crashing the plane." Dylan noted the next problem they faced as both twins crawled back in to the car. Dylan even failed to ask if his brother was physically all right. He didn't have to because he knew that he was from his jokes and general demeanor. Had Payton really been hurt, Dylan would have known in an instant from the grimace on Payton's face from trying to hide the pain. Dylan's final relief came when he saw none of these telltale signs from his brother.

Neither spoke on the relatively short ride back to the airfield waiting the questioning sure to greet them upon their return. It went without saying that if Payton was thrown out of the program that Dylan would leave too. Many soldiers formed the bond of brotherhood with their fellow platoon mates. The crucible of battle forged a bond among men only replicated by blood in its strength and loyalty. At WestPoint the instructors had drilled in to the cadets the importance of team work and trusting the guy next to you. The unit had to work as a whole with each part doing its job correctly for the whole to function properly. Dylan and Payton had operated as a unit since the first time they'd discovered as toddlers that if they tugged on the door together they could get out of the house. They were a team, and their unspoken terms were that they would only get through this war together.

As they arrived back at the airfield Dylan pulled straight over to the hangar and they both marched directly in to Captain Benson's office. To their surprise, Captain Benson looked more contrite than anything. He did not immediately begin a tirade about the importance of each and every airplane. Instead, he simply asked the twins to follow him in to the classroom where the other three recruits waited.

"Flight Leftenant Anders, I'm pleased that you seem well after this afternoon's flight." Captain Benson began. "Next, I also want to point to two very important lessons from the incident that we all need to take care to learn. One is operational, and the other more strategic. First, the operational or tactical lesson, and this is a failing on my part for not teaching it to you sooner. The Spitfire has one flaw, and that is the carburetor. Most other airplanes are fuel injected so they needn't worry about it, but the Spitfire will starve itself if you dive straight down at too steep an angle. The petrol literally is forced out of the engine. Jerry has learned this and begun the tactic of diving for the earth to avoid an attack from a our boys in the Spitfire." Captain Benson continued. "Fortunately, the issue is simple to solve. You just have to pour gas back in to the carburetor before you dive with a simple maneuver. To do this, you half roll the plane to the right before diving and you should have no problems.

"Does the roll have to be to the right?" Baker asked.

"Yes, the fuel line to the carburetor is on the left, so you have to pour it in. Otherwise the maneuver doesn't work." The Captain replied.

"And the second lesson?" Dylan asked

"Yes, the second lesson is just as important, and far simpler to explain. Planes are easy to replace, we have citizens all over Great Britain working hard to produce them. However, top notch pilots are much more difficult to replace. Always bail out if there is any question as to your survival. Planes can be replaced, pilots can't. Don't get too attached to your planes and make some kind of heroic attempt to save them at the expense of your life. We can replace planes faster than we can replace pilots. Dismissed for the rest of the day." The Captain finished.

"Thank you, sir!" All five men stood and saluted before hurrying out of the room to digest the hard lesson of the day.

CHAPTER 20

June 21st, 1940

On the Friday of their third week Captain Benson surprised the group. They had completed their training and each pilot received their assigned squadron where they were to report, but not until Monday. Each pilot would have the majority of three days to themselves before joining their combat groups. Dylan and Payton felt fortunate to receive assignments to squadron 610 which was detached from No13 Group RAF to No. 11 Group RAF. The squadron had recently moved to Biggin Hill about fourteen miles south of central London in the borough of Bromley. They could easily spend the weekend with Anne and Clara before reporting for duty.

With a phone call to Timothy the boys had a ride back to London to surprise the ladies along with plenty of flying stories to tell them. It had not dawned on them that maybe girls don't want to hear flying stories. As Timothy pulled up he barely had to slow down before the twins had thrown their bags in the back and clamored in to his car.

"To London, Jeeves." Payton joked.

"Arse, you are. But good to see you as well." Timothy ribbed back.

"Thanks for picking us up. I hope we didn't interrupt anything important." Dylan added.

"Of course you didn't. Simone is out of town at her father's country place, and I'm just looking to stay out of trouble. You got your squadron assignments?" Timothy asked.

"Yes, we'll be at Biggin Hill." Payton answered.

"Excellent, Biggin Hill guards London from the southeast, directly in line with Jerry in France. You'll be my personal defenders. Clara and Anne will also have the pleasure of knowing you are in the skies above us." Timothy nearly beamed at the thought. "It can't hurt to have friends in the sky."

"Glad to oblige." Dylan offered, also pleased that he'd have a direct hand in defending Clara and knowing Payton would probably think the same about Anne. "Where are we headed?"

"The ladies have to work at the hospital until about 8pm tonight, but then we can meet them there for a late supper." Timothy answered. "We'll have a few hours in London to knock around before we meet them. You boys look like you're ready for the town. I'll swing by my place and switch out to something more suitable and we'll find a place to get a drink. In fact, we'll make it tradition. Whenever you are on leave in London I'll have the pleasure of buying your first beers upon your successful defense of my sorry arse."

"We'll take the beers, but you are in charge of defending your own rear." Payton laughed back at his friend. Just like with the girls, more than two weeks had passed since the twins laid eyes on Timothy, so falling in to the same camaraderie felt good.

The three passed the rest of the car trip chatting aimlessly about Timothy's wanderings through the great city. The twins told him a little about flying, but the intense training seemed like drudgery to Timothy so they mostly avoided the subject. The country side slide by like a green quilt with low hedgerows serving as stitch marks across the patchwork. The straight lines reminded the twins very little of the rugged and jagged lines of their home in Oregon. The soaring pine trees of the Willamette Valley presented a different texture of green background and even though they'd also grown up on a farm, these smaller patches of land still seemed a little foreign. The pastoral setting stood in stark contrast to their memories of the deep forest and even more contrasting to the imposing skyscrapers of London forming their own steel forest. The twins knew that they'd defend these farms, this quilt, the steel forest, just as if it were their own farm amidst their own forest. Nothing else could even come close to accomplishing the mission they set out for themselves in New York knowing that they had to do something for the world state of affairs.

Once they arrived at the small studio flat Timothy had rented for the remainder of the summer near the hospital Payton took the chance to write home to his father since he hadn't written since before sailing for Dunkirk.

Dear Dad,

I hope you and mom are getting along okay. Last I wrote we were headed to Dublin. You may have read about the evacuation of Dunkirk, so I thought you'd like to know that Dylan and I helped by sailing between Dover and Dunkirk several times on a couple of borrowed boats. We saved nearly a company of men with each trip that we took. We finished after one of our boats took a shell while empty. That seemed like a good sign to pack it in.

After we returned to London we managed to secure a commission to the Royal Air Force. For the last three weeks we've learned the basics of aeronautical warfare, and after this weekend we'll be posted to a squadron at Biggin Hill, southeast of London. We'll help defend the seat of the empire.

On a slightly different note, Dylan and I have both met our own wonderful girls. I met Anne while we were in Canada and she followed us here to London to volunteer with the Red Cross. She must be as crazy as me. I'm sure you will like her. Dylan met Clara in Dublin and is head over heels. She's a spitfire and I'm sure you'll like her too.

We'll do our best to write more often. Give our love to Mom.

Love,
Payton

***

The boys arrived at the hospital early enough to walk around some before finding the girls. They passed wards full of injured men convalescing after battle. The grim looks of survival mixed with glassy eyed shell shock as well as those relieved to simply hold on to their lives. These men survived the horrors with the scars to prove it, but the worst scars did not clearly show on skin but on psyche. The twins recognized one of the men they'd brought back from Dunkirk and stopped to chat. He sustained a glancing ricocheted piece of shrapnel through the thigh, but otherwise counted himself lucky and well on his way to being healed. The man didn't say much otherwise, but he did relay his gratitude and included that he'd be back in the battle soon not because he wanted to, but because he needed to protect his family in London. In England not only were they fighting the tyrant of Berlin, fighting for freedom and fighting for their way of life, but they also fought to defend their families. They didn't have the choice that so conflicted Roosevelt and the rest of America. Payton and Dylan came because they knew it was right and they wouldn't wait for political indecision. Even though came to keep war as far away as possible from their mother and father half a world away, they now were fighting for Anne and Clara, too.

Finally, the girls emerged from their training rounds in their long skirts and aprons.

"Hello, my love." Anne beamed at Payton when she walked up and wrapped her arms around his neck for a kiss.

263

"Hello, Anne, I'm pleased to see you." Payton said, unable to really think of anything else to say while both acted rather shy in their moment of tender reunion.

Clara, meanwhile, dispensed with the greeting and went directly for a passionate embrace and kiss of Dylan.

"It's nice to see you, too." Dylan deadpanned with a sly grin in between kisses.

"No hug for your brother?" Timothy complained mildly.

"Hello Tim. I see you often enough." Clara chided her brother.

"Tell me about your nursing courses." Payton asked of Anne.

"These poor men, with their horrid wounds, please don't ever end up here." Anne responded. "That's not much of an answer." She sheepishly conceded without prompting.

"Well, it's true." Clara jumped in. "But the training has been adequate, considering the circumstances. We've learned to staunch any bleeding and recognize shock. Other than that we mostly just comfort the men and follow the directions of the doctors."

"I'd imagine no one can comfort more easily than the two of you." Payton attempted a compliment. "You can practice tonight on us!" he finished with a joke.

"I'd ask about your flying, but honestly at this point I'm too tired to care. Please forgive me." Anne said, and for the first time the four reunited paramours took a moment past the rush of the greeting to see the same looks on the opposites face and body language. They were all tired from the intense training, drained physically but buoyed by the emotional energy of contributing to the cause as well as the joy of the unexpected sight of their new loved ones.

"I hadn't much felt it until now, but I haven't felt this tired since our first year at the Academy." Dylan admitted. The small group lingered in the hallway where they'd met for a moment longer before mustering the energy to move on. Without much in the way of plans, they ate a simple dinner at a local pub and meandered through conversation. Shortly after the stately grandfather clock in the corner struck ten, the quintet heard low rumbling in the distance.

"I didn't think we'd have thunder tonight." Anne thought out loud. "I know it's warm, but the forecast called for clear skies the rest of the weekend."

"Thunder here is rare." Clara added.

"That's not thunder." Payton stated quietly.

"They're bombs." Dylan added somberly.

"Bombs? From training?" Anne asked.

"No, from Germans." Payton said knowing that the bombing meant that they finished their training just in time. "The low sound means they are a long way off, so we should be safe here for the moment. My guess is that the air fields are taking a pounding in these night raids. The Germans have stuck to strategic bombing during the blitz krieg, so they might want to knock out the air defenses."

"Must you leave then?" Clara asked tentatively.

"Not yet. We don't have any place to call. Captain Benson just gave us orders to simply show up at Biggin Hill Monday morning. We'll finish dinner and make some calls after we drop you back off at the hospital." Dylan answered.

"Don't go without saying goodbye, then." Anne more ordered than requested.

"Of course we won't." Payton responded quickly and patiently. "Duty calls, but we don't want to leave you either."

The rest of the dinner passed with the intermittent rumbling moving further afield and very little conversation as they tried to soak up every moment together. All involved hoped that this wasn't the last time they'd see each other before taking on the next rigors of war.

Shortly after walking the ladies back and lingering on the doorstep of the hospital dormitory, the twins rode quietly back to Timothy's flat. Dylan took the reins and called back to Middle Wallop. The duty officer seemed somewhat distracted, most likely by the reports of bombing, and simply gave the number for the duty officer at Biggin Hill before hanging up. Payton took his turn and called Biggin Hill. With a quick introduction and question to the duty officer all Timothy and Dylan heard was Payton replying "Yes, sir." several times.

"Verdict?" Timothy asked after Payton hung up.

"We go tonight." Payton answered in the clipped military tone he usually used only to answer a superior officer.

"Had they been hit?" Dylan asked more pointedly.

"They were targeted, but no direct hits. The officer just asked us to be there by midnight so we could get all our documentation and settling done before heading to the squadron first thing in the morning. We'll have to leave in about an hour to get there in time." Payton reported.

"At least you didn't unpack. I'll run you out to see the girls and then on to Biggin Hill. That should give you the most time to say goodbye." Timothy offered.

"Thank you, that's kind of you." Dylan genuinely thanked his friend for helping even in the small thing of avoiding a cab ride in the middle of the night.

Back at the hospital, the boys realized they had no idea which room in the dormitory belonged to Cara and Anne. The doors were locked and they couldn't simply find a window to tap on in the age old tradition of a boy showing up in the middle of the night. They found the night nurse, a matronly lady advancing in years, who listened to their story sympathetically and knew precisely where to find Anne and Clara.

"I feared you'd be back tonight." Anne said with a sigh as she walked out of the dormitories with Clara.

"Parting is such sweet sorrow." Payton offered in return.

"Don't you quote Shakespeare at me." Clara quipped back, clearly perturbed that their weekend was about to be cut short. "His heroes usually die."

"Well, hopefully this isn't a tragedy then." Dylan tried to add cheerfully to Clara's dark proclamation. "The man did write some comedies if I recall."

"This is not exactly a midsummer's night dream, nor is it St Crispin's day." Anne finished the Shakespeare talk. "You must go tonight?" she asked.

"Yes, we're to report at midnight." Payton answered.

"I wish I could tell you not to go, but duty calls for us all." Clara relented. "Let's walk for a minute and then off with you."

Dylan and Clara walked north along the street while Payton and Anne turned south. "I guess I'll just stay here then." Timothy muttered to himself as he found a bench to wait on.

"I'm sad to see you go again." Anne admitted as she and Payton found a blacked-out lamppost to stand under. "This time I don't know when I'll see you again."

"I don't know how often we'll get leave. I'd guess it depends on how often we have to fly." Payton thought out loud.

"You mean how often the Germans attack." Anne clarified with just a hint of trepidation in her voice.

"Yes, I suppose that's true. Whenever they come whoever is on duty must scramble to meet them. You'll be working too, and doing something important. Hopefully that will help pass the time." Payton said.

"Come visit whenever you can, even if it is just an afternoon. Promise me that. Letter's won't do when you are so close." Anne asked earnestly.

"I have nowhere else to go. I promise to be here whenever I can, but it is most important for me to cover the air above you."

"Thank you, but don't be a hero. I'd rather take my chances in the bomb shelter and have you back."

"If I can, I'll fly over the hospital whenever possible and waggle my wings. I'll have Dylan do the same for Clara, so whenever you see the two of us waggling our wings you'll know we're on our way back to Biggin Hill and okay. I can't promise that we'll always fly by this way, or that we'll have enough fuel, so don't worry if you don't see us, okay?" Payton said to try and ease the fears building in Anne.

"Yes, of course, it will be reassuring but I won't worry." Anne lied for both of their sake. "Now, just hold me here for a moment before you go."

"I can offer you one better." Payton said as he leaned in for a kiss followed by the requested embrace. They lingered there for several minutes, with his arms wrapped around her waist and hers around his neck.

Dylan and Clara said even less as they sat together on a bus stop bench several blocks in the other direction down the same street. They simply sat together quietly as close as they could. Clara, almost never at a loss for words, didn't want to express the anxiety she felt at the wrenching departure hanging over them. She felt a black, deep pit in her stomach knowing that Dylan left her to fight this time. She hadn't felt the same on each of the voyages across to Dunkirk because she knew he wasn't a combatant, a target. This time, however, she knew any German that even saw him would shoot without hesitation. She'd worried about her brother and father on their clandestine runs before, but knew that they'd mostly have the occasional nasty business partner or pesky law enforcement officer. Thinking even for a moment that Dylan might not return turned her cold in side like no feeling she could have ever fathomed.

"Come back." Clara managed to say without breaking down.

"I will." Dylan answered with the only words he could manage as well.

And with that, they walked back to the hospital arm in arm as slowly as they could manage. Payton and Anne arrived at the same time in the same quiet state. After insuring that the ladies safely entered the doors of the hospital, and each lingering for one last kiss, Timothy pulled the car around for the longest ride across town any of them ever imagined. The twins left the army, snuck in to Canada, sailed across the Atlantic with a king, met two women that they loved deeply, helped evacuate an army in retreat, but now they finally stood on the precipice of the challenge they came for. They came to fight the Nazis, and now they would have their chance in the skies over London.

CHAPTER 21

June 22nd, 1940

The twins arrived at Biggin Hill at the appointed time, and although they hadn't expected much activity, the airfield was eerily quiet. Timothy bid them good bye in the way most men do, with a slap on the back and a joke, before driving back towards London. Figuring it was their best bet, the twins walked toward the large main building beneath the tower. They walked past a low building labeled WAAF headquarters and another unmarked building with blacked out windows indicating some sort of covert operations inside. They also passed the Officers Club, which they surely to noted for when they sought food other than the mess hall. All of the buildings appeared to date within the last decade or so, including the long standard barracks and the large hangars at the far end of the airstrip. The twins even took the extra time to note the particulars of the air strip, such as where the small lights of the buildings stood in relation to the airstrip and where the windsock flapped to tell them the direction of the wind.

When they walked in the front door of the command building a WAAF officer greeted them and managed to stay pleasant despite the late hour intrusion. She led the boys to the watch officer.

"Flight Leftenants Anders reporting for duty, sir." The twins said in unison as they saluted the watch officer. The man looked like he might still be young, but the fatigue around his eyes and the rumpled uniform belied his actual age. He half saluted the twins back without rising from his chair.

"Welcome, you will need that kind of energy to keep up here." The watch officer said flatly. "Thank you for coming in promptly. You'll be assigned to fighter squadron 8, in the north barracks, number 42. I've had the supply officer send up flight suits for you based on the sizes you gave me over the phone. They are in the packages at the desk on your way out. Find a bunk in the barracks and rest of the remainder of the night. Your squadron leader, Major Phillips, will give you the run through in the morning." The officer finished and indicated for the twins to move along. He probably relished a quiet night before the anticipated storm in the morning. Dylan and Payton begrudged him nothing and quickly followed orders.

The next morning the twins woke early, with the sun low in the sky, and dressed quietly expecting the rest of the unit to start buzzing about soon. Of course, they found none of the other pilots rose from their beds before the sun climbed several more rungs higher up its endless arc of a ladder. By the time the twins had identified Major Phillips and the man had risen, they'd already had breakfast and played catch to pass the time. Major Phillips, a bear of a man, came out of the barracks in just an undershirt, pants and suspenders to assess his new pilots.

"When did you two arrive?" he inquired in a thick Scottish accent. "I wasn't expecting any new pilots until Monday."

"Last night, sir." Dylan answered. "We heard the bombing in London and called in."

"We got a few of those Jerries, all right." The Major grinned quickly and then frowned as he said "but a few of them snuck through. I hope they didn't hit anyone."

"We heard on the radio that the bombs fell mostly in to the Thames, harmlessly." Payton said. "I suppose they were looking for the blackest area to bomb thinking it was a blacked out factory."

"Of course, that must be it." Major Phillips really did chuckle this time. "We've been down several men since flying cover in Dunkirk, so we're glad to have you, even if you are Yanks."

"I'm sure the evacuating men appreciated the cover." Payton said while intentionally leaving out their role in the rescue. Both twins knew from WestPoint and from their father that junior officers should always stay modest and humble. They wanted to the Major to know that flying and helping the war effort topped their priorities, not making heroes of themselves.

Only those that come to war to serve become heroes. Those that come to be heroes died relatively quickly.

"Now then, we've got two relatively new Spitfires waiting for you. Let's show you off to your planes." Major Phillips said as he turned nonchalantly towards the hangars and sauntered away from the barracks with a yawn. "We are on call whenever we are on base, so when you hear the claxons you scramble to the planes without hesitation. Whoever gets to the planes first takes off first so we aren't waiting around on the ground. Once four planes are together, you head to the target. Chain Home command will order your intercept coordinates and away you go hunting. It's all very informal."

"How often do you scramble?" Dylan asked.

"We try to get some rest in between sorties, but we fly whenever we have to. If they keep coming, then we'll just re-fuel and fly again. To date, I've only had one instance of going up twice in a day. It's quite draining. Seconds count, though, so you must never hesitate." Major Phillips answered.

"Yes, sir. Who maintains the planes?" Payton asked.

"Excellent question, the maintenance crew is headed by Sargent Blinn. They think of these as their planes, and despise when they get shot up." The Major chuckled again.

"I'll be fairly upset if I get shot up too." Dylan noted dryly.

"Yes, of course." The Major returned the dry note.

"Forgive the directness, but what's the best way to make friends with Sargent Blinn?" Dylan followed up his brother's question. When someone else took charge of maintaining the planes their lives would depend on, the twins wanted to make sure it was someone they could trust, someone that knew them and would take extra care on their planes. And, they knew a friend might be able to get their planes fixed faster if they needed it.

"I'm told he likes whiskey." The Major grinned back, most likely because he'd used the same trick.

"We know just the man to help with that." Dylan said as he made a mental note to call Timothy later in the day for a case of Bushmills, the fine Irish whiskey.

"Here we are, your aircraft. All the eighth squadron planes start with an eight. One of you will be 842 and the other will be 810. Unfortunately, from our standpoint, you are a bit interchangeable at the moment. I can't imagine anyone other than your mother being able to tell you apart, so choose whichever plane suits you. These Spitfires just arrived, so your luck runs you into brand new aircraft of the highest quality." Major Phillips finished.

"These are splendid, sir, thank you." Dylan said with true admiration for the war machine in front of him.

"Don't thank me, thank the factory workers." Major Phillips said. "I've a report to write this morning, and then I will meet you two for lunch to talk about dogfighting. My understanding is that you received very little instruction on anything other than the basics of flying and gunnery, correct?"

"Yes, sir, that is correct." Payton affirmed.

275

"We'll talk it over this afternoon and see if we can keep you alive until the end of the week, then." Major Phillips said lightly, never changing the mood of his voice despite his dark prognostication.

Left again with no direction until the afternoon Payton and Dylan took the chance to go over every detail of their new planes. They walked around the elliptical wings scanning for any cracks or inconsistencies in the metal. They pulled and tugged on the flaps and ailerons to insure that they moved freely. They pushed the tail rudder back and forth. They looked for ways to improve the planes, even if just a little. They sanded small metal burrs off the leading edge of the wings, and they greased the hinges of all the control surfaces just to get the extra swift movement that might lead to an advantage in the air. Payton even hit on a simple idea to add a touch of sharpness to their reflexes. They found a can of hydraulic fluid sitting near their planes and filled the reservoirs to their tops. By increasing the amount of hydraulic fluid they ran the risk of bursting the lines, but with a light touch they could move the control surfaces with smaller, more precise movements. In essence, they could save the split second required to move the stick or pedals a half inch further. The planes would respond more quickly, so the twins would have to be careful not to overcorrect or push too hard, otherwise they would lose control and fall from the skies.

After walking through the outside of the plane, the twins crawled in to their cockpits. The planes sat side by side in the hanger with only the wingspan separating them. They left the wind shields open and talked back and forth to reaffirm the details of their training in their minds. They double checked the sighting on their guns, though all they could do was line up the crosshairs and hope that the machine guns did the same. They wouldn't learn how accurately the factory workers had done their work until a German Messerschmitt sat in their bullseye. After a while they both just sat, quietly, in their planes and contemplated what it would mean to fly them. What it would mean to see a Luftwaffe insignia on another plane with cannons and machine guns pointed not just at each plane, but also at the plane carrying their brother.

"Dylan" Payton said.

"Yeah" Dylan answered.

"If I go down you keep fighting." Payton said, stating simply the hard truth about their situation.

"Same for you." Dylan said quietly back.

***

The twins found Major Phillips sitting at the bar of the officers club waiting for a shepherd's pie when they came around to discuss dogfighting. He sat by himself at the bar, but where one would expect to find a beer he simply had a tall glass of water.

"Sir." Dylan and Payton said in unison as they came to attention despite the awkward idea of saluting another man at a bar.

"We have a rule around here, no saluting in the O-club." Major Phillips said. "This is the one place we come to relax. Best just to show respect and go about your business in here."

"Yes, sir." The twins said in unison again.

"Curious habit, that." Captain Phillips noted. "Do you do everything together?"

"No, sir. It just happens sometimes when we have the same answer." Payton answered.

"Yes, of course. Now, to dogfighting. The easiest way to defeat another fighter is for him to never know you are there. Ideally you attack from above because you can use the altitude to gain enough speed to fall on your prey and maintain the speed to get away from anyone of his wing-mates lurking nearby. Altitude equals speed and speed means you stay alive." Major Phillips continued his abbreviated tutorial. "Failing the height advantage, your next best option is to sneak in from below. You'll really have to push your airplane to gain altitude and still keep up with your prey, but the idea is to stay hidden below and behind him until the other fellow can't do anything about it."

"What do you do if you get spotted before you can take the shot?" Dylan asked.

"He'll have to turn in to you to shoot, so do your best to stay behind. Turn with him. His best move is a loop to come down on you, so you might be able to loop too. If all else fails, dive for the waves and turn tail towards home, live to fight another day." Major Phillips responded.

"Thank you for the advice, Major." Payton said as the major rose to indicate the lesson was done.

"We'll try to keep you alive. We need all the pilots we can get. That is why a newly minted Major such as myself is still flying, instead of commanding a whole group." The Major noted dryly. "One other thing, don't drink beer unless it's a day you know you won't fly, and those days only come when you are on leave. Drink water, beer will slow you down. Don't drink too much of anything, though. You can fly patrols for hours and urinating in your flight suit is frowned upon. At the very least take an empty canteen to use if necessary. It will probably freeze by the time you land, but at least it will allow you to relieve yourself if you keep it against yourself during the patrol." The Major then stood and clearly displayed what had brought his last point to mind by heading directly to the restroom. "Your first patrol is tomorrow morning. In your planes by 0700 please." He finished over his shoulder as he wandered away.

***

The next morning dawned beautifully like every summer day seems to as a child. The air warmed as soon as the sun peaked above the horizon. By 0700 it glinted off the windshields of the spitfire cockpit canopies as it marched higher in the sky at the accelerated summer pace. No sirens cut the night before to send the men scrambling, so the whole squadron turned out relatively well rested for the morning patrol. The twins walked around their planes running through the pre-flight checklist as they always did. As the rest of the squadron turned out Major Phillips motioned for everyone to come together before takeoff for a quick briefing.

"Gentlemen, and I use the term loosely" he started with a joke, "First, let's welcome our fresh recruits. Flight Leftenants Anders. I'll let them tell you which is Payton and which is Dylan, and I'll ensure that their fight suits are thusly labeled."

"Dylan." He said raising his hand slightly.

"Payton." He followed his brother.

"Thank you gentlemen. For the benefit of our new pilots, this is Blue Section of the squadron, we six. There are another six aircraft making up red section. We'll take the first flight this morning and they'll take the afternoon patrol. Now, we've been assigned sector 36, over the channel just outside of London. I'm sure most of you know the way. The new recruits will fly in formation with me." Major Phillips finished the very short briefing. "Off to your planes."

The twins hurried to their planes to get the propellers spinning before the major could get out too far ahead of them. All six planes took off without incident and formed up to head southeast to the channel. The twins flew in tight formation with the Major and elicited a mild "Well done" over the radio before they flew out over the water. The sun glinted off the shimmering surface below them reminding the whole of the fine midsummer's day that lay before them. Blue section took station several miles above the English Channel and began making lazy circles in the sky waiting to either catch a stray German squadron or to receive directions from the Chain Home command radar center. However, on this day, Blue section merely flew in circles for four hours. On the return to Biggin Hill Major Phillips decided to put the twins through their paces in a mock dogfight.

"Gentlemen, your job now is to kill me. You two against me with no real rules attached. In a true dogfight there is only one rule, kill or be killed. We start now." Major Phillips said and executed a steep turning climb to try and get behind the twins. Dylan immediately pulled back on his controls and followed the Major as if he'd fought dozens of dogfights. Payton followed his brother in text book wingman position without requiring any direction.

Both Americans felt confident that they'd have the Major quickly enough with their two to one advantage. The Major held a few tricks up his sleeve, though. First he leveled off his climb and feinted left by dipping a wing without using the rudder before climbing again. The maneuver nearly shook the twins, as it had many Germans, but they were able to recover quickly enough to maintain the chase.

Next, the Major pulled hard to starboard to try and get around the twins in the horizontal space, but again he was unsuccessful when the twins were able to keep up with his tight turn. With the horizontal maneuver out the Major went vertical again and performed a half loop with a roll at the top to completely change directions, almost like a u-turn in a car. The twins nearly lost him again, but were able to climb just a little bit higher than the Major before they rolled to stay on his tail.

Finding no room to shake the twins, but never giving them a clean shot either, the Major decided that only an unexpected move might shake the precise flying of the Americans. So, the major dove hard in a downward spiral for the ground. The twins followed hoping to get the kill before the Major could level out. However, to their great surprise, the Major pulled out of his dive after only 10,000 feet and pulled hard back on his controls. The G-forces on him must have cause him to nearly black out, the twins though afterward, but Major Phillips was able to use his downward momentum and fight his way through a tight loop and gain the advantageous tail position on the twins.

"With that, my young friends, let's call it a day. Head back to base please." The Major ordered. "I may not have gotten a clean shot on you immediately, but we are running low on petrol." He explained.

"Yes, sir." Both twins replied over the radio hiding the disappointment in their voices at having been dispatched with the advantage on their first patrol.

***

"That was disheartening." Dylan said as he and Payton walked back to the barracks from the airstrip.

"We've got to figure out the dogfighting pretty darn quick, or we'll end up in the Channel, at best." Payton answered. "The Major beat us because he didn't follow the book. He beat us because we were thinking too much."

"Flying is the easy part. How do we get in the other guy's head?" Dylan thought out loud. "It's like playing chess with Dad. We have to think out past the next step."

"And we need to do it as a team. Mom always said stick together." Payton said. "I think we'll have to start playing cat and mouse. One of us is going to have to be the bait."

"That just might work. We'll try it next time we're up."

Chapter 21

June 30th, 1940

For the past week Blue Section had flown several sorties, alternating between morning and afternoon, with nary a German in sight. The Luftwaffe had concentrated their efforts on other sectors leaving London relatively quiet. In fact, the Luftwaffe had focused heavily on shipping ports, relentlessly bombing Porstmouth and other vital harbors trying to blockade supplies and strangle the island nation in to submission.

With little fight in their sector, the twins had even taken a twelve-hour pass and snuck down to London to visit the girls. They caught Clara and Anne as they walked back to the dormitory after finishing their shift.

"Fancy meeting you here." Payton called out before the girls saw them.

"Well aren't you a sight for sore eyes." Anne teased playfully as he reached out to pull her close.

"You're not so bad yourself." He answered as Dylan and Clara dispensed with the pleasantries all together and went straight for a long kiss. A little warm halo enveloped the four young people and pushed out any thoughts of the people around them, let alone the war surrounding the globe. However, the moment and halo broke quickly as the air raid claxons blared out their unwanted song again.

"This way!" Clara insisted as she grabbed Dylan's hand. He hadn't even said a word yet and she was ushering him towards their room. Payton and Anne followed quickly as they entered the door as the all too familiar sound of faint thunder indicated that bombs were falling on another part of the city. "Please tell me you don't have to go." Clara said as the four tumbled in to the small room assigned to the girls. "I could barely stand to see you go early last time. If you are only here for a few minutes I might lose my senses."

"No, we have a true pass for the next 10 hours. They don't need us and we won't rush to get back." Dylan finally got a word in.

"I think the squadron might be upset if we got ourselves killed on the ground, too." Payton added. "So, we'll happy hunker down in here with you, and if the bombing gets closer we'll find the nearest shelter. One thing we have learned, though, is always have food." Payton said as he reached in to his knapsack and pulled out four sandwiches from the deli down the street and a bottle of sparkling cider. "No Champaign, but this will have to do." He smiled as he poured the drinks in to four paper cups.

"A feast." Anne smiled warmly. "We don't even make it down the street that often. We usually end up with the cafeteria food. They've started rationing, so some days even the cafeteria is a bit bland."

"I'll never look at potato soup the same again. And I'm Irish!" declared Clara. "It could be worse. We've been treating men nonstop since we saw you last. I guess the motto around here is learn by doing. The older nurses teach as we go. The doctors are always rushing to the next patient." Clara finished as the whole group fell silent. The happiness at the simple reunion came tinged with melancholy punctuated with each rumbled of a bomb finding its mark.

"Have you seen your brother?" Dylan finally asked Clara to break the low moment.

"Yes, he and Simone dropped by yesterday. He was rather cryptic though, saying that he wouldn't see us for a month or so, but that Simone would come round to check on us while he was gone. Honestly, I've never really known what he's up to our whole lives." She finished with a chuckle. "I hope he hurries back and is alright, though." She added.

"Timothy can take care of himself, of that I'm sure." Payton stated simply. "Have you any word from your brother, Anne?" he finished.

"No, not a peep. I'm so worried about him, and that goes doubly for you." She smiled, half sadly, half ruefully at the thought.

"It sounds like the raid is coming to an end. The blasts are receding and further apart." Dylan noted.

"We'll start seeing overflow patients if they can't handle them in whatever hospital is closest to the bombing." Anne said quietly in an almost resigned voice. However, she added with more vigor "We best go check in the with the head nurse to see if they need us. You boys can stay here while we are out." She finished with a smile at the thought of coming back to them soon. And with that, the girls who had left their last shift only a short time before found the resolve to head back to the hospital floors where they could help.

Dylan and Payton sadly watched the girls leave, but then sacked out quickly in their beds and fell asleep with the sweet, delicate smell of their loved one taking them off in to a much needed rest. Although they eagerly served, the first week flying mostly routine patrols showed the twins what lay ahead in the form of utter boredom occasionally punctuated by heart pounding bursts of adrenaline whenever they spotted an enemy flight. They hammered the mix of tension and fear down so they could function as credible pilots. Neither spoke much of the mettle required for such a task, but they knew they at least had each other, which helped more than any of the other new pilots could know. Escaping the tension for just a few hours could only recharge them in their resolve to fight.

The clock passed midnight before Anne and Clara returned. In a minor scandal, at least if the head nurse found out, they simply slide in to bed beside the warm bodies they adored and thanked the Lord that they could rest, together again for at least a few more hours. However, the sun lifted itself above the horizon early, as it was wont to do in the summer, and bade Dylan and Payton back to their squadron. They both quietly readied themselves to leave so as not to wake the ladies. Each leaned in for a whispered goodbye and a quick peck promising to return as soon as they could manage. Anne and Clara both managed the universal half asleep smile and goodbye before falling back in to their dreams.

With that, Dylan and Payton snuck out of the hospital dorms and found their way back to their squadron.

***

Timothy had very little trouble procuring a case of bushmills for Sargent Blinn the first time a week prior, and he was only too happy to oblige is American friends for their defense of The Realm. Now, however, Timothy wanted to show off a bit for both Sargent Blinn and the twins. Timothy walked in to a shoemakers shop just off of Picadilly Circus on the way to Leicester Square. As it happened, the shop owner had a cousin in America willing to ship him cases of the American whiskey made by Jack Daniels. Timothy had no idea whether the stuff was any good, but he thought he'd at least let Sargent Blinn give it a taste so as to link the yankee whisky with the yankee pilots whenever they needed help. He might even save a bottle for himself and Simone, Timothy thought.

Timothy adored Simone, but he'd never let it show. He figured as soon as she knew then she'd want to move on to something different. For her class, the hunt held more appeal than the kill. As luck would have it, Simone wanted to meet for dinner that night before he left. Rationing cut deeply in to the usual lifestyle Simone generally led, but when she rang him earlier her convivial request clearly communicated something special afoot. After a show of trying to rearrange his schedule to accommodate her, Timothy gladly accepted. Now he just needed an acceptable offering to thank her.

"Hello Tim!" the shopkeeper greeted him warmly.

"Mr. Cain, a pleasure as always. I'm always pleased to see you. Let me say again how much I appreciate your help in this matter. Nothing is too good for our boys protecting the city!" Timothy responded.

"Only the Lord knows what the city would look like without them. It's bad enough as it is. Anymore and I'm afraid the blitz would break the city forever." Mr. Cain sighed heavily.

"I don't think Old London will break that easily." Timothy offered sympathetically.

"But, you are correct; we can take all the help we can get. Speaking of help, I might ask for a small bit of further help from you. I'm to escort a find young lady to dinner tonight. I'm not sure where, but I was hoping to be a proper gentleman for once and not show up empty handed. Have you anything that might fit the bill?"

"You have splendid timing, my young friend. I happen to have the scarcest thing to a fine young lady. Silk stockings are as rare as gold these days. The military requisitioned all they silk to make parachutes." The shopkeeper grinned somewhat sheepishly talking so candidly about a garment so particular to the ladies.

"Brilliant!" Timothy exclaimed, but on consideration asked "You don't think it too forward to offer to a young lady? Her class far outranks mine."

"Times change, Tim, her smile at the gift will outweigh any impropriety. Take them my boy, and I hope they bring her great joy. You will certainly have paid for them after we confirm our other delivery." However, Timothy wasn't bringing anything to Mr. Cain's shop. He was delivering for him, in France.

***

"How on earth did you get these?" Simone asked. Stunned at the coveted gift, she wore the silk stockings that evening. "I'd dreaded pulling on my old pair one more time, but our destination simply calls for a finer dress than one can get away with bare-legged. Your suit looks smashing, and will fit in perfectly. I've reservations for us at the Savoy."

"Excellent choice, my dear. I so enjoyed our last time there with our friends." Timothy offered back a bit sheepishly. "I hope you did as well."

"I enjoyed my time there with you, very specifically, that is why I chose it." Simone said with just a hint of a smile on her reserved, aristocratic face. "Let's walk, though, such a beautiful evening shouldn't be wasted before you leave." With both hearts buoyed by the thought of such a fine evening ahead, Simone took Timothy's arm as they emerged in to the warm summer's eve.

CHAPTER 22

July 3rd, 1940

Payton and Dylan pointed the nose of their aircraft up and climbed in to a sky wild with late afternoon sunshine. With the memory of the night in London providing mixed feelings from seeing the girls but also hearing the bombing, the twins felt even more urgency to propel themselves into the fight. With Anne and Clara below each sortie took on personal meaning. Still, no German managed to wander through their crosshairs the two days previously. Today would be different.

Not twenty minutes in to their leisurely racetrack loops around their station in the sky Chain Home Station radioed a heading directing them over the city and out to sea to intercept a flight of German bombers headed directly at London. The twins curved out of their pattern behind their flight lead and followed a half dozen other planes in formation slightly south of east. Several of the other pilots chattered on the radio in anticipation until Major

Phillips ordered radio silence until spotting the enemy. The other pilots were veterans, but the surge of adrenaline from an imminent fight caused some men to verbalize everything. Payton and Dylan were in fact the opposite. They tempered their adrenaline with silence and continually scanned the skies above, below, and ahead for enemy aircraft while occasionally stealing a glance at each other. Each knew exactly where the other flew at all times, but it never hurt to check.

Finally, Dylan broke the silence and called out "Bogies at 11 o'clock, slightly low."

Major Phillips replied "Thank you gentlemen, guns free, Tally Ho!" And with that, Dylan and Payton took up arms against the Nazis.

Payton followed Dylan as he altered courses slightly to his left to match the incoming Luftwaffe flight. At such a distance, they looked like small dark specks moving in unison high above the glistening waters below, something like bugs on a lake. The RAF squadron garnered two further pieces of luck in that the radars at Chain Home Command had directed them on target, and also in that the pristine weather allowed them to see the combatants while the sun obscured their position from behind. The luck held only until the Spitfires closed to within a mile of the attacking squadron before the Messerschmitts detected the threat and rose to protect the lumbering bombers. Payton estimated eight Messerschmitt BF-109s and two dozen or more heavy Heinkel bombers.

As the northern most element of the squadron, Dylan and Payton settled in to attack the left most enemy flights. "Just like reading a book, we'll attack left to right." Dylan directed over the radio.

"Yeah, but let's flip lead attacker every other. The wingman can get a quicker jump on the next plane that way." Payton concluded. The twins had come up with a serviceable strategy in the moment, and now looked to play out the action in their first real fight.

Enemy canon fire began exploding between their two planes, reminding the pair of the fire superiority they heard rumors about. The Messerschmitt BF-109 could not match the Spitfire for pure speed, but still carried its own advantages, such as a smaller turning radius, and of particular interest to the twins at the moment a heavier armament in the form of a single ballistic cannon fired through the nose cone. Dylan and Payton immediately took evasive action and banked hard right, then ducked back to the left to maintain an attacking course. Dylan let loose with a short machine gun burst to remind the enemy that he intended to fight, though the head-on closing attitude and speed left little hope of a direct hit.

As the three planes (of the many in the sky) converged at a closing speed roughly equal to the speed of sound the twins split horizontally to try and loop behind the fighter while the German went in to a vertical loop to try and gain the advantage. From the ground, it looked as if the three planes traced out a three-leaf clover. Unfortunately for the German, his vertical loop took longer than the horizontal loop the twins traced and Dylan timed his shot perfectly as he rounded in to place behind the enemy aircraft. The tracers found their mark in the tail and wing and Bf 109 burst into a mighty fireball.

Anticipating his brother's success, Payton immediately banked back to the right and found two more Luftwaffe planes immediately in his sights enroute too late to help their fallen brethren. Through luck and no skill, he found himself in perfect firing position. Through skill and no luck, he brought down the first, then second attackers with short machine gun bursts.

"Leftenants, we have engaged the remainder of the fighters, please turn your attention to the bombers before they cross the coast." Major Phillips clipped out as an order over the radio. With a simple click of the radio in the affirmative Dylan and Payton reformed up quickly and turned for the flight of two dozen bombers below. If they could bring down some of these giants, then perhaps the rest of the squadron and the anti-aircraft fire over the city could finish off the rest before any bombs could lay waste to lives and structures below.

"Best to take two at a time each, if we can." Payton radioed his brother. "They'll be in upper and lower tiers, so you take the left and I'll take the right, upper to lower. Be careful of the tail gunners." He finished.

"Roger!" was the only response he received. Both aircraft roared like mechanical lions as they dove towards the bombers while herking and jerking to avoid the maelstrom of machine gun fire aimed at their death. Dylan lined up the farthest left bomber and fired a sustained stream, then re-aimed and fired at the next bomber down until his machine guns clicked loudly from a lack of ammunition. He'd fired every bullet he had. Both German planes sagged, and then seemed to peel off to the left before settling in to fiery death spirals towards the sea. Dylan didn't wait to see if any men were able to escape as he continued his dive and raced to the wave tops to avoid any further fighting while out of bullets.

Dylan didn't have to wait at all until he sensed more than saw his brother on his wing. Payton had followed the exact same route, taking out two bombers, on the right side of the formation and now both were headed back to Biggin Hill elated to survive their first battle, but worried about the bombers still in the sky. They prayed first that none arrive over the city, and if they did that the bombs would miss the hospital holding Clara and Anne. They raced over the city ahead of any bombers to avoid the anti-aircraft fire that would thunder to life as soon the Luftwaffe appeared. At the last moment, the twins deviated slightly from the direct heading to the aerodrome. They flew right over the hospital and waggled their wings slightly just in case the girls watched from below. Both hoped that they already sat in a bomb shelter that would prove unnecessary.

His heart rate slowing as he approached the airfield with the adrenaline wearing off, Dylan asked his brother "Did we miss anything?"

"Yes, we ran out of bullets." Payton answered quickly. "If we can hit the weaknesses in the Messerschmitt with fewer rounds expended, then we can attack more bombers. I think we wasted some early shots." He concluded.

Although they'd put a dent in the bandits, Dylan knew his brother was right. Cold hearted as it may be, their job was to shoot down as many of the enemy as possible. The euphoria of the first battle dissipated as both twins landed smoothly, and the self-reflection left a hollow, cold pit gnawing at each stomach as they taxied off the runway. Sargent Blinn indicated that they should taxi to the hangar, and that red section had already scrambled so they wouldn't take off again immediately.

Payton crawled out of his cockpit after parking outside the hangar just as Sargent Blinn ambled up to the inspect the Spitfire.

"Looks like you did okay for your first fight." The Sargent stated flatly. "But you brought my new plane back with holes." He finished gesturing at several quarter size bullet holes in the tail section of Payton's plane.

"I didn't even know I'd been hit." Payton admitted. "I don't know if they are from the bombers' machine guns or the Messerschmitt."

Dylan walked over just then "I've got holes in mine too." He sheepishly divulged.

"Most come back with more holes than this. You've done well. From the radio reports it sounds like you each got two bombers, and one of you got one fighter while the other got two. That will put you on the path to ace shortly." Sargent Blinn informed them.

"It looks like we're the first back, have you heard how the rest of the squadron made out?" Dylan asked.

"Or if any of the bombers got through?" Payton asked before Sargent Blinn could answer, but then heard his answer in the form of a low rumble a long ways off. "Oh no." he sighed quietly.

"Heads up boys." Sargent Blinn answered. "We can't get them all. But that was the sound of a job well down. The explosion you just heard came from the southeast, over water. I'd wager a bomber was hit and dropped its payload to lighten up and head home. As for the rest of the squad, they are headed home now. One or two are limping, but should have no problem getting back safely. We'll have everyone patched up for morning, including your two swiss cheese tails. London should sleep well tonight after the bloody nose we've given those Jerrys today!" He finished triumphantly.

Heartened by the words of encouragement, Dylan and Payton walked back to the squad room in silence, each lost in his own thoughts at what they'd accomplished that day. They knew they'd have to survive many more days like this one to survive the war. Wave after wave of Luftwaffe fighters and bombers crashed against the thin RAF line in their heads like sledgehammer blows aimed at crushing not just the physical war making machines on the island, but their will to fight as well. Winston Churchill called this the Battle of Britain, and now the twins knew why.

CHAPTER 23

July 4th, 1940

Both Anne and Clara vaguely understood that it was an American holiday that might be important to the twins, but neither cared much at the moment. Though the clock hands indicated midmorning, and the sun indicated the truthfulness of the clock, both nurses fought off yawns and fluttering eyes as they attempted attentive wakefulness amidst the disheartening ward around them. The vicious air battle successfully diverted the afternoon before over London only presaged more brutal attacks at other ports and airfields. The overflow of wounded in various states of blood and shock soon flowed steadily in to their hospital. They spent the night triaging patients, bandaging wounds, and soothing souls long after their original shift had ended.

The charge nurse eventually issued orders "Off with the both of you. You've done enough for today and are no more use." She intoned sternly, but with a hint of thanks and admiration for the hard work. "I shall see you again tomorrow morning. No arguing."

"I'm so tired I'm not sure I can sleep now." Anne said as they changed out of their uniforms. "Let's go for a walk, if you are up for it." She suggested.

"Of course." Clara responded. "Laying around our room will do us no good now. Better to try and make it through the day and aim for a full night's sleep." Clara finished, leaving unsaid the two thoughts that it would be the first full night's sleep in a week and that the Germans might interrupt their plans anyway.

As they walked out to the sidewalk and headed towards the river both could feel the sun begin to break through their own grey overcast of the previous night. Neither hurried too quickly, so they enjoyed a leisurely stroll along the sidewalk headed south from St. Thomas'. They spoke little of work, and little of the boys they both missed dreadfully. Simple banter floated lightly behind them as they forgot all their cares in the world.

"Tell me more about Canada." Clara prompted.

"Only if you tell me more about Ireland" Anne responded.

"Lovely my dear, not only shall I tell you about it, the next chance we have we can sneak off from here and I'll show you Dublin at the very least."

"That does sound tempting. Let's go right now." Anne joked with a sigh. "Well, I grew up on a ranch in Alberta, one of our western provinces. Its about an hour south of Calgary, on the eastern side of the Rocky Mountains. Father inherited the ranch from his father, he called it Fog Ranch, for Fields of Gold. Grandfather loved that because it was a play on the grazing land around us and the family name." Anne said.

"Well then, perhaps I shall start calling you Anne Fields of Gold!" Clara teased.

"Father has grown it from two thousand head of cattle when he took over to almost six thousand now on ten thousand acres. The grazing lands are so pretty with the mountains in the background. I love watching the sunset behind them." Anne continued.

"That does sound lovely." Clara added.

"Father has been taking orders non-stop to help supply the army. I think he'd trade the extra business to have my brother back home safely, though. The ranch house has been expanded several times, but it is still comfortable and cozy and rustic. Open roughhewn beams in an open great room that covers most of the downstairs. Most of the walls are covered in dark wood paneling. The kitchen in one corner, with an enormous dark wood scroll leg table just off the pantry. I'd sit at that table for hours as a child reading, or drawing. Mother and Father always seem to have people over, from just a few of the ranch hands to the Prime Minister. He came for dinner one night when I was a child though I can't for the life of me tell you why." Anne explained. "Once I was ready for university I wanted to live in a big city, so I went to McGill in Montreal. I'm almost done, but will have to finish one more term."

"Maybe they'll count nursing as part of the curriculum!" Clara laughed. "I don't think it will fly there, or at Trinity. I'm in the same state, as I must make sure and finish up otherwise what was the point?"

Before Anne could reply, the air raid sirens blared their usual song of impending agony. Through mutual, silent consent neither girl hurried their pace towards a bomb shelter. The morning was too pleasant to even think of bombs falling near them. They waited for the usual far off rumble that signaled the start of a raid, but generally it took several minutes for the show to start. This time, however, the rumbling never came because a whistling sound presaged the bomb that fell just outside the nurse's dormitory.

***

Dylan and Payton had been vectored to the incoming bombers not long before the klaxons went off in London. This particular flight had escaped the notice of both the radars at Chain Home Command and the Coast Watchers sitting on the beaches with radios to call in any raids. Major Phillips had spotted the flight sneaking in behind them while hiding in the sun. The raid was small by the most recent standards which, along with the uncharacteristic early hour, probably explained the surprise. Only eight bombers flew with no Messerschmitts as escorts, and they must have taken off in the dark to arrive so early. The raid already touched the outskirts of London and would start dropping bombs before long.

"Quickly now lads." Major Phillips said "Those ruddy bastards are close to sneaking by us. Tally Ho!" he finished.

The twins pushed the throttles to the stops and climbed after the bombers. The tail gunners would see them any moment and let loose a stream of tracers in defense. Blue Section tore after the bombers in desperation, and began firing before they truly were in range, but they were not in time. The lead Luftwaffe aircraft opened his bomb doors, and moments later two thousand pound bombs began dropping in rapid succession. The next two aircraft followed suit, dropping their entire payloads on to the civilians below.

Blue section managed to take down the trailing aircraft before their bomb doors opened. Dylan and Payton each took one of the next two planes, while the rest of Blue section took out the rear of the attacking Luftwaffe formation. The twins circled back down in altitude to survey the gruesome damage. Buildings on both sides of the Thames billowed smoke. A deep crater indicated an explosion just outside Buckingham Palace they noted and prayed that the King was somewhere else. As they adjusted course across the river, the twins realized with horror that St. Marks was directly in the path of the bombs that had fallen. They could only waggle their wings over a smoldering column of smoke and fire as they raced overhead. Anxiety grew in their stomachs like ice encroaching from the edges of a wintry lake. Fear pulled at them as they rushed to land and find out what destruction had been wrought on the hospital and their loved ones.

The twins landed in parallel on the run way at Biggin Hill, despite the standing order to only do so in an emergency. They figured this qualified. Just as they slowed, Sargent Blinn raced up in a lorry and directed them just off the runway far enough for other planes to land. With the blades of their airscrews still turning, the twins scuttled out of their planes unsure what to do next.

Sargent Blinn already knew. "Go, take the lorry. I'll get your planes parked and make sure the Major knows you aren't awol. Check in later." Was all the omnipotent Blinn had to say.

"Thank you!" leapt from the twins lips simultaneously as they dashed to the car and drove off, on the wrong side of the road, without another word.

With the roads mostly clear due to the air raid, and the gas petal permanently against the floor, Payton managed to make the usual 45 minute drive to St. Thomas' hospital in under thirty minutes, but that only got them close. Traffic slowed to a crawl as they approached along the river. Abandoning the lorry in favor or walking, they twins made better time trotting in the direction of the smoke filled air. From the time the bomb hit the hospital grounds barely forty minutes had passed.

"Normally I'd say we should split up and search for the girls, but I think if we split up in this chaos we won't be able to find each other again." Dylan commented.

"Yes. We'll assume the girls are together and in one place. Stay close and start asking around about the nurses." Payton answered.

After making it to the hospital grounds proper both Dylan and Payton noticed the scene was eerily quiet. With so much damage around the city the boys had beaten the already thin emergency response teams to the hospital. Soon, sirens would wail and the injured would stream in they were sure, but for the moment it was quiet except for the occasional crackle of a small fire. A few dazed souls had shaken off the shock and begun looking back at the charred blast site, and a few braver souls had even begun pulling away at the rubble to help in any way they could. Dylan helped a small old man pull away some rubble piled up next to him that trapped him on a park bench. Payton pulled down a pile of rubble built up around the base of a tree like a fortress freeing a young lady in the process.

As the smoke cleared, the boys could see the nurse's dormitory from two blocks away slumped in on itself on the river side like a giant thumb had pressed in the middle of a soft cake and left a massive indentation. Anne and Clara's room had been on that side, the side where the bomb had gone off and blown away a side of the dormitory. Fighting off the rising fear by praying the girls had been out of the room working, or anywhere else, the boys kept pressing closer to blast site. The expected sirens came as hundreds of emergency workers and regular citizens came pouring on to the hospital grounds to help. With the threat of the bombers gone, the regular British citizens thumbed their noses at the Third Reich and pulled together to help in any way possible. All were relieved to see that the bombs had done little damage to the main hospital. It would keep operating as normal with a few pieces of plywood to replace some blown out windows. The small blessing meant that the injured in the hospital and the newly injured from all around the city could continue to seek care.

With no better plan, Dylan headed for what he thought was the general area of the girls room and began pulling away rubble and digging with all his heart. Payton continued asking passerby's if they had perchance seen a chestnut haired nurse with another redheaded nurse. No one had. Finally, after several futile minutes, he joined his brother. It had been nearly an hour since the initial bomb blast and the fear was turning in to a deep seated anxiety for both boys. As they dug deeper they began to find some of the things they knew belonged to their beloveds. A handkerchief of Clara's that she'd used to wipe away blood from Dylan's arm. The scarf that Anne had been wearing when Payton first saw her in the lobby of the Savoy....

"You'll not find us in there." Dylan heard a voice trying to be defiant behind them. Payton turned at the same time as his brother to see Clara and Anne arm in arm holding each other up in scorched uniforms, the sun shining brightly behind them. The twins reached the girls at the same time, and held them up as they sagged into their arms in pure shock. Without a word, they held each other for several minutes, each thanking God the others were all still alive.

"I'm so thankful you weren't in that room." Payton finally managed.

"We'd just gotten off extra shift, and were walking along the river." Anne answered. "Luck more than anything." she finished quietly.

"We were about a block away. The blast knocked me out." Clara said, regaining her courage. "I woke up next to Anne, next to the wall down to the river. It's another lucky thing that we didn't get blown in to the river."

"I don't remember anything other than sitting up next to you, so I must have been knocked out too." Anne added. "We checked each other, and don't seem to be any the worse for wear."

"Thank the Good Lord for that." Dylan finally managed to get the lump out of his throat. "Come with us, we've got a lorry, let's get out of here."

"We should stay and help." Clara protested.

"You've earned a break to get your strength back, and there is plenty of help here at the moment." Payton said as he motioned at the swarm of people around them.

"Where shall we go?" Anne asked.

"Anywhere but here." Clara finally consented as they headed for the lorry. "Simone's, take us to Simone's, we should check on her." Clara said suddenly as she thought of it.

***

No one gave the lorry with two officers and two nurses in it a second look as it wound its way across the river and through London. As they drew closer to Simone's home the quartet were relieved to see that her neighborhood had remained largely untouched.

The butler opened the door and ushered the shabby looking pairs in to the house while also calling for Lady Simone. She rushed down the stairs and threw herself in to the arms of the girls.

"I'd just heard about the hospital. I was on my way out the door to find you. I'm so relieved you are here!" Simone nearly wailed.

"We used a bit of Clara's Irish luck, but made it through okay." Anne replied.

"Have you seen Timothy?" Clara asked anxiously. "I haven't seen him in nearly a week. I've no idea where he is."

"He went back up to Dublin yesterday." Simone answered. "He said not to worry, but that I wouldn't hear from him for several weeks. I've no idea what he's up to either." She finished, unconsciously mimicking her friend. "No need to worry about him, at the moment. Come up with me, ladies, we'll get you changed and we can rest here for as long as you like. Boys, you can raid my father's closet if you need anything." Simone finished as she whisked the girls upstairs.

"Thank you." Both twins said to the three as they disappeared.

"We'll report back in tonight." Dylan thought out loud.

"Yeah, that should work. They won't need us before then. This is as good a place as any to relax for a bit and make sure the girls are well and truly okay before we head back. Let's go change. I wonder what Timothy is up to?" Payton wondered as they followed the butler up the stairs themselves.

CHAPTER 24

July 14th, 1940

The air raids only intensified. The Luftwaffe targeted both military installations and London, softening the Brits for an anticipated invasion. After Dunkirk, every last citizen felt the invasion was a question of when, not if, the Germans would come. The continual bombings only reinforced that feeling. What was becoming known as the Battle of Britain around the world continued high above the ground unabated against this tense backdrop.

Dylan and Payton continued patrolling over the English Channel in protection of London. As a matter of recourse, Blue Section began venturing further out over the Channel after the bombers slipped through ten days previously. They hoped to intercept the enemy flights earlier and enhance their chances of fully denying any bombs falling on the city. While largely successful, the Luftwaffe committed so many aircraft to each raid that it became impossible to engage them all, so London suffered as a consequence.

Each of the brothers had brought down two more Messerschmitts and two more bombers in a ferocious display of flying the day after they'd returned from finding Clara and Anne alive and well. Since that day they'd earned the reputation in the squadron for at least two kills per air raid attempt, so Major Phillips had started referring to them as Anders Squared, meaning two times two, for a total of four kills at a time. Eventually he just shortened it and just called them Squared. They had become so skilled, in such a short time, that on good days they doubled that kill total. In the eleven days since the raid they had each totaled 27 confirmed kills, tops in the squadron. The twins also earned a reputation for going directly after the bombers at the expense of bullet holes in their fuselage from the tail guns of the big planes. Three quarters of their kills had been heavy bombers. They reasoned that the bombers were the only targets that mattered. The Messerschmitts weren't going to do any harm to the people below. Major Phillips endorsed the idea and assigned other squadron members to first engage and peel off the fighter coverage so the rest of the squadron could go after the lumbering bombers. The strategy worked, and the kill rate went up, but not enough to discourage the Luftwaffe from sending more bombers to devastate the city.

Whenever the twins flew back to base they saw the steel forest of London pock marked with craters, leveling a block like clear cutting an old growth forest. They would land exhausted, and thankful for another safe landing. They had stopped counting the bullet holes in the fuselage after each attack.

Sargent Blinn and his crew continued to patch up each hole and paint over it so the planes had a mottled almost camouflage look from each shade of blueish grey paint denoting the length of time since application.

Each day the squadron woke more tired than the last, but energized by the urgency of their mission. Sometimes they were awoken by klaxons summoning them immediately to their aircraft. Other days they would eat a languid breakfast or lunch before climbing in to their cockpits at an appointed time to relieve the current patrol. About half of the squadron had been shot down since the twins joined, though a few of those men had been able to ditch and parachute out over the channel to be rescued. New recruits replenished the ranks at a steady trickle, but no end stood in sight, so onward they all pressed. No one stopped to think which side was the unstoppable force and which was the unmovable object.

Remarkably, the postal service around London remained unchanged. Each day the twins scrawled out a few words on a postcard to Clara and Anne (they usually shared one for economies sake) and it would magically appear at the hospital, care of Simone's address. A response always came two days later, postmarked the next day after the twins had sent their card. The singsong card and response reassured each party that the other pair still roamed the earth. Since the bombing had taken out the dormitory Clara and Anne wrote that they had more or less taken up residence at Simone's house at her insistence. They could walk to the hospital across the river in less than an hour, or if it was night they could usually catch a ride back across the Thames with an empty ambulance headed out on patrol. If they stayed on in to the night shift, they slept on sofas and cots in the nurse's lounge. Clara wrote in her last missive that Timothy had dropped a postcard to Simone from London, but only mentioned that he was safe and would be out of contact for another couple of weeks.

With the afternoon patrol assigned to Blue Section, Dylan and Payton formed up as lead and wingman just behind Major Phillips and his wingman. The Major had again taken a green pilot as his wingman hoping to keep the newly minted pilot alive for at least one patrol.

"Follow me out to the southeast, if you please gentlemen." Major Phillips clipped over the radio once the squadron fully formed behind him. Each plane followed his steep climbing turn out to sea while bantering lightly about the unusually cool, clear day. The sky above remained blue, but once at altitude each could see the line of clouds forming over the continent. Weather systems usually moved from west to east, covering the UK first, but this system must have come from the south. While not concerning, it was worth noting to each pilot. Cloud cover could nullify any bombing attempts, so the whole of Blue Section hoped that the clouds would shift back west over the channel to hide London from her enemies for a little while at least.

The Luftwaffe had other plans. As Blue Section reached mid Channel a massive sortie of bombers and covering fighter aircraft burst out of the high clouds. They'd used the cloud cover to hide as long as possible. However, such a large force could not hide forever.

"Bogies dead ahead. Estimated strength 120 aircraft." Dylan barked.

"Roger, relaying to Chain Home command and requesting all available resources" Major Phillips answered. "Tally Ho!"

The clouds had so well hidden the enemy forces that Blue Section had only moments to vector an attack. Each lead/wingman pair drove headlong in to the enemy formation and opened fire. Dylan quickly brought down an advancing Messerschmitt while Payton clipped a bombers wing followed by a quick kill shot at another Messerschmitt. As Payton rolled back on to Dylan's wing he saw two more Messerschmitts pulling behind his brother looking for a shot.

"Dylan, pull right!" Payton ordered. Before his brother had finished his thought Dylan banked hard to the right, putting the two Messerschmitts in line with Payton's gunsights. He pulled the trigger and watched as one, then the other exploded.

"I get one of those kills." Dylan deadpanned in the heat of the battle while quickly lining up a shot at another bomber. Payton followed his line and between the two of them shot down the right side of a diamond flying formation. Moments later, the left side of that flying formation let loose a withering fusillade of bullets aimed at the twins. They expertly split, but not before each took several bullets to the tail sections of their planes. As they pulled back together, two more Messerchmitts dove out of the sun, headed directly for Dylan's plane with gun barrels spitting tracers directly on target. Dylan's plane immediately caught fire and began streaming flames behind it as he valiantly fought to keep it airborne.

Dylan righted his plane briefly and slowed his descent enough to try and get his bearings. In his struggle to gain control of the damaged plane he'd drifted ever closer to the French coastline. Dylan pulled hard to the right on the stick, and mashed down on the rudder pedal trying desperately to head back west. If he survived at all, ditching in the ocean meant a chance of rescue by a British ship while ditching in France meant capture by the Nazi's. The battered aircraft failed to respond. Severed control lines spewed hydraulic fluid in to the flames. At 10,000 feet the flames began licking the cockpit, and the remaining ammunition in the wings starting popping in their canisters like popcorn. Left without a choice, Dylan unstrapped from the plane fought to keep control of the stick with his knees while he pushed on the canopy.

The angle and speed of his aircraft made opening the canopy exceedingly difficult under normal circumstances and more so under Dylan's current duress. Letting the stick go with his knees Dylan heaved with all of his strength against the warped metal and glass holding him hostage. The canopy creaked open slightly, and then blew completely off. The front edge barely missed knocking Dylan unconscious as it flew scant inches above him. The wind screeched passed the young pilot's ears with the howl of a hundred hurricanes. The better than gail force winds tried to root him in place, but Dylan felt the plane begin to roll. If he didn't get out now, he'd be trapped in the cockpit facing earth unable to jump. Dylan planted one foot firmly on the edge of the cockpit, grabbed the front of the windscreen with his hand, and pushed with all of his might. Now the wind and momentum worked in his favor. The plane continued its death spiral while he was pushed clear of the flaming fuselage. He pulled the ripcord of his parachute and prayed.

***

Payton watched in horror as his brother's plane faltered, then recovered slightly as the flames engulfed the fuselage before gravity reasserted itself. Feeling helpless in the 10 seconds it took Dylan's plane to cycle in to catastrophe, Payton could only attack. He saw Dylan's attacker pull back around to finish off Dylan's already dead plane and confirm a kill. Thinking he was alone, the German pilot never saw Payton attack at right angles from above, perfectly timing his shot to puncture the canopy and wings of the aircraft before it exploded. The revenge gave Payton no pleasure as he continued diving towards his brother's plane.

Dylan never saw the explosion above him, nor thought to be thankful that no one continued shooting at him. Payton caught up in time to see the canopy on his brother's plane fly off, and he had to adjust course quickly to make sure it didn't hit his plane. Pulling level just above the aircraft that looked more like a fireball now, Payton saw Dylan exit the cockpit and prayed along with him that the parachute would open, just as his parachute had during training.

The white silk canopy opened beautifully, round and full like the top of a cotton bud. Dylan felt the jerk as his fall suddenly slowed dramatically, and both twins breathed a momentary sigh of relief. The relief, however, was only momentary. The prevailing winds immediately began pushing Dylan towards the beaches of the French coastline.

The Germans had begun building the famed Atlantic wall, and since neither twin knew exactly where they were on the French coast, Payton assumed that as soon as he came in to sight his brother would draw fire from the machine guns on the high cliffs at best. At worst, the Germans would send a squad of SS men after him. Payton reacted quickly. He dove for the narrow stretch of beach where he guessed his brother would eventually land. Pulling up perilously close to the ground Payton commenced strafing the cliffs above the beach. He took three full runs attempting to negate any hidden emplacements before he ran out of ammunition. As he pulled up from his final attack Payton saw Dylan land gently on the beach, safe as could be. The wind shifted and Dylan's parachute canopy pulled him slightly along the beach towards the south. Payton thought of the windsocks at the rutted dirt runway at home. Without hesitation, he swooped above the beach, put his landing gear down and commenced emergency landing procedures. His brother needed a ride and he would give it to him.

***

Dylan touched down immediately grateful to feel solid ground under his feet again. During his float down to the ground Dylan watched his brother attack the cliffs over his not very intentional landing spot. Although he knew the foolishness of expending all of the remaining ammunition, Dylan appreciated what his brother did for him. He also knew he would have done the same thing if their situations were reversed. What his brother did next simply confounded Dylan, though. He watched Payton line up a landing approach and watched as his landing gear came down. The beach appeared big and flat from the air, so the inclination to land in his brother's head was understandable. However, the moment Dylan saw the landing gear he realized the sandy beach was too soft. The tide flowed out enough that wet sand seemed firm and at fifty yards or so from cliff to water it was plenty wide enough, so Dylan fervently hoped he was wrong enough that his brother could land safely. Wanting to get out of the way, Dylan quickly gathered up his parachute and scurried towards the cliffs, once again glad that no one shot at him while doing so.

Payton roared down the beach and touched down just past Dylan's original landing spot. In a deft moment he flared the plan mere feet above the sand before settling down as gently as possible. But, it was not enough. As soon as the plane touched down the tires used to concrete sank deep in sand, slowing the plane almost instantly. Payton jerked forward against his restraints, and the landing gear buckled from momentum of the plane pushing against the nearly stopped struts. It seemed like the fuselage kept flying a few feet forward while the landing gear remained in place. All three wheels sheared off from the bottom of the plane before it settled on its belly in the sand. The airscrew still spun until it too dug in to the sand, twisting the blades at grotesque angles and rendering them useless. Now Payton's aircraft would never fly again, just like Dylan's.

"Nice landing. What the hell were you thinking?" Dylan said exasperated as he trotted up to his brother's plane.

"I thought you might need a ride. It didn't go as I expected it to." Payton cheerfully answered as he scrambled out of the cockpit. Both twins hunkered down on the ocean side of the fuselage for cover and removed their Mae West life jackets. "At least we are both momentarily alive." Payton finished in the same cheerful voice.

"Grab your back up chute, it might be useful. I've got mine." Dylan ordered as he pointed at his spare chute nicely tucked in its bag.

"Good idea. Where'd you think of that? I'll grab the emergency kit too." Payton answered.

"I had plenty of time to think falling from the sky." Dylan answered, starting to feel a little better at their predicament. His anger at his brother for landing and putting them both in danger subsided at the thought of knowing he wouldn't have to go through whatever lay ahead alone.

"Let's get off this beach, then we can take inventory." Payton said. "The Germans will probably notice the downed planes soon enough. Eventually, the tide will wash over my plane, so I don't think we need to blow it up." He finished.

"Right, the cliffs here aren't going to let us up, so let's get under them as best we can and follow the beach." Dylan continued his brother's line of thinking. "I think I saw a fissure in the cliffs about a half mile up. Maybe we can get up there." He concluded hopefully and set off towards the cliffs. Payton followed a half step behind, marveling at the massive luck that had gotten them this far, and hoping that it would hold out.

The boys scrambled from wet sand to dry, and then across a small rocky section until they reached the base of the towering cliffs. The small rocks made for easy passage, almost a gravel trail, a small blessing instead of slogging through the sand. In short order they reached the fissure that Dylan had spotted from his parachute landing. They glanced briefly around the corner to insure no ambush awaited them, and seeing no one stepped in to the relative cover of the gap in the cliffs.

"Would you look at that!" Payton exclaimed.

"What?" Dylan asked.

"Stairs, right to the top." Payton said, satisfied at the discovery of a way off the beach.

"They're no elevator, but they'll due." Dylan noted dryly as they started scampering up the long, straight stone stairs carved in to the fissure in the cliffs. A platform with a railing at the top of the stairs announced their arrival on the bluffs. The lush countryside spread out in front of the twins and gave them their first true view of where they'd landed. Fortune again shined on them as they'd landed in a sparsely populated area clearly used for farming. A small trailhead extended from platform headed inland, with a small arrow sign pointed to the south east.

"Octeville Sur Mer." Dylan read. "We're a lot further south than I thought. Le Havre should be four or five miles south of here." He concluded.

"Yep." Payton confirmed. "Good to know, at the very least. Maybe if we make it there we can steal a boat or something and head back west."

"That's as good a plan as any." Dylan agreed as he looked further afield to see if he could see anything else useful. As we looked back north, he spotted a small column of black smoke rising from the edge of the cliffs about two hundred yards away. "Either someone is over there making s'mores, or you shot something." Dylan noted pointing to an area that Payton had strafed minutes before.

"I hope it's Nazi, or I'll feel badly for shooting it." Payton said a little nervously. "Let's go see, quietly. If it isn't German maybe it will be someone that can help us. If it is an occupied German post, we'll head back south and have a better idea what to look for as we make our way down to Le Havre."

Without answering, Dylan set off down the trail towards the column of smoke. Before long, Payton tapped him on the shoulder and indicated a gap between the few trees and tall brush as a good place to enter the woods for concealment before they got too close. The two spent the next several minutes picking their way quietly through the coastal foliage until they saw the smoldering remains that had drawn their attention. It was a fortified Nazi machine gun outpost that surely would have fired at Dylan as he descended, or waited until he was on the ground and fired at point blank range.

"Good thing you got this one." Dylan said quietly. "Do you see anything useful?" The small post contained the remains of a gunner, loader next to a machine gun, and what the twins assumed must have been the post commander sitting at a field desk inside a dug in and fortified timber enclosure. Payton had strafed right through the middle of the roof, killing all three in a hail of bullets.

"I'll check the desk. See if you can scrounge up some food." Payton ordered thinking of primary needs first. This was war, no time for sympathy to ones enemies. Payton strode to the desk and began opening desk drawers while avoiding looking at the body slumped over the side of the chair. The simple metal desk had three drawers down the left side. The top drawer held some extra ammunition for a luger, which reminded Payton to reach over and secure the officers handgun for himself. The next drawer contained a treasure trove. "Maps!" Payton held up triumphantly for his brother to see.

"Good find, anything else?" Dylan asked.

"Nothing, no code book, no letters, this is it. You?" Payton asked.

"A loaf of bread, and a couple of cans that maybe contain sausage, but I'm not sure. Hopefully not sardines." Dylan answered. "What all do we have?" he asked as he walked over and laid out his supplies on the desk.

"Our two colts" Payton said, referring to the not exactly standard issue Colt model 1911 that each had brought with them for just such an occasion. "And our spare clips make twenty shots each. Plus, I just pulled a Luger and two spare clips from the officer. That's another twenty one shots, I think. We've got our knives, and reserve chutes, but other than the food, map, and medical kit that's about it. Anything I'm missing?"

"Sadly, that's about it." Dylan confirmed. "Looks like you got the radio too, so we should have a couple of minutes to get out of here before the cavalry arrives." He added pointing to the bullet riddled radio set in the corner. Without another word the twins quickly packed up and headed out in the direction of Le Havre. They followed the original path inland while carefully keeping an eye out for anyone or anything. After about a quarter hour, they reached what appeared to be the main road running along the coast. Sticking to the culvert along the road provided a measure of cover, but it proved unneeded as the two made it almost an hour before a small truck rumbled by them. It was the first and only vehicle they saw that afternoon.

As the sun began to set, the boys reached the outskirts of the city. They doubled back to a couple of small farm houses they'd just passed to seek shelter. Although it was only early evening both boys understandably felt exhausted. They carefully moved in tandem, using anything for cover, until they reached the barn out back of the farm house. They snuck in to the mostly empty barn, and climbed quietly in to the hay loft. The silence continued as both tucked themselves in to the far corners of the hayloft and fell instantly asleep, oblivious to their precarious situation for at least one night.

CHAPTER 25

July 15th, 1940

The day dawned bright, and the twins woke with the sun. Although both had slept, neither had relaxed. "We probably should have slept in shifts and had a rotating watch. That was dumb. Now what?" Payton thought out loud. "Any better plan than yesterday, because I've got nothing." Payton continued.

"Nope, me neither. Let's head in to city and discreetly see if we can come up with something. We'll need a change of clothes first." Dylan answered. "Keep an eye out for a clothes line. Maybe we'll get lucky." He hoped as he opened one of the cans they'd taken from the Germans. "Sardines, not exactly breakfast food." Dylan moaned slightly as the salty smell assaulted is nostrils more harshly than even the dense sea air creeping inland from the English Channel.

"Not ideal, but manageable. I'd rather have some smoked salmon from home, too." Payton responded, reaching for his half of the morning meal. After gulping down the fish and swallowing the remnants in their canteens the twins quietly crept out of the barn before the tiny farm came to life. The next farm house over forgot to bring their laundry in the night before, so the boys stole a brown shirt and corduroy pants along with a peasants linen vest for Dylan and a loose light weight sweater for Payton. They felt bad for stealing from the meager looking farm, and from the occupied French people in general, but the with the clothes they passed as indistinguishable from any of the other common folk in the area as long as no one asked them anything in French. The twins set off down the road without hiding in the bushes. They were more confident that they looked like a pair of laborers on their way in to work. Covering ground more quickly they easily reached the city center just as the usual bustle began for the day.

Eventually, they crossed the mouth of the Seine River before it poured out in to the English Channel. Following the river, they made their way to the harbor proper. The few fishing boats were not brave enough to risk a torpedo, so they remained anchored in the mouth of the harbor while various merchants set up booths for the day's business in an adjacent market. Their wares included everything from fresh baked bread to hand crafted clothing and small farming tools. The twins noticed that about half of the available space stood empty. The normally lively market operated under a cloud, as if in a mild stupor, afraid to step too far out of line by lowering their grim guardedness.

Heads stared at the ground, uniformly bowed, grimaces transfixed upon faces, and eyes screwed nearly shut in squints that would deflect the sun, the sea salt air, and any questions.

Soon, the twins saw why. A cortege of automobiles flying red Nazi swastika flags began rolling through the streets. Some stopped and took things from the market, while others headed directly to the largest building near the port. It appeared that the Nazi's had taken over the admiralty building for the port as their local headquarters. The local citizens showed the deference of the truly frightened. No one wanted to enrage the men holding absolute power.

While casually walking through the streets, the twins picked out the usual Nazi hangouts, sympathetic bars, large confiscated houses quartering particular occupation units, and the large movie theater sure to show the latest propaganda. Marked as places to avoid, the twins went in other directions, hoping to find some way home.

"Let's have a closer look at some of those boats still anchored in the harbor." Payton suggested.

"But not too close." Dylan quietly cautioned, indicating two Nazi foot patrols marching back and forth along the harbor sidewalk and sea wall above a short sandy beach with a long wooden pier jutting out perpendicularly in to the water.

"Perhaps we should wait until this evening then." Payton thought out loud. "When the sun sets we'll slip out on the pier and see what we can see. Until then, let's see if we can hide under the pier somewhere. We can stay out of sight there but keep an eye on the harbor while we wait. The fewer Germans we talk to the better." He said warming up to the mediocre plan.

The two lingered quietly in the shadow of a doorway until the sentries passed each other and disappeared briefly out of sight. Without hesitating the twins took advantage of the window afforded them to walk briskly to the seawall's edge, and slip over the side down to the beach. From there they ran until they could hunker down in the shadows of the sturdy timber pilings holding up the creosote soaked planks of the pier above. They found a shallow depression in the sand above the high tide line for further shelter. The relative safety of their new hiding place allowed the twins to relax for the first time in twenty four hours.

"Some shot down pilots we are." Dylan ruminated after a few minutes. "I don't even have a picture of Clara. I don't think there are even any pictures of the two of us together in existence. We never went anywhere with a photographer for the few dinners we had together."

"You can fix that when we get back. I don't have any of Anne either." Payton answered showing a surety in their survival that neither necessarily felt. With the full day spread out in front of them, the twins reverted to wiling away the hours as they used to when they were working on the farm. They talked of baseball, debating teams and players while also reminiscing about some of their own exploits. They talked of their parents, hoping that they were not worried about them. And, they talked of the girls. They knew Clara and Anne would be worried about them, but hoped that they could get back to England before they were truly missed.

Clara screwed up all here courage, walked to the telephone, and dialed the number for the squadron base at Biggin Hill after dinner.

"Major Phillips, please." She said ever so sweetly to the enlisted man that answered the phone. He complied readily, without even inquiring about whom might need the Major at the phone.

"Phillips." The Major intoned flatly as he picked up the receiver a few moments later.

"Major Phillips, this is Nurse Clara O'Ryan. One of your men we patched up here yesterday afternoon, a Flight Sargent Quarles, said you were the man I needed to talk with because two of your men I'm interested in went down over the Channel. I need to know what has happened to the Anders twins." She was barely able to get it out without breaking out of the professional nurse's tone.

"I know who you are lass. I'm sorry about your boy. I saw one get shot up, but I saw the parachute open. The other plane crashed on the sand. I didn't see anything after that, but I know they were both alive the last time I saw them. That should give you some hope."

"Thank you." Clara blurted and hung up before she crumbled to the floor. Anne hadn't even managed enough courage to leave the room, but she rushed out when she heard the muffled thud of Clara slumping against the wall.

"What?" Clara asked with the fear evident in her voice.

"France, they've crashed." Croaked Clara

"Oh, no." Anne almost sighed as she slumped next to her friend. Neither said anything else until they slowly rose, overwhelmed and numb, hugged each other and slowly pulled themselves in to bed for the night.

***

As night fell the twins slowly crept out of their hideout under the pier and made their way up the seawall without incident. They swayed a little bit like drunks, which they'd decided much earlier in the day for their disguise, as they walked brazenly down the pier doing their best to pick out any possible escape vessels. As discreetly as they could manage they scanned each small fishing vessel and tramp in the harbor.

"I don't see anything close enough to shore that we can swim to that will be big enough to make it across the channel but not so big that we can't handle it." Dylan surmised. "Do you see any dinghy's that could get us to some of the fishing trawlers on the other side of the harbor?"

"No, I think we'll have to come up with a different plan, or wait until any of the boats turn over and come closer." Payton said dejectedly. "Let's head back under the pier and regroup."

Dylan swayed as convincingly as possible before he turned and headed back towards the shore. Payton followed, stumbled a little on purpose, and leaned against the railing for a moment as his brother swerved forward a few steps. As they prepared to edge over the wall Dylan scanned down the path one more time. "Halt!" commanded a stern German voice. Trailing Dylan by a step and half shielded from the challenger, Payton simply drew his gun and shot the German soldier without mercy twice in the heart.

"Run!" Dylan commanded immediately. He knew his brother had made the right decision, they had no way of passing any kind of a challenge from even the lowliest soldier, but now the only thing they could do was get out of Le Havre before the SS, or worse the Gestapo, started searching for the two men who had shot one of their own.

"Wait!" Payton slowed after the first three running steps he'd taken. He knew just as well as his brother that the sound of gunfire would soon bring a swarm of attention. However, shooting the German soldier also meant he had to slow down and think. He ran back and pulled off the dead man all of his papers and, seeing he was an officer, his sidearm before reconsidering. "Run toward the admiralty building, and let's ditch the weapons for now. If we hide them, and then hide ourselves in plane site where most of the Nazi's are we can try and slip out of town early in the morning when the shot has worn off the investigation some." Payton finally explained to his brother. They found an alcove of large stone three blocks south that had been attached to a building housing some kind of shops before the Nazi's artillery had leveled everything except the entry way. The twins found a loose stone near the base, dug a small hole underneath, and hid their small stash of food and weapons as well as the papers of the dead man. With that done, they tried to walk towards the admiralty building as drunkenly as possible before acting as if they were collapsing in to a doorway and passing out. The doorway, conveniently, allowed a near perfect view of the admiralty building and the entire surrounding square. The twins didn't have to decide who would take first watch because on this night two sets of alert eyes would stay open.

***

The frenzied activity surrounding the shot German died down around midnight. The last lights in the Admiralty building switched off around 1am as the last hard working bureaucrat in the Werhmacht decided to seek at least a few hours of sleep. Only one or two patrols wandered the streets of the slumbering city. Around 4:30 am, the twins silently nodded to each other and accented to move out of the city after gathering their provisions and weapons from the lackluster hiding spot. They crept slowly along the boulevards of the silent French town, avoiding the halos cast by the few street lights and listening for any sign of human movement ahead of them. Once they reached the outskirts of the town, wary of roadblocks after the shooting, the twins slowed their pace even more. Dylan crept forward slowly with Payton ten steps behind lurking in the shadows and ready to pounce should they run in to any trouble. The Germans confidence in their iron grip on the local population only served to aid the twins. No challenges or roadblocks appeared as they escaped the city unchallenged. Slipping out of town gave them a moments relief, but then they set their course south and disappeared in to the hedgerows and lanes as best they could for the next part of their unknown journey.

CHAPTER 26

July 16th, 1940

Clara awoke early with a pit in her stomach. She'd slept fitfully, tormented by dreams of her missing beloved, her mysteriously absent brother, and the crater that used to be their dormitory home at the hospital. After the destruction of the dormitory the nursing staff understandably faced a critical shortage of trained women to run the hospital. Simone even volunteered to help, so both Anne and Clara tutored her as best they could. She learned quickly in the dozen days since the decimation of the nursing staff. Clara and Anne tried to ignore the thought of how many bright young women just trying to help had been killed. And, that they'd almost been killed themselves.

After a few moments of sleep filled reflection Clara roused herself from bed and mumbled quietly to Anne.

"I'm awake." She replied. "I was trying to hold it all together silently so you could sleep a little longer." Anne offered quietly.

"We must hold it together a little longer. The hospital needs all three of us today." Clara answered a little sternly, if only to mask her own pain. "I'll get Simone and we can start on our way." Clara said as she headed out the room. Just then, the phone rang. It was a bit early for a call, but Simone's butler answered quickly.

"I'll find her immediately" Clara heard him say. "Ah, splendid, Miss O'Ryan, there is a call for you." He said as she rounded the corner in to the hall with the telephone.

"Thank you" she replied as she picked up the handset. "This is Miss O'Ryan." She stated somewhat flatly with just a hint of a question at such an early call.

"Miss O'Ryan, this is Flight Sargent Quarrels. I'm sorry to bother you so early, but I've just returned from a dawn patrol." The caller explained.

"Why Flight Sargent, I hadn't realized you'd been released back to duty so soon." A surprised Clara replied.

"You did a fine job patching me up, and then I snuck out." The small man grinned through the phone, ruefully. "I wanted to get back to flying. This was my first mission, and I couldn't help myself, but I flew out over where Flight Leftenants Anders went down. I'm afraid I didn't see them, but their plane was also missing. And I don't mean parts of it, I mean the whole thing. The tide must have taken it out to sea, meaning the Germans didn't blow it up. There was no wreckage floating in the surf. Along with a smoldering pill box above the cliffs, I'm forced to conclude that they escaped." He finished hopefully.

"That is very kind of you Flight Sargent. I hope you didn't put yourself in any danger to come by this information." Clara said.

"No more than the usual." The pilot lied. "I must be off. If I find out anything else I will certainly let you know as soon as I can."

"Thank you so very much." Clara said with true heartfelt thanks before hurrying off to relay the glimmer of hope to Anne.

***

The twins continued along their general southerly route at an amble that they hoped would fool any passersby in to thinks they were just local farm hands going about their business. Any further investigation would reveal the stolen rifle Payton hid down his trousers to the knee and strapped to his shoulder under the workmen's jacket and the lugers both sported in those same jacket pockets. After leaving Le Havre proper, they found more and more evidence of the brutal war at hand. The German plan to invade France, Plan Yellow, included an immediate dash to the coast to take Le Havre. The importance of the deep-water port as a military objective was obvious. The Wehrmacht invaded the north of France through the Netherlands, while sending an army directly across Luxembourg straight for La Havre. The twins saw the devastation first hand. The Wehrmacht pincer from the south started at Le Havre and along with the northern arm enclosing from the Dutch border compressed the British and French forces around Dunkirk. Knowing full well the destruction in Dunkirk, Dylan and Payton saw the continued destruction this far south.

Clusters of mangle and burnt out tanks, both French and German, lined the sides of the roads like grotesque medieval gargoyle statues. Pretty estates and farm houses alike stood half tall, with entire sides caved in by large caliber shell fire. Like a forest fire, war left a black mark on everything it touched.

As mid-morning approached they had managed to travel about twenty miles south of the city and decided to take a break in the shade of a low stone wall running along the deserted lane marking their path. "I figure we're making about 3 to 4 miles an hour at this pace." Payton surmised. They'd been walking for nearly six hours, proving his internal calculator remained well calibrated. "Any faster and we risk detection. I'd figure it's a shade over 100 miles to Carentan judging by the maps we took off the Germans. If we can manage fifteen good hours of walking a day, with the other nine for finding food, shelter, and sleep, we should be able to make it by the day after tomorrow or so. If we head there we can try to find Donna's family and find out if there is any resistance in the area that might be able to help us back across the Channel." Payton finished laying out the plan slowly forming in his head.

"Okay." Dylan answered. "We probably don't want to try and catch a ride. Even if we found a friendly Frenchman, cars are more likely to be stopped by the Germans." Dylan concluded.

"Once we get to Carentan, we'll have to discreetly find Donna's family." Payton continued thinking out loud. "But one problem at a time, I guess. At least we don't have to worry too much about navigating. Ocean on our right means we are still headed in the right direction, more or less." With that, he heaved himself up from the ground, and stretched out a hand for his brother. They both took one final drink from the liberated canteen and hoped to find another well or faucet soon. If they noticed the far-off rumblings of a car soon enough, they jumped behind a tree or wall to conceal themselves as they went. If their senses failed to warn them early enough, the twins shambled along the roads with their heads down and hoped for the best. None of the cars even slowed down through the heat of the day and in to the evening. The twins walked steadily with few breaks until the late evening light indicated the sun would set soon.

As usual, and with only a hint of competition to see who could walk the farthest, the twins exceeded the fifteen hours a day goal by a good two hours. With the sun already set and the remaining light barely illuminating the countryside, the twins found a small ravine off the main road and close to the beach. A small creek ran from the hills down to the ocean below creating an ideally sized depression for the two to hide. Several tall trees created a canopy over them as a gentle rain began to fall. Dylan found a flat rock and dug in to the depression even more.

"I think if we get this down a foot or two we can have a fire. The trees will cover smoke coming out and we'll be in the ravine enough that no one will be able to see the glow from either the road or the beach." Dylan explained as he used the rock to lever out some soft dirt next to the creek.

"I think you are right." Payton answered. "We haven't seen any pillboxes on this stretch of the coast, so it must be all right. The trees will keep the rain off, too. I'll go find some firewood."

With the fire made, the twins settled in just as if they were boys again camping on the coast of the Pacific Ocean in Oregon. They ate most of the last vestiges of the rations they'd taken the first day, and saved just enough for breakfast in the morning along with filling their canteens from the stream. Payton took the first watch, picking a spot just above their camp outside the glow of the dying fire that afforded him a full view in all directions without sticking much more than his head outside the small ravine. The brothers would take turns listening intently for any man made sounds, and constantly watching for any hints of light headed towards them. Every four hours they switched, and survived one more restless night before continuing their trek south into more of the unknown.

***

Clara softly dabbed a damp cloth around the ankle of her patient as she changed the dressing around the shrapnel damage. Usually that meant she was helping a young soldier recover, but the increased bombing around London meant that today she was helping change the dressing of a young girl of no more than eight years old. Her family home sat adjacent to a building that took a direct hit, so she was lucky to get away with just a lacerated ankle. Others in the building had not been as lucky.

"There you go love." Clara cooed quietly at the little girl. "You are good as new. I'd guess they'll let you out of here soon."

"Do you know where my parents are?" The little girl asked ever so softly. "I haven't seen them since the bombing.

"I haven't, but I'm sure they'll turn up." Clara lied as her stomach turned over in torture for the poor little girl. She leaned forward and gave the girl a hug, more so for her than the most likely new orphan. Tears sprung from both sets of eyes as Clara held the small child for a little bit longer. After a moment, Clara got up and gave the girl a reassuring smile before heading back to the nurse's station. The long shadows from the last vestiges of the setting sun hid Clara's concerned face from the other patients as she walked down the hallway.

Leaning against the small desk that passed as the nurses station, Anne saw her friend approach looking exhausted and knew she must look nearly the same. Without a word, the two embraced long enough to fight off the outside world and continue on with their duties. The small hope that Dylan and Payton might still be alive gave them some reason to go on, but at this point they were pushing through for each other. They never even said a word as they continued on with their duties.

Clara moved on to a young soldier with a large hole in his shoulder. She changed the dressing and humored the poor boy when he asked when he could get back in the fight. "Any day now" she always answered him.

"Excuse me, Miss?" Clara heard a voice behind her. "I'm looking for a Miss Fields. Can you help me?" As she turned Clara saw a young man that looked vaguely familiar. He wore the uniform of a Captain in the commonwealth armies, and he had deep brown eyes with close cropped chestnut hair. For a moment, Clara froze thinking that this man brought bad news about the twins, but then she realized his accent was Canadian.

"You must mean Anne, she's a friend of mine. I'm sure I can find her in a moment, what is it you need with her?" Clara responded politely.

"I'm her brother. Captain Jack Fields." The man said, surprising Clara so much that her mouth nearly dropped open.

"Oh My Word!" Clara exclaimed. "She's been worried sick about you! After Dunkirk no word had come. Her father sent word that he thought you'd made it out, but with no more details. She didn't know what to do. Come with me, she must be just over here." Clara said as she hurried the man between the beds of the hospital ward. Captain Fields disguised a limp as he rushed to keep up with Clara.

Anne also sat low on a stool tending to the medicine for a severely wounded patient. She finished with the syringe and turned to dispose of it just as she caught sight of her brother.

"Jack!" She bellowed in shock and delight. "You're okay! Where have you been? Why are you limping?" Anne demanded of her older brother all in one breath.

"I'm pleased to see that you are okay too." He started. "I didn't know you were here. I wrote father and he just telegraphed me back that you were in London. I was shot in a rather delicate place and have been recovering down in Dover for the last several weeks."

"You were shot? Where?" Clara interrupted.

"There are two answers to that question." Captain Fields answered slyly. "One is far less embarrassing. I was shot on the beach in Dunkirk. Our unit was one of the last to evacuate. They pulled me on to the boat as we sailed away. The second answer is somewhat less than I would share with anyone, but I was shot in the arse, to be terribly precise." He finished while both Anne and Clara failed to suppress giggles.

Anne flung herself in to her brother's arms and hugged him fiercely, happy at the unexpected reunion. "Now I just need Payton back, and I will ask for no more as long as I shall live." Anne mumbled in to her brother's shoulder.

"Ah, yes, father did mention something about a Yank you chased after to wind up here." Jack chided as he glanced at Clara for support.

"You'll get no support from me." Clara bluntly answered the glance. "I'm in love with his twin brother." She said as her smile broke through ever so briefly before fading back to a concerned visage.

"Well, I'll have to give both these boys a good thrashing. Where are they now? Let's have dinner!" Jack declared before noticing the sorrowful look on the faces of both girls.

"They crashed, in France. We don't know where they are." Anne answered, deflating some of the buoyant mood from finding her brother alive and well.

"I'm sorry to hear that." He answered quietly.

"They know their way around, they're twins, and they helped at Dunkirk, pulling boatloads of men off the beaches with my brother." Clara offered in the sincere hope that she could talk herself in to believing that the twins were okay.

"I heard about that!" Jack exclaimed. "A set of twins kept coming inland to get more men until one of their boats exploded. I was set to be on their next trip before things went awry. I'm quite pleased to hear they made it back to England intact." Jack grinned. "I'm sure two resourceful chaps like that can navigate France and find a resistance group to get them home." He said reassuringly, though none of them felt nearly as strongly about it as they wanted to.

"We're off in an hour." Clara said to change the subject. "We'll round up Simone find something to eat after that, if that suits you Jack?"

"That suits me fine. I would never think to keep my saintly sister from her duties." Jack teased lightly. "I'll meet you at the hospital entrance then." He smiled as he limped slightly back the way he came.

***

Both twins were already awake when they heard the first truck of the morning rumble by on the road a quarter mile inland from their little camp. The burning embers of their small fire gave off no visible smoke, thankfully, so they quickly buried it with sand to further avoid detection as the sun barely crested in the east. Quietly, they waited for any other sounds betraying anyone approaching. After a full five minutes, they silently looked at each other and simultaneously consented to head out. The early morning sun indicated a general direction, which again simply meant keeping the ocean on the right, and the sun on their left during the morning. When the sun made it all the way to their right, they knew it would be time to rest. But, resting stood a long way off. After a few minutes stretching out creaky and sore muscles from another night sleeping on the ground, the twins picked up the pace for their continued trek south. Amazingly, the twins managed to eat up ground at nearly a double time pace despite the rough terrain needed for stealth until they reached the road and resumed their shambling jaunt imitating local workers.

The twins said little as they meandered towards what they hoped would be a way out. A German soldier overhearing them speak English surely led to the end. A grim stoicism crossed both faces as they mentally searched for their next move once they reached Carentan. After a couple of hours on the road, Payton nudged his brother and gestured toward the coast. Dylan focused on the small column of smoke rising from the beach. They clambered off the road and up a dune without arousing suspicion. To their surprise, they saw the smoldering ruins of another Spitfire half in the surf.

Payton refrained from stating the obvious, that the scene looked familiar, and simply asked "Do you see the pilot?"

"No." Dylan answered simply. "He may be dead or alive, but we should go check before the Germans arrive."

"Are you sure?" Payton asked quietly, already knowing his own answer. "The Germans will be here soon, and he may already be dead."

"Yes, I'm sure. You came to help me, so we should go and help him if we can." Dylan finished as he started toward the downed plane. Payton followed not far behind, but then stopped.

"I'll find a vantage point up here and cover you while you investigate. I'll signal if I see anything coming." Payton explained to his brother.

"Right, I'll see what's up with pilot and then search for any supplies we might use." Dylan said over his shoulder as he started again at a trot down the beach. Payton turned around and climbed back to the top of the dune before finding a solid tree to hide behind that afforded him an expansive view in all directions. Using the Zeiss binoculars that he had taken off the Germans in the pill box on that first beach he resisted the urge to simply watch his brother and began to continually sweep the area for any signs of approaching complications. Every so often he snuck a peek at his brother, and by the time Dylan reached the plane Payton began to hold out a small hope for the other downed pilot.

Unfortunately, the feeling was not to last. Just as Dylan looked up from where he'd climbed to the cockpit and signaled his brother in the negative about the pilot and with hand signals indicated the hazard of a leaking fuel tank. Payton caught site of an approaching patrol a little less than a mile away and approaching fast from the road towards the beach. Dylan saw his brother wave frantically at him as he grabbed the small supply bag under the pilot's seat. He jumped down and ran over the pebble strewn beach as fast as his legs would carry him over the three hundred yards between him and his brother. Dylan thought

343

their only hope was if he could safely reach Payton and hide. Payton stared intently at the approaching patrol and knew it would be a close thing for Dylan to hide before he was noticed. Fortunately, the patrol seemed in no hurry to reach the beach. Payton considered a diversion to ensure his brother's escape, and decided he had to take the risk. If he could put a shot in to the plane's exposed and leaking fuel tank the ensuing explosion would surely allow them to escape, and hopefully startle any smart Wehrmacht soldiers enough that they would go directly to the plane and not discern the gunshot first and follow that sound. At worst, if the self-sealing fuel tank held up like it should, nothing would happen.

Payton took careful aim as his brother continued at a breakneck pace over the beach, thankful that the rocky beach meant no footprints for Dylan to leave behind. Payton exhaled a half breath and pulled the trigger. Only an instant after he fired he knew that his aim held true as the smoldering plane spewed forth a tremendous explosion that only a direct hit could deliver. Evidently the self-sealing fuel tanks had already ruptured well past failure, or such minor shot would not cause nearly the conflagration that leapt forth from the already damaged plane. Quickly picking up the Zeiss glasses and turning toward the patrol Payton first saw the men duck, and then race toward the sound of the explosion. Dylan arrived moments later, and the two beat a hasty retreat over the dunes and back to their southerly course.

"All I managed was his emergency pack, but I didn't look in it." Dylan said after the two felt far enough away and safe enough to stop for the night more than several hours later. The twins had settled on a dilapidated shed in the far corner of field that was the only building standing on an estate the Germans had shelled. The shed was barely more than a roof and four walls, but it was large enough to conceal the twins and remote enough to make any approaching sounds obvious. The roof overhead managed to keep out most of the sputtering rain, and the walls stored enough heat to obviate any need for a fire. As both twins felt raggedly tired, avoiding the search for firewood came as a welcome relief.

"At the very least we'll have a few bandages. Not much to show for the close scrape with that patrol." Payton conceded. "Let's have a look."

Dylan pulled the small canvas bag out from under his jacket and poured the contents on the floor in the waning sunlight. As Dylan suggested, two small medical kits fell out first. Each twin grabbed one for their pockets. Scissors, gauze, and tape certainly would come in handy, but hopefully not for patching up a wound.

The only other thing to fall out of the bag was a small chocolate bar. Without saying a word Dylan broke it in half and the boys enjoyed a meal for the first time since crashing in France. A small grin creased Payton's lips as he thought out loud "Not exactly dessert at the Savoy, but at least it is real chocolate and we don't have to share with the girls!"

Dylan laughed at the joke and returned his own "And at least we didn't have to steal it from the pantry at home, so Mom can't be mad at us either!" The small chuckles relieved the grimness of their situation enough that they reminisced some about their parents and home before both twins fell fast asleep, not even bothering to post a guard. Carentan lay only a morning's walk away.

CHAPTER 27

July 18ᵗʰ, 1940

Very few people knew where Timothy was at the moment, and that was just the way he preferred it. Other than the man on the boat with him, only his father knew exactly where he was going and why. In truth, running the boats in to Dunkirk exhilarated the small man, and he wanted to find that rush again. His new American friends inspired him, so all the while they flew above, Timothy discreetly inquired around London about ways he could make himself useful to the war effort, Ireland's neutrality be damned. In the end, his service came down to what he knew best, smuggling. After making the right connections; such as with Mr. Cain, Timothy now smuggled guns in to occupied France and the Resistance.

The man with him on the boat was named LeMark, and other than being French and part of the Resistance Timothy knew absolutely nothing about the man. This was their second such voyage, and the two survived the first so Timothy figured they made a good team. The taciturn Frenchman contrasted greatly with the boisterous Irishman, but both knew their work. Timothy handled the shipment and brought the boat, and LeMark handled the connections in France and captained the boat due to his local knowledge of the coastline that barely outpaced that of Timothy. Both men could accomplish the other's task if necessary.

In the early morning darkness, several hours before sunrise, LeMark looked hard towards the French coastline in search of the small inlet that the resistance covered with camouflage netting to hide the boat from the Germans as they unloaded the guns. The shipment was large enough that it would take several hours to unload by hand. Also complicating the timeline were the tides. LeMark dare not bring the boat close to shore under anything other than minimal steerage power, so they were at the mercy of the rising and falling tides. They timed their trip to arrive during the flood tide, and must hide the boats during the day and wait for the late ebb tide to slip away unnoticed.

"Where are we landing tonight?" Timothy inquired quietly as LeMark continued concentrating on the coastline.

"Carentan, contact is a family called Henri." LeMark answered quietly.

***

Payton and Dylan slept the sleep of the weary more so than safety allowed. They'd endured battle by air, escape from the beach with a gunfight on the cliffs, followed by their furtive and tense trip south punctuated with moments of frenzied fighting for their lives. Both twins slept well past sunrise, and only awoke at the sound of a medium size truck rumbling by. The sound woke Dylan and Payton with a start, but both had the presence of mind to stay silent as they abruptly woke from their deep slumber in case the truck led a German patrol. Payton signaled to his brother, and they each crept silently to opposite corners of the shed. They scanned the hedgerows around them through the openings between the slats of the shed.

"It's just a farm truck." Dylan breathed with a sigh of relief to his brother.

"Good, that was close." Payton replied. "Let's get some breakfast and get on the move." He urged his brother. "The longer we hide in a shed the longer we look guilty."

"Fine by me. I think our options for breakfast are sauerkraut or sardines." Dylan replied wryly.

"Let's make a feast and have both." Payton jabbed back. "I think we'll hit the outskirts of Carentan later this morning, and be in the town proper by lunchtime. We'll have to make reservations for our next meal." A grinning Payton said to finish the joke.

With the saltiest breakfast that either twin could remember down the hatch, the peaked out the shed again before embarking further in to the unknown. After working their way mostly west again for another two hours the twins began encountering the edges of Carentan. They'd strayed further from the coast to reach the town, but scarcely noticed as they'd been able to follow the road for most of the morning. The widely spaced farm houses turned in to small cottages marching towards the beach on sparsely lined roads. Once the cottages began packing together, they knew the center of town must be close at hand. The sun had yet to reach its full apex, so they had made good time, not that it mattered. They arrived almost directly west of Carentan half a day earlier than they anticipated.

"We're here, now what?" Payton wondered aloud.

"Two options that I can see." Dylan answered. "We can head for the coast and have a look around, or we can head for the center of town and see if we can find the Henri's."

"I'm not sure which will be more heavily patrolled, the coast or the town." Payton mused aloud. "I'm guessing we'll be less conspicuous in town though. I vote we head that way."

"I'll second that. We'd be more exposed than a failed suicide squeeze if we get caught on the beach a mile from town."

"Town it is then." Payton said with a flair as if they had just made plans for a double date with Clara and Anne. "I think we should stick together. Any roadblocks or alerts might only be for one person. If we are a pair they might not pay us any mind." Payton reasoned.

"I wasn't planning on leaving you." Dylan answered a little mischievously.

"Didn't Donna mention an old church with a spire when she described the town?" Payton asked after ignoring his brother's comment.

"Indeed she did. She said it covered one end of the town square." Dylan answered. "It would be a good place to get a bird's eye view of the town since we seem to be fresh out of airplanes for reconnaissance." Dylan answered continuing his mischievous streak that belied his buoyant mood. In fact, both twins seemed relieved to accomplish the first step in their escape plan. Step two still had yet to be fully defined, but they felt happy for being one step closer to returning to England, to getting back in the fight, and to holding their beloveds in their arms again.

***

Clara, Anne, Simone, and Jack gathered again a morning and a day after the first reunion and dinner. Jack sensed the pallor hanging over the three young ladies, and although he knew why he still tried his best to liven things up a bit.

"I know the three of you worked all day yesterday, but how about showing a young lad around London?" He asked.

"We promised to make plans together for the next day that we all had off, but never did." Simone said. "And I still haven't heard anything from Timothy in more than a week, so I guess I'm free if everyone else is." She finished. The other two girls assented as well, but more so out of a sense that that they needed to soldier on than anything else. Jack suggested a trip across the Thames to see Buckingham palace and Parliament at Westminster.

"I've never seen the Commonwealth seat of government, so I might as well see it now." He reasoned. "They certainly didn't get us in to this war, but perhaps they can find a way out of it for us." He thought out loud, though unconvincingly. The others agreed and scattered off to make themselves ready for a day out. Jack dressed quickly in his uniform, while Anne wore a pale blue, low wasted cotton dress with short cap sleeves and a sweetheart neckline under a yellow crocheted cardigan. She looked very much like the student she had so recently been. Clara wore a simple white short sleeve blouse with a slightly daring cut out and loosely tied neckline over a light grey wool summer weight pencil skirt, along with a bright emerald green cardigan. Simone took a little longer, and overdressed slightly in a full length empire wasted dress in a very faint lavender color better suited for early cocktails, but she seemed not to notice as she covered her shoulders with a velvet shawl. She seldom wore her full wardrobe anymore, so she was happy to dress up a little. Jack took no notice, and the girls enjoyed her elegance with no hint of envy.

The quartet walked through the chic neighborhood where Simone had spent all of her life (at least the part of her life when she was in London) and counted their blessings that the Luftwaffe had focused elsewhere. They knew from the patients entering their wards every day that the wounded were coming from the industrial east end, and around the Thames as their ordeal at the hospital had attested. They eventually found an underground station that took them under it all before they departed at a Westminster Station.

"Before the war I would never have taken the tube." Simone admitted guiltily.

"The war has changed us all, henceforth and forevermore." Jack mumbled in reply as if he were repeating something someone else had said.

"Two years ago I was contentedly studying art history." Anne said. "Now I think I'll go back to school and change to medicine. I see its power to heal now, the opposite of this bloody war. Funny, I just thought of that." She laughed slightly at herself. "And here I am, walking towards Buckingham Palace with a fantastic art collection. I just can't bring myself to care. We didn't get to see much of it when we saw the king and I don't mind so much now."

"You saw the king?" Jack asked, incredulously.

"Yes, with the boys." Clara responded somewhat sheepishly. It was amazing, but it also made her long for Dylan.

"Well, I would have thought that's a story you would have shared earlier." Jack said as he looked at his sister with a reproving frown.

"I'm sorry. It wasn't long ago, but it feels like ages. The king greeted us warmly and clearly felt strongly about the information the twins gave him. He's as worried as we are, and hopefully he can do something about it." Anne answered.

"Well, if you've been to Buckingham Palace, then let's move along to Westminster." Jack suggested. All agreed and they kept walking past the guards in their tall black fur hats and red uniforms.

"Simone!" The quartet heard from behind. "I haven't seen you in ages!" As they turned all saw Maggie waving happily in their direction. "What on earth are you doing down here?" She finished.

"We were headed to Parliament to have a look around." Simone answered. "This is Clara, Timothy's sister. This is another friend of ours, from Canada, Anne Fields and her brother Jack." Simone continued by way of introductions.

"A pleasure to meet you all." Maggie replied, with a sideways glance at Jack admiring either his uniform or the man inside it. "I'm just coming from the war department. Father is doing some job there and he's asked me to fill in for his secretary this morning while her husband is home on leave."

"How very kind of you." Jack returned the glance and comment charmingly. "What does your father do for the war department?"

"He works for a department on Baker Street, but I can't tell you much other than that." Maggie answered.

"Ah, excellent. I know of the group. The Baker Street Irregulars. We fed them information while I was in France and they gave us back very useful information as well." Jack replied in a way that implied he knew the function of the department without letting his mouth runaway with itself. In fact, Baker Street was the headquarters of the Special Operations Executive, or the SOE. The Ministry of Ungentlemanly Warfare was in charge of espionage, sabotage, and raiding parties. There was precious little they could do now to stop the Luftwaffe as it flew overhead, but any network of informants tipping off bombers taking off or saboteurs disabling ground equipment or airfields could help tilt the odds on any given day.

"Father just pops in on them. He keeps an eye on the group as a member of the House of Lords for Uncle Winston."

"Uncle Winston?" Anne asked.

"She does mean Churchill." Simone giggled. "Their families are old friends."

"It does seem odd, we've known him since we were little girls." Maggie said.

"Nothing surprises me anymore." Jack laughed. "First the king and now the Prime Minister. Anne, we are out of our league here. We're used to running around a ranch!"

Anne and Clara exchanged glances, as they had for most of the morning. They'd enjoyed the distraction, but every time they glanced at each other both thought a variation on the same thing: I'd rather be with my love.

***

As they drew closer, the coastal town of Carentan seemed almost deserted. With no one to ask for directions in their dead giveaway English, and only a smattering of German and no French, the two followed a wide canal further south and west from the coast until they found a main thoroughfare. The twins slouched in to town as inconspicuously as they could, and managed to avoid arousing any suspicion mostly because they only saw a group of school girls and an older couple walking through the square as they made their way to what they hoped was the center of town and the town square. As soon as they crossed the canal (which they had no idea the name, all the signs had been removed to slow the Germans, and not replaced to slow any future British invasion) Payton spotted the spire towering over the flat brick buildings that constituted the urban core of Carentan.

As they shambled down the road they hoped led to the church, the twins passed a monument about 20 feet high. On the top of the pedestal stood a winged goddess wearing a helmet and wrapped in traditional robes. She reached forward with her right hand as if urging the twins on in their journey.

"Perhaps that is lady liberty herself. Place de La République, Carentan it says." Dylan muttered lightheartedly.

"I don't think so." Payton answered quietly in case anyone was within earshot. "The only part I can make out on the statue base is 'La France, 1916-1918.' That means it must have something to do with the Great War. I think she's raising her hand in victory." He observed as they continued on without stopping.

A few minutes after they passed the monument they came upon a massive stone church. Romanesque arches and peaked windows nearly covered the front façade as the spire stretched out to the sky from the middle of the building. Built in the 11th century, Notre Dame de Carentan still left the twins awestruck as an exquisite piece of architecture. Columns and carvings ornately decorated nearly every inch of the church and the roofline was magnificently decorated in front of several smaller arched peaks coming off the main roofline like freshly dug rows in a field waiting to be planted.   At the main peak above a stunning large window which must have shed light on the main nave of the church, stood a statue of an angel, a cherub really, so small and innocent that it surely hadn't noticed the war around it.   The conical shaped spire stood maybe four stories high at the peak, but still stood high above the rest of the mostly squat coastal town. Without saying a word the twins agreed that it was indeed a magnificent piece of medieval architecture, and the perfect place to celebrate Jesus Christ. They took a moment of prayer, without interrupting each other.   They prayed that the other would make it out alive, and that they would make it both back to England for their beloveds, but also someday back to Oregon in a world at peace. A sense of calm settled over them, and as if on cue, they headed for the west door, the main entry to the church.

At best, they sought a friendly, English speaking priest. At worst, they hoped no one was inside, but of course it could be much worse if Wehrmacht soldiers took the time to seek communion or confession. As they approached the door, Dylan stopped momentarily

"Should we both go in, or should one of us keep a lookout here in case something goes wrong?" he queried his brother.

"We are in France, so the Musketeer motto shall rule, All for one and one for all." Payton replied glibly. "In we go, and pray for the best."

Payton pushed open the massive church door and walked in as naturally as he could muster. At first, the church was quiet and dark. As their eyes adjusted to the dim light and their ears adjusted out of the wind they could see the large nave, and the door to a small vestry off the side, but still no one to be seen or heard. Not wanting to rouse anyone for any reason, the twins remained silent. Payton thought about the layout of the church they observed from outside and took a guess at the general location of the stairs to the central spire. After motioning Dylan to follow, he strode down the right side of the pews and found a small door where he'd expected. Out of sheer luck, he found after opening the door quietly, Payton did indeed find the stairs leading skyward.

Dylan followed his brother through the door and closed it quietly behind him, not at all impressed that his brother found the stairs so quickly. Taking the stairs two at a time the boys reached the landing atop the church before the spire began to narrow. They could go no higher. Feeling relatively sure no one could hear him, Dylan took his turn in charge.

"You look west out over the town, and I'll look east. Stay low so we aren't spotted, and then circle round clockwise back to the door. I'll go the opposite to minimize our exposure." Dylan instructed. Without hesitation Payton nodded agreement and followed his brother out on to the landing. Dylan followed his circuit quickly, keeping his head down and noting anything of interest. As he scanned down near the statue they'd passed his heart sank. What appeared to be company of Wehrmacht soldiers marched in their direction and began to spread out in search of something. He hoped it wasn't them.

With only his eyes over the parapet, Payton quickly scanned out towards the ocean, and then worked his way around his side of the spire. He didn't see the soldier that Dylan spotted, but he stopped, nearly frozen and dumbstruck for a moment before as he followed a small road out towards the sea and a small truck bumping up the road towards the town. He quickly pulled out the Zeiss binoculars to confirm his first intuition about the redhead in the truck. With only a moment to recover he scurried back to door and met Dylan.

"I think we're in trouble." Dylan reported first. "There's a company of soldiers headed directly to the church."

Still a little dazed from his discovery, Payton answered "I think I saw Timothy in a truck coming up the road from the beach.

CHAPTER 28

July 18ᵗʰ, 1940

"Thank you, Monsieur Henri, for the ride in to town." Timothy said in nearly flawless French to his host driving the truck. The man was not much older than Timothy, but his hard blue eyes indicated the daily strain of fighting the Germans. He was tall and lean with wavy dark brown hair offsetting the blue eyes.

"You are most welcome, Monsieur O'Ryan. The Parisians would never say so, but your French is excellent. Where did you learn it?" his host asked.

"Mostly from pirates and thieves, sir, but also a little bit at Trinity College."

Timothy joked.

"Funny thing about languages, one learns to speak them best out of school, and please call me Joseph." Monsieur Henri replied in perfectly clipped public school English.

"The pleasure is mine, Joseph. Please call me Timothy. Where did you learn your English?" Timothy inquired.

"Oxford. Papa was determined to give us all a worldly education. My sister, thankfully and Bless the Lord for it, is studying safely in Canada at the moment, at McGill." Joseph answered.

"I just met someone from McGill. Ann Fields, she's the girl of one of my American mates flying spitfires." Timothy thought out loud, wondering at the connection.

"I know that name!" Joseph nearly shouted, his heard eyes softening with a bit of glitter behind them. "She's friends with my sister. They study together. At least that's what the letters home say."

"Small world, and getting smaller." Timothy answered before looking ahead on the road.

Several German soldiers stood in their path, erecting a crude roadblock.

"No trouble, I'm sure." Joseph said without conviction.

As they slowed to a halt next to a Wehrmacht corporal he motioned for them to turn off the engine and get out of the car.

"Papers, please." The Coporal demanded imperiously. Joseph handed his papers over easily, as they were authentic German issued papers showing him to be a resident and farmer who occasionally brought his produce in to town for sale or use by the Germans.

Timothy, just as casually handed his papers over as well. Joseph Henri admired the nonchalance with which Timothy handed over his surely forged papers. Of course, Joseph didn't know that Timothy had been dealing in forged papers for his whole life, or that these papers were the very best available. Timothy's papers probably looked more authentic than Joseph's. Whether German identity papers, or forged shipment manifests for their wine, or even officially stamped customs papers for whiskey delivered across the English Channel, Timothy had seen them all and knew he would have no trouble with this German conscript.

However, Timothy occasionally took a sideways glance and warily eyed the fat sergeant sitting to the side of the road on a tree stump. Timothy fervently hoped the red nose on the man meant his hangover could be counted on to keep him from rising off his stump to search the back of the truck. If he opened the flap and looked more than two boxed deep the load of Enfield Rifles, hand grenades, and two radio sets might get them shot immediately, or worse yet taken to the SS for interrogation.

Both the actual Frenchman and the masquerading Frenchman showed just the right amount of deference and irritation to the Corporal as he handed both of their papers back to them and waved them on.

Just down the road, Timothy sighed in French "Monsieur, we had a bit o luck there. Best get in to town and rid ourselves of this cargo. I've never seen a roadblock there before. Any idea as to why?"

"I heard two soldiers were shot up in Le Havre a couple of days ago, and the culprits escaped. The search may have expanded to here if they are still on the loose." Joseph guessed.

"Interesting." Timothy answered. "The enemy of my enemy is my friend. Anyone who shot a German must be on our side."

"Yes, perhaps." Joseph answered without another thought to the subject. "Carentan is ahead. We are almost there. You can see the church spire in the distance. Our destination is up the block from there."

***

"Who gets here first, Timothy or the soldiers?" Dylan asked immediately.

"Let's hope Timothy, but for now we need to get out of this tower and out of sight." Payton answered as we slipped back through the door to the stairs. Dylan never hesitated and followed his brother as they bounded down the stairs twice as fast as they had climbed them. The ruckus caused an elderly priest to investigate, and he nearly ran in to the twins as they opened the door in to the nave. Both boys grinned awkwardly at the kindly looking grey haired man and prayed hard that he would not raise any sort of alarm. The priest simply raised his hand, and made

363

the sign of the cross blessing both boys without a word. Using their limited French, both boys mumbled "Merci." and quickly marched to the front of the church. After clearing his throat to get their attention, the priest pointed toward the vestry, indicating a better way to exit.

The twins followed his instructions and exited in to a small side court fenced off from the ally. The gate door provided access to the ally, so the twins took a moment to listen for any telltale noises before slowly easing the gate open. They resumed their casual saunter up the ally, hoping no one noticed two workmen out strolling in the middle of the work day. As they neared the end of the ally they began to hear sounds that reminded them of their days at Westpoint: marching boots.

"Back up the alley?" Payton asked.

"Maybe they are a block over, let me peak around the corner to see." Dylan answered, and began to edge around the corner. Peering ever so briefly around the corner, Dylan saw an empty street. "Come on." He said to Payton before fully turning the corner and moving off with his head down.

Half way down the block Payton muttered "Might not have been our best choice, the boots sound like they are getting closer."

At just that moment, salvation appeared. The truck that Payton had seen from the church rounded the corner just in front of them. Payton recognized Timothy in the front seat as easily as he would recognize is brother. He grabbed Dylan and ordered a touch too loudly "Run!" but it came out as more of a grunt than anything.

Understanding his brother, and seeing the opportunity, Dylan scrambled to get even with his brother's head start as they ran for the back of the truck that began accelerating out of the corner. This was their only opportunity to catch the truck. If it pulled away they'd be stranded.

Payton jumped on to the bumper with one hand firmly on the bar holding up the canvas cover while he held out his other hand to drag his brother up. Their hands clasped and the combined momentum catapulted Dylan in to the tiny gap between the tailgate and the false front of produce. Payton quickly occupied the rest of the opening and pulled the flap shut over him.

Dylan snuck a look outside the flap to see that their escape had indeed been by the skin of their teeth. He saw the first of the soldiers appear around the corner opposite from where the truck had come. The soldiers began to spread out over the street and quickly made their way up the ally and in to the church.

To the twins dismay, the truck stopped not much more than a couple blocks from the church. They heard the driver downshift, and felt him pull in to another ally before hearing a large door open and the echo of a garage before the engine shut off.

"Best get out before we surprise poor Timothy and get ourselves shot." Dylan surmised as soon as the engine had died.

"Hold your hands up and go to the passenger side, in case the driver is jumpy." He finished.

The twins hustled out of their cramped, short lived escape truck and turned the back corner of the truck just as Timothy stepped down from the cab of the truck.

"Hello Timothy, good to see you again!" Payton said as casually as if in the bar of the Savoy.

"Oh Bloody hell! What are you doing here?" Timothy asked, flabbergasted, before regaining his composure. "It is nice to see you, but better circumstances might have been nice. How on earth did you get here?"

"We might ask you the same, but I'm guessing there are more than groceries in the back of the truck, so that might explain you." Payton offered.

"True, guns and such in the back." Timothy answered.

As Timothy finished Joseph stuck a pistol in Payton's back. "Keep your hands in the air, both of you." He said in his perfect English.

"You can put the gun away, Joseph. May I present to you the chaps I spoke of earlier, Messrs. Anders. Your gun is in the back of Payton and Dylan, over there inching toward you to try and knock you unconscious with whatever implement is up his sleeve, is his brother. Gents, this is Monsieur Joseph Henri."

"Henri!" Both boys exclaimed at the same time. "Do you know Donna Henri at McGill?" Payton got out before his brother.

"She is my sister! You've seen her?" Joseph said, but before they could answer he lowered his gun and hugged Payton like old family.

"We do, but we'd better do something about the guns in your truck before the Wehrmacht gets here. They started searching in the block of the church where we jumped on your truck. I don't know if they are looking for you or us. We crashed up near Le Havre four days ago. We met a little resistance and killed a soldier on our way out of town." Dylan said, heightening the urgency of their situation past the small world joy of finding friends.

"Yes, we must work quickly. It does not matter who they are looking for." The Frenchman answered as the twins took their first opportunity to look at where they actually were. The truck had pulled in to a large garage, but it looked more like the garage to a private house than to a commercial business. It barely held the truck, and there was just one door leading in to the main building.

"My great grandparents owned this house before us. They bought it as a business office to run the sales portion of the farm closer to town. The oversize garage has been very helpful over the years. We should have no trouble hiding everyone and everything. Fortunately, this is the last load out of the shipment. We only have four boxes of rifles and two more small boxes of the other supplies Timothy so kindly brought us. My compatriots should have scattered and concealed the rest already." Joseph said as he moved to the back of the truck and lifted the flap. He nearly jumped to the back and began unloading the produce to the twins and Timothy, who quickly stacked it off to the side with boxes that appeared similar and must have been used for the same purpose in the past.

"Follow me please." Joseph quickly commanded after he handed down the contraband. He led the quartet through the door in to the house, renovated to serve as an office and entertaining space, towards the kitchen on the opposite side of the house from the garage. In the kitchen he opened a door that disappeared in to the darkness below. As they reached the bottom the walls held rows of shelves indicating the little basement served as the pantry.

"Surely they'll search here." Timothy said skeptically.

"But perhaps not here." Joseph answered with a grin as he reached underneath the lowest shelf to reveal a small notch in the edge of a board that he pulled up giving way to an opening in the floor. With the floor board removed, a short ladder gave access to a cleverly concealed sub-basement. "Before there were refrigerators, this was the cold storage sub-basement." Joseph explained, indicating for the twins to climb down. Dylan climbed down first, and noticed the roughhewn wood walls holding back the earth that crept through between boards in several places. He felt like he'd climbed in to an abandoned mine, though the space was probably only eight feet square and barely tall enough for him to stand. Moments later Dylan accepted the first crate handed down to him by his brother. Not wanting to waste any time, Timothy and Joseph went back for the last two crates while the twins worked to lower the other three crates of rifles down into the sub-basement.

After the last of the crates were safely stacked in the sub-basement, Payton followed his brother down the ladder. Joseph lowered the cover, which blocked out most of the light to the twins.

"Off to the salt mines, I suppose." Payton joked quietly.

"As long as we don't stay six feet under, I'll take it." Dylan responded wryly.

While the twins were cracking wise, Timothy reached in to the very much above ground refrigerator and pulled out two bottles of beer and plopped them on the table to show two workers casually taking a break.

"No, wine." Joseph ordered as they heard an ominous knock at the door. Timothy scrambled to make the correction so they appeared as two Frenchman and poured the wine as Joseph headed for the door. Although he expected them, it was still a shock to see the three German soldiers standing on the doorstep.

"Monsieur, we are looking for gun runners." Said the oldest looking of them, in halting French. "Step aside while we inspect your house." Joseph judged he couldn't have been much more than 19 or 20 years old, but showed the proper deference.

"Of course, come in. Search wherever you like. We don't want any trouble." Joseph answered in passable German.

"Danke." Replied the boy, looking more relieved that his French would no longer be called in to use than he was at the lack of resistance. One private went to the upper floor to look, while the nominal head of the operation/translator stood guard over Timothy and Joseph drinking their wine in the kitchen. The third boy rummaged through the main floor. When the other two reported back after finding nothing, the head boy asked a question of Joseph: "What is behind that door?" and in doing so began to regain some of his air of authority.

"The Pantry is just down the stairs behind that door." Joseph answered concealing the uneasiness he felt with so thorough a search.

"And where is the door to the garage?" the head boy asked as well.

"Down the hall, back that way, on the right." Joseph indicated by pointing behind the three Germans. Now feeling fully in command, the head boy indicated to his two subordinates to further search both places. Had it not been a dead giveaway, Timothy and Joseph might have held their breath as the soldier descended the stairs in to the pantry.

As they heard the stairs creak above them, the twins both instinctively held their breath for just a moment. They held every other muscle in their bodies absolutely still. The floorboards creaked, and a shadow cast over them for what seemed like an eternity. A can fell from one of the shelves almost directly above them, nearly startling the twins, yet they stayed resolutely quiet. Both saw the German soldier through the small cracks in the floorboard as he bent over and picked up the fallen can, and prayed that he would not see them. A moment later their prayers were answered. The soldier stood up, replaced the can on the shelf, and backtracked to the stairs to meet his comrades above. The creaking on the floorboards confirmed their safety, and the boys let out small, soundless sighs of relief.

Several minutes later, after much shuffling and a door slam emanated to the sub-basement, Timothy creaked down the steps and lifted the floor boards. The twins emerged and shook Timothy's hand.

"No problems?" Dylan asked.

"Never are!" Timothy lied enthusiastically through his teeth.

"What next?" Payton followed up.

"That, my good friend, is up to Joseph. I have a boat well-hidden at the coast that I had planned on sailing out with the tides in an hour or so, but I'm not sure we'll make it past our German friends to make it in time. Unless Joseph has a trick up his sleeve to get us there, LeMark, my partner, will sail and we'll be stuck here for another two weeks, at least." Timothy summed up.

"How far is it from here to the boat?" Dylan inquired.

"I'd say about five miles, by road. Maybe a shade less than that over land. I'm not worried about the distance, I'm worried about the Germans." Timothy furnished.

"I'd suggest, my friends, that going for the boat is your only chance. With the enhanced searches, such as we just experienced, I don't believe we can hide two non-French speakers in town for very long. I've heard rumors that the Germans intend to close the beaches, but that isn't the case yet. I think I have a plan." Joseph grew more confident as he spoke, and a faint smile broke out across his lips as he motioned for the others to follow him.

CHAPTER 29

July 18th, 1940

"Have you finished your duties for your father for the day?" Jack asked the leading question of Maggie, still standing outside Buckingham Palace.

"Why, yes I have, I was just headed out for some lunch then back home." Maggie answered, taking the bait.

"Would you mind terribly showing us around Westminster and Parliament then? I'm terribly keen to see it." Jack only half lied. He wanted to see it, but perhaps he was more terribly keen on Maggie.

"Of course, I'd be happy to. I don't think they are in session, but I can show you around the building." Maggie graciously answered.

With that, the newly formed quintet made their way to Parliament. Along the way several younger lads noted Jack's crisp uniform and quartet of beautiful companions with more than just a little hint of envy. He might as well have been a recruiter for the army as they walked jovially along the sidewalks in an otherwise shell shocked city. To look at them, one would think the war was well in hand.

After the short walk to their destination, Maggie gamely showed her friends around the famous legislative building. She showed them the empty chambers from the visitor's balcony, explaining this was where the debates and legislation took shape. She then took them down the long halls of individual Members of Parliament's office suites. Staffers hurried around them amongst the hallways, and except for the ornate building and decorations it may have been nearly any busy, prosperous office building in the city.

As they finished their personal tour, a rotund man in a well-tailored grey pinstriped suit and a neatly clipped mustache. "Hello, my lovely, I thought you'd gone off home for the day." The man said, addressing Maggie.

"Hello Daddy, you know Simone, and these are her friends, Clara O'Ryan of Dublin, Anne Fields, and her brother Jack Fields from Canada. Everyone, may I present the Baron of Dover, my father, Sir Gregory Fitzwater."

"A pleasure, sir. I've crossed paths with some of your men at Baker Street while I was in Normandy." Jack said, bowing slightly and offering his hand to the older man.

"Excellent, a fellow ungentlemanly warrior." Sir Gregory said with a smile.

"If you don't mind me asking, sir, what's your connection? How did you get in to this line of work?"

"My father was a minister in the House of Lords before me, so that's how I ended up here. For the irregulars, I'm good friends with Sir Charles Hambros, of the banking family that we do business with, who introduced me to Lord Hankey, who set up the outfit for Sir Winston. Then, those two scoundrels introduced me to Sir Frank Nelson, the head of the department. Turns out Hambros is his man for Scandinavia at the moment, and they recruited me to keep an eye on France over the last couple of months. It's all very new, and secret, so I'd appreciate your discretion." Sir Gregory summarized quickly.

"Of course, not another word, my apologies." Jack offered sheepishly.

The old man took another look at the group and settled his gaze on Clara. "My dear, did I hear correctly that your name is O'Ryan of Dublin? Perhaps with a brother named Timothy?" he asked several questions at once.

"Why, yes, on all counts." Clara answered, too surprised and disarmed by the charming man to let out one of her normally clever retorts.

"If he hasn't told you, and he seems like a good chap so he hasn't, he works for me." Sir Gregory said with a twinkle in his eyes. "He's probably in France right now."

"Timothy! In France?" Clara said, astonished. "I thought he'd stopped going over after Dunkirk. One more loved one under the thumb of the Germans, if they are even still alive." Clara said with a resigned tremble in her voice. Although she couldn't find her voice, Anne clutched Clara's arm and held her close so as to support each other physically and emotionally.

"They?" Sir Gregory asked with a raised eyebrow.

"Payton and Dylan." Simone interjected.

"The Americans Caroline and I met at the Savoy with Simone, Daddy." Maggie said to jog his memory.

"Yes sir. Two American fellows, pilots. They crashed four days ago around Le Havre." Jack added. "They also seem to have taken the hearts of my sister and Timothy's sister with them."

"I heard reports that a couple of unknown actors shot their way out of Le Havre two days ago." Sir Gregory said. "Let's hope it's your boys making an escape. My contacts haven't heard anything about captured pilots, so they must still be on the loose. If I hear anything else, I shall let you know. Also, Captain Fields, if you are interested in some work, please come see me at Baker Street. I'd be interested to hear your assessment of the coastline. For now, I'm off to a meeting. A pleasure to meet you all." Sir Gregory finished as the rest of the group murmured their goodbyes, still shocked by all the news, and the sudden injection of hope.

***

Joseph led his three compatriots/charges out the back door after grabbing a medium size duffle bag. Once through the garage, to assure no more Wehrmacht soldiers lingering about would spot them, he kept to the allies and led them back to the block with the church. Instead of going in the house of worship, he led them around the block to what was unmistakably a school. He entered one of the side doors with the practiced ease of someone who had done so many times.

"I went here as a child." Joseph mentioned off handedly, but then remembered their mission. "But, that is not why we are here. My wife teaches here, follow me." He commanded as they wound through the hallway to a door on the left.

Joseph barreled through the door without knocking, and immediately smiled upon seeing his petite wife seated behind the teacher's desk. As she stood the visitors saw a slightly short woman with dark brown hair, dark brown eyes, and slightly Mediterranean features. She wore a fashionable long sleeve, mid-length, yet slightly worn, navy blue dress with chalk dust around the elbows.

"My love, you work too hard. Let's go to the beach, right now." Joseph said coyly in French. "Gentlemen, my wife, Genevive" Joseph said in English turning to his own charges.

"The pleasure is all ours." Timothy said in French with a slight bow. "Unfortunately my heathen friends here only speak English." He finished while indicating the twins.

Finally given the chance to speak, Genevive said "Joseph, what have you gotten yourself mixed up in this time?" She spoke as if to one of her students, but slightly more exasperated because she was speaking with her husband.

"Just some friends that we need to help get back to the beach. Those two are American pilots, and this one with the smooth tongue is one of our delivery men from across the channel." Joseph answered cheekily, but truthfully.

"Then why are you here asking me to go to the beach?" She demanded.

"If you don't mind, let's round up some of your single teacher friends to go with us. We'll hide in plain sight and just walk down to beach like we are taking the afternoon off. But we must hurry, we've only an hour to get them there."

"Joseph, that is a terrible idea." Genevive stated matter of factly. "We can't get everyone rounded up and in to believable beach attire that quickly, and we would put all of them at risk. Someone must be above reproach at this school to look out for the children." Joseph shrugged his shoulders and gave the half admiring, half amused look of a highly accomplished man who had an even more highly accomplished wife. "Gentlemen, if you would follow me." Genevive continued in English as she walked out from behind her desk. "I think I have a better idea, but we must move quickly."

"Thank you, Madam, my name is..." Payton started, but Genevive waved her hand at him briefly wishing to speak.

"Please don't tell me your names, I don't need to know them." She said firmly, showing her full grasp of the precarious situation. "Underneath the school is a basement, with a tunnel that goes underneath the church. From the church basement, we can access the old roman aqueduct tunnels that run along the river. From there we can emerge on the outskirts of town and follow the foot trails over the hills to the coast."

"That's amazing." Timothy said, utterly astonished by the quick wit and brilliant sounding plan.

"Did I not tell you about my brilliant wife." Joseph beamed. "Perhaps I forgot to mention that..." he trailed off.

"Ma'am, one question, please?" Dylan said, nearly raising his hand to ask the teacher.

"Yes?" she responded naturally.

"How do you know about all of this? I don't doubt it will work, but it almost sounds too easy." Dylan said in the most deferential way he could manage.

"I'm hoping it is that easy. This is how we used to sneak out of school as girls to go to the beach when I was young." Genevive replied with a gleaming smile, remembering the better days as she strode out the door.

All four men followed the teacher down the hall without hesitation and stayed close as she descended to the basement on a rickety set of wooden stairs. They moved passed the boiler for the school and in to a tight, low ceiling passage lined with bricks. The twins produced three small flashlights for all to use, one each from their flight kits and a third from the plane they'd scavenged on the beach. Genevive continued ahead until a few minutes later, when a forbidding timber door to the church basement with steel straps blocked their path.

Undeterred, Genevive simply looked at her husband and nodded as she said "Joseph, the door please." Without further urging Joseph used his sturdy work boots and kicked open the door with a single blow. The quintet then quickly crossed the basement and followed their leading lady down a half flight of stairs that seemed to lead nowhere.

"This is the tricky part." She said, indicating a round grate drain at the bottom of the stairs. She looked at Joseph again, who bent down and removed the grate. "The key, to avoid detection, is for the last person to replace the grate. We used to bribe one girl to stay behind, but that won't work here." She stated. "The drop is not far, maybe three meters. We'll figured something out." Genevive finished before hanging her legs over the side and sliding off feet first in to the dark hole. After a soft splash, she signaled for the next person to follow. Timothy heartily followed the intrepid woman with Joseph coming next.

Payton and Dylan hesitated, examining the problem of the grate as best they could.

"Go next." Payton said to his brother. "I'll slide the grate as close as I can and then try to grab it from underneath and pull it over before I fall. I might look like I'm on monkey bars, but I think it will work. If not, at least I'll have it far enough over that we can put Timothy on our shoulders to move it over."

Dylan never said a word and proceeded down the hole. Payton followed, and with his legs hanging in the abyss he used his body weight to pull the grate after him. He managed to get the grate halfway over the opening before lowering himself down with a hand on each side of the rim of the hole. Hanging from one arm, he used all his strength to pull the grate further in to place until just enough space was left for him to pull his other hand under the grate. Payton pulled himself close to the great, and then with one quick, jarring push used his swinging momentum to jump the grate up and over in to place.

After Payton fell to the ground Dylan said "I guess all those pull ups they made us do finally came in handy!" with a grin.

"Other than being noisy, that worked. Follow me please." The no-nonsense Genevive said, bringing everyone back on task as only a teacher of wayward students could. She set off at a brisk walk, and the men had to half trot to catch up with her along the dry sides of the aqueduct.

After catching up with Genevive, the twins explored the tunnel with their torches. Long past use, no water ran through the tunnels save for a damp, slim stream of condensation down the middle of path. The ceiling vaulted in an arch above their heads, cresting at over 9 feet, just as Genevive had said. The stonework lining the walls and ceiling were a dark slate grey from lack of sunlight and worn smooth from the centuries of flowing water before the French had installed their own modern water works. Both Americans admired the engineering and precision construction involved in building such a tunnel with only primitive tools centuries before this group laid eyes on it. Now, they had to use it as a tool to escape.

***

"After the tour, I believe you still owe me lunch." Maggie said to Jack playfully as they walked out of Parliament in to Westminster. "And, I'm quite famished." She added. Clara,

Simone, and Anne followed them out of the broad doors and down the steps out on to the street where the post midday sun shone brightly before them.

"How ungentlemanly of me. Of course, where shall we go?" Jack responded back in a very serious tone.

"I think it's a lovely idea to have lunch out, but I'm not terribly hungry at the moment." Anne said, leaving unsaid that she wasn't hungry because of their brief meeting with the Baron of Dover and his news about all three of the boys in France.

"I'm not either." Clara added. "I'll go with you on the underground back to the house." She offered.

"I'll join you." Simone said to the two girls because she didn't much feel like eating and felt even less like being the third wheel for the burgeoning interest between Jack and Maggie.

"Suit yourselves. Lead on Mademoiselle." Jack said without a hint of regret as the others left. So, Jack and Maggie walked away flirtatiously close.

"We may have trouble with those two." Clara noted as the three girls walked toward the underground entrance.

"I've never known Maggie to take such a shine to anyone." Simone added. "She is usually such a snob about men and bats them away with a stick." She finished with a small giggle.

"She seems lovely. Jack usually has good taste in women." Anne said of her brother.

"Good for him, after the horrid ordeal in France I'm sure most any company is welcome." Clara added.

"She is lovely," Simone said "but you two are more so. She didn't catch the eye of either of your men the first night we met. Timothy had invited me to dinner and said to bring two friends, so I brought Maggie and her sister Carolyn. That was when I met Payton and Dylan. We had a splendid evening, but no sparks flew between the twins and the Fitzwaters."

"I'd wondered what she meant when she told her father about the American's at the Savoy." Anne mused.

"They were perfect gentlemen, but I half expected to never see them again after that night." Simone said with a shrug. "I was a little disappointed, and quite frankly so were the Fitzwaters. However, with Jack in tow it seems there will be no rivalry."

"I don't think it would be an issue anyway." Clara offered as they settled in to their seats on their train. "The way Dylan looks at me makes me feel safe even amongst this chaos. He's not just handsome, he's kind and devil may care exciting. I can't really describe it but the first time I saw him I knew it, even as his twin stood next to him I knew he was the one. I just wish he wasn't so brave. Then he would be here and not lost in France." Clara nearly sobbed out the last few words.

"I know how you feel." Anne continued her line of thought quietly. "You'd think that they are so alike that you could fall for either of them easily enough, but Payton is the one I knew I'd love. I agreed to meet them again after only meeting them for a moment. I would never do that, but Payton had such intelligent eyes, and such a passion for making this world right that I couldn't say no. He makes me see things differently, through his deeply thoughtful words and his truly caring actions. I just want him back. I want all three of them back for all of us, so we can all have a future together." Anne finished, fighting back tears but with a resolute statement declaring the future for all of them. Neither Simone or Clara objected, and they rode quietly back to the house. These women rarely cried or fought back tears. They were strong, independent women. The Germans, that devil Hitler, and their war brought about theses trying times that tested even the strongest wills.

***

The small group continued to follow Genevive through the maze of tunnels, making sure to stay close to her quick turns left and right. The pace quickened, but to the twins amazement the aqueduct remained the same throughout. No growing or shrinking, just standard uniformity throughout. The engineering was marvelous, they thought again, but the navigation would fall somewhere past impossible without Genevive.

At last, they saw the literal light at the end of the tunnel and nearly ran to the drain run out. However, as they approached the daylight the men saw heavy steel bars blocking their path.

"What now?" Timothy asked anxiously. Without answering, Genevive walked to the prison like bars on the far right of the tunnel and reached through them, under the lip of the tunnel structure sticking out slightly above a small pond below. She felt around momentarily, then muttered a small curse to herself before standing and walking to the far left set of bars. She repeated the process, but this time came back through the bars with a four-foot length of rebar and a medium size rock. She walked back to the right side of the tunnel and tapped the rock carefully along the bottom of the penultimate bar from the edge. Once she found her spot, she rapped the stone against the bar as hard as she could.

Dylan saw immediately that the bar had dislodged slightly from the base and walked forward to help by pulling opposite of her strikes.

"Not that way, it won't move. Hold the rock against the next bar, please, here." Genevive ordered Dylan. He followed her directions and held the rock about two feet off the ground against the third bar. Genevive wedged the four-foot length of rebar between the rock and the outside of the third bar. She then tugged on the end of her little lever mightily until the bottom of the prison bar move aside by two feet. With a smile and a flourish Genevive turned and accepted the applause of her companions for the ingenious use of the simplest tool.

As he clapped, Timothy quoted Archemides "Give me a big enough lever...and I will move the world."

"Well done, I thought we might be at the end there for a moment." Payton added lightly.

"Let me go first. I'm the smallest." Timothy said, not thinking of the diminutive Mrs. Henri. Timothy deftly slipped between the grates and slithered down the small embankment to the pond. After a moment of scouting, he returned to the opposite sides of the bars and reported back. "I know where we are, I can lead us from here. No sense in the Henri's being seen in public. Merci and bend the bars back in place once the twins are out." He concluded.

Without another word the twins slipped through the bars, far less deftly due to their size. However, both scraped through after a little more pulling on the bar.

"Godspeed, my friends. Au Revoir." Said Joseph. He slipped the duffle bag off his shoulder, and handed out three short stock carbine rifles to supplement the handguns the boys carried. Each rifle had two clips, which was enough. If they needed more than 30 shots between them hey weren't going to make it anyway. And with that, Joseph and his wife disappeared back down the tunnel from whence they came.

"Do you really know where you are going, or are you just trying to save them?" Dylan asked Timothy immediately after the Henri's departure.

"A little of both." Timothy said jovially. "The beach is west, and we are west of town, so it shouldn't be too hard to figure out. The cove where we unloaded is just south of the main headland, so it shouldn't be too hard to find once we get to the coast."

"With only 40 minutes we best be on our way, then." Payton said stridently. He knew Timothy was right, but also would have appreciated the help of the Henris. With no margin for error, the trio needed all the help they could get. With no better option, he began walking around the pond.

For the first time, the triumvirate looked around the edges of the small pond. They found themselves marching along the sunken shell of a small dell about forty feet across, with high grass at the top, and the thirty-foot pond forming the bottom of a bowl about eight feet deep. The edges of the bowl sloped gently up, so traversing the sides proved no problem. As they approached the far edge, a well-worn path appeared to apparently mark the best exit. Payton held up his hand indicating for the others to stop as he crept up the edge of the bowls rim to scout for any German soldiers. Peeking just his head above the lip of the pathway, Payton saw nothing. He stood to his full height and motioned the group forward.

Mrs. Henri had been true to her word. The trail led the group to the beach in less than a quarter mile. "South is left, I believe." Timothy smiled triumphantly as he started out for the sandy expanse.

Before Timothy took a step, though, Dylan grabbed his shoulder and indicated quietly for the group to stick in the high dune grass. "More concealment." Payton added under his breath. Even in a low crouch, the three moved quickly until they couldn't anymore. Payton heard them first, the unmistakable sound of a Wehrmacht patrol. Of course, if they came to the town they would come to the beach as well. Boots scrapped against the sand like scouring paper, and German guttural voices rose above the crash of the ocean on the shore. Signaling the others to stay put, Payton crab walked to the edge of the dune. Burrowing as deeply as possible in the sand, he moved several large stocks of the dune grass aside. Immediately, he saw only a corporal and two privates walking slowing down the beach from the north. No older than the boys they hoped they didn't find, the soldiers marched briskly down the middle of the beach about a hundred yards north, and fifty yards west of Payton.

Moving only the necessary body parts, Payton slithered back to his companions and gave a quiet, concise report. "Three Wehrmacht, coming down the beach, we have about thirty seconds until they reach us."

"Stay hidden?" Timothy asked without much hope.

"No, even if they don't find us now they may find the boat or us again on their way back." Dylan surmised quickly.

"Work the compass. Shoot in 15 seconds" Dylan said before scampering north among the grass as he unslung the carbine from across his back.

"What does he mean by work the compass?" Timothy asked urgently as he saw Payton unsling his carbine and begin to move south at an angle towards the edge of the dune grass.

"Shoot the guy in the middle. 10 seconds." Payton said over his shoulder as the group became the smallest semblance of a fighting line.

Timothy shimmied down the dune until he could see his target, and lay prone in the classic soldiers firing position. He aimed, took a deep breath, and finished his count to ten before pulling the trigger. He heard only the bang of his own gun, but saw all three soldiers all to the ground. The three timed their shots perfectly. That's what they meant, Timothy thought after a moment. North shoots east, south shoots west, following the compass clockwise. They'd just left Timothy in the middle to shoot the soldier in the middle. Then, realizing he'd just shot some poor boy, Timothy nearly threw up.

Dylan emerged from his spot no more than twenty yards north and hustled down the beach.

"Run!" He shouted as he passed Timothy's position. When Timothy didn't move he double back quickly. Timothy sat up, in shock. Dylan grabbed him by the collar and shoved him down the beach. "You didn't have a choice, move now before the city patrols can get here. They heard our shots and are for sure on the way." Timothy came to his senses and began running, knowing his life depended on it. They soon caught up to Payton, who waited for them another twenty yards down the beach. With no attempt at hiding, they ran down the edge of the beach.

"The cove, where is it?" Payton asked urgently.

"The treeline, those dogwoods, just up around that bend. We're almost there." Timothy said nearly grinning ear to ear. His smile faded quickly as her heard loud intermittent pops coming from the dunes. Then, the repeating chatter of a German submachine gun. The three automatically began to zig and zag down the beach, hoping to throw off the fire of the Germans while gaining a little distance for themselves.

The sand kicked up by the approaching Germans crept closer and closer to the group. Payton yelled "Keep going!" As he executed a perfect bent knee baseball slide to stop himself. He popped up to one knee while pivoting in the direction of the fire.

He let loose with four precise shots, emptying his clip in to the advancing Germans. Two Germans fell, clutching their chests. The rest of the advancing squad immediately dove for the ground. Payton stood and ran in a straight line to catch up with Timothy and Dylan.

The three burst through the line of trees and saw the small pier below extending out to the open waters. LeMark, having heard the gunfire, had already cast off the lines and begun to drift away from the pier before applying the throttle. In desperation, the three ran faster than any of them thought they could go. Their boots pounded on the first planks of the pier as the Dylan began to pull ahead of Timothy's shorter legs. Payton followed behind, mostly caught up after his diversion.

Thirty feet from the end of the pier, Dylan leapt for the side of the boat. He landed cleanly halfway up the gunwale, but he knew the boat was gaining speed. Timothy jumped next, and landed just on the edge of the hull with only ten feet left on the pier. Payton, knowing that he was out of room, ran to the last corner of the pier before leaping with every ounce of strength remaining in his legs. Dylan scrambled back to the stern of the boat and reached for his brother. Payton reached forward as the boat accelerated away from underneath him and caught his brothers outstretched hand. Dylan pulled with all his might, and pivoted as hard as he could. The combined momentum swung Payton hard in to the side of the boat, but between holding on to his brother and reaching and arm over the side of the hull rail he managed to stick long enough for Dylan and Timothy to pull him in   with   only   up   to   his   knees   getting   wet.

LeMark burst from the wheelhouse to find out what in the devil had thumped on to his boat to find the three laying flat on their backs, gulping down huge mouthfuls of air in to their heaving chests.

"Sorry to be late, old chap." Timothy grinned between gasps. "Full throttle ahead, no need to let them take any more shots at us." LeMark shook his head, and returned to the wheel. The twins rolled over and assumed firing positions below the stern wall. The Germans, however, never got another shot off. By the time they'd cleared the tree line and could see the boat the sun was low enough in the sky to blind them, and the boat was far enough out to see to effectively put it out of range. The sun quickly sank below the horizon, and the boys all prayed grateful thanks for their safety, and quick return to England.

CHAPTER 30

July 19th, 1940

Just after midnight, LeMark pulled his boat in to the same Dover harbor that Timothy and the twins had used during Dunkirk, not much more than a month before.

"Home sweet home." Dylan cracked wry. "This must be our lucky port of call." He finished. Luck had run with them. No U-boat found them, or thought enough of the small fishing boat to waste a torpedo. They hadn't even bothered to surfaced and fire their deck guns. Maybe they thought the small boat was bait, ready to radio a torpedo plane or destroyer just over the horizon as soon as a U-boat revealed itself. In any event, the safe return to British soil seemed the greatest blessing possible. William the conqueror and his army they were not, but safely ashore all the same.

"What now?" Payton asked with exhaustion written all over his face. "Its only another hour and a half to London, if we can find our way." He finished.

"I wouldn't mind telling Clara I'm alive in person." Dylan said with a sly grin.

"You might be sorry. She probably found someone much better while you were gone. I'm sure any officer at the hospital would be happy to oblige replacing you." Timothy teased his friend. With the worry and tension left behind in France, the three resumed the normal good natured ribbing standard to their friendship.

"London it is then." Payton said before adding with true sincerity "Mr. LeMark, thank you for allowing us on your boat and bringing us back safely. I don't know what we would have done without you."

"It's my boat! Who do you think dragged you back here!" Timothy nearly shouted with mock indignation.

"Well then, Timothy, thank you for not getting us shot." Dylan said ruefully as all three burst in to laughter. LeMark just grinned, which was as close as he ever came to laughing.

After finding all cabs unavailable, either because they were busy picking people up at the pubs or because they knew discretion was the better part of valor and stayed home during the blackout, the trio left LeMark and walked in the general direction of the train station. Nearly an hour later, they found their way in to a small local train stop. Nothing more than a ticket office next to a platform the three happily noticed that their arrival barely preceded the northbound train they heard about a mile away.

Timothy quickly walked to the blacked-out ticket window and rapped on the glass. Almost as quickly, a small, bald, bespectacled man moved the blackout curtains aside and eyed the three strangers arriving in the middle of the night.

"London, please." Timothy said without indulging the man's curiosity.

"Papers, then." The man answered just as curtly.

"You gents might be in trouble. He wants passports to prove you didn't just sneak in the country. I'm getting on the train either way." Timothy answered cheekily while handing his passport over.

"Not a problem." The twins answered in unison as they dug in their pockets and produced their military ID cards. "We kept them in case we needed them, though probably would have been smarter to sew them in to clothes we borrowed." Payton finished.

The ticket clerk immediately brightened as he saw the RAF cards, but then a questioning looked passed over his face as he compared the cards to the two battered pilots in French farm peasant clothing.

"We were shot down in France, and just found a boat home." Dylan furnished by way of explanation without the clerk even asking.

"Yes yes, I heard something about that. Welcome home, I dearly hope you shoot down many more of those bastards." The clerk replied in a pleasant, professional tone despite the deadly sentiment. He then quickly issued three tickets and shut the curtain before they could even pay their fare. The three ran for the train as it began pulling away from the station and quickly collapsed in the third class cabin. All three fell asleep before the train had even left the city limits.

Back at the ticket office, the clerk watched through a slit in the curtain until he was sure the boys had all made their train. Then, he lifted the receiver on the phone and dialed a number he knew from memory.

"I've found them. They are on the 1:30 from Dover." Was all he said before he hung up.

***

The local train from Dover took much longer than estimated to reach London. However, Dylan, Payton, and Timothy never new it. They slept like logs the whole way, and only woke up when a kindly conductor saw London on their tickets and shook them gently as they pulled in to the station.

"Splendid." Timothy said as he stretched and walked down the train stairs to the platform. Dylan and Payton followed along groggily, the newly risen sun forcing them to squint out on the platform. As they exited to the street with no luggage, all three stopped dead in surprise. Mr. Smith, the King's chauffeur stood at attention next to his prized Lanchester limousine.

"Welcome home, my boys." Mr. Smith said with a smile and the slightest glistening of a tear in his eye. The standard British stiff upper lip forbade much more. "If you will follow me,

395

I will take you wherever you please. The King has put me at your disposal until I am to bring you to see him for luncheon at noon."

"How on earth did you know we were here?" Dylan asked in amazement.

"We don't even know exactly where we are!" Payton added with some exasperation.

"His Majesty learned of your disappearance from Sir Dowding. Sir Dowding had a Flight Sargent Quarles assigned along to your squadron to keep an eye on you, per the King's orders." Mr. Smith explained. "Once you went missing, the King ordered that all rail stations around Dover keep an eye out, in case you made your way backs across. We heard nothing until a ticket clerk in Dover telephoned early this morning. Thus, here I am, at your service."

"But of course." Timothy laughed merrily. "Can you take us to Lady Simone's then, please?"

"Yes, please." Payton said. "As I doubt the tailor is open this early, they will have to take us as we are."

The three fell in to the backseat of the limousine and waited impatiently, though politely, as Mr. Smith drove them through the surrounding neighborhoods. Even tired, they stared out the windows at the damage done by the Luftwaffe bombers. Though the bombers mostly attacked military targets, stray bombs still destroyed blocks like the tide destroys sand castles. Whole buildings and blocks reduced to mounds of rubble. The randomness of pristine blocks next to what looked like ancient ruins brought the bombing damage home in stark relief.

Sensing the changing mood, Mr. Smith commented "Its not as bad as it seems. We carry on, and thanks to you boys and your pilot friends we are giving more than we are getting from the Jerries." The small consolation felt good, and reignited the small spark of fight in the passengers.

"Britain must hold on." Dylan said forcefully. "Hitler must be stopped, on the shores here before we can go back and get him on the continent. We'll go back and fight. We owe it to the people we care about, the people that risked to get us back here." He finished with passion rousing him out of the all encompassing fatigue of the last few days.

Payton nodded agreement with his brother, and then like a child remembering candy in his pocket, he pulled out the papers they'd found in the first machine gun nest on the beaches in France. "We might start here." Payton said as he spread the sheaf of papers on the floor of the limousine. While running for their lives they hadn't bothered to look at what they'd picked up. Now, they poured over the papers.

The first, an order of battle, grabbed their attention immediately and struck them dumb all at once. It was titled "Operation Sea Lion."

"I don't know much, and I don't speak German, but this looks important." Timothy said first.

"It's an operational plan, from the Wehrmacht." Dylan said.

"It's their plan to invade Britain." Payton said quietly as he read down the page that consisted of unit strength, arms allotments, deployment plans, and objectives for the first hours of the Germans attempting to recreate 1066 ad and the Norman conquest.

"Wait, Payton, why would a machine gunner on the beach need these plans. They must be fake." Dylan said.

Payton didn't answer immediately, until he came to a paragraph on the bottom of the third page. "This is why." He said with a finger pointed at the section titled "Praxis und Probe"

"That means practice and rehearsal. They must be practicing the water landings on the beach we landed on."

"You landed, I crashed." Dylan joked, even amongst the dark mood.

"Yes you did. Germany is mostly landlocked. They must want to practice the amphibious assault before crossing the Channel. And it says here, the practice is tonight. They let the gunner know not to shoot his fellow Wehrmacht soldiers. Look, here is the map, along with the marked machine gun points."

"Mr. Smith, as much as I hate to say this, could we please re-route. Sir Dowding please. We need to order up an attack for this evening." Dylan asked.

"Of course." Mr. Smith responded, smiling like the Cheshire Cat. "I suspect he will be pleased to receive you. He's usually in early, so I'll take you straight away."

"Quite the find." Timothy mused with pride at his friends.

"Yes, if it proves true we might wreck their rehearsal and prove to the Germans that any crossing is a bad idea. At the very least hopefully it will delay them long enough to rebuild the army here after the Dunkirk debacle." Payton offered up his hopeful analysis in his own rehearsal of what he would say to Sir Dowding.

"What else have you got in those papers?" Timothy asked.

"I grabbed all the maps I could. Each of you grab one of these and see what they say." Payton handed each the last of the papers.

"Not much here." Dylan said immediately. "This was their attack plan around Dunkirk. Useful a month ago, but not much now other than to analyze their tactics."

"Mine might as well say Spain is Neutral. It's a map of southern France with a bold black line along the Spanish border. It must mean, stop here, do not attack." Timothy said a little dejectedly.

"One out of three isn't bad. Mine's a map of the French coast from Calais up through Normandy. It shows the temporary strong points, and I think these are the new to be built machine gun nests and artillery positions. It's their Atlantic wall to stop anyone from coming back to the continent. I don't know who to give this to, but I'm sure Sir Dowding does. That's two pieces of intelligence. Dylan, crashing might have been the smartest thing you've done." Payton teased his brother with a smile.

***

Nearly two hours later then they originally planned, Mr. Smith dropped his charges off on the steps of Simone's stately residence.

Fortunately, the visit to Sir Dowding resulted in at least three successes. The head of the RAF immediately saw the value in attacking the rehearsal and sent one of his deputies off in a hurry to make the attack happen. Medium bombers and ground support attack fighter planes would lay down a formidable barrage on the beaches that night. His only regret was that he couldn't get the Royal Navy destroyers to steam off the coast close enough to bombard the beach as well. That might have been too much of a giveaway and tipped the Germans to cancel the fake assault.

The second success, equally important, sent the what had become known as the Atlantic Wall map off to the intelligence department on Baker Street. Sir Dowding figured they would at least find a way to slow down the construction before passing the information on to the military planners for an eventual invasion when it came to that. In his understated way, Sir Dowding praised the boys for giving Britain a fighting chance to not just stay in the war, but win it. "Excellent Show, glad you are back." Said all that needed to be said.

Finally, the third success, meant less to the war but more to the twins as they stood before the door. Sir Dowding had arranged for a hot shower, some bandages for their small scrapes and cuts after living on the run, a meal, and clean pressed uniforms for the them to don before returning to their loves.

Even two hours later, the clock just crossed eight in the morning when Dylan quietly rapped on the door. Nobody said it, but all were thankful the house still stood proud and unbowed by the Luftwaffe attacks. A very professional butler opened the massive oak doors and showed not an ounce of surprise at the three military men standing on the front veranda.

"Please come in, the ladies are having breakfast in the dining room. I'll fetch them immediately to the drawing room." The butler intoned in a stately manner with his deep baritone.

"Thank you." They all mumbled as they shuffled in to the drawing room. Anticipation kept them standing, and before long they heard hurried footsteps coming down the hallway.

Clara burst through the door first. "It is you, thank God!" She said and nearly ran to Dylan, grabbing him tight with no intention of letting go.

"We do turn up like a bad penny." Dylan managed to say while holding Clara with equal lack of intention to disentangle the embrace.

Anne and Simone entered just behind Clara, with similar sentiments and actions. Outside of a few stifled sniffles amid held back tears, the room stayed quiet for a long time as the three couples relished the reunion. The spell broke when Jack entered the room, followed by Maggie. They both looked a little sheepish interrupting such a moment, even if wholly by accident. Payton politely responded first "Maggie, a pleasure to see you again. I don't believe I know your friend."

"That's my brother, Jack." Anne said by way of introduction.

"Captain Fields, it is certainly a pleasure to meet you." Payton said as he saluted and then shook hands with Jack.

"The pleasure is all mine." Jack answered. "Anne must be in heaven with your return, so anyone that makes my sister happy is all right by me. She has told me a lot about you over the last couple of days." He finished.

"She spoke of you often as well. I'm so pleased to see you here, alive and well if you don't mind me saying so." Payton responded.

"Not at all, I'm happy to be alive and well, too!" Jack joked back.

"You boys take nothing seriously." Simone chided mildly. "But, since we have the morning off, let's finish breakfast and then we'll worry about the rest of the day."

"That sounds splendid." Timothy immediately agreed.

"However" Payton interjected "We do have luncheon plans at noon."

"Plans?" Anne asked incredulously. "When did you get back? If you didn't come straight here you are in deep trouble."

"We got back to London at five this morning, and didn't want to wake you. The plans, however, were made for us before we even returned." Payton answered a little sheepishly.

"I'm sure they were." Clara replied, growing indignant as she looked at Dylan. "Now you are going to tell us that we are having lunch with the king. I don't care who it is, you aren't leaving my sight today."

"I don't know this for sure, but I'd say we are all invited. And yes, it is with the King again." Dylan replied casually.

"I can't believe I know you aren't joking." Simone replied. "Very well, ladies, we can finish breakfast and I am sure we will find something suitable to wear for luncheon."

***

The three women wore very fashionable gowns from Simone's closet. Simone wore a pale ivory clingy sheath with a slight train that clung and draped in all the right places. Anne wore a slightly more traditional yet highly elegant low necked gown in a very pale canary yellow that made her look like the radiant early morning sun. Clara had chosen a slightly daring high wasted gown with cap shoulders in a deep shade of merlot red that offset her hair splendidly. Maggie had rushed home and returned in a blue cap shoulder gown the color of pale blue moonlight. All four were a touch overdressed for midday, but none cared.

Captain Fields and the twins all donned their dress uniforms. Fortunately, Sir Dowding had provided these for the twins as well, and they were close enough to standard size to not require any tailoring. He would not allow his men to show up shabbily dressed to see the King. Timothy, eschewing the formal top and tails or formal morning wear, wore his tuxedo with a black bow tie.

Mr. Smith, as ever, arrived at precisely half past eleven. He smiled and said not a word when eight people piled in to the back of the limousine chattering happily like a flock of geese at a family reunion. Despite the daunting tasks ahead, this happy moment belonged just to them, just to the overwhelming relief and gratitude for the safe return despite its temporary status.

As they arrived at Buckingham Palace Mr. Smith merely opened the door without giving directions. Everyone except Jack and Maggie knew their destination already. They followed the butler quietly, following the rules of any library or museum, for which the Palace surely counted even if the monarch lived there. As they reached the anteroom to the Kings office chambers, his private secretary waved them through.

"He's been expecting you, and quite pleased to have you." The kind man said as they passed through the massive oak doors.

As if on cue, the king stood from behind his desk and motioned for them to join him on the richly upholstered sofa sets around an equally massive fireplace.

"I am so very pleased to have you here, safely returned from your, ah, travels I suppose." King Edward the VI said as he smiled graciously at his guests.

"Thank you, your Majesty. May I introduce you to Captain Jack Fields, of the Canadian army and Anne's brother, as well as Lady Margaret Fitzwater, first daughter of the Baron of Dover." Payton said as he glanced over at Simone, greatly relieved to see her smile and nod approvingly. He hadn't bungled the titles or introduction, so no hell to pay later.

"My pleasure to to meet you. Lady Margaret, I've met your father and have seen some of his work coming out of Baker Street. Quite remarkable. And Captain Fields, you must have come back over from Dunkirk?"

404

"Yes, your Majesty. I'm one of the lucky ones." Jack replied a little nervously.

"Indeed, we failed too many men over there." The King answered like he had a sour taste on his tongue. "I would like, however, a brief report of your activities. I've had the basic outline from Sir Dowding, but I'd like to hear anything else you have to add."

"Yes, your Majesty, of course. As you seem to know, we crashed on the beaches outside of Le Havre, and then made our way down to the Carentan where we met Timothy, wholly by accident, and hurried our way home. The most important things we saw were of course the maps, and the resistance building in France. The maps show Hitler is building an Atlantic wall, and that he is planning on coming across the Channel as soon as he thinks feasible. I would gather that he is just waiting for the Luftwaffe to soften us up." Payton responded.

"I would agree, your Majesty." Dylan added "And I would also add that the timing is important. If he can't get wound up for a crossing by early this fall, the weather in the Channel will hold him off until late next spring, at least. That time could be crucial to rebuild your Army."

"As for the resistance" Payton picked up where his brother had left off "it would appear that the French, at least on the coastlines, have no love for the Germans. They should be cultivated and supported for use when necessary. In other words, give Baker Street whatever they want." He finished.

Timothy shifted a little nervously on his feet at the last comment, and so did Captain Fields. "It would appear that we have a couple of recruits for you." Payton smiled widely as he said it.

"Of course, I'll put in a word with Sir Fitzwater, or perhaps you might, my dear?" The King said to Maggie.

"Of course, your Majesty. I would be pleased to help both my father and these men." She said with a twinkle in her eye. She clearly had designs on keeping Captain Fields close at hand.

"I already, informally, work with some of the Baker Street contacts, though would gladly make it a more formal arrangement." Timothy spoke up to avoid any confusion.

"He offered me yesterday as well, though I'm sure Maggie's kind words will surely help." Jack finished to round out the conversation.

"Excellent, and thank you, all. I think your assessment of the situation warrants action now, as you've persuaded Sir Dowding. We must destroy the rehearsal today, and then fight in the skies to the last pilot so Goring can't claim that we are softened up. Of that, I put the utmost faith in the RAF. We shall persevere, as we always have." The King said resolutely. "The Atlantic wall concerns me. Once we survive this, at some point we will have to get back to the continent. That may require America."

"Yes, sir. We agree." Payton said quickly, nearly not minding his manners.

"We'll report back as such to our contacts at home." Dylan added. "I'm sure General Bradley's interest will be piqued."

"Excellent, that was the answer I had hoped to hear. My sincere thanks for that." His Majesty responded before turning to the ladies. "Simone, Clara, Anne how are things at the hospital? Is there anything I can do to help?"

"That is very kind of you, your Majesty. As you can imagine we are dreadfully short of nurses, so anything you can do to lift morale and boost recruitment would be very kindly appreciated." Simone answered.

"Yes, of course, morale for both the patients and staff would greatly lift if you are able to visit." Clara said boldly, to which both Simone and Maggie looked somewhat horrified.

"Of course, that is a splendid idea. I'll have my secretary arrange it." His Majesty answered without ever batting an eye.

"Thank you, your Majesty, that will mean a lot to our patients and staff." Anne said "And it will mean a lot to their families. Everyone has a piece in this, all over the empire."

"Indeed, and well put Miss Fields. And now, I have a task that shall please me to no end." The King continued "I have something in particular for the other three fine gentlemen on their return from galavanting around France." The King continued, with a sly smile. "We usually do these at an official ceremony, but with the approval of Sir Dowding after his effusive praise, I have something for the three of you."

King Edward VI walked back over to his desk and opened a small drawer. He returned to place three small black velvet boxes on the table between the seated audience.

"If you would please, gentlemen, stand." The King ordered. Timothy, Payton, and Dylan all stood in unison. He reached for one of the boxes and opened it so only the standing could see inside. "Do you know what this is?" He asked them. Looking inside the box the three saw a crimson ribbon holding a burnished bronze cross with a lion and crown laid across the top. Beneath, an inscription read "For Valour."

"Yes, your Majesty. It's the Victoria cross." Payton answered quietly.

The seated audience gasped slightly, it was the highest honor awarded by the British for valor in the face of the enemy.

"Sir Dowding agrees with me that your incredible intuition in gaining the aforementioned intelligence, your fight to get it home safely, and your urgency in bringing it to light so quickly has given us a chance to give Hitler a real bloody nose and regain our footing. Along you're your work at Dunkirk, and your story of brushing aside the incredible odds to return home and rejoin the fight are the very definition of valor in my book, so it is with great honor that I invest the three of you with the order of Victoria's Cross. Thank you, from everyone in the realm for what you have done and what you will do, and may God Bless you as you go forward."

"But I'm Irish...." Was all Timothy could mumble "And not even in the military." He finished.

"We did consider that, but the award can go to any civilian under the command of our military, in this case your twin friends here, and without you putting yourself at great risk they would not have brought home what they did." The King answered in an almost insisting way.

"Thank you." All three said after that sternly as King George placed the medal over their heads and shook the hand of each. There was not much else they could say.

When his Majesty finished, the three women nearly leapt from the couch and cradled their loves with pride, and joyfully kissed each according to their hearts.

"The medal is nice, but I'm just happy you are home." Anne said tenderly to Payton low enough that no one else could hear.

"You know, this does not mean I have to call you sir." Clara pointed out to Dylan.

"Timothy, you rogue." Simone merely stammered out as she threw hundreds of years of etiquette aside and kissed the Irishman in front of the King, who nodded approvingly.

Payton held on to Anne at his side, and thumbed at the medal almost as if he didn't believe it was real.

"I rather doubt they will trade that for one of you baseball rings. World Series, they call it correct?" The King asked. "I think you are stuck with the VC, no world championship ring." His majesty teased the twins, clearly remembering his baseballs lessons with more than a little fondness.

"I don't think the Dodgers will make the series this year anyway." Payton grinned back at the monarch. "I think we'll be okay settling for this."

***

After returning to Simone's house, Payton took his turn writing a dispatch to General Bradley, knowing full well that they were remiss in writing over the last several weeks.

To: General Bradley

From: former Lt. Payton Anders.

RE: Flight Commissions, Training, and Follow on Actions

The purpose of this note is to inform the General of relevant notes from our continuing mission in Europe. Upon last communication we made contact with an associate of Air Marshall Sir Hugh Dowding. He provided an introduction letter for us to take to the Air Marshall, who immediately commissioned us in to the RAF. We undertook several weeks of training before transferring to our assigned squadron group.

Luftwaffe tactics appear focused on RAF bases, attempting to limit the effectiveness of the air defenses before an invasion. After several missions, we made independent forced landings on the French coast at Normandy, from which we escaped several days later.

Relevant observations:

1. Pilot training is critical. Machines can be replaced, pilots cannot. We urge in the strongest terms possible to begin covert pilot training ASAP.

2. British Spitfires and German Messerschmitt are generally an even match. Lesser planes will not survive against these foes.

3. French resistance will be a powerful ally.

4. We have obtained maps/directives describing the "Atlantic Wall" as well as the German invasion plans for Great Britain during our time in France. English operatives will share with USA government/military officials ASAP.

5. When the US enters the war (we believe that is when, not if) invasion of the French coastline will be a daunting task. Recommend considering Normandy landing instead of Pas De Calais. Landing sites will have less open ground to cover, beaches are passable, though with high cliffs that will require neutralizing hardened emplacements, and Normandy will be less well defended than the more obvious Pas De Calais. Carentan and Cherbourg will make suitable harbors before pursuing a deep water harbor at Le Havre.

We will return shortly to our squadron. Continuing updates to follow.

***

"What happens now?" Anne asked quietly as the sun began to set quietly outside the windows of Simone's drawing room. She sat nervously on Payton's lap, while Clara and Dylan sat opposite them on a small sofa framing the large, marble encased fireplace. Jack and Maggie had gone out for dinner, while Simone and Timothy had gone out for a walk. The entirety of the ride back from Buckingham Palace had consisted of Jack and Timothy discussing their future collaboration at Baker Street.

"I was thinking of asking Simone if we could stay here forever." Payton responded flippantly.

"You know what I mean." Anne responded with a hint of irritation.

"I do, I just don't want to think about it." Payton responded, apology in his tone.

"I believe we have until midnight until we have to return to Biggin Hill, and you report back to the hospital in the morning. From there, one foot in front of the other." Dylan said blandly.

"Yes, we must continue fighting. England can't fall, Hitler has take so much he must be stopped. Kristalnacht, Poland, the Sudetenland, Paris. Who know's where he'll go next." Payton said, feeling the burning passion rise again in his chest. Dylan agreed, and didn't have to say it.

"But what about us?" Clara said. "That evil man can't be let to keep us apart."

"He won't." Both boys promised both girls.

"We'll win." Payton said forcefully. "We'll do our part, and we'll win. The sooner we can get the US in to this war the sooner we can get back to you. And I promise you, Anne Fields, that I will come back to you. Every time." Payton promised with equal passion.

"I know, when you can control it you will come back. But you don't control it. Every time I think of you in France I start sobbing." Anne answered. "And I don't sob."

"Neither do I." Clara added.

"We control what we can, and we come back. Each day. I won't live without you." Dylan said, holding Clara's hand tightly. "We will find a way."

"Then we'll keep the time we have. Come on Dylan, just you and me for a moment." Clara answered while faking a smile. She stood and they left the drawing room, arm in arm, with no real plan.

Anne rested her head on Payton's shoulder, curled herself up as closely as she could to him, and said "This is all I want, right now."

And that was how they stayed, in to the night until each returned to their part in the fight.

ABOUT THE

AUTHOR

This is Ian Lindsey's first novel. He lives and works outside of Portland, Oregon with his family. Ian's fascination with WWII era aircraft started when he was in high school and blossomed as he studied aeronautical engineering at California Polytechnic State University, San Luis Obispo where he earned his BS in General Engineering. Given the chance, he recommends the Boeing Flight Museum outside of Seattle, WA and the Evergreen Aviation Museum outside of McMinnville, OR. Also, Ian does have a twin brother named Collin, and he does in fact root for the Dodgers.

Made in the USA
Middletown, DE
23 July 2018